Joanna

my double lifer

2 books in 1

Two years in the so-called life of RACHEL RILEY

OXFORD
UNIVERSITY PRESS

OXFORD
UNIVERSITY PRESS

Great Clarendon Street, Oxford OX2 6DP
Oxford University Press is a department of the University of Oxford.
It furthers the University's objective of excellence in research, scholarship,
and education by publishing worldwide in

Oxford   New York

Auckland   Cape Town   Dar es Salaam   Hong Kong   Karachi
Kuala Lumpur   Madrid   Melbourne   Mexico City   Nairobi
New Delhi   Shanghai   Taipei   Toronto

With offices in

Argentina   Austria   Brazil   Chile   Czech Republic   France   Greece
Guatemala   Hungary   Italy   Japan   Poland   Portugal   Singapore
South Korea   Switzerland   Thailand   Turkey   Ukraine   Vietnam

Oxford is a registered trade mark of Oxford University Press
in the UK and in certain other countries

British Library Cataloguing in Publication Data

Data available

ISBN: 978-0-19-272921-7

1 3 5 7 9 10 8 6 4 2

Printed in Great Britain by CPI Cox and Wyman, Reading, Berkshire

Paper used in the production of this book is a natural, recyclable product made
from wood grown in sustainable forests. The manufacturing process conforms
to the environmental regulations of the country of origin

Contents

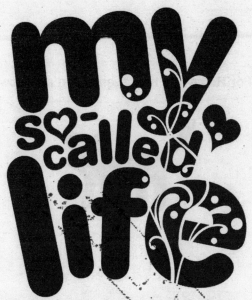

my so-called life

The Tragically Normal Diary
of Rachel Riley

december

Saturday 25

Christmas Day

Christmas presents asked for:

- mobile phone
- *O.C.* Complete First Season boxed set on DVD
- Chanel No. 5, as worn by Marilyn Monroe
- Touche Eclat to cover up hideous dark circles inherited from Granny Clegg
- hair straighteners to tame hideous curly hair inherited from Grandpa Clegg.

Presents received:

- Mum and Dad—BBC *Pride and Prejudice* boxed set. Apparently *The O.C.* has been added to Mum's list of proscribed items (also featuring *EastEnders* (common), *Coronation Street* (northern and common) and Ribena (purple, causing stain issues)). When I asked her why, she said it gave teenagers an unrealistic image of life in a seaside community. This is because she grew up in Cornwall where Granny Clegg made her wear a balaclava to school.
- James, my brother—*What Not to Wear* by Trinny and Susannah. This is rich coming from a seven year old who has been known to go out dressed in a Virgin Mary outfit.
- Grandpa Riley—a box of toffee with 'Thank you for looking after my dog' on it, which is weird as I have never looked after his dog because it *a*) is sick all the

time; *b*) looks at me menacingly; and *c*) ate one of my pink Converse low-rise. Maybe it is a plea. I hope not.

- Granny and Grandpa Clegg—a £5 WHSmith token and a Selection Box (sell-by date last August). The concept of inflation has clearly not reached St Slaughter yet, along with central heating and Channel 5.
- Auntie Joy(less) and Uncle John—a junior New Testament. They are severe Methodists and force my cousins to go to a cult church in Redruth where they dip you in a pool in all your clothes and talk in tongues.
- Uncle Jim—nothing. I don't think they celebrate Christmas in Tibet.
- Scarlet, my best friend—this diary.
- Sad Ed, practically next-door neighbour and second best friend—*The Bell Jar* by Sylvia Plath. Ed's ambition is to become an alcoholic genius and die in a car crash by the age of thirty. He has no chance. He passed out at Scarlet's birthday party after two martinis, can only play 'Bobby Shaftoe' on his guitar, and came third last in the school poetry competition last year.

Emailed Scarlet. She got: a Nokia with an inbuilt MP3 player, camera, and the *O.C.* theme as the ringtone; *The O.C.* Complete First Season boxed set; a Cure T-shirt and a pair of enormous skate trousers (she is thinking of

becoming either a goth or Avril Lavigne); and a book called *Let's Talk About Sex*. This is typical. Scarlet's mum is a sex therapist and her dad is a gynaecologist, which sounds exotic, but is, as Scarlet points out, actually gross. Especially when they start talking about pelvic floors at breakfast.

Casually mentioned Scarlet's new mobile phone to Mum. She said Scarlet would fry her brain with radiation. I said if I had one I would only use it to text people but Mum said I would get RSI and fail my GCSEs (which, I might add, are two years away). So now I am the only thirteen year old in Saffron Walden forced to use the public phone box to call Dad for a lift, which is embarrassing, not to mention unhygienic. I know for a fact that Mark Lambert once got his thing sucked in there by Leanne Jones for £2.50 and a Westlife CD.

Ate Bounty, Twirl, Mars bar, and half a Twix from out-of-date Selection Box whilst reading *What Not to Wear*. Apparently I am committing a litany of crimes against fashion. Under no circumstances should someone of my height (157 cm—only five cms off being a medical midget, according to James) wear cropped trousers. Looked in wardrobe to assess situation. Own three pairs cropped trousers, one pair of jeans (with a burn hole in the knee where James tried to invent inkstain remover), a bridesmaid's dress left over from Uncle Jim's second wedding, a kilt (don't ask), four assorted Marks & Spencer jumpers, a hoodie, seven T-shirts (three black,

7

one grey, one Brownies, one Saffron Walden Carnival, and one 'I Love Bodmin Farm Park'), and my school uniform. Not promising.

10 p.m.
Feel a bit sick. Maybe should have stopped at the Mars bar. Sylvia Plath would have stopped at half a Bounty. Or, probably, would have chosen an apple instead.

. . . .

Sunday 26
Boxing Day
A terrible thing has happened. Grandpa Riley's dog has been banned from the Pink Geranium sheltered housing complex after eating the turkey for the communal Christmas lunch. Grandpa says it wasn't the dog, but, according to the warden, Mrs Peason, a pile of incriminating sick was found outside Elsie Stain's porch. Apparently it is the last straw in a long list of canine misdemeanours. She has asked Dad to come and pick it up this week or it will be sent to the dog home. That box of toffee must have been a premonition.

Also, a giant tidal wave has washed away Thailand. Mum says that's the problem with choosing the third world as a holiday destination—not only are the toilet arrangements suspicious but it is ravaged by freak weather, which is why Cornwall is ideal. James pointed out that Granny Clegg still had an outside toilet and

that it had rained persistently on three out of the last four visits to Cornwall, at which point he got sent to his room to reflect on world disaster.

Emailed Scarlet but no reply. She is obviously too busy watching *The O.C.* whilst wearing enormous skate trousers and reading about her G-spot. Went round to see Sad Ed. He was depressed, as usual. Mainly because he got a David Beckham calendar and a machine that dispenses miniature Dairy Milks for Christmas. He had asked for a stuffed crow and a box of Slimfast (he wants to get in shape for his tragic untimely death—he says he cannot be a revered genius with fat upper arms). He has not liked David Beckham since Year Five but his mum and dad are in denial. He said the Tsunami is a symbol of globalization and the capitalist society eating itself. I had to leave as he was making me depressed as well.

Monday 27

Bank Holiday (UK)

Gave up waiting for email reply and went round to Scarlet's. Suzy and Bob (Scarlet gets to call her mum and dad by their first names) are frantically setting up a Tsunami appeal fund with the Saffron Walden Labour Party and Suzy's tantric yoga group. Scarlet was too busy to watch *The O.C.* as she was helping Suzy write letters to Sainsbury's and Tesco's demanding they hand over tinned oriental produce for immediate repatriation. Even

Scarlet's brother, Jack, is doing something. His band, Certain Death, are playing a charity gig at the Bernard Evans Youth Centre next week.

I tried calling my mum Janet once and she banned me from watching *Dawson's Creek* for two weeks.

Dad is going to fetch the dog tomorrow. Mum is not happy but has agreed, under a three strikes and it's out rule regarding food theft and vomiting.

Tuesday 28

Bank Holiday (UK)

Went to collect Grandpa's dog from the Pink Geranium sheltered housing complex, which sounds like an exotic gay nightclub but is a three-storey concrete block of flats on the site of the former gasworks. Mrs Peason the fascist warden was waiting at the front door with Grandpa and the dog, who looked very sad. (Grandpa, not the dog. The dog was eating a Mars bar and was too busy to look sad.) Mrs Peason said, 'At last. This dog is a menace to health and safety. I hope you have a ready supply of Jif.' Grandpa shook his head and said things like, 'It's all over for me and you now, pal. Don't pine yourself to death.' But the dog just climbed in the boot. I think it was glad to get away from Mrs Peason.

Mum has told Dad that the dog is not allowed into the lounge, dining room, or bedrooms, except in cases of absolute emergency (what would these be, I wonder?).

10

She has put up James's old stairgate on the kitchen door to restrict its activities.

8 p.m.
The dog has chewed through the stairgate and is locked in a stand-off situation in Mum and Dad's bedroom, where it is growling menacingly from under the sprig-patterned duvet cover.

Wednesday 29

Went into town with James and spent my £5 WHSmith token on *Sugar Rush* by Julie Burchill. Scarlet has read it twice and says it is seminal. James bought a dictionary of Elvish and a Carol Vorderman Sudoku puzzle book.

Rival Tsunami appeals are appearing all over the place. I counted at least five in the space of 500 yards, including one by Les Brewster and his wife, Ying, who own the Siam Smile Thai café on the High Street (formerly the Dog and Bucket pub). Les (overweight, bald, fifty-seven) divorced Mrs Brewster (also overweight, bald, and fifty-seven) two years ago and married Ying (thin, full head of hair, twenty-one) after a holiday in Phuket with the pub darts league. They are raising money to rebuild the sex bar where they met.

Got back to find that the dog had eaten the DVD player and the *Pride and Prejudice* boxed set. Dad claims it is not the dog but there is a pile of sick by the dog's bowl with a picture of Colin Firth in it. Mum says it is two strikes down but James says DVDs do not count as food.

Thursday 30

Tomorrow is New Year's Eve. I have still not been invited to any parties but I know that Jack is having all the members of Certain Death over for a jamming session and that will include Justin Statham (lead guitar) who can play the solos out of 'Stairway to Heaven' and 'I Believe in a Thing Called Love'. Scarlet says Jack says he is going out with Sophie Jacobs whose dad invented Microwave Muffins and who was once in a Fairy Liquid advert, but everyone knows she is still in love with Chris Cross (seriously), who is in quarantine for glandular fever, so as soon as he is given the all-clear it will all be over with Justin and I will be there to comfort him. I just need to lay some groundwork now. I will call Scarlet in the morning and get myself invited over.

Read three pages of *Sugar Rush*. Scarlet is right. It is clearly a modern classic. Why, oh why, can we not move to Brighton, which is full of exotic and tragic people like blacks, lesbians, and the homeless? All Saffron Walden has is Barry the Blade, the notorious town madman, who eats leftover falafel from the dustbin outside Abrakebabra. Where is the urban degradation? Where is the multicultural melting pot?

Friday 31

New Year's Eve

11.45 p.m.

New Year's Eve has been a total disaster. I should be at a house party having meaningful conversations on the stairs with Justin Statham but am, in fact, at home watching Jonathan Ross. Scarlet was too busy to celebrate—Suzy and Bob are holding a candlelit vigil with Les Brewster and Ying in the Siam Smile (they have joined forces in an attempt to form one giant Tsunami Appeal and weed out the pretenders). I asked if I could go but Mum said that the sex bar being washed away was probably a good thing and that anyway, she needed me to babysit so they can play Giant Jenga with Clive and Marjory next door. Sad Ed came over for a bit and we played his Leonard Cohen CD (he is a total Emotional Music Obsessive) but he has a 10 p.m. curfew. He says that we are both the products of depressingly unbroken homes and that is why our existence is so meaningless. Although his plight is worse than mine as his parents are both forty-eight, which makes them practically pensioners, and they are in the Aled Jones Fan Club.

Ed is right, I need more tragedy in my life. Why is life never like it is in books? Nothing Jacqueline Wilson ever happens to me: I am not adopted, my mum is not tattooed, I am not likely to move to the middle of a council estate or be put into care. My parents are not alcoholics, drug addicts, or closet transvestites. No one in

13

my family is brown, gay, interestingly autistic, or even mildly retarded (although James won't eat fruit and meat on the same plate and can sing the books of the Bible off by heart, which is a bit *Curious Dog*.) Even my name is pants. Why didn't my parents call me something exotic like Lola? (Actually I asked Mum that once and she said that no daughter of hers was being named after a transsexual prostitute.) In other words, my life is earth-shatteringly NORMAL.

This cannot go on. Something deep and life-changing has to happen. Thin Kylie (Britcher) was put into care for a week when her mum's breast implant burst. Even Fat Kylie (O'Grady) has suffered tragic loss—her dad Les choked to death on a Findus Crispy Pancake last March.

Next year will be different. It has to be. Starting tomorrow.

PEANUT →

COFFEE

PRIDE & PREJUDICE

january

Saturday 1

New Year's Day

8 a.m.

My New Year resolutions:

1. Drink coffee. Tragic heroines do not start the day with Cheerios and lemon barley.
2. Get boyfriend, i.e. Justin Statham.
3. Buy flattering clothes as suggested by Trinny and Susannah. Am not going to have a life-changing moment in a Brownies T-shirt and science experiment jeans. Am going to go vintage and look pale and interesting and incredibly literary.
4. Train dog. So far it has eaten, ripped up, or otherwise ruined: the DVD player, the *Pride and Prejudice* boxed set, a giant tin of Quality Street from Dad's work, two pairs of washing-up gloves, a bar of Clearasil soap, and a giant poster of Elijah Wood (James's, not mine. He is obsessed with him. His bedroom is a shrine to all things hobbit).
5. Get period. I am officially a freak of nature. I saw Fat Kylie's sister Paris-Marie buying Tampax in Boots three weeks ago and she is only 11.
6. Befriend more tragic and interesting people.
7. Visit Paris—centre of literary romance (e.g. *Sex and the City* final episode).

9.30 a.m.

New Year resolution amendment:

17

1. Drink tea. Tried making black coffee with Mum's Nescafé Gold Blend but felt a bit strange and had to lie down for half an hour. I think it is like drugs. You do not start off by injecting heroin. You need to try the softer stuff first. Tea is very vintage anyway. I bet Sienna Miller drinks tea.

2 p.m.
Tried training dog to no avail. It just wagged its tail when I told it to sit, then it lost interest and went off to chew some more of the kitchen wall.

. . . .

Sunday 2
Took the dog to visit Grandpa Riley. Grandpa's care worker Treena was there, smoking a Benson and Hedges. James pointed out that forty-nine per cent of smokers die from lung or heart disease and that, anyway, Mrs Peason had banned smoking in the flats after Grandpa accidentally set fire to himself when he fell asleep during *Cocoon*. Treena muttered, 'Flaming weirdo,' and opened the window. She is not very caring for a care worker.

The dog seemed happy to see Grandpa and Grandpa got all teary like it was Lassie coming back home but then it ate Treena's cigarettes and was sick on the rug. Treena said, 'They cost me £5.15 they did.' So Grandpa gave her

ten pounds, which made her a whole lot more caring. She gave Grandpa a kiss and offered to 'do his feet' later. Vile. I have seen Grandpa Riley's feet. They are huge and the toenails are yellow.

Monday 3
Bank Holiday (UK)

Auntie Joyless and Uncle John were supposed to be coming to stay this week but she rang to say they couldn't as they were having discipline issues with Boaz (who is also thirteen, but three months younger than me in actual time and about three years in mental time). Apparently he is refusing to go to Bible camp this Easter. Anyway it is a relief as Auntie Joyless would be bound to ask me if I was reading the New Testament and I would have to tell the truth (she has a spooky sixth sense about lying) and say I was reading *Sugar Rush*, which is about lesbians and sex, and then she would make Mum ban it, like she did with Boaz's *Harry Potter*.

The dog and James are best friends. He speaks to it in Elvish, which seems to calm it down. It will not leave his side and follows him when he goes to the toilet, guarding the door like Cerberus at the gates of hell. He has trained it using biscuits (it gets a digestive for sitting, and a custard cream for lying down. James is thinking of patenting the method).

Tuesday 4

Bank Holiday (Scotland)

Mum has banned the biscuit method. She says she is not forking out £2.33 a day on dog treats. (The dog ate two packets each of digestives and custard creams plus four Duchy Originals chocolate ginger things that only come out when we have guests.)

Wednesday 5

Two days to go until Jack's gig. My clothing options are: grey T-shirt, hoodie, and kilt or outlawed cropped trousers. Looked in Mum's wardrobe for possible vintage outfits. Could only find a hideous mint-green jumpsuit with criminally tapered legs left over from the eighties. I have to go shopping.

4 p.m.

There is a distinct lack of vintage clothing in Saffron Walden unless you count Gray Palmer, which only sells Aertex and tweed. Went to Oxfam in the hope of unearthing a beaded flapper dress or ethnic-print kaftan. Mrs Simpson was in there. She smells of wee and wears white flares all year round, which is not a good colour when your hygiene is questionable.

There was no flapper dress or kaftan. Bought an enormous jumper, a crochet top, a suede miniskirt, and some furry boots. Mrs Simpson bought a pair of tap shoes

20

and a Wonderbra. Maybe she is auditioning for the Amateur Operatic Society's production of *Chicago* (starring forty-seven-year-old Co-op cashier Maureen Tyler as Renée Zellweger).

Wore my giant jumper. James said I looked and smelt like the dog and Dad asked if I wanted to go for a walk (ha ha).

8 p.m.
I have three bites on my stomach. That dog has got to be defleaed.

* * *

Thursday 6
Epiphany
What is epiphany?

Went round to Sad Ed's to show him my new vintage look. He agrees it is more tragic and literary than my old style. He is not coming to the gig as he has to go to his cousins' in Leighton Buzzard. He says he doesn't care because Certain Death are just amateurs and he is getting tickets to see Pete Doherty at a secret Babyshambles gig in London. (In his dreams. The last concert he was allowed to go to was the Teletubbies live at Harlow Playhouse.) He is just jealous because he once auditioned to play lead guitar but they picked Justin because his dad's company has got a Transit van. Also, Justin is quite good and Ed is truly crap.

Two more bites, including one on my neck. I am going to be disfigured at this rate. I hope it is dark at the gig. Justin is not going to want to cry on a spotty shoulder.

Friday 7
6 p.m.
Am wearing crochet top, suede skirt, and furry boots. Scarlet is wearing her Cure T-shirt and giant skate trousers. She says she is hovering more towards goth but that Suzy won't let her dye her hair black so she needs a back-up in case the other goths reject her. Suzy said my vintage outfit was 'fabulous' and said she would look out some old Monsoon skirts for me. Jack said 'Interesting boots, Riley,' but I couldn't tell if he was being sarcastic or not because his hair is so long it covers most of his face. He got sent home from school once to get a haircut, but Suzy set up a protest group and the headmaster, Mr Wilmott, was forced to retract the suspension for fear of mass hair growing. Am staying at Scarlet's tonight, which means I get to stay and help the band pack up. I am almost a groupie.

10 p.m. Scarlet's bedroom
The gig was a disaster. Sophie Jacobs and her minions Fi and Pippa were there. They were all wearing pink in unironic homage to *Mean Girls*, which they have seen thirty-seven times. Sophie was draped over Justin looking

all blonde and ethereal (Chris Cross is still bed-ridden). She asked me why I was wearing her gran's boots. I told her they were vintage but she said, 'No they're not, they're Clarks, my mum took them to Oxfam last week.' Then she and Justin laughed and they walked off together to the VIP area (aka the parent and toddler room).

Scarlet is still in the bathroom being sick. She got the goths to buy her two rum and blacks. Then she tried to stage dive but no one caught her and she hit Sophie Jacobs and passed out. Her dad had to take us home before Certain Death had even got on stage. She threw up in the map pocket on the back of her dad's seat on the way, but I don't think he noticed as he had Coldplay ('middle-class semi-talented bandwagon-jumping sellouts' according to Sad Ed) on very loud. At least Sophie has a black eye, so something good happened, anyway.

Saturday 8

Scarlet didn't come down for breakfast so I ate croissants with Bob, Suzy, and Jack. They were discussing literature so I said I was reading *Sugar Rush*. Bob said Julie Burchill is a man-hater with a voice like she's breathed in too much helium. Suzy narrowed her already cat-like eyes and said that Bob was only saying that because Julie Burchill used to be married to Bob's hero Tony Parsons but dumped him because he was a misogynist with a fake

cockney accent. Jack said 'Whatever' and rolled his eyes at me. Why don't we have heated debates like this at home (or croissants, for that matter)? The closest we get is when Mum and Dad argue over who should be Round Table chairman now that Tony London has defected to Lions Club, and whether we have to visit Granny and Grandpa Clegg this year and, if so, do we take the M4 or A303?

Bob gave me a lift home. He asked if I could smell something funny but I diverted the question by pointing out some new graffiti on the bus shelter.

· ·

Sunday 9
1 p.m.
Scarlet is not allowed over. Her dad has found the Volvo sick. The rum and black has stained the beige leather indelibly.

The dog is in the shed and is refusing to come out. Mum tried to deflea it, which sent it into a wild panic and it made a bolt for freedom. It has changed colour from muddy grey to white, with all the powder. James is in the shed with it, talking Elvish to try and soothe it.

3 p.m.
The dog and James are out. They were won over with a packet of bourbons. They would be useless in a hunger strike.

24

5 p.m.
I have six more bites. The powder has not worked. Mum is taking the dog to the vet's next week while we are at school.

. . . .

Monday 10

School. Tried to wear my enormous jumper over my uniform but Mum said it was called uniform for a reason. She does not understand vintage. She buys all her clothes from Marks & Spencer in the sale. How will Justin notice me now?

Registration was awash with Christmas iPods and mobile phones. Fat Kylie's Samsung plays a video of her little brother Brady (O'Grady, seriously) shouting, 'I don't want f**king Fruit Shoot, I want Cheese Strings.' He has a wide command of swear words for a three year old. Thin Kylie is not back from Lanzarote yet. Scarlet suggested Ms Hopwood-White report Mrs Britcher to social services, but Ms Hopwood-White is scared of the Kylies' mothers ever since parents' evening when she suggested they might like to stop smoking on school premises. We are getting someone new in our class called Davey MacDonald. He is being transferred from Mrs Duddy's Special Educational Needs group (aka Retards and Criminals). Maybe he will be an idiot savant like in that film with Tom Cruise and Dustin Hoffman. He will be tragically misunderstood but will go on to win the Nobel Prize. I shall befriend him.

. . . .

Tuesday 11

Davey MacDonald is not an idiot savant. He is just an idiot who has a habit of getting his thing out in class. He was back with Mrs Duddy by 11 o'clock after he showed it to Scarlet in the language lab and asked her to help him with his 'special needs'. Ms Hopwood-White said he wasn't ready to be integrated yet. She told Scarlet to see the school counsellor (and woodwork teacher) Mr Doddington (aka Doddy) for trauma. Scarlet said she wasn't traumatized and that it looked bent and that he could suffer sexual problems later in life. She should know, she has seen hundreds in her mum's manuals at home. I haven't seen any. Except James's when Mum made us share a bath in one of her economy drives. I don't think that counts. I hope not.

The dog does not have fleas. Mr Mercer the vet says they must be from another source. He also said the dog has to stop eating so much, apparently it is showing signs of obesity, sugar addiction, and canine tooth decay.

Wednesday 12

Thin Kylie is back from Lanzarote. She is the colour of a Footballer's Wife. Sad Ed said he hoped it was from a bottle or she will be riddled with life-threatening moles by Year Twelve, but Kylie said, 'No, it's f**king real, you fat poof. I spent six hours a day on this.' She and Mark Lambert were all over each other in break. They have been going out six weeks. She has got a badge on her

Burberry parka from him for every time she has let him touch her minky. Which makes ten (five McFly, three Busted, one Girls Aloud, and one 'I've seen the lions of Longleat!'—I counted them in food technology). I heard her tell Mark she nearly died being parted from him. But later she showed Fat Kylie and Tracey Hughes pictures of a waiter called Jose.

The dog is sulking. Mum is forcing it to eat dry dog biscuits. It is used to three cans of Pal and several Penguins a day. It lies in front of the fridge, eyeing it mournfully. Mum says the dog will cave in before she does.

Thursday 13

I have four more bites. Where are these things coming from? Maybe there is a dead animal in the house. Clive and Marjory next door once found a dead squirrel under the drinks cabinet. Apparently it had got in through the window after seeing a packet of cashews. It still had the empty packet in its claws. Mum did a thorough sweep of the house after that and put locks on all the windows. I don't think the squirrels will be breaking in to get at her mung bean cultivator.

Friday 14

Oh my God. The source of the fleas has been identified. It is the enormous fluffy Oxfam jumper. Mum tried to

handwash it and the fleas all jumped out of the sink and scattered around the kitchen. Rentokil have been round and fumigated the place. Mum made them park round the corner and take off their badges so that Marjory won't think her domestic hygiene has lapsed. Going vintage is fraught with difficulties.

. . . .

Saturday 15

Went to see Grandpa Riley. The dog was not allowed to come after last time's cigarette fiasco. Grandpa and Treena were on the sofa watching T4. She was sitting very close to him. Clearly smoking has compromised her sense of smell or she would have kept away from the overpowering odour of Old Spice and athlete's foot powder. Grandpa says he is applying for a home visit next Sunday. I said I thought you only had to do that if you were in prison but Grandpa said Mrs Peason used to work at HMP Holloway and is implementing a strict new regime.

. . . .

Sunday 16

The dog is victorious. Mum left it alone in the kitchen while she was on the phone to Granny Clegg (topics discussed: 'Why in God's name have Persil changed the smell of their washing powder?' and 'the impending downfall of St Slaughter now that Hester Trelowarren

has turned one of her battery chicken sheds into a holiday home') and it managed to eat the entire, uncooked, Sunday lunch. Dad says it is Mum's fault for depriving it of real meat. It is back on Pal. Mum says she cannot afford to lose £10 worth of Waitrose organic lamb every week.

Monday 17

A life-changing moment has occurred, without the aid of vintage clothing: Justin Statham spoke to me. To be fair, I was behind him in the queue for the Coke machine and his exact words were, 'Got two fifties for a pound?' But Scarlet and I think it is a breakthrough, none the less. Sophie still has a black eye. If it lasts much longer he will chuck her for sure. She looks like a panda in a wig.

Tuesday 18

Scarlet and I lurked by the Coke machine all break and lunchtime in case Justin needed any 50ps but there was no sign of him. He must be getting his refreshment from other sources. Sad Ed says I am delusional, but how would he know? He has only ever been in love with Willow off *Buffy*, and she was a lesbian.

Grandpa Riley rang. Mrs Peason is allowing him out for four hours on Sunday. He has asked if he can bring a guest. I hope it is not his neighbour Arthur Edge. He has

29

a colostomy bag and Parkinson's, which is potentially very messy.

. . . .

Wednesday 19

Scarlet has tracked Justin down to Mr Patel's opposite the lower school gates. He goes there with Jack at lunchtime. Under interrogation from Scarlet, Jack has disclosed that he buys a Coke (full fat) and a Snickers. I am going to start eating Snickers to bond with him. I hope I am not allergic to peanuts. Ooh, if I was, though, he could heroically give me mouth to mouth when I collapse on Mr Patel's sticky lino.

. . . .

Thursday 20

Went to Mr Patel's at lunch and bought a Snickers, right in front of Justin and Sophie. But it turns out I am not allergic to peanuts. For a minute I thought I might be because I went all red and started coughing, but it turned out that a peanut had lodged in my throat. Sad Ed hit me on the back and the peanut flew out onto Sophie Jacobs's pink puffa. Sophie said, 'Gross, you loser'; Justin flicked the peanut on the floor for Sophie; Jack smiled and said, 'Nice one, Riley'; and I stood there with Snickers dribble running down my chin. It was not the bonding moment I had hoped for.

. . . .

Friday 21

I am avoiding Mr Patel's and peanut-based products for a while. Scarlet agrees I need to lie low at least until Sophie's coat is dry-cleaned. At the moment the peanut residue is still very much in evidence.

Saturday 22

A life-size cut-out of Des Lynam and a Will Young doll arrived today addressed to James. Mum has now added eBay to her banned list. She is writing to ask them to review their security arrangements, which are clearly insufficient if a seven year old can evade them. She has also asked Grandpa Riley to review his own security arrangements, as apparently he let James use his Mastercard after the sellers refused to accept £17.23 in small change and a Boots token. Dad just said, 'That boy is not normal, Janet.'

Sunday 23

Grandpa Riley's guest was not Arthur Edge; it was Treena. Mum went very tight-lipped when she saw her. She does not approve of Treena, who is not only northern, but watches *EastEnders*, smokes, and wears mauve leggings (even I would ban these). They brought a four-pack of Red Bull and a box of Ferrero Rocher with them. Mum asked Treena where her

husband was and she said he was busy working for the post office. This is not strictly true. Grandpa told me later he is in prison but sews mailbags. So it is not a total lie either.

Lunch was a disaster. The dog got overexcited about the Ferrero Rocher and knocked over Treena's Red Bull in its frenzy to get at the table. Red Bull has been added to the proscribed list on account of its persistent stickiness.

. . . .

Monday 24

I have chosen my GCSEs. I am doing the same as Scarlet and Sad Ed. Except for art, which I have been actively encouraged not to choose by Head of Art Beardy Morris, and music, which would be pointless as I can only play 'Twinkle Twinkle Little Star' on the descant recorder. I am doing: English literature (of course), English language, maths, French, biology, history, geography, drama, and rural studies (Jack says it is a cinch—all you have to do to pass is clean out the school chickens and grow some potatoes).

. . . .

Tuesday 25

Robert Burn's birthday

There is an apostrophe in the wrong place in Robert Burns. Mum says it is symptomatic of the decline in educational standards under New Labour (she voted Lib

Dem). She is writing to Lynne Truss and WHSmith to inform them of the error.

* *

Wednesday 26

There is uproar at school. Mr Patel's shop was burgled last night and is closed for police investigation, and the Coke and crisp machine is out of everything except plain chocolate Bountys and Polos. Lessons were disastrous on account of the sugar and caffeine withdrawal. Mr Wilmott has been forced to demand an emergency machine restocking.

Mr Patel is hoping CCTV footage will identify the thieves. Apparently they stole £12.37 from the charity jar (the sex bar Tsunami appeal), six cartons of Marlboro (high tar), four bottles of cherry brandy, and a jumbo box of Wotsits.

* *

Thursday 27

The robbery has been solved. According to Tracey Hughes, whose mum is the receptionist at the police station, the CCTV wasn't working but they still know it was Stacey O'Grady (another of Fat Kylie's many brothers) and Darryl Stamp who works at B&Q. Darryl dropped his balaclava at the scene, which still had his name sewn in it from primary school. He buckled under interrogation and named Stacey as the ringleader. I

wouldn't want to be in Darryl's shoes. Stacey once broke Fat Kylie's nose when she grassed him to her mum for stealing her fake Chanel handbag and Tiffany heart necklace and selling them to Darryl so he could give them to his mum for Christmas.

* * *

Friday 28

Mrs Hughes has been suspended from receptionist duties for disclosing police information. Tracey says she is only allowed to make tea and feed the police dogs for a month.

* * *

Saturday 29

The O.C. Season Two begins on Channel 4 tomorrow. My life will be complete once more. Although I will have to view it at Scarlet's every week as Mum is refusing to remove it from her banned list despite my pointing out that one of the lead characters is called Seth, which is Grandpa Clegg's middle name, i.e. as backward Cornish as you can get.

* * *

Sunday 30

Went to Scarlet's for the second annual *O.C.* opening episode ceremony. Suzy watched it as well. She is addicted to teen television. She was inconsolable when

Joey picked Pacey over Dawson. Even though Dawson's forehead was unfeasibly large. *The O.C.* was excellent and inspiring. Life would be so much better if I lived in California and had an ex-criminal living in my pool house or an ex-porn star for a mother.

Monday 31

Mum has written to the paper to complain about the increasing quantity of dog mess on Battleditch Lane (aka Dogshit Alley). She stepped in no less than three piles of poo on the way to St Regina's C of E primary today. She says if she can stoop to clear up after the dog, then so can everyone else. This means I will have the dog-owning mafia on my back at school come Friday once the paper is out. My week is doomed.

Tuesday 1

Scarlet says the paper will call her mum and dad about the dog poo for a comment (they are both Labour councillors). I told her to tell them not to say anything but Scarlet says it is anti-social behaviour as well as environmental damage so they will probably demand a crackdown and on-the-spot fines.

Wednesday 2

I phoned the newspaper to try to recall the letter but the woman at the other end said the paper was going to print and the only changes from now on were tonight's lottery numbers. I asked her what would happen if a serious front-page crime were committed right now. She said it would appear on page seven next week. I told her the *Guardian* did not get where it is with this lax attitude to breaking news. She said she wouldn't know, she only read Mystic Meg.

The paper does not get delivered until after school tomorrow, so I will only have Friday to suffer. I have to be grateful for small mercies.

Thursday 3

Mum's dog poo letter has made the second page of the *Walden Chronicle* under the headline 'Dog Mess Mania',

alongside a photo of some poo, possibly on Battleditch Lane, but feasibly anywhere.

The letter said:

DOG MESS MANIA

The state of Battleditch Lane, popular with parents for walking their children to school

(and with the Kylies for snogging during the lunch break)

is a disgrace to the town. It is high time that the council took the menace of dog mess seriously. It can cause blindness, stomach upset, not to mention the damage to footwear. The council must be urged to provide extra pooper scooper bins and to patrol the area day and night for lawbreakers.

Under the letter was a comment from Suzy. She says it is all the fault of the Tory council and has demanded that Hugo Thorndyke MP (Con.) lobby parliament for a dog poo crackdown and on-the-spot fines.

Under her comment was a comment from Hugo Thorndyke MP (Con.) who said it is all the fault of the Labour government for allowing anti-social behaviour to run riot in market towns.

This is humiliation beyond anything I have ever known. This is worse than when I had to partner Peter Foster (aka Stinky Pete) in country dancing at primary school, only an hour after he'd wet himself (again). Not even Scarlet would touch my hand for ages. I had to disinfect it with Dettol.

I cannot go to school tomorrow. This calls for desperate measures.

Friday 4

My ploy of claiming a stomach bug failed, despite using Scarlet's tried and tested method of throwing a glass of water down the toilet whilst retching to make it sound like you are really being sick. Mum said there were no telltale vomit splashes on the toilet surround so she wasn't falling for that one. The police should employ her in forensics, she is like Amanda Burton.

School was predictable. Fat Kylie (whose dog, Tupac, is responsible for at least half the mess) said, 'They got to go somewhere, innit.' When I suggested she could just pick it up she said, 'I ain't touching no stinking dogshit, loser.' And Tracey Hughes said her mum said the police have got better things to do with their time than patrol for dog poo. I have seen the police dogs pooing down there as well so it is fair to say that would be pointless.

I told Mum what trauma her campaign was causing me but she said their reactions were typical of today's irresponsible dog-owners and that they should bring back the dog licence and raise it to £100. She is going to suggest it to the Lib Dems for their next manifesto.

Thank God it is Friday.

Saturday 5

Scarlet and Sad Ed agreed I need to keep a low profile in Saffron Walden so we got her dad to drive us to the cinema in Cambridge. (Our cinema shut down in 1984 and is now a branch of Halfords.) Scarlet's dad's Volvo still smells, despite three Feu Orange air fresheners. But when we got to the cinema the man with the ginger toupee who runs the Odeon wouldn't let me see any vaguely interesting films as he said I didn't look twelve and would therefore need parental guidance. I told him I was nearly fourteen (in August) but he said he had never seen a thirteen year old with so little make-up and so many clothes (I was wearing one of Suzy's Monsoon dresses and the boots). Scarlet and Ed were allowed in as they both had eyeliner on. The only film the toupee man would sell me a ticket for was *Spongebob Squarepants* so I had to watch that with a cinema full of eight year olds full of nachos and pick-and-mix. I do not think it should have such a low certificate, it is full of sexual innuendo—he lives in Bikini Bottom, for goodness' sake—plus it is clearly drug-influenced, involving a pineapple under the sea. I left before the end after a Magnum stick got

entangled in my hair and went next door to Boots to buy some 17 make-up. Got supercurl mascara, a lipgloss called 'Juicy Lucy', and a green eyeshadow, which the assistant claimed would go with my hair, but which looks suspiciously like three-day-old bruising.

Sunday 6

Wore green eyeshadow to breakfast. Dad asked if I had been in a fight (ha ha). James said, 'Don't think you're going out looking like that,' and Mum just tightened her lips. What chance do I stand against this kind of opposition?

Took the dog for a walk to the Pink Geranium sheltered housing complex so Grandpa could talk to it through the fence. The dog wasn't very interested, it is still recovering from its starvation diet, and it was too cold for Grandpa's bunions so there was not the emotional reunion I had hoped for. Grandpa asked if I had been bullied at school. Came home and removed green eye shadow. Will stick to mascara and subtle lipgloss, as worn by natural beauty Sienna Miller. Eyeshadow will be emergency cinema make-up only.

Monday 7

Grandpa Clegg rang after school to moan about the hunting ban. He wants Mum to pass on his outrage to

Suzy in the hope she will tell Tony Blair. (Suzy met him once at a Gala dinner at the Chelmsford Moat House. Scarlet says she had to take a valium afterwards to calm down.) I don't know why Grandpa is up in arms, he has never been on a hunt in his life. The closest he gets is the Fox and Hounds in Camborne. He and Granny Clegg are joining the Countryside Alliance. I do not see them fitting in with the 4×4 set. They live in a 1950s terrace called 'Bellevue' (overlooking Hester Trelowarren's battery chicken farm) and think that the Harvester in Bodmin is posh.

He says they are thinking of going on the pro-hunting march in London on Saturday. Mum urged him not to. This is because it will involve them taking the train, and they got lost the last time they went to Plymouth and called 999 from a payphone. The policeman who took them back to the station told them not to leave the Redruth area in the near future except under strict supervision. Also, Grandpa Clegg is notoriously racist so Mum is worried he may say something untoward on the underground and get mugged or happy slapped.

Tuesday 8
Shrove Tuesday

Ate compulsory pancakes. The dog got worked up with all the tossing and singed itself on the gas trying to

intercept a pancake in mid-air. It looks weird. I am not walking it until the hair has grown back.

. . . .

Wednesday 9
Ash Wednesday

Have decided not to give anything up for Lent. The list of proscribed items in our house is now so lengthy that I don't think I need to deny myself anything as Mum is already doing it for me.

Sad Ed is giving up watching *Buffy* reruns. He will not last. He has no stamina when it comes to Willow in a lesbian clinch.

. . . .

Thursday 10
Islamic New Year

Ms Hopwood-White caused a stir by wishing Happy New Year to Ali Hassan, our Iraqi refugee. The Hassans are Church of England. Ali said she had insulted his religion and demanded an apology. Then Jade McDonald, whose mum is a quarter Jewish, asked her why they hadn't celebrated Hanukkah, and said that Ms Hopwood-White was clearly racist. Then Fat Kylie demanded Catholic concessions like Filet O'Fish on a Friday. Mr Wilmott had to be called in to calm everyone down. He said he was minded to instigate a no-religious-celebrations rule at school but then Sad Ed pointed out that he would have

45

to cancel Year Seven's production of *Jesus Christ Superstar* so he is having a temporary suspension until people can be sensible.

. . . .

Friday 11

Mum has rung Grandpa Clegg again to plead with him to reconsider the hunting march. Grandpa Clegg says it is all arranged. Auntie Joyless is picking him and Granny up at 8 a.m. to take them to Truro. They are going to get the direct train to Paddington and will then follow the crowds to Hyde Park. Mum said she doubted there would be hordes of huntsmen walking through West London but Grandpa said, 'Well, if the feeling in St Slaughter is anything to go by, I think you will surprised, Janet. We are right livid in Cornwall. That Mr Blair is going to ride roughshod over our rural history and sell our souls to Brussels.' (Grandpa reads the *Daily Mail* religiously.) Mum pointed out that it was Margaret Thatcher who signed us up to the Common Market but then Grandpa Clegg put the phone down as he won't hear anyone speak ill of Mrs Thatcher.

. . . .

Saturday 12

Granny and Grandpa Clegg did not make it to London. Apparently Auntie Joyless got her Mini Metro stuck behind a herd of 'new-fangled' organic sheep and the trip

46

was aborted in favour of a shopping trip to Trago Mills. Grandpa says he got a seven-pack of pants for £3.99 and a jumbo box of Christmas crackers for £2.50.

Sunday 13

Tomorrow is Valentine's Day. I fear the worst. Last year Scarlet and I got no cards. The Kylies got seven each. Scarlet says it is because they are so liberal with their sexual favours.

Monday 14

St Valentine's Day

Not a single Valentine card. It is the school's fault for scheduling half-term to clash with this crucial occasion. If I was at school, someone could have put one on my locker. James got three. He is strangely popular for a nerd.

Rang Scarlet. She got a card but it is from Davey MacDonald in special needs—the idiot signed it. Scarlet says Valentine's Day is meaningless capitalist nonsense perpetuated by Clinton's Cards and Cadbury's in order to boost sales in the Christmas to Easter lull. She has put her card in the recycling bin.

Scarlet is right. I do not care about not getting a card, not even one from an exhibitionist retard. I am far too literary and interesting for such commercialism.

Read some more *Sugar Rush*. Maybe I should try lesbianism. I could be like Madonna when she kissed Britney, or the ginger one off *Sex and the City*.

3 p.m.
Tried thinking about naked women, but the only minky I have seen close up belongs to Thin Kylie who charged 50p to look at hers behind the mobile science labs last summer (I did not pay, I stumbled across it on my way to feed the locusts). I just kept hearing her voice saying, 'Piss off, Brian, it's one pound to touch it.' Anyway, she is definitely not gay and has the badges to prove it. The only possible lesbians at our school are the PE teachers Miss Beadle and Miss Vicar, who live together, and Oona Rickets in Year Ten who is a feminist and won't wear deodorant because it is masking woman's true nature. Mr Wilmott was forced to intervene during a heatwave last year. I hope I am not a lesbian. I do not want to have to kiss Oona Rickets.

4 p.m.
My lesbian phase is over. A valentine card has arrived, posted by hand! I interrogated James as to who had delivered it but he says he was too busy phoning his admirers. The card is of Millais's painting of Ophelia drowning after she goes mad because she is socially inferior to Hamlet etc. Inside it just has a question mark and a sticky stain, possibly a lover's tears, although it

smells like caramel. The £2.20 price sticker from Mr Patel's is still on the back, so it must have come from someone at school i.e. Justin! Justin is secretly in love with me! I am his Ophelia. Rang Scarlet and she says Jack says that he and Justin are doing *Hamlet* for GCSE, plus I am totally socially inferior to him! Scarlet agrees that, as the card came from Mr Patel's, it is helping keep corner shops alive against the omnipresent out-of-town supermarket giants (or Waitrose in our case), so it is OK to keep it.

I have pinned the card to my notice board.

Tuesday 15

Could not sleep for thinking about my card. If only I were a Shakespearean heroine. Life would be so much more interesting if my father was fatally stabbed by a tormented Justin in a case of mistaken identity, and then I went mad and drowned in a brook (i.e. the shopping-trolley-clogged Slade behind the police station), although I cannot see James piercing Justin with a poisoned rapier.

Decided to become more like Ophelia so I lay on the bed with my eyes shut in what I imagined was a sort of deathlike calm. But my hoodie and John Lewis duvet set didn't feel very Shakespearean so I put on my bridesmaid's dress and scattered some leaves and a bit of potting compost in the bath. It was a bit weird wearing

clothes in the water at first because air came out from the bodice and made noises, but then I imagined Justin mourning my innocent body and got quite into it. The moment was ruined when Mum came in for an emergency wee (the downstairs loo has been blocked since Grandpa Riley's last home visit) and screamed blue murder. I assumed she thought I had committed suicide but apparently it was panic at the compost. She made me Cillit Bang the bath immediately. If I had slashed my wrists she would have got out her Stain Devils collection before calling an ambulance.

Sad Ed came over to see if I'd got any cards. I showed him the Ophelia one. He agreed that whoever sent it must be sensitive and meaningful. I said it was Justin and he said that that was impossible as Justin likes The Darkness who are pseudo-musicians. He is just sulking as he only got a card off his mum and dad, again.

Wednesday 16

Went round Scarlet's. Apparently Suzy and Bob are not speaking to each other. It is all after last night's emergency Labour Party meeting. Both of them want to stand in the next election and cannot agree as to who will best represent a forward-thinking Saffron Walden. Bob says Suzy, being *a*) female and *b*) a sex therapist, will put off the crucial pensioner vote. Suzy says pensioners will not vote for an abortionist who likes Tony Parsons and

smoked cannabis until he was thirty-eight (i.e. last year). Scarlet says the whole thing is hypothetical anyway as neither of them have a hope of beating Hugo Thorndyke MP (Con.) as he has a majority of 21,000, and the town only has 22,000 people in it.

I was hoping Jack would be there so we could get more information about my card but he was at band practice at the Air-Training Corps hut (a youth group for the criminally weapons-obsessed) so we went upstairs and listened to Sad Ed's new vintage Smiths CD instead. It was about being run over by double-decker buses, which was all a bit depressing, so I went home to look at my card again but the dog had got into my room and smelt the caramel and now Ophelia's head is a bit chewed and wet so she looks more like Jocelyn Wildenstein. Nothing is sacred in this house.

. . . .

Thursday 17

Went to town with Scarlet to lurk outside Goddard's Butchers. Justin has a holiday job there mopping up meat blood and operating the mincing machine. Was hoping for some words of confirmation that he is my Hamlet, but Sophie was in there with her mum buying fillet steak and swishing her bottom-length blonde hair everywhere (which is unhygienic in a butcher's—no one wants Herbal Essences in their pork belly). Justin is obviously having to keep up a pretence with Sophie to spare her the devastating truth. She is notoriously highly-strung. She once tried to kill herself with a bottle of Junior Vitamin C tablets after she failed an audition for *Grange Hill*. Bought a scotch egg so as not to give the game away. I will bide my time. My day will come. Gave scotch egg to dog. It has been sick on video of *Heartbeat*.

Friday 18

Hunting has been banned from the British countryside (except for drag hunting, hare coursing, and if the fox dies before the hounds get to it and shred it to pieces). Went round Scarlet's as Suzy and Bob were having a party to celebrate this historic occasion. They say it is all about the miners, really. I am not sure what they mean. I did not think miners went hunting, unless they are talking about pit ponies. They have resolved the election issue. Suzy is going to stand and Bob is going to be her Chief of Staff if she gets in. Scarlet says that it was settled because the hospital said they couldn't give Bob time off in March and April due to the seasonal rush of abortions following Valentine's Day. Suzy will still be able to do her therapy in the evenings at the Bernard Evans Youth Centre and will do phone counselling while she is on the campaign trail.

Grandpa Clegg called to mourn the loss of an 'ancient tradition'. I pointed out that he had bought pants instead of marching in London and he said he was keeping the

rural economy afloat and saving Cornwall from the evil grasp of Europe. I said that £3.99 was not going to turn around the Cornish economy and anyway, the pants probably came from China. He said would I rather he spent £10 in Marks & Spencer in Truro, and what did it matter if the pants gave good support and aeration? At which point I had to call for Mum as the thought of Grandpa Clegg's aerating pants was too much.

Saturday 19

Took James into town on pretext of mind-expanding trip to library but in reality to lurk outside Goddard's again. Justin was elbow deep in mince. I think I love him. I will wait for ever if that is what it takes to have his muscular, mince-stained arms around me.

Sunday 20

Grandpa came for his home visit with Treena. Why does she need to accompany him? It's not like he needs any extra caring for at our house. He only eats and watches telly. Mum was visibly put out. Especially when Treena said her peas were all vinegary and had Mum checked the sell-by. Mum smiled as if talking to a three year old or someone in Criminals and Retards and said they were capers.

Monday 21

There is a sex scandal in 9 Hopwood-White. Thin Kylie came back from Formentera with a badge of unknown provenance. (How can they afford to go on so many holidays? Her stepdad is a plasterer and her mum does Ann Summers parties. We have been abroad once—to Normandy, and we had to drive there and James was travel sick eleven times on the ferry.) The badge is of Kenzie. Mark Lambert has chucked her. He says she is a badge slut.

Tuesday 22

It was a false alarm. Apparently the badge came free with four Hooch bottle tops. Kylie brought in the CD that came with it as evidence. She and Mark were reunited (quite revoltingly) behind the mobile science lab at first break.

Wednesday 23

Watched *Jamie's School Dinners*. He is a legend in Saffron Walden as he used to live near here. The only other famous people are Marlon off *Emmerdale* and a McGann brother. Jamie Oliver should visit John Major High School. Mrs Brain's idea of nutrition is apple doughnuts. Thank God Mum was busy at her evening class (conversational French for the over-forties). She would be writing to the Prime Minister by now.

Thursday 24

Scarlet and Sad Ed saw *Jamie's School Dinners* as well. At lunch Scarlet asked Mrs Brain how much she spent on ingredients. She said she didn't use ingredients, it all got sent in giant trays from Chelmsford. Then Scarlet wanted to see the packaging for the veggie nuggets (the Stones are strict vegetarians) to check for transfats and monosodium glutamate but Mrs Brain said it had been put in the giant bins next to the lower school playground (aka Rat Corner). So Scarlet demanded statutory fresh vegetables. Mrs Brain said she could have chips, baked beans, or spaghetti hoops. Scarlet was about to point out that spaghetti hoops did not, in fact, contribute to the recommended five-a-day but Mrs Brain pointed her bean-encrusted spoon menacingly at us so we got pizza and Alphabites before they sold out.

When I got home, Jamie Oliver was all over the *Walden Chronicle* under the headline 'Local Hero Gets Turkey Twizzlers in a Twist'. Mum is bound to get interested.

Friday 25

Scarlet is boycotting school meals. She has brought in hummus sandwiches and is trying to rally support for change. She will not have much success. There was resistance when Fruesli bars turned up in the Coke and crisp machine. Mr Wilmott had to get the vending company to put back King Size Mars bars after Stacey O'Grady threatened to riot.

. . . .

Saturday 26

Went to WHSmith and bought Dad a DVD of Great Golfing Moments (his birthday is on Monday). I do not understand golf. Scarlet says it is an evil misogynistic sport perpetuated by Pringle-clad clones in Audis. She is probably right. Mum is only allowed in the clubhouse after three on a Saturday and then only if she is wearing a knee-length skirt or culottes.

. . . .

Sunday 27

Grandpa is in trouble with Mrs Peason for persistent abuse of the emergency buzzer system. He has used it to complain about loss of reception during *Neighbours*, to demand a bottle of stout, and to ask who played Bergerac in the eponymously titled TV series (during *Who Wants to be a Millionaire*). He insists they were all emergencies but Mrs Peason has put him on a written warning. Mum has told Dad to talk to him about his rebellious behaviour. She is worried he will be sent the same way as the dog.

. . . .

Monday 28

Dad's birthday. He got Great Golfing Moments (me), a golf club (Mum), a packet of three novelty golf balls

(James), and a tee holder (the dog). Officially he is forty-one. But James pointed out that really he is only ten because his birthday is actually on February 29th and so, by rights, he should only have a birthday every four years. He is a stickler for rules. He gets it from Mum. I think Dad was glad he was going to work.

Tuesday 1

St David's Day

Mum has cancelled her French conversation evening class so she can watch Jamie Oliver tomorrow. I fear the worst.

· ·

Wednesday 2

The predictable has happened. Mum, along with half the country, has gone Jamie mad. I watched her face throughout. It was all contorted like a Scream mask. She asked me if we had Turkey Twizzlers on the menu at school. I said yes, but that I didn't eat them (they are sold out by the time we get to the front of the queue). She said that is not the point and has written to Mr Wilmott demanding their immediate removal from the school premises, along with a rethink of the school catering contract. She has drawn up a suggested menu. It includes pasta, fresh fish, and risotto. Mrs Brain struggles with Bachelor's Savoury Rice.

I offered to hand deliver the letter for her tomorrow (i.e. put it in bin) but she says she will do it herself. She is not bothering with St Regina's primary. James takes sandwiches after a stand-off over some roast pork and apple sauce.

· ·

Thursday 3

Left the house early before Mum could try to walk me to school. She wears a cagoule, which is a criminal offence at John Major High.

61

With any luck the letter will be lost in the school office for years. Mrs Leech, the school secretary (bad hair; too much face powder; biscuit habit) is notoriously bad at filing. She once lost all Year Eleven's GCSE results under a tin of assorted shortbread.

. . . .

Friday 4

Watched *Bring It On* on DVD tonight while Mum and Dad played gin rummy at Clive and Marjory's. Scarlet had to smuggle it in inside the case for *Harry Potter*—Mum would never have let it in the house.

Why can't we do cheerleading in PE instead of hockey? Since the school sold off the playing fields to be turned into executive housing we have to do games on the sheep field, which is fraught with dangers like the electric fence and sheep poo.

. . . .

Saturday 5

Got Mum a Mother's Day card in WHSmith. It has a picture of a single daffodil on the front. It took a long time to choose it. Mum does not like cards involving whimsical kittens, puppies, overambitious floral arrangements, rude jokes, or nudity in any form. Also got her a box of Black Magic. Scarlet did not get anything for Suzy, as Suzy says every day should be a celebration of motherhood, it should not be reduced to a single Sunday,

a mass-produced card, and a box of cheap chocolates. Felt guilty about the Black Magic, but Mum doesn't like Thornton's Continental since they changed the packaging.

Sunday 6

Mothering Sunday

Gave Mum her WHSmith card and Black Magic. James gave her a painted pottery ashtray he made at school. Mum had to pretend to be pleased and said she would use it as an olive dish, but I could sense she was planning a letter to St Regina's to complain about them encouraging smoking.

Scarlet came over to escape her house. Neither she nor Jack had got Suzy anything and Suzy had locked herself in the home office and was playing Suzanne Vega albums at full volume. Mum let us eat a layer of Black Magic. I hope she wasn't feigning delight at my present as well.

Monday 7

Mrs Leech has clearly tidied up her act. I fear Mum's Jamie Oliver frenzy letter has reached Mr Wilmott after all and that he is putting pressure on Mrs Brain to amend her saturated-fat-focused menu. There were bananas (brown) on offer for pudding next to the chocolate sponge and pink custard.

Tuesday 8

Mr Wilmott has definitely shopped me to Mrs Brain. She gave me a very shrivelled sausage and only five chips for lunch. I am going to have to join Scarlet and her hummus sandwich rally if this goes on.

Wednesday 9

Today is the anniversary of Fat Kylie's dad's fatal encounter with a Findus Crispy Pancake. She had a letter to get off games. Considering the way in which he died and Kylie's veering towards childhood obesity this seems highly inappropriate.

I asked Miss Vicar (stick-thin; no breasts; facial hair) and Miss Beadle (overweight; bulgy eyes like Joey in *Friends* or rabbits with myxomatosis) if we could do cheerleading like in *Bring It On*. They have clearly seen the film, possibly several times, as Miss Beadle said: 'This is not California and you are not Kirsten Dunst. Now stop shivering and partner up with a netball.'

Got burnt nuggets (possibly chicken, but with the flavour of pork) and an odd-tasting yoghurt for lunch. Am definitely bringing sandwiches tomorrow.

Thursday 10

Was sick four times in the night. It was the yoghurt. Mrs Brain is poisoning me to make me pay for Mum's

letter. Mum demanded a vomit sample for laboratory inspection but I flushed it away and got out the Cillit Bang before she could take a swab. I do not want to aggravate Mrs Brain further.

Lay on the sofa sipping Evian and watching daytime telly. Why, oh why, do we not have satellite? Actually, I know the answer to that and it is because it is on Mum's proscribed list due to *a*) cost and *b*) shopping and porn channels and *c*) excessive sport. *This Morning* has definitely gone downhill. It is all about sex and angels. Even the dog got up and left.

Friday 11

My so-called life, as I know it, is over! We are moving to London! Dad has been offered a new job but he has to start in a month. He and Mum are going house and school hunting on Monday in a place called Dulwich. It is bound to be full of gangsters and ASBOs. I cannot wait to tell Scarlet. I will be devastated to leave her and Sad Ed behind, but they can come and see me in the holidays and meet all my black friends and we can hang out on the King's Road or the giant Topshop. Maybe I will have a leaving party and Justin will confess his true feelings for me.

Granny and Grandpa Clegg are coming to look after us while Mum and Dad house hunt. Last time they came Granny Clegg let James ride round into town in her wicker shopping trolley. I hope she does not bring it this time.

Had cheese and tomato sandwich at lunch. Am not risking the wrath of Mrs Brain again. I expect my school in London will have a multicultural menu like rice and peas and healthy lentil daal. I will not have to eat shrivelled sausage and life-threatening yoghurt again.

Saturday 12

Dulwich is not a ghetto. It is an upper-middle-class suburb and is where Margaret Thatcher and Tom Cruise have houses. James googled it. But on the plus side it is very close to Peckham and has an above-average car-crime and burglary problem.

Sunday 13

Granny and Grandpa Clegg have arrived. They got a bus all the way from Newquay to Stansted Airport where Dad picked them up. The shopping trolley was thankfully too big for the luggage compartment on the coach. They have just brought Spar bags instead.

Grandpa Clegg says he does not understand why we want to go and live in a city that is being overrun by 'gyppos and darkies' (he means asylum seekers and Muslims) thanks to Tony Blair. James told him he was being racist but Grandpa Clegg said he couldn't be racist

because his grandfather was a midget. He is a racist. He thinks Saffron Walden is dangerously exotic. But compared to St Slaughter it is. We have the Hassans; the Hangs, who run the Mandarin Palace; Ying from the Siam Smile; Mrs Wong the sadistic dentist; plus some Asian families on the Whiteshot estate. The closest Grandpa gets to a foreigner is the Australian barmaid in Truro, and he thinks she should be deported.

Was not allowed to go to Scarlet's due to presence of Cleggs so that is another episode of *The O.C.* that I will never get to enjoy.

. . . .

Monday 14
Commonwealth Day

Mum and Dad left after breakfast. Granny Clegg insisted on walking me to school. I told her this was not necessary but she said I could get mugged or raped or run over and she didn't want to have to explain that to my mother. She seemed alarmed to see Ali Hassan and the Wongs walking in the gates and clutched her Spar bag tightly to her chest. God knows what she thinks they are going to do. Grandpa Clegg took James so it could have been worse. He has been known to feign a Chinese accent at inappropriate moments.

Told Scarlet about London. She is devastated and is going to organize a leaving party at her house. Then I told Ms Hopwood-White who announced it to the class. Fat

Kylie cheered but Ms Hopwood-White gave her an immediate detention. Mark Lambert said he was a cockney. Then he tried to prove it by stabbing himself with his compasses and yelling that there was 'claret all over the gaff'. He is not a cockney. He is from Braintree.

When I got home Granny Clegg had fed all the Waitrose pasta sauce, asparagus, and half-fat fromage frais to the dog and replaced it with Fray Bentos pies and Viennetta. Granny Clegg only serves sandwiches, cold meats, and ready-meals. This is since the mythical occasion on which she Tried to Make Rice Pudding and forgot the rice, so we had to eat boiled milk skin. (She won't throw anything away—it is her working-class upbringing. Mum is the same, she will store half a leftover boiled potato in Tupperware for a week rather than waste it. The dog always gets it in the end, though.)

My room smells of Fray Bentos and liniment. I have lit one of the incense sticks that Scarlet got at the Cambridge Folk Festival last year to get rid of it.

. . . .

Tuesday 15

Mum rang before school. Granny Clegg has reported me for smoking drugs. I told her it was incense to banish the smell of Fray Bentos and old person. She told me not to do anything new-fangled with Granny Clegg in the house. That includes using the internet and microwave or talking about iPods.

68

Nine Hopwood-White has gone London-mad. Mark Lambert is now talking in rhyming slang and the Kylies think they are black. They are calling each other 'nigger' and 'girlfriend'. It is pathetic.

· ·

Wednesday 16

There has been a terrible accident. Granny Clegg let James put food colouring in his bath. I pointed out the dangers of E-numbers but she said she had drunk blue milk for fun when she was little and it hadn't done her any harm (this is the limit of things to do for amusement in Cornwall). But then she left James unsupervised while she went to check the Fray Bentos and he added the entire bottle and now he is tinged yellow. Granny has showered him three times but it will not come off. He will have to go to school like it. I hope for Granny Clegg's sake that it has worn off by Friday when Mum and Dad get home.

· ·

Thursday 17

St Patrick's Day. Holiday (N. Ire.)
James got sent home from school with suspected jaundice. Granny Clegg explained the food colouring thing but Reverend Begley, the head teacher, said it would cause a panic among the other parents and he didn't want a health scare on his hands.

I suggested Granny Clegg should try to dull it down a bit by giving him a bath in another colour. But the Co-op only had blue (Granny Clegg will not shop at Waitrose) so now James is green. Mum is going to go mad. They are back tomorrow. I cannot wait to find out what my new school is like. I wonder if they scan you for guns and knives when you go through the gates.

Friday 18

Change of plan. We are not moving to London. Mum and Dad got back looking very angry and weary. The only houses they could afford were in a place called Tulse Hill, which Mum said she recognized from several reports on *News at Ten*. There were no places at the girls' grammar either. The only school she could get me into was Peckham Academy and that only had a place because one of their Year Nines was pregnant *again* and the pupil crèche wasn't opening for three years and Dad refused to pay for me to go private on principle when there was a perfectly good school place for me in Saffron Walden (he does not come to parents' evenings). Dad is going to stay at his old job. So my life is once more one of middle-class market-town misery. Grandpa Clegg is overjoyed. He sees it as a victory against Tony Blair.

Rang Scarlet to tell her. I thought she would be happy I was staying but she is annoyed at having to cancel the

leaving party. I asked her to come over but she said she would be too busy apologizing to the caterers (Suzy).

Mum is so pleased at not having to move to London she did not even tell Granny Clegg off for James looking like an alien. But then she asked where her manuka honey had gone and Granny Clegg said she had thought it was off and had given it to the dog. Mum said it cost her £7 a pot and Granny Clegg said the dog was clearly undernourished and that if Mum couldn't look after it then she would be happy to rehome it at Bellevue. James started crying but Mum said he was in no position to complain because he was green. So that is it. The dog is moving to Cornwall. I hope it knows what it is letting itself in for.

Saturday 19

The dog has gone. Mum is visibly relieved. I think it was costing her a fortune in cleaning products. She won't be so calm when Grandpa Riley finds out. He hasn't spoken to Granny and Grandpa Clegg since an argument about Terry Wogan in 1985. James has shut himself in his room and is talking Elvish, presumably to his Elijah Wood poster—I don't think Des Lynam or Will Young look like hobbit fans.

I don't understand all this worry over the dog, when we should all be mourning the fact that we are stuck in Saffron Walden instead of trudging the mean streets of

London. Scarlet said we should try to make Saffron Walden more urban and edgy. So we tried hanging around the bus shelter like disenfranchised youths. But we got bored after an hour and went to Eaden Lilley's for smoothies.

. . . .

Sunday 20

Palm Sunday
First day of spring

James has an imaginary friend called Mumtaz. At breakfast Mum asked him if he was feeling better and he said, 'Only Mumtaz understands me.' Mum (who has been glued to *Supernanny*) said we should humour him and treat Mumtaz as if she were real until he has got over the trauma of the dog moving.

. . . .

Monday 21

James is back at school. The green has finally worn off his face so, unless he has PE, he will pass Reverend Begley's colour test. He asked if Mumtaz could come for tea on his birthday on Thursday. Mum smiled through gritted teeth and said she could and asked what she liked to eat. He said Shreddies and Marmite soldiers. These are James's favourite foods. I have never had an imaginary friend. Sad Ed says he had one called Geoffrey who wore a suit and read Enid Blyton books. I asked him when Geoffrey

had gone and he said two years ago, when he briefly got into death metal. Apparently the noise was too much. At this rate we will have Mumtaz for years.

Told Ms Hopwood-White I was not moving to London. Thin Kylie booed so Ms Hopwood-White sent her to see Mr Wilmott. Mark Lambert said it was because I didn't have cockney blood like him and anyway my Bristols were too small. So Ms Hopwood-White sent him to see Mr Wilmott as well. They have been given detention for a week because Mrs Leech caught them groping on C corridor while they waited for punishment.

Tuesday 22
James has ordered Mum to purchase a present for Mumtaz as it is her birthday on Friday. He says they can have a joint party so they will need two cakes as well, and two kinds of jelly. Mum is beginning to regret her decision to humour him. I predict Mumtaz will be sent packing by Thursday night.

Wednesday 23
Went into town to get James a present. Mum wearily told me to get something for Mumtaz so I got her a Beach Babe Barbie for £12.99. Mum said it was a bit much to spend on a figment of James's imagination but Dad said, 'What price sanity?' and I pointed out she could take it

back next week once James had got over her. Got James a laminator. He has wanted one for ages. God knows what he will do with it.

Thursday 24
Maundy Thursday
James's birthday
Mumtaz is real! It is Mr Patel's niece who arrived from Birmingham three months ago. This is typical. Why does James get to have a best friend of colour? I tried to befriend Ali Hassan once but he said he would rather I didn't talk to him about *The O.C.* as it was meaningless American propaganda. Also, he is in the maths club, which is sad.

James got the laminator, a cereal selection pack containing forbidden Frosties (Grandpa Riley), a *Lord of the Rings* calendar (last year's) (Granny and Grandpa Clegg), a Jesus Loves Me car sticker (Auntie Joyless), and a season ticket to Mole Hall wildlife park (sum total of wildlife: ten marmosets and an otter) (Mum and Dad). He has laminated all his pictures of Elijah Wood. Mumtaz was delighted with her Barbie. Mum glared at Dad. He hid behind the *Walden Chronicle*, which was leading on the under-fives Easter bonnet competition. It is so unfair. If we were in London our local paper would be full of shoot-outs and gang wars.

74

Friday 25
Good Friday
No school.
The Barbie is back. Mumtaz's dad came round this morning and said he didn't want Mumtaz being corrupted by the Western lack of respect for women and money. Mum is livid. She can't take it back now as there is jelly on Barbie's bikini. Also, James has laminated the receipt.

. . . .

Saturday 26
Dad is beside himself with delight because something called *Dr Who* starts on telly tonight. He says James and I will be scared out of our wits and will be hiding behind the sofa. Mum said if it was that traumatic the BBC wouldn't put it on at 6.35. I don't know what the fuss is about. If it is anything like *Dr Quinn, Medicine Woman* it will be so rubbish that no one will watch it anyway.

8 p.m.
Mum is writing to the BBC to complain about screening *Dr Who* before the 9 p.m. watershed. It was not like *Dr Quinn, Medicine Woman*. James was so shocked that he dropped his milk all over the sofa. Dad's viewing was suspended while Mum washed it off before it went sour.

I may well write to the BBC as well, as there were some serious flaws in their plot, like how will Billie Piper wash her clothes on the Tardis? By the end of the series she will be like Mrs Simpson. No one in telly thinks of these things. Like in *24* (which I watched illegally at Scarlet's)—no one went to the loo for a whole day, when, in reality, with all that excitement, they would be queueing up for a wee.

Sunday 27

Easter Day
British Summer Time begins
10 a.m.
Got five Easter eggs: one Green and Black's Organic (Mum and Dad); one wooden with a picture of Jesus on the cross (Auntie Joyless); one Creme Egg (James); one KitKat (Grandpa and Treena—what is she doing giving me eggs?); and one Smarties, sell-by date last April (Granny Clegg). Am going to ration them. Only small children and Fat Kylie eat all their Easter eggs on Easter Sunday.

4 p.m.
Have eaten all eggs. Sad Ed came over and said it was better to do things by extreme in this life and to eat it all in one go. He had already eaten a giant Dairy Milk and two Lindt rabbits. Felt so sick that we could not even make it to Scarlet's. Had to lie on the bed groaning instead. Also, Ed has chipped a tooth trying to eat Auntie

76

Joyless's wooden biblical egg. Next year I will nibble only 70 per cent cocoa solids dark chocolate a square a day, no matter what Ed says.

. . . .

Monday 28

Easter Monday

There is nothing to do in Saffron Walden on a bank holiday. If we had moved to London I could have gone to Harrods or Topshop. Here only Mr Patel's and the DFS on the Bishop's Stortford ring road are open. So I am OK if I want a sherbet dib-dab, a pornographic magazine, or a leather sofa.

Went round Scarlet's. Suzy was busy plotting her election campaign. She is sure Tony Blair is going to announce it next week. The kitchen was full of Labour Party members drinking lattes and phoning people up on their BlackBerries. Bob had been called into work for a complicated breech birth. Suzy said that the baby's bottom was lodged in the vaginal canal. So me and Scarlet left before she got more graphic. What is a vaginal canal? It sounds horrible. We went for a boat trip down the canal in Northampton once and we saw a shopping trolley and two dead pigeons in the water.

Scarlet had also eaten all her Easter eggs. She says she is full of self-loathing. She thinks we should become anorexic for a bit because it is a rite of passage for any prospective goth or tragic literary person. She is right.

77

Lots of famous and brilliant people are anorexic. Suzy had made Nigella's melting chocolate puddings for tea so we are going to wait until next week to try it.

- -

Tuesday 29

Grandpa has been ordered to leave the Pink Geranium sheltered housing unit. He has been given until Saturday to pack his things. Mum says he is not coming to live here, not over her dead body. Dad is going to see Mrs Peason after work to reconcile their differences.

8 p.m.

Grandpa is moving in with us, temporarily, until Mum can find him suitable accommodation. He has caused a scandal amongst the elderly citizens of the Pink Geranium by having an affair with his care worker, Treena. Apparently they have been doing it since February. Grandpa insists he is the victim of an ageist hate campaign but Mrs Peason said he had been caught with his trousers down, literally, and that it was not a pretty sight. Mum is in shock. Not only is there a forty-five-year age gap but Treena is from Bolton. I think Dad is secretly jealous. Treena is younger than Mum and she wears a Wonderbra. Personally, I am on Mum's side. At least her nails are real.

- -

Wednesday 30

Told Scarlet about Grandpa Riley. She says it is a classic Lolita complex. Suzy said Grandpa should be careful in case he has a heart attack in the middle of relations. She said ambulance men had to rescue one of her patients last year when her eighty-two-year-old husband died mid-session. He was wearing handcuffs at the time and had to be sawn loose.

Thursday 31

James has laminated the contents of Mum's purse. Mum went to use a £20 note in Waitrose but the cashier said she couldn't accept it as it might be a clever ploy to disguise fake currency. Mum demanded to see the manager. He agreed with the cashier and confiscated the plastic £20 note pending police investigation. Mum says she will be glad when the school holidays are over.

april

Friday 1
April Fool's Day
9 a.m.
It is Anorexia Day. Scarlet and I are going to start starvation this morning. I ate two bowls of Shreddies to prepare. Sad Ed is going to invigilate in case we get hypoglycaemic and try to binge on bourbons.

12 p.m.
This is easy. We have drunk three cans of Diet Coke each and eaten some toothpaste. Scarlet says your breath smells when you are anorexic. I am not hungry at all.

2 p.m.
Sad Ed has eaten three portions of Suzy's lentil moussaka and a bag of Cheetos he had brought for an emergency. My stomach is rumbling. But I will not give in. The Olsen twins did not get where they are by eating Cheetos.

4 p.m.
We have finished the toothpaste.

5 p.m.
I feel faint. Scarlet is very quiet.

7 p.m.
It is all over. Suzy came in with a Waitrose pizza. We are

not cut out to be anorexics. Sad Ed says we can try out alcoholism in a few years instead.

. . . .

Saturday 2

Went to pick Grandpa up from the Pink Geranium sheltered housing complex. He was standing outside with his suitcases and Mrs Peason, looking sorrowful (Grandpa, not Mrs Peason—she looked triumphant). There was no sign of Treena. Mrs Peason said, 'Never in all my years have I come across such a poorly behaved pensioner. He is more of a menace than that dog.'

When we got back, Grandpa asked where the dog was so he could be reunited with the only living thing that cared about him. Mum said it had broken all its house rules and had been sent to Cornwall to live with her mother. Grandpa said the dog would pine itself to death living with those two inbreds (Granny and Grandpa Clegg) and demanded its safe return forthwith. Mum said he was in no position to make demands (I notice she did not correct him calling Granny and Grandpa Clegg inbreds). So Grandpa has shut himself in the spare room and is smoking Benson and Hedges. Mum has festooned the landing with Glade plug-ins but I guarantee she will cave in before Grandpa does.

3 p.m.
Grandpa is victorious. He got all teary and said that both

he and the dog were on their last legs and one of them would probably die in the next few months. I don't think this is true but Mum felt guilty and has agreed to let it return, provided that Grandpa keeps it under strict control and that smoking is confined to the back garden in the dark so that the neighbours can't see. Dad is going to drive to Cornwall tomorrow to fetch it. He is not happy, it is a twelve hour round trip. James is going with him. He is taking his Elvish book and a packet of digestives as a welcome home present.

Sunday 3

The dog is home. It is sitting on the sofa next to Grandpa eating Werther's Originals. Dad is in bed. James made him listen to *Lord of the Rings*, as read by Stephen Fry, for twelve hours and the dog was sick on the M25. Also Granny and Grandpa Clegg did not give the dog up without a fight. They want visiting rights.

The Pope is dead. I do not see what all the fuss is about. He was very old and they can pick another one.

Monday 4

The Pope's death was more significant than I thought. Fat Kylie and her many brothers and sisters are off school. Maybe I should become religious. You get loads of concessions.

Tuesday 5

The election has been declared. It is on May 5th. Ms Hopwood-White let us watch the news at lunchtime. She is running mock elections at school. Mark Lambert said he was going to organize an Anarchist Party. Sad Ed said 'How anachronistic.' And Mark Lambert said, 'No, anarchist, you deaf retard.' So Ms Hopwood-White sent him to Mr Wilmott.

Fat Kylie was back in school. She had a note for Mr Wilmott saying that she needed to be able to sip Coca-Cola throughout the day to keep her strength up at this traumatic time. Even Mr Wilmott is too scared of Fat Kylie to say no.

There was an anti-Hugo Thorndyke leaflet on the doormat when I got home. Scarlet says Suzy says 'going negative' is the only way she will win in this town. She is hoping a sex scandal will rear its ugly head. Scarlet is worried it could all backfire. If Hugo Thorndyke goes negative on Suzy the results could be disastrous. She has heaps of skeletons in her closet including a lesbian experience and hallucinogenic drugs.

Wednesday 6

Fat Kylie could not do PE because of the Pope. Miss Beadle said that she had better be over it by next Wednesday or she would put her on the school hockey team. They are crap and always lose and it means you have to go to school on Saturday.

Mum has banned Grandpa and the dog from excessive daytime telly and biscuits. They were getting through four packets of Gypsy Creams during *LK Today*, *The Jeremy Kyle Show*, *This Morning*, *Neighbours*, *Doctors*, and *Murder She Wrote*. She is enrolling him at the Twilight Years Day Centre, starting on Monday. Grandpa says he will be forced to make raffia owls by over-jolly do-gooders and that the tedium could kill him. I think Mum is hoping this is the case.

Thursday 7
Suzy is in trouble with Labour Party headquarters for her anti-Hugo leaflet. They have written her another one all about extra nurses and tax credits for poor people. It has a picture of the whole family on it, but it has been doctored to make Jack's hair shorter and get rid of Scarlet's goth make-up.

Friday 8
Election fever is sweeping school. Jack is going to be the mock Labour candidate. He is standing against Ali Hassan (Conservative), Pippa Newbold (Lib Dem) and Oona Rickets (Green Party/Lesbian and Gay Alliance/Stop the War). Ms Hopwood-White has banned the BNP from fielding a candidate.

Sad Ed says he is not voting because tragic geniuses are above such a cheap media circus. He is right. I will abstain.

I bet Julie Burchill doesn't vote. She will be too busy enjoying lesbian sex on Brighton beach.

8 p.m.
Scarlet rang to say that Justin is going to be Jack's campaign manager. I have volunteered to help with leaflets.

Saturday 9

Charles and Camilla got married today. Grandpa is outraged. He is still mourning Princess Diana. He says he doesn't blame the Queen staying away from the service. Dad said that, no matter what the Queen thought, she should still have turned up. But Grandpa pointed out that he had a hard job persuading Grandma Riley to turn up at the church when Dad married a Clegg. Luckily Mum was busy descaling the kettle and didn't hear him.

Sunday 10

The dog has done a poo in Clive and Marjory's tulips. It was poking out of one of the flowers. Grandpa said it was an artistic triumph and James took a photo to send to the local paper's 'Fancy That' competition page but Mum says it could jeopardize her dog-poo campaign and deleted the picture and cleared the poo up before Marjory noticed. It has left a smear on the petals. I

hope Marjory does not cut the flowers for the dining table.

· ·

Monday 11

Mum's Day Centre plan has backfired. It turns out that Treena has got a job there after being sacked by Mrs Peason for sexual misdemeanours. Grandpa is jubilant. He says his flames of passion are rekindled. So Mum and I left the room before he got any more graphic.

· ·

Tuesday 12

Went round to Scarlet's after school to help plan Jack's campaign. He is having to use his bedroom as Suzy has taken over the kitchen, cellar, and second bathroom for her campaign. It is painted black. I am going to ask Mum if I can paint my room black. I am too old for stencils of ladybirds.

Justin and Sophie were both there as well. She laughed and said, 'Oh God, the peanut girl,' and tossed her Barbie-blonde hair so that it swished in Justin's face. Jack told her to shut up and that he needed all the help he could get in the fight against fascism (Ali Hassan and the maths club geeks). Ha. She won't be laughing when I am snogging Justin at the victory party in the lower school canteen.

Jack said he is veering towards a Marxist campaign. Justin agreed and said that Karl Marx could well be the

key to cracking the impressionable lower school as well as the über-left anti-Blairite upper sixth. Who is Marx? I am going to have to politicize myself fast.

Asked Mum if I could paint my room black. She said she would compromise on magnolia, apple white, or butterscotch. I do not think they are much of a compromise.

Wednesday 13

Went to the library at lunchtime. The hairy librarian Mr Knox said the only Marx they had was in the video section. It is a film called *Duck Soup*. I said that would do.

Watched the film with Grandpa after school. He said it is a cinematic classic. He laughed so hard he said he had nearly wet himself. I don't know which one is Karl. Probably the one that looks like Robert Winston. He seemed to be in charge. I do not see the political relevance. It must be subliminal, like in Pringles adverts, which make you eat the whole tube. But Justin is right, the madcap humour could win over Year Seven and some of the more idiotic sixth formers. I will take the video to tomorrow's campaign strategy meeting. I bet Sophie hasn't done any research.

Thursday 14

Karl Marx is not one of the Marx brothers, as Justin pointed out after he, Jack, and Sophie had finished rolling round the floor in hysterics. That is the last time I use Mr Knox as a reference tool. I shall only use Google from now on. It is infallible. Except that time me and Sad Ed tried to find the Waterboys' official fanpage and got a disturbing website about men weeing on each other. Jack said that I was a perfect example of the depoliticization of today's youth and that I was exactly why this election was so necessary, to get people to stop worrying about *I'm A Celebrity* and start worrying about big brother (they are doing *Nineteen Eighty-Four* for GCSE and all think they are living in a fascist police state). Sophie said that should be their slogan and Justin agreed. Sophie is a hypocrite. I know for a fact that she voted seventeen times for Jordan last year. Then Justin started to do a Groucho Marx/ Robert Winston impression and they all got hysterics again so me and Scarlet went down to the cellar to help Suzy telephone-canvass disillusioned former Labour voters (all forty-five of them) instead.

Jack came down later and said, 'Sorry, Riley.' But Scarlet told him we are going to work for a real politician (i.e. Suzy) from now on, unless he disbars Sophie from the campaign. Jack asked on what grounds and Scarlet said on blondeness and idiocy. Jack said you can't get rid of someone on the grounds of them being blonde and idiotic and Scarlet said what about Anthea Turner and Jack had to agree. But he is still not going to sack her because Microwave Muffins are sponsoring their posters.

Friday 15

Treena is in Grandpa's bedroom. James says he brought her back from the Day Centre along with a raffia owl (now hanging on the downstairs toilet wall). He says he has not been able to ascertain what is going on in the room due to Neil Diamond being played at high volume but there is possibly sex happening because at one point the dog got shooed out and Grandpa was only wearing a string vest, pants, and socks. I said Treena might be giving him a therapeutic massage for his arthritis. But James said Treena was in her bra and that no one got arthritis 'down there'. (How does James know about things like this? I blame the internet. Mum should put stricter parental controls on it. It still allows access to medical sites.) I asked James where Mum was and why she was allowing this activity to go on, and he said she had called Dad back from work as a matter of emergency and was now Cillit Banging the downstairs loo to block out the horror.

4.30 p.m.

Dad has cautioned Mum over the use of term 'emergency'. Mum says it is an emergency when there are impressionable children in the house. (I hope she is not talking about me. I am not likely to want to go out and snog old men or northern care workers after witnessing Grandpa and Treena's sexploits. And James is only interested in male celebrities and fictitious midgets.) Grandpa said he can't go to Treena's house in case Kelly next door sees him and tells

her husband who is in prison with Treena's husband Des for the same attempted burglary. Mum has compromised. Grandpa is only allowed conjugal visits at pre-arranged times when all under-fourteens can be supervised in a distracting activity. Grandpa says Mum is worse than Mrs Peason. He is right. At least Mrs Peason did not ban Ribena.

Saturday 16

Granny and Grandpa Clegg rang to check up on 'Valerie'. I assume they mean the dog. It must be named after Valerie Singleton, their all-time favourite TV presenter (now a lesbian, but this news does not seem to have reached Cornwall yet). I told them 'he' was fine. I asked how Granny Clegg was and she said she was sick of all the canvassers. Apparently the Lib Dem candidate for Redruth had asked for her vote earlier. He won't get it. She does not approve of Charles Kennedy. Her motto in life is 'Never trust anyone ginger or with a beard. Or, worse, with a ginger beard.' I asked her if she had considered voting Labour but she said, 'Not likely. That Gordon Brown has no neck and greasy hair. You'd think that Sarah would buy him some Vosene.' I pointed out that Gordon Brown was not the leader of the Labour Party and she said, 'That's what you think.' (What does she know, I wonder?) She and Grandpa Clegg are voting UKIP.

Told Grandpa Riley about Valerie. He said no dog of his was going round with a name like that and what was

wrong with 'dog'? Dad said we should have a vote on it and that we could all put a name in a hat (actually a large Tupperware container). I put in 'Byron' after the romantic poet.

The dog is called Frodo. It got off lightly. Mum had put in 'Jeremy', as in Paxman.

. . . .

Sunday 17

Went round Scarlet's. Jack was there with Sophie and Justin. Sophie's dad has printed a hundred 'Turn off *I'm A Celebrity* and tune in to big brother' posters. They have the Microwave Muffins logo at the bottom. Scarlet pointed out that they didn't actually say 'Vote Labour' anywhere on them but Sophie tutted and said the message was implicit. I think she may have overestimated the electorate at John Major High.

. . . .

Monday 18

Jack's election campaign has been derailed. The 'Turn off *I'm A Celebrity* and tune in to big brother' posters have caused confusion. Most people seem to think it is an anti-ITV campaign by Sean Cummings in Year Twelve, whose mum is an accountant at Channel 4. Mr Wilmott has made Lou the caretaker (formerly of Mrs Duddy's Criminals and Retards) take the posters down, as commercial advertising is banned from school premises.

This debacle has cost Jack dearly. The maths club, who are doing daily polls, are putting Pippa Newbold in the lead, down to her free Chomp bars at first break.

Scarlet says Jack has considered sacking Sophie, but that her dad has promised to sponsor T-shirts and free jolly bugs. Sad Ed said he should have more principles but Scarlet said electioneering isn't about principles it is about rich donors and celebrity endorsements.

That is it. I am going to get a celebrity to endorse Jack. Then Justin will be thanking me not Sophie Microwave Muffins Jacobs.

Tuesday 19

Grandpa got a letter today from the hospital informing him that his grommet operation has been cancelled. He says the NHS is going down the pan and that no one cares about pensioners any more and that people like him fought in two wars to put people like Tony Blair in Downing Street instead of Helmut Kohl. Mum pointed out that Grandpa was only seven when the Second World War started. Grandpa was about to reply but Mum's lips went super thin and she did that glary thing with her eyes so he went to take the dog for a walk instead. When he got back he was happy again though. He said he had met a very nice man on the street who had listened to all his problems and agreed with him about the NHS. Mum asked him his name. It is Hugo

Thorndyke, evil Conservative MP for Saffron Walden and environs.

. . . .

Wednesday 20

The election is inescapable. James has joined the Conservative Party, the Liberal Democrats, the Green Party, and Veritas. He says he is keeping his options open. The only party that has not accepted him into its ranks is Labour. You'd think they would want all the support they could get, even from an eight-year-old hobbit obsessive. I said I didn't think he was allowed to sign up until he was of voting age. He said he had used a false name and age, i.e. Grandpa's. I said that was identity theft but he said it was in a good cause because he is going to campaign to get the voting age lowered. I don't think that primary school children should be allowed to vote. Mum doesn't think anyone should be allowed to vote unless they have passed an intelligence test. That would rule out all the O'Gradys and possibly Granny and Grandpa Clegg.

The dog is not responding to its new name. I tried to get it to stop chewing Mum's *Woman and Home* magazine by saying, 'Down, Frodo,' in a commanding but loving voice as recommended by my dog training book. But it totally ignored me and swallowed a picture of Gloria Hunniford and then Mum came in and shrieked, 'Get out of here, you hairy halfwit,' and it stopped what it was doing immediately.

. . . .

Thursday 21

Queen Elizabeth II born (1926)

Grandpa is on the front page of the local paper under the headline 'Ernest's Ear'! There is a photo of him and the dog in our living room. They are looking sadly at the camera. Grandpa is clutching his ear like it is in agony. The article says:

> Ernest Riley (pictured left) has been hit by a cruel double whammy from local NHS and care services. Already reeling after being denied a place at the Pink Geranium sheltered housing unit, Ernest was knocked for six when he found out that a vital ear operation had been cancelled for the second time. Ernest says he is relying on the goodwill and patience of family members but that he fears it could run out at any time.
>
> Local MP Hugo Thorndyke said that this showed just how low Britain's provision for pensioners had sunk at the hands of the Prime Minister. He is spearheading the campaign to get Ernest's Ear on the operating table before election day.

Mum is hopping mad. She said it makes it sound like she is going to throw him out on the street. I think she is thinking of throwing him out now. Grandpa said it wasn't his idea to be in the paper, that Hugo Thorndyke had suggested it. Then the doorbell went and it was Suzy and Scarlet. Mum does not like Suzy very much, she thinks she is too permissive, but she got the Duchy Originals out anyway, so she may be softening. Suzy flounced in in a cloud of Opium and said that Grandpa is being used as a pawn in Hugo Thorndyke's giant game of political chess. She says that Hugo Thorndyke doesn't care if Grandpa lives or dies (I didn't think grommets were life-threatening). Normally Grandpa doesn't like women in politics but Suzy was wearing a daringly low V-neck so he went all teary and let her hug him. He is so transparent.

Suzy has a weird effect on people. It must be her aura of sex counsellor. Or the large breasts. Because then Grandpa admitted to her that his operation hadn't been cancelled, that he had missed it, twice, because they had clashed with crucial storylines in *Neighbours*. Mum made him get the letter out and it was true. It was a stern warning about wasting NHS resources. Suzy is keeping it as evidence. She says Ernest's Ear is going to be the nail in the coffin of Thorndyke's campaign. Then she said she had to go because she had a meet and greet at the Golf Club and a group orgasm session at the Bernard Evans Youth Centre. I hope she doesn't get them muddled up.

Friday 22

Suzy was on Radio Cambridge this morning talking about the Ernest's Ear scandal. She says it was a typical Tory anti-NHS smear and that what Hugo Thorndyke really wanted to do was to shut down the NHS and make Grandpa pay £1,000 to get it done on BUPA instead. Then Hugo Thorndyke came on and said he had been misled by Grandpa. So Suzy asked him if he was accusing a vulnerable elderly man of lying. And then Hugo got all flustered and the presenter tried to cut in because it was time for listeners' recipes but Suzy got the microphone and shouted, 'Are you listening, Saffron Walden? Your MP is trying to get a confused seventy-three year old to shoulder the blame for his own deceit.' Then there was a crashing sound and Brenda from Royston started talking about cauliflower cheese.

Saw Jack on the way to school. He said, 'Nice hit on the Tories, Riley.' Then I remembered that I am supposed to be getting him a celebrity endorsement to lure Justin away from Sophie Jacobs so me, Scarlet, and Sad Ed decided to track one down this weekend. The choices are Marlon out of *Emmerdale* or the McGann brother. We are going to go for Marlon as none of us can remember what the McGann was in or what his name is.

Saturday 23

St George's Day

Went into town with Scarlet and Sad Ed to search for a celebrity. We have ruled out Stead and Simpson, Oxfam, New Look, the shop that has giant pants in the window, Gordon Bennett fabrics, Star Burger, Gray Palmer (no celebrities wear Aertex or tweed), and the library. The locations are: Waitrose (upmarket delicatessen shopping possibilities), Moss Bros (in case he has TV award do to go to and needs to hire a dinner suit), and Sketchleys (in case he needs to get the suit cleaned).

5 p.m.

Walked around Waitrose for two hours without seeing a single celebrity. Miss Beadle and Miss Vicar were in there buying exotic vegetables and Nutella. How can teachers afford to shop in Waitrose? I thought they were all impoverished and had to buy in bulk from Lidl or Netto. Then Sad Ed remembered that Tracey Hughes's brother, Seamus, works on the fish counter on a Saturday. He was gutting a turbot. I asked him if he had ever seen Marlon buying salmon or lobster (expensive celebrity fish) and he said that he had it on good authority (Gary Fletcher who stacks the pet food aisle) that he gets his shopping delivered. So Scarlet asked if he could get his home address but he said it was more than his job was worth. (He has an inflated sense of worth: he wears white wellies for God's sake. Anyone would think he had signed an

100

official secrets act.) So we bought some mini Victoria sponges and came home.

Sunday 24
First Day of Passover

Grandpa is demanding to be taken to the St George's Day parade to show patriotic spirit. Mum said she had a roast to do and Dad is playing golf with Clive so I am going with James and the dog. I do not see what the fuss is about. All it involves is the Brownies and other military-style youth groups marching up the High Street to the church. It is very disappointing. One year James was in it but he has left Cubs because the religious element clashes with his Elvish tendencies.

1 p.m.

The parade was a disaster. I am too weak to relay details but to cut a long story short, Grandpa had a fight with Hugo Thorndyke and the dog savaged Marlon from *Emmerdale*. On the plus side, Hugo Thorndyke was caught on mobile phone camera by Fat Kylie who is going to sell the pictures to the *Daily Mail* so Suzy will be pleased.

Monday 25

Fat Kylie has not sold the pictures to the *Daily Mail*. Brady deleted them by mistake trying to take a photo of his

bottom. I declined to see the picture. Scarlet says Hugo Thorndyke's political career is over anyway. Margot Gyp, who is the Ladies' Captain at the Golf Club, saw the fight and she is the most influential woman in a twenty-mile radius.

. . . .

Tuesday 26

Mr Wilmott has found out about the election betting. He has banned gambling from school premises. Ms Hopwood-White looked worried. She has £5 on Ali Hassan.

. . . .

Wednesday 27

A lot of post arrived for Grandpa, thanking him for supporting Charles Kennedy, Michael Howard, George Galloway, and Robert Kilroy-Silk. He is livid as he has never been a member of any organization in his life, not even the RSPB, on the grounds they might fritter his money on pigeons, which he does not approve of and which are honorary rats anyway. Mum looked at the letters. One of them said, 'Thank you for your interesting suggestion of using "Evergreen" by Will Young as a theme tune.' James has been banned from political activity until he is eighteen. Mum is going to buy a shredder from WHSmith this morning to prevent further identity theft.

6 p.m.

Mum has shredded the entire contents of Dad's filing cabinet plus a letter from Granny Clegg to the dog. What is anyone going to do with that?

8 p.m.

Mum has agreed not to shred anything of Dad's before he has rubber-stamped it. In her enthusiasm she shredded the pin number to Dad's new credit card, before he had memorized it. James said it was 8187.

Thursday 28

Suzy is threatening to take the *Walden Chronicle* to the Press Complaints Commission. Their lead story was the new bollards on the High Street—love them or hate them? There was no mention of the St George's Day Parade gang fight. She has accused the editor, Deirdre Roberts, of running a media cover-up because Deirdre's cousin is married to Hugo Thorndyke's sister. She said that Saffron Walden is like Baghdad and the Thorndykes are the Husseins, with fingers in every pie and spies on every corner. Personally, I think this is stretching it a bit far.

Friday 29

Scarlet has done a terrible thing. She let one of the senior goths pierce her nose with a pair of compasses in the

lower school toilets at first break. It is lucky they did it in there because she was sick almost immediately because of the blood. The goths had to call for the school nurse (aka Mrs Leech, the school secretary) to administer revival techniques. Mrs Leech just wafted her with a maths text book and told someone to get a Coke out of the machine to boost her blood sugar. I hope that is not what Tony Blair is training all his extra nurses to do.

Scarlet revived after the Coke and a Galaxy Ripple. She said it was a rite of passage for the goths to be pierced in as many places as possible. I assume she means body parts, rather than various toilets. Suzy is going to go mad. This could be another major setback in her election campaign.

. . . .

Saturday 30

Suzy has ordered Scarlet to put a plaster over the stud because she has an important public appearance at the Town Hall tonight. It is going to be like *Question Time* on telly, with Deirdre Roberts as David Dimbleby. Scarlet, Sad Ed, and I are going to watch.

8 p.m.

Things did not go according to plan. Suzy has revealed herself to be a former drug taker and sexual deviant. Everything was going OK after the first few questions ('What is your favourite Saffron Walden landmark?'

'Should so-called graffiti "artists" be locked up?' and 'Is France our friend or foe?'). Then Deirdre asked the panel if they had ever taken drugs. Suzy said, 'Yes, and yes I did inhale, does that make me a criminal?' Deirdre said that yes, actually, it did. Suzy should have known better. Deirdre thinks speeding should carry a minimum of life. The next question was about the bollards, but Suzy got an emergency counselling case on her mobile. So, when Deirdre got to Suzy's answer, all everyone could hear was Suzy shouting, 'Dennis, I really think you should consider using more lubricant.' Deirdre looked as if she was going to faint and Hugo Thorndyke seized his opportunity and took over the microphone. He said that Saffron Walden should send a message to Tony Blair that normal middle-class law-abiding citizens won't tolerate this kind of perversion. Margot Gyp, the influential Ladies' Golf Captain, said, 'Hear, hear.' Sad Ed said it was the sound of the fat lady singing. He is trying to be poetic in everyday situations.

Sunday 1

Rogation Sunday

Looked rogation up in the dictionary. It said supplication. So I looked that up. It is something about thanking the gods for victory. I suspect Hugo Thorndyke is doing that right now.

Treena came for her conjugal visit. She looked very pale and worried. She and Grandpa went for a Benson and Hedges in the garden. I heard her say, 'December, Ern. What are we going to do? All the sick and the shitting everywhere.' Her husband, Des, must be a heroin addict. I have seen it on TV. She is going to help him go cold turkey when he gets out in December. When Grandpa came back in he looked pale as well. I'm not surprised. I've seen a photo of Des and he has a tattoo on his neck and wears a Burberry baseball cap. I don't think they did any conjugating today.

Scarlet is out at CHURCH! Suzy is trying to revamp her image after yesterday's disaster. I don't think Scarlet is going to sway any old ladies with her pierced nose, though. It has blown up and gone septic. She looks like Shrek.

Monday 2

May Day Holiday (UK)

Yet another tedious provincial bank holiday. Went over to Sad Ed's but he was feigning illness under threat of being taken to an Aled Jones Fan Club (Essex branch) meeting in Harlow. I asked what he was pretending to have and he said scurvy. Mr and Mrs Thomas are easily duped. Mrs Thomas had gone to Mr Patel's for emergency orange juice.

Took the dog out for a walk into town. Something odd happened. We saw Grandpa and Treena coming out of the emergency chemist's and I am sure Grandpa saw us but he hurried Treena over the road into the White Horse pub instead. The dog tried to follow and wanted to wait outside until he came out. But Fat Kylie was also out there with Paris-Marie and Brady, waiting for their mum and I didn't want people to think I was related so I went to Mr Patel's and bought some Gypsy Creams and we ate them at home while we watched *Chitty Chitty Bang Bang*. I do not think that film should be shown before the watershed. I had to close my eyes on several occasions and the dog whimpered throughout the whole of the child catcher scene. I think it brought back memories of Mrs Peason.

Tuesday 3

Scarlet's nose is horrendous. It is actually seeping green stuff now. Ms Hopwood-White demanded that she remove the nose stud but Scarlet refused on the grounds that it was regulation gold. Ms Hopwood-White pointed out that the rule referred to single ear piercings only but Scarlet said she was being body-partist and possibly

anti-Hindu. So Ms Hopwood-White sent her to Mrs Leech to get some Savlon.

· ·

Wednesday 4
The nose stud is out. Suzy said the deformity could cost her the election, plus Scarlet got mild septicaemia and went all shaky during *BBC Breakfast*. Bob had to take her to work to get it treated so she missed PE this morning (hockey—result 27–2 to Fat Kylie's menacing team, plus two minor electrifications). When she came back she had a bandage across her face like Britney after her nose job. Thin Kylie was instantly impressed. She is already planning extensive surgery. Her mum has saved her child benefit since she was two so she can get a boob job. I said I didn't think that was what the government had hoped she would spend it on. Kylie said what could be more beneficial than a career-boosting DD cup, look at Jordan? Scarlet says she is going to get the nose stud done properly at Camden Market as soon as it is healed. That is like a goth pilgrimage site.

· ·

Thursday 5
Ascension Day
Election Day
8 a.m.
Grandpa is refusing to vote. He says no one has offered him anything worth leaving his *Daily Mail* and bowl of

111

Grape-Nuts for. I said, 'But the political future of Saffron Walden hangs in the balance.' Dad said, 'Yes, between a drug-addled nymphomaniac and a pensioner-beating madman.' James offered to use his vote for him, but Mum shredded the voting card before he could try.

10 a.m.

The John Major High polling station (i.e. a cardboard box outside the lower school canteen) is a hive of political activity (i.e. handing out free things). Ali Hassan has Michael Howard protractors, Pippa has badges with a pop star of your choice (using her sister's badge machine and a pile of *Heat* magazines), Oona Rickets has Stop the War organic lesbian-made flapjacks and, shamefully, Jack, Justin, and Sophie Jacobs are handing out Microwave Muffins (cooked in the sixth form common room microwave, which is ten years old and is under investigation for leaking radiation by the science club). The maths club are running exit polls. They say it is too close to call but that a change from blueberry to double chocolate could swing it for Jack.

3 p.m.

Jack has won the election! He has a majority of thirty-one. Pippa Newbold came second and Ali Hassan and Oona Rickets joint third with twenty-seven votes each. Oona claims she got at least thirty but that several Criminals and Retards spoiled their ballot papers. I lurked near Justin hoping that the post-election madness would rub off on

him and he would throw me against the Coke machine and kiss me passionately, but he was too busy fending Year Seven girls off Jack.

This is all a good omen for Suzy though. I predict she will beat Hugo Thorndyke and join Tony Blair's babes in the Houses of Parliament tomorrow.

2 a.m.
Scarlet rang. Suzy did not win. She says the tweed Saddam Hussein got in. I assume she meant Hugo Thorndyke but Mum came down in her Marks & Spencer's dressing gown and told Scarlet not to ring at such an ungodly hour and then put the phone down.

. . . .

Friday 6
Scarlet says Suzy has taken to her bed. She is playing Sheryl Crow albums and compulsively eating sesame snaps. Bob wants her to stick to sex instead of politics.

Jack says it is the last time he enters a political contest as well. He says there can be no victory in leading an electorate who are swayed by convenience cake. He is not leading an electorate anyway. Ms Hopwood-White failed to secure permission from Mr Wilmott to grant the winner any powers so he is a straw doll (I learnt that from Jeremy Paxman).

Granny and Grandpa Clegg rang in a panic. They are thinking of moving because a Lib Dem got in in St

Slaughter. Mum went pale and warned them that the Lib Dems were strong in Saffron Walden but Granny Clegg said they would rather move to Wales than Saffron Walden and anyway they were thinking more of Camborne, which is Conservative, bordering on BNP. Mum looked relieved. Then Granny Clegg said she and Grandpa wanted to come up and exercise their dog visiting rights in a fortnight and Mum looked weary again.

Saturday 7

I am glad the election is over. Now I can concentrate on more pressing matters. Like, where is my period? Scarlet got hers over a year ago. She is already using organic tampons. She says Miss Vicar told the ski-trip girls that cold weather could bring it on. Why are we having a clement spell? This is typical. I am going to have to wait until November or pray for an unseasonal snowstorm. I have looked it up on the internet. There is even a name for sad people like me. Apparently the two main causes are anorexia or genetic inheritance. I don't think six hours of anorexia count so it must be Mum's fault. It suggests that I ask her when she got her period. Gross. I expect Granny Clegg banned periods in St Slaughter anyway. They probably still call it the 'curse'. I will suffer in silence like Joan of Arc.

Sunday 8

Treena came over for lunch again. I don't think she likes lemon meringue pie. She went all pale when she saw it and ran out and threw up in the downstairs loo. Mum was annoyed. She sees it as a waste of food. I don't know why. It comes out at some point.

At least she has given up smoking though. Mum asked her why she had finally come to her senses and she said, 'It weren't my flaming idea. It's those bloody doctors.' But when Grandpa went out for a Benson and Hedges I noticed she stood in the cloud of fumes, passively inhaling furiously.

Mum says the sooner smoking is banned the better. She says it is anti-social behaviour. She is thinking of starting a catalogue of anti-social incidents in the area. It will be enormous. She thinks Clive and Marjory should get an ASBO for owning a caravan.

Monday 9

We are having a sex talk at school on Wednesday. Ms Hopwood-White gave us all a note to get permission from our parents. Scarlet says Suzy won't let her go. I said I thought Suzy would be all for it but Scarlet says Suzy is of the opinion that the school sex education curriculum is outdated and could set her back years. I am going. I do not have the advantage of a liberated mother or a library full of sex manuals. Sad Ed is going to forge his mum's signature. She still thinks Aled Jones is a virgin.

· ·

Tuesday 10

Everyone has gone sex talk mad. Sad Ed says that at his cousins' school in Leighton Buzzard everyone put anonymous questions in a hat and the 'sexpert' person answered all of them, even whether you should take out your braces when you give a blow job. Mark Lambert said, 'You don't wear braces, fat boy, so you'll be all right.' So Ms Hopwood-White sent him to Mr Wilmott. I don't think he and Kylie should be allowed to come to the talk—they have an unfair advantage. Scarlet says we are all going to be disappointed.

· ·

Wednesday 11

Scarlet was right. I might as well have sat in the library with her, Ali Hassan, and the Jehovah's Witness children. There was no sexpert. It was Miss Beadle and a plastic penis model. I think Mr Wilmott should have chosen a more appropriate teacher. Everyone knows she has no experience with male genitalia. There were no free condoms and no questions about blow jobs. Sad Ed was visibly disappointed.

A mattress has been dumped outside Clive and Marjory's. It appeared overnight. Marjory says it is the

116

O'Grady brothers. They have been running a black market waste collection and disposal firm. Mum is beside herself with potential ASBO excitement. She has catalogued the mattress in a WHSmith notebook and is going to write to the council. (Marjory has palsy in her right hand from excess Jenga playing.)

Thursday 12

The mattress is still there. The dog has taken to sitting on it. Grandpa says he is thinking of joining him. He says it gets the sun most of the day and Mum can't tell him off for spilling Hobnob crumbs.

Friday 13

I hate Friday the thirteenth. Every time anything odd happens at school everyone says, 'Ooooh, Friday the thirteenth!' in a stupid voice. At first break Tracey Hughes dropped her Mars bar and it landed end up on the piece of gum she had just spat out. She might as well have twisted her head around 360 degrees by the reaction from the three Year Eights who saw it happen. They watch too much *Most Haunted*.

Scarlet is celebrating though. It must be some sort of goth festival day. She has got out *Scream 3* and *I Still Know What You Did Last Summer* to watch later. Sad Ed says they are Hollywood trash and that we should watch the

Wicker Man or *The Exorcist* if we want to watch real horror.

10.30 p.m.
Have just got back from Scarlet's. I am never watching horror films again. Even Sad Ed got scared and had to hold my hand. I notice he did not hold Scarlet's hand though. Maybe the studded glove put him off. Scarlet made Bob bring us home in case evil forces were lurking in Waitrose car park. Bob accidentally drove over the mattress when he was reversing up Clive and Marjory's drive to turn around. One of the springs got caught in the undercarriage of the Volvo and the mattress is now stuck on Marjory's flower bed. Bob drove off quickly before anyone could see.

Saturday 14
Marjory is all het up. She claims mysterious Friday the thirteenth forces have moved the mattress. She has asked Mum if she thinks an exorcism is necessary. Mum gave her a glass of cooking sherry and said it was probably just anti-social council estate children or cats. I did not tell her that it was a thirty-nine-year-old gynaecologist in a sick-smelling Volvo. It would have ruined her image of today's youth. How could cats move a mattress anyway? They are not co-ordinated enough. Mum has catalogued it under subsection A of the mattress misdemeanour.

Sunday 15
Whit Sunday
9 a.m.

Barry the Blade is asleep on the mattress. Mum has called 999 but the police said that sleeping vagrants were not an emergency, beard or no beard. Mum said that he was a known knife fetishist and might have progressed to guns but the policeman laughed and said, 'This isn't Hackney, love.' How right he is. Mum said he will be laughing on the other side of his face when he is mopping up blood on Summerdale Road. I think Barry the Blade looks peaceful though.

11 a.m.

Grandpa has been sent to his room. He made Barry the Blade a cup of tea and took him out two Duchy Originals. I'm not sure if Mum is more angry about Barry the Blade or the biscuits.

Am going over to Scarlet's for ritual TV viewing. I hope Barry the Blade is still there when I get back. He is the most interesting thing to happen to our road since the legendary gnome stand-off at Number 38. Maybe he is not a mad murderer after all but a misunderstood philosopher type who has fallen on hard times, like Stephen Hawking but without the keyboard and wheelchair. Maybe he is out there thinking about the space-time continuum. I could engage him in philosophical discussions and discover his genius and then I could be his muse. I told Scarlet on the phone and she said the mattress could be a live art installation. Apparently, Suzy once went to look at some ginger actress asleep in a box. We could become millionaires for our mattress art, especially with a philosophical tramp sleeping on it.

4 p.m.
Barry the Blade has gone. Clearly he wasn't having philosophical thoughts. He started singing 'I'm Just a Love Machine' so Marjory hosed him down on the pretence of watering the tulips. I told Mum about the live art installation and phoning the Tate Gallery but she said the only people she was phoning were the council first thing in the morning.

Monday 16
Mum has called the Uttlesford environmental health department re. the escalating mattress situation. They have not agreed to remove it but are sending someone out to inspect it and assess its position. Apparently, if the majority of the mattress is on Clive and Marjory's garden then they will have to dispose of it themselves. Mum measured it. It is fifty-six centimetres on Marjory's poo-smeared tulips and seventy-two centimetres on the council-owned pavement. She is triumphant.

Tuesday 17

The man from the council came and looked at the mattress after school. He says it is definitely a menace but that he can't get it moved until at least next Monday. Mum threatened to call the *Walden Chronicle* and he said he could probably fit it in tomorrow. Mum rang the *Walden Chronicle* anyway. Her anti-social behaviour crusade knows no bounds.

Wednesday 18

The mattress is gone. The dustbin men took it away. Mum asked if they were going to check it for forensic evidence. They said no, they were going to take it to a junk shop in Cambridge. Apparently students will pay good money for a second-hand mattress. Even one covered in Hobnobs and dog hair.

Thursday 19

The mattress has made the *Walden Chronicle* under the headline 'Dumped Mattress Madness'.

Mum has rung the paper to complain. She says the piece makes her sound like she is the anti-social one. She is never satisfied.

Personally I think a mattress is an ideal object to trip up on, providing an instant crash mat to break the fall.

DUMPED MATTRESS MADNESS

A mattress left abandoned for literally a week has finally been removed following pressure from anti-social campaigner, Janet Riley. Mrs Riley, 40, said the mattress had become a health, crime, and environmental hazard. 'It could have seriously hurt someone if they had tripped on it, not to mention the potential of it being set on fire by thugs.'

Friday 20

Granny Clegg rang to make arrangements for their dog access visit. Auntie Joyless is going to get her 'hooge' verrucas prayed off at a church convention in Newmarket, so she is going to drop her and Grandpa on the M11 at 9 a.m., traffic and foot pain pending. Granny wants Dad to pick them up from the Junction 8 services and to bring 'Valerie' with him. She says they want some time with it alone, out of the brainwashing grip of Grandpa Riley. Grandpa Riley says he is going to train the dog to attack anyone who thinks 'hooge' is a word.

I can tell Mum is dreading the weekend. She has hoovered the stairs three times and cleaned out the cupboard under the sink. At least she doesn't have to share a room with James.

. . . .

Saturday 21
9.30 a.m.

Junction 8 services. There is no sign of Granny and Grandpa Clegg so we are eating proscribed Egg McMuffins. Dad says it is payback for making him wait around a motorway service station when he could be at home reading the motoring section of the *Telegraph*.

10 a.m.

Dad has phoned Mum but it is engaged. It is probably Auntie Joyless from a payphone on the A30 saying they have diverted to Trago Mills.

11.45 a.m.

Still no sign of Granny and Grandpa Clegg. Phone is still engaged at home.

Motorway services are a hotbed of adulterous sex. I have seen at least three suspicious couples running into the Travelodge next door and then coming out an hour later, including Tracey Hughes's mum and one of the traffic police. I will not blab though. Tracey Hughes's mum is hard as nails.

123

2 p.m.
No sign. Have eaten a Little Chef omelette and a chocolate ice cream sundae. The dog has eaten four bags of Doritos and an Early Starter Breakfast.

2.15 p.m.
Dad finally got through to Mum. Apparently James has been online all morning learning about Middle Earth. Dad said that was a good argument for broadband but Mum said she was not going to fork out an extra £7.99 a month to encourage an eight year old's Tolkien habit. Then she told Dad to widen his search. Dad said he was not going to cruise up and down the motorway looking for a pair of yokels. Mum then said something severe because we are back in the car heading towards London.

5 p.m.
We have been to every service station on the M11. No one has seen two short pensioners with odd accents carrying Spar bags. We thought we had struck lucky at Junction 3 but it turned out to be two Romanian panel beaters. Dad says he is going home.

5 p.m.
Granny and Grandpa Clegg were already at home. They arrived in a police car fifteen minutes ago. Auntie Joyless got confused and dropped them at the Q8 Garage in

Stansted. Mum asked why they hadn't rung and Granny Clegg said she had, but it had been engaged. (James has been sent to his room and internet access has been reduced to half an hour, off peak only.) Apparently they walked all the way from Stansted but got lost and scared near the Whiteshot Estate when a 'darkie' (possibly Mrs Wong or one of the Hassans) tried to help them so they called 999 again.

They were overjoyed to see 'Valerie'. But the dog got excited at the smell of Fray Bentos and immediately threw up its Doritos and Early Starter Breakfast. Grandpa Riley said he felt like joining it. So Mum sent him to his room.

I said it was all a lesson in the importance of mobile phones. Which was when I got sent to join James. Mum is just annoyed because Clive and Marjory saw the police car and now probably think she is harbouring criminals.

I do not hold out much hope for tomorrow. Treena is coming for tea. They are not likely to see eye to eye.

* * *

Sunday 22
Trinity Sunday

Woke up with a giant Des Lynam lying next to me and the dog drooling on my face. I don't know how James gets any sleep, the dog has to be let out to wee at least twice in the night.

The day got progressively worse from there. Granny and Grandpa Clegg wanted to take Valerie for a walk but Grandpa Riley said they couldn't be trusted on their own not to steal him or teach him Cornish gibberish so he made me follow them round Saffron Walden. I hid several paces behind with my hood up. When we got back, Treena's Datsun was on the drive and she was snogging Grandpa in the back seat. Granny Clegg said, 'Shut your eyes, Norman,' and Grandpa Riley wound the window down and said, 'You're just jealous, Joan,' so Grandpa Clegg told him to get out of the car and say it, so he did, but luckily Mum came out and said lunch was ready.

No one spoke during lunch. It was punctuated only by the sound of Treena throwing up in the downstairs loo.

Then, Auntie Joyless arrived early from Newmarket. She makes Mum look permissive. Her lips are so thin they are non-existent and she wears men's shoes. She asked if I had got to Corinthians 3, Chapter 4 yet. I said I had yet to enjoy that part (or any part). I asked about her veruccas and she said they were definitely smaller, thanks to the power of Reverend Billy's prayer. Grandpa Riley said that Reverend Billy sounded like a charlatan and that a good dose of Bazuka would work wonders. James asked if Auntie Joyless had checked Reverend Billy's ecclesiastical credentials. Auntie Joyless said that God didn't need to hand out identification cards and

126

that Reverend Billy had cured Barbara Pengelly's women's troubles and that was good enough for her. Then Treena came out of the bathroom after being sick again and said, 'Christ on a bike, I'll be throwing up my arse if this goes on.' Auntie Joyless snapped 'Blasphemer' at her. Grandpa Riley said how dare she shout at someone in Treena's condition. I said 'What condition?' but no one heard me. Mum said it might be a good idea if Treena went out for a little while but Grandpa Riley said it was 'pissing down' and she wasn't to know Auntie Joyless was a god botherer. Which would have been bad enough, except that he actually called her 'Joyless'. Auntie Joyless stormed out to the Mini Metro and said it was the last time she was leaving Cornwall, verrucas or no verrucas. Granny Clegg said, 'Get the Spar bags, Norman, we're going home.' Grandpa Clegg said something unrepeatable about Grandpa Riley and Auntie Joyless said she would pray for us all. Then the dog saw that Granny Clegg was leaving and made a run for the Mini Metro but Auntie Joyless slammed the door and the dog hit the side panel making a huge dog-shaped dent and knocking off the wing mirror. Granny Clegg screamed 'Valerie!' but Auntie Joyless drove off quickly before she could get out.

Mum says she is banning Treena and ending dog visiting rights. Dad says it shows why Rover have gone out of business if a dog can cause that much damage.

I think Treena is bulimic. It is very Jacqueline Wilson. I will try to get on her side and help her overcome her awful 'condition'.

. . . .

Monday 23

There is no justice in the world. Thin Kylie has won the lottery. She was not in school to share the joyous news, she is on a celebratory week at Disneyworld, but, according to Fat Kylie, her stepdad Terry got a million on the lottery on Saturday. Why don't we do the lottery? Actually, I know why and that is because Mum says there's more chance of being killed by a donkey and she would rather put the £1 into her Barclays Saver Account. Where is the fun in that? If I won, I would buy a mansion in Derbyshire like Mr Darcy's where I could languish about looking tragic and give the rest to poor people.

Mark Lambert is dead excited. He reckons he is going to get a minibike and a season ticket to West Ham. Scarlet says he is an idiot and that Kylie will dump him the minute she gets back. She can afford to now. The money will move her up a social circle, like Heather Mills McCartney. She will be able to buy real Burberry instead of the Made in Taiwan stuff off the Saturday market.

To add insult to injury, I have a dentist's appointment tomorrow with sadistic Mrs Wong. I have tried to change dentist several times (every six months, in fact) but the only other dentist with space was Mr Webb, who is a renowned drunk and once tried to snog Leanne Jones, according to Leanne. So Mum won't let me see him. I would rather run the gauntlet of a drunken child molester than Mrs Wong. She is evil personified. I may well write to Hugo Thorndyke MP to complain about the general lack of suitable dentists.

Tuesday 24

I cannot speak. One side of my face is swollen and I keep drooling down my chin. Mrs Wong gave me two fillings. I asked if I could have a second opinion but she pointed her drill at me and said, 'Don't be silly, little girl. You want more pain when teeth go black and drop out then I have to give you crown?' I did not want to argue with a madwoman with what looked like a Black and Decker, so I let her give me two injections and then lecture me on the perils of the western diet and why all my teeth will fall out by the time I'm forty if I don't give up Coke. Clearly she has not seen the relationship her son Alan has with the school vending machine. He has been known to eat three Mars bars in one break. Luckily I was so disabled I could not go back to school. I am on the sofa with a tea towel to catch the dribble (Mum's idea) watching *Bargain Hunt*. That man's hair is unfeasibly large.

Sad Ed came round in the evening. He is devastated. Mrs Noakes from WHSmith (no chin; bad perm; calls trousers 'slacks') rang his mum to tell her that he had bought a copy of *Lady Chatterley's Lover* in his lunch break. She is concerned that he bought it for the sex parts not the literary merit (she is right). He has had his pocket money stopped and his bookshelves checked for further potentially damaging material. *Romeo and Juliet*, *The Sleepover Club*, and *You and Your Body* (pop-up version) have been confiscated pending closer inspection. He says it is like *Fahrenheit 451* in his house, even Enid Blyton is under suspicion. I'm not sure what he means. But it is very hot in there. Mr Thomas always has the heating on full because of his bonsai collection.

. . . .

Wednesday 25

School is still awash with lottery madness. I hope Mrs Britcher did not tick the 'no publicity' box on the ticket because, according to Fat Kylie, the *Walden Chronicle* is camped out on their doorstep awaiting their return. Tracey Hughes told her mum who told the police who told the fat traffic warden who told his wife who is the receptionist at the paper. Nothing is secret in this town. How I long for the anonymity of London, where the newsagent is not likely to inform on you for buying a sex book and your neighbours are more likely to be drug dealing terrorists than Jenga-playing accountants.

. . . .

Thursday 26

Thin Kylie's mum, Cherie, is on the front page of the *Walden Chronicle*. It is a picture of her dressed as Britney Spears in last year's carnival looky-likey competition (she came second after Les Brewster as a bald John Prescott) and the headline 'She's So Lucky'. (I think the reference to Britney's minor hit will be lost. They should have put 'Toxic'.) The *Walden Chronicle*, in a never-before-seen act of investigative journalism, managed to trace the Britchers to Disneyworld (Mark Lambert told them Kylie's mobile number) and interviewed Cherie at the poolside bar. I think she may have been drunk at the time because a lot of the words had asterisks in the middle.

Mum said it was proof there was no God and that they will only spend it on gold taps and Austrian blinds. James said that, statistically, most lottery winners spend their money on holidays and cars and that he hoped that Auntie Joyless did not know she felt like that about our good Lord. Mum did not look pleased at his cavernous knowledge or new-found religious leanings. I think she is rueing the day she bought *Encyclopaedia Britannica* on CD-Rom and sent him to a primary school with a vicar as the headmaster.

Friday 27

Thank God it is half term next week. I do not want to see Kylie or hear about her again. Everyone is mad with anticipation for her return, even Melanie Bazley in Year

Eight whom she beat up last week for getting the last Double Decker out of the Coke and crisp machine (note correct use of whom, as learnt in double English today before it got suspended when Mark Lambert tried to belch 'Whole Again' and was sick by mistake).

I am all alone for a week as well. Sad Ed is going to Butlin's in Minehead and Scarlet is going on a tantric sex retreat in India with Bob and Suzy to help her recover from the election disappointment. (Scarlet is not going to do anything tantric, she is going to commune with indigenous cultures.) I asked Mum if we could go on holiday and she said we were, in August, as usual. I said that Granny Clegg's was hardly a new experience and she said there was nothing India had that Cornwall didn't. I said exotic wildlife and curry and she said, 'Looe Monkey Sanctuary and the Rajpoot in Truro.' I will never get to Paris at this rate.

. . . .

Saturday 28

Grandpa has broken up with Treena. I asked if it was to do with the throwing up and he said 'kind of'. I am not surprised. It is very offputting. She was sick seven times last Sunday, beating the dog's record. It is very disappointing from a tragic and interesting point of view. Mum is relieved though. I think the whole thing was jeopardizing her reputation as a law-abiding puritan.

. . . .

Sunday 29

Grandpa is moping round the house. I asked if he wanted to watch *The O.C.* with me (Mum had taken James to the museum with Mumtaz to look at its vast collection of old coins and a stuffed lion). But he said all the age-gap relationships reminded him of himself and Treena so he turned it off. He is deluded. No one on *The O.C.* would wear nylon for starters. Or say 'bag of shite'.

Monday 30

Spring Bank Holiday (UK)

No school and no friends. I am going to devote this week to bettering myself through literature. I am going to read *Emma*. Which is apparently just like *Clueless* but set in England.

5 p.m.

It is not like *Clueless*. There is too much fainting. And the men sound awful. But it is good for me. So I am going to persevere.

Tuesday 31

Mum's WHSmith ASBO catalogue is out again. There is a dodgy man with tattoos loitering with intent outside the For Sale house over the road. It has been empty for months since Mr and Mrs Lawson got divorced and moved to Haverhill and Benidorm respectively. James says it is overpriced for a four-bed semi with a through lounge, but it does have the advantage of a south-facing garden.

10 a.m.
Mum has called 999. The man has gone through the side gate and has not been seen for seven minutes.

11 a.m.
It was not a burglar. It was a prospective buyer. Apparently he got tired of waiting for the estate agent and was just having a look through the patio doors to see whether his L-shaped sofa could fit it. Mum said L-shaped sofas were a crime in themselves. She is annoyed because the police declined her offer to see her ASBO catalogue. It is now several pages long.

Wednesday 1

Grandpa is missing Treena. I caught him sniffing an old cigarette packet earlier and his daytime TV viewing has gone through the roof because he is refusing to go to the Twilight Years Day Centre in case she is working. I hope they get back together soon. I cannot watch *Neighbours* twice in one day.

Also, I have given up on *Emma*. It is totally implausible and not very tragic. Am reading Dad's *Da Vinci Code* instead. It is set in Paris so is bound to be good.

Thursday 2

That tattooed man must have bought the house opposite. The For Sale sign has come down. Mum says she thinks he is a cash buyer—probably a gangster from East London spending his ill-gotten gains. I hope so, he might have Ray Winstone or Guy and Madonna round to dinner. Or he might have a glamorous gangster daughter my age, which would be excellent. There is nothing to do round here when Scarlet and Sad Ed are away.

Grandpa has caved in and called Treena. Even he couldn't cope with that many makeover programmes. He is going to see her on Sunday. They are meeting on neutral territory (the White Horse). He says he is willing to meet her demands, whatever the consequences. What is she demanding? More food?

Friday 3

Our new neighbours have moved in. They are not gangsters from East London, they are Kylie Britcher and her lottery-winning mum and stepdad! James and I watched in horror from my window as the removal men carried in a flab-buster machine, a tropical-themed drinks cabinet, and a four-poster bed with leopard-print canopy.

James says it is the beginning of the end of Summerdale Road. He is right.

7 p.m.

Cherie just came over to invite us for cocktails and karaoke tomorrow to 'celebrate' her and Terry's arrival! She has invited Clive and Marjory as well but they said they had a regional Jenga bout in Bishop's Stortford. Mum was too slow trying to think of an excuse so we are going to have to go. Kylie is going to go mental when she knows I live here.

Saturday 4

Sad Ed rang and asked me to go over to commiserate over his week of hell at Butlin's (i.e. group activity and swimming, revealing flabby upper arms). Told Ed about Kylie and he agreed it was a life-threatening situation. He said I can stay at his if I want. But his spare room is taken over by his mum's Aled Jones memorabilia collection, and last time I stayed I got the feeling Aled

138

was watching me sleep, so I said I would take my chances.

James has got out of going because he is only eight and Mum does not want him exposed to karaoke or too many E-numbers. Mum made Grandpa promise to put him to bed at 8.30 and not to let him watch anything on ITV. There is no hope. Grandpa is addicted to *You've Been Framed*.

11 p.m.
I should have gone to Ed's. Even a night with forty-seven Aled Joneses would have been better than that. The Britcher's house is Mum's Room 101. Their doorbell plays 'Rule Britannia' and they have Alsatian dog statues guarding the porch. Cherie came to the door wearing a figure-hugging halter top and miniskirt. It was in stark contrast to Mum who was in figure-concealing beige Marks & Spencer's linen and Clark's sandals. At first I thought I had had a lucky escape because Kylie was nowhere to be seen, but Cherie said she was in her room playing Nintendo and I should go and join her. I looked to Mum to get me out of it, but she was too busy staring in horror at the Austrian blinds so I had to go upstairs.

Kylie was on the phone, presumably to Mark Lambert. She said, 'F**k off, I ain't telling you . . . no, I ain't . . . no I ain't . . . oh, all right, Wonderbra and a thong . . . the black one from BHS.' Then she saw me and said 'Oh . . . my . . . God. There is, like, a retard in my room. Laters.'

Then she looked at me menacingly and said, 'What . . . the f**k . . . are you doing in 'ere?'

I explained the proximity of our houses, now that her family had had the good fortune to win the lottery, and she said, 'Don't tell me that fat poof friend of yours lives near here as well. This is, like, sadland central.'

I told her that indeed Sad Ed did live two hundred yards away on the corner of Loompits Avenue, but that he was neither fat nor gay. And she said, 'Are you, like, blind?'

I suggested we should go downstairs and do the karaoke and ignore our differences but she said, 'Yeah, right. I'm going down Barry Island in half an hour to see Mark, I ain't singing no Amarillo shite.'

I said wouldn't her mum mind (Barry Island is the car park on the Common where the O'Gradys and similar youths go to rev up their Fiestas and have sex) but she said, 'She'll be pissed in half an hour and forget I'm in anyway.'

At that point I left and went downstairs to find Dad singing 'Is This The Way To Amarillo?' and Mum sipping Appletise with an umbrella in it. Cherie cheered when Dad finished and put her hand on his arm. I noticed Dad did not try to remove it. He is easily swayed by tight clothes.

Then Cherie said, 'It's *Grease* next, who wants to do that?'

So before she could make me sing 'You're the One That I Want' with Terry I said I would go home and check on James and Grandpa.

Cherie said, 'Oh, I didn't know you had two, Jan. How old is he?'

Mum went all tight-lipped (name shortening is one of her banned activities) and said he was eight. Cherie said, 'Oh, an accident. One was enough for me, all that sweating and heaving and pain. It's not natural, is it?'

And Terry said, 'And that was just the conception!'

Dad laughed and Mum shot him one of her looks so he pretended to have a coughing fit instead.

Cherie said, 'Not like now. When our girls get pregnant they can book 'emselves in for the slice and they get a tummy tuck at the same time. I've got stretch marks the size of dinner plates right down to my hoo-ha.'

Mum said she didn't think I was planning on pregnancy any time soon and Cherie said, 'But you can't stop their urges, can you, Jan. They're all at it.'

Luckily, before Mum could highlight my lack of experience at even snogging anyone, James arrived to say that Grandpa and Treena were in the bath with a box of Celebrations (Treena showed up unannounced—apparently she couldn't wait until tomorrow to see Grandpa's grisly bits) so he couldn't do a poo (downstairs toilet blocked again). Mum said she had better sort Grandpa out so that James could poo in peace. But Dad, who had just been handed a pint glass of Bailey's and what looked like fruit salad, said he would stay.

I don't know exactly what happened after that, but Treena has gone home, Grandpa is on a caution for attempting conjugation outside previously agreed terms and conditions, and Dad is asleep on the sofa.

Thank God Scarlet is back from Bob and Suzy's tantric sex retreat tomorrow. My life on Summerdale Road has become fraught with danger.

Sunday 5

Went round to Scarlet's with Sad Ed to hear about the tantric sex week. Suzy is definitely back to normal. She came downstairs in a kaftan looking red and sweaty and said, 'Oh, Rachel, my beautiful child, you must go to India, it is so liberating.' Then she danced back into the bedroom where I could clearly see Bob naked on the floor reading a sex manual. Scarlet says they have been at it for forty-seven hours now, including on the flight from Mumbai.

Ed says he saw a programme about tantric sex once on Discovery Home and Leisure. He says it sounded painful and boring to him. Scarlet said she wouldn't know, she spent all her time lying on her mat in the hut and reading Kafka. I said I thought she was going to commune with indigenous cultures. She said she went outside once but she passed out because her goth clothes were too black and heavy in the heat.

Got home and the two Kylies were sat on the front wall drinking Shandy Bass. I have catalogued them in Mum's ASBO book for underage drinking and loitering. Treena was in Grandpa's bedroom, conjugating again.

142

I have a mind to catalogue them as well. It is highly anti-social to have sex when everyone else is trying to watch *Antiques Roadshow*.

. . . .

Monday 6

There has been a stand-off at school over the seating arrangements in the lower school canteen. It is over the free school dinners table. Mrs Brain makes all the poor people, like the Kylies, Ali Hassan, and the rest of the Whiteshot Estate, sit on one table so she can monitor who doesn't have to pay. But now that Thin Kylie is rich she has been ejected and has to sit with normal people instead. Fat Kylie is up in arms. She was used to getting all Thin Kylie's leftovers.

Sad Ed said it was like South Africa before they banned apartheid and accused Mr Wilmott of being a white supremacist. So Mr Wilmott gave Sad Ed detention but Scarlet told Mr Wilmott that he was as good as holding him political prisoner and that she was texting Suzy immediately for Labour Party back-up. Mr Wilmott panicked and agreed to end the 'povvy table' but Mrs Brain went mad and said it would be a free-for-all with the free meal tokens (this is after Stacey O'Grady forged two hundred last year and no one paid for food for two days). So now there is going to be a discussion at next week's PTA meeting.

Scarlet has diverted her hummus sandwich rally to an anti-class-segregation one. She says she will not rest until

the Kylies can sit where they like to eat their chips and processed meat products.

- -

Tuesday 7

I am finally getting to go to Paris! There is a school trip at the end of the month for anyone doing French GCSE. Ms Hopwood-White is jubilant—she had to get Mr Wilmott to lift his ban on school outings, imposed after last year's Year Ten Geography field trip to Wales when Darren Woodley accidentally set fire to the youth hostel trying to light his farts. Me and Sad Ed are going but Scarlet says she will be at Glastonbury with Bob and Suzy. (I asked Mum if I could go to Glastonbury last year but she said it was a hotbed of illegality and potentially eardrum-damaging music and reminded me that I had only lasted three hours in a tent in Granny Clegg's garden: Hester's cats were pawing the canvas, it was terrifying.) Mark Lambert and the Kylies are going as well. I am staggered that they have been allowed to take GCSE French. Mark Lambert falls about laughing every time Ms Hopwood-White says '*Oui*'. Hugo Thorndyke is right, school standards are falling.

- -

Wednesday 8

Mum is not happy about the Paris trip. She thinks it will be racked with teenage sex and alcohol. I think she has been panicked by Cherie and her 'urges' speech.

I pointed out that *a*) I had no intention of having sex with any of the morons in my year until I was at least sixteen, if ever and that *b*) it could harm my GCSE result if I didn't go. Mum said she would think about it. Anyway—there is no chance of me being a teenage mother until I get my period, which is still freakishly absent.

. . . .

Thursday 9

The shopkeepers of Saffron Walden have followed the lead of fellow shopping Meccas Lakeside and Bluewater and have banned hood-wearing. It is on the front page of the *Walden Chronicle*. Mum says it is a vital blow for anti-social youths.

. . . .

Friday 10

Mum is writing to the council and to the Saffron Walden Chamber of Commerce to complain about the hood ban. She was ousted from Boots for having the hood up on her cagoule. I took the opportunity of her being blinded by anger to get her to sign the Paris trip note. Now all I have to do is get a cheque off Dad.

. . . .

Saturday 11

Went round Sad Ed's to plan what we are going to do on our Paris trip. Ed is overexcited because some dead singer is buried there. Ed said he isn't any old dead singer—he is Jim Morrison, legendary drug-abusing sexual deviant who died prematurely in mysterious circumstances. Ed is hoping some of these qualities are going to transfer through the grave into him. I said I didn't think Ms Hopwood-White would agree to visiting a graveyard but he said that Chopin was buried there as well so we could use that as a lure.

More importantly—what am I going to wear? I am not sure that the French appreciate vintage, let alone Brownie T-shirts. They all wear tight black things. I am going to have to persuade Scarlet to lend me her goth outfits.

Sunday 12

Went round Scarlet's. She is refusing to lend me goth clothes. She says she needs them for Glastonbury and that all she can spare is a pair of school plimsolls and a beret she wore on no-uniform day last year when she went as Che Guevara. She says it will be ironic.

Watched *The O.C.*, which was full of glamorous alcoholics and charity balls. I wish my mother was more American. She could stagger around the house in kitten heels and Gucci, clutching a champagne flute, instead of the Dettox spray which is usually welded into her hand.

Treena was round ours when I got back. Her bulimia is not working. She is definitely putting on weight.

Monday 13

Jewish Feast of Weeks

Something is wrong with Thin Kylie. She was suspiciously quiet at school and didn't even make a comment when Emily Reeve turned up wearing knee-length socks (not in a fashionable Japanese way). Now she is sitting on the front wall crying. Fat Kylie is trying to comfort her whilst simultaneously smoking a cigarette and eating a packet of Skittles.

Maybe I should try to befriend her. I could be like Cher in *Clueless* and mould her into a better person. Plus she might be a chav genius—like Ms Dynamite, only white. Yes—that is it! I am going to do a good deed and help her out of her meaningless existence. This is my one chance to make my life more Julie Burchill and less Enid Blyton.

5 p.m.

That did not go according to plan. Something very bad has happened. It turns out that the giant Justin Timberlake badge was significant and that Kylie's relationship with Mark Lambert has moved beyond the minky-touching stage but not, apparently, to the buying condoms stage because she needs the morning-after pill. I told her she could get it from the chemist but she said she had got it four times this month already and is on a blacklist at Boots and Superdrug. I said, couldn't Fat Kylie get it for her? (I didn't say 'Fat'.) But Fat Kylie said, 'I'm

Catholic, innit, I don't believe in contraception.' Then they both stared at me waiting for me to say something. Their tightly gelled hair and giant hooped earrings were so menacing I ended up offering to get the pill for Kylie. I have made a doctor's appointment for tomorrow lunchtime. Boots will never believe I am sixteen.

Tuesday 14

7 a.m.

Woke up feeling sick. I have made a terrible mistake trying to befriend someone from a council estate. Scarlet would never make me do this. But then Scarlet would never sleep with anyone without several methods of contraception, especially with Mark Lambert. Plus her dad is an abortionist so she has options. I thought about trying to get off school but, even if I did get past Mum's forensic vomit checks, the Kylies would kill me.

4 p.m.

I have done something truly awful. I have given Thin Kylie breath mints instead of the morning-after pill. It is Dr Potter's fault. She was away so I had to see Dr Braithwaite (huge hands; lazy eye; bottle of whisky in desk drawer) who plays golf with Dad and is renowned for his inability to abide by patient confidentiality rules. If I had asked for the morning-after pill half of Saffron

148

Walden would have known by tomorrow morning. So I feigned a stomach bug and got a prescription for milk of magnesia, and a lollipop (for not crying). But on my way back to school I had a vision of my life when Kylie found out so I diverted via home and told Mum I had a headache and that Mrs Leech had run out of painkillers following last week's inter-year hockey tournament. (It is surprisingly easy to lie when your life is under threat.) I had planned to give Kylie some vitamin tablets or something else harmless but possibly resembling morning after pills but all Mum had was bright pink liquid Calpol so I dispensed a load of Grandpa's Smint-type things into one of Mum's miniature Tupperware containers and took those back to school instead.

The Kylies were waiting in their headquarters (aka the lower school toilets). When I gave them the pot Thin Kylie said, 'They didn't look like that last time?' And Fat Kylie said, 'Why are there so many?' Why, oh why, didn't I check how many pills is normal? Any other nearly fourteen year old would be familiar with this kind of thing. I told her I had got her some for next time and changed the bottle so her mum wouldn't find out. Luckily, the Kylies are easily fooled—Thin Kylie said, 'Wicked,' and took one of the mints immediately.

Oh, God, I am a bad person. What if she really is pregnant? It will be all my fault. Maybe I can blame faulty drugs.

6 p.m.
What if Cherie threatens to sue the pill company? They
will test the pills and find out they are no more potent
than TicTacs. I am doomed.

Wednesday 15
Kylie was off school today. I hope she has not had a bad
reaction to the mints.

Thursday 16
False alarm. She was in London at her mum's *X-Factor*
audition. Cherie has no hope if her karaoke is anything to
go by.

Friday 17
Am still in morning-after pill panic. Sad Ed and Scarlet
asked me what was wrong. I lied and said the dog had got
a miniature orc model stuck in its throat and might have
to have an operation. I felt awful afterwards but if I tell
them the truth they will be all weird anyway. Anyway, it
is not a total lie, the dog did eat an orc but threw it up
during *Countdown*.

Thin Kylie beat up Dean Denley, the one-eyed midget
in Year Seven, at last break. I am hoping it is a sign of PMT.

Saturday 18

Tried to spy on Kylie from my bedroom but their Austrian blinds were in the way. James offered me his binoculars but I declined. I do not think even they can get past two metres of pink ruffle.

. . . .

Sunday 19

Father's Day

Forgot Father's Day in the pill panic. Had to make an emergency outing to Mr Patel's (the only shop open at 7.45 a.m.) to buy a card. He had obviously experienced a last-minute rush as the choice was limited to a racing car design with 'from your loving son' inside or a giant padded Care Bear one with 'You're my best friend'. I chose the racing car one (£1.79). The padded one was £5.99. I will swap it with James.

10 a.m.

James had made Dad a card with a glued-on picture of Carol Vorderman (Dad's favourite intellectual TV presenter). He agreed to swap for £3.50 and my copy of *The Princess Diaries*. So it would have been cheaper and less weird to get the hideous padded bear card. Dad said the Carol Vorderman card was very artistic. He is good at lying. They teach him to do it at work.

. . . .

Monday 20

It is SATS week. Oh, God. How could I have forgotten this as well? It is all the stress from Thin Kylie and her morning-after menaces. Mr Wilmott gave us a talk in Assembly how it wasn't about not letting the school down, it was about not letting ourselves down. That is rubbish. He is just worried about being replaced by a superhead like at Harold Wilson Modern in Bishop's Stortford (now the Burger King Sports Academy). I have English and Science tomorrow. I am going to have to revise all night.

7 p.m.
Have stocked up with banned Red Bull from Mr Patel (smuggled it into the house inside a pomegranate juice carton). Will start revising after *Watchdog*.

8 p.m.
James and dog have drunk all the pomegranate juice/Red Bull. They are disturbing my science revision by jumping on the bed next door and singing 'Light My Fire' (Will Young version).

8.15 p.m.
Not the dog, obviously. It is barking.

8.30 p.m.
Will just watch *You Are What You Eat*.

9 p.m.
And *Supernanny*.

10 p.m.
OK, am definitely going to revise. Have drunk two cups of Nescafé.

* *

Tuesday 21

First day of summer
7 a.m.
Aaaagh. Nescafé was decaffeinated. It is all over. I am going to fail my SATS and get sent to a pupil referral unit. Actually that might be interesting. I bet they are full of misunderstood youths. Although I know Stacey O'Grady has been in one three times and he is not misunderstood, he really is an idiot.

James and the dog are still asleep. They did not go to bed until midnight. Mum thinks they might have diabetes. Or sleeping sickness. Have hidden the incriminating carton in the dustbin in case Mum finds it and dusts it for clues.

Will read *To Kill A Mockingbird* on the way to school to make up for lost time.

4 p.m.
Walked into lamppost trying to read on way to school and missed English exam due to blood pouring from gash on forehead. Then could not concentrate in science due to

153

itchy bandage haphazardly put on by Mrs Leech. So now am disfigured and a moron with the SAT results to prove it. Plus Thin Kylie is still showing no signs of having period and I know Fat Kylie is on because she had to leave the exam twice due to period pain. Although Sad Ed says it may be because she ate five packets of Skips in registration.

Wednesday 22

7 a.m.
Maths. At least you can't revise for maths. You either know it or you don't. That's what Sad Ed says anyway.

4 p.m.
Sad Ed is wrong. You can revise for maths. At least I would have known what a quadratic equation was if I had bothered to check last night. I am doomed. I will be at the bottom of the league table, condemning Mr Wilmott and John Major High with me.

Thursday 23

Scarlet has gone to Glastonbury. Suzy faked her a sick note claiming she had diarrhoea. Scarlet tried to get her to change it to TB but Suzy was adamant that diarrhoea was more convincing. Tony Blair has no hope of tackling truancy if would-be Labour MPs are going to flout the

laws to take their children to drug-addled music festivals.

Thank God it is Paris tomorrow. Maybe the change of climate will bring on Thin Kylie's period. And even mine!

* *

Friday 24

10 p.m.

Am in Paris. Romance of city blighted only by having to share a room with Emily Reeve who has brought her entire doll collection with her. Sad Ed has a room of his own. This is because Mark Lambert said he might accidentally try to stab or maim Ed in his sleep as he is learning combat training with the ATC. Ms Hopwood-White, vaguely aided by hopeless student teacher Mr Vaughan (twenty-three; earring; Gitanes and possible drug habit) has put them at opposite ends of the Travotel corridor.

Tomorrow we are going to the Louvre and then the Eiffel Tower. I expect they will be full of long-haired mysterious French students who want to whisk vintage English girls off to drink espressos by the Seine. It is a shame my hotel window does not have a view of Paris by night, as advertised on the hotel's website. Instead it has a view of the hotel bin area, which is not at all picturesque.

* *

Saturday 25

Midnight

Oh, my God! Fat Kylie is having an illicit affair with Mark Lambert. It is like Brad and Jennifer and Angelina but with ugly fourteen year olds. Here is how the drama unfolds:

8 a.m.

Kylies' sleeping arrangements amended after they drank the entire minibar at a cost of €78.48 (my calculations—they should give you questions like that in the SATS, it is far more useful than quadratic equations). I am now sharing with Thin Kylie, and Fat Kylie is in with Emily Reeve. This is not ideal but at least I can keep a close eye on her menstrual cycle.

9 a.m.

Absence of Mr Vaughan noted.

9.15 a.m.

Mr Vaughan roused from Gitanes and Pernod stupor by Sad Ed.

9.30 a.m.

Class takes le Metro under guidance of Ms Hopwood-White and Mr Vaughan.

9.40 a.m.

Class exits le Metro so Mr Vaughan can be sick on le platform.

10 a.m.
Mr Vaughan is revived by pain au chocolat, purchased by Sad Ed, and miniature whisky, stolen by Mark Lambert, and class boards le Metro again.

10 a.m.–10.50 a.m.
Class circles Paris on le Metro looking for correct stop.

11 a.m.
Class arrives at Louvre.

11.30 a.m.
Class asked to leave Louvre due to overexcitement at nude paintings.

12 noon
Thin Kylie refuses to eat in authentic brasserie 'Les Deux Puces' because she is 'allergic to garlic and frogs'.

1 p.m.
Class eats in McDonald's on Champs Élysée.

1.15 p.m.
Class leaves McDonald's following pommes frites fight with boys' school from Edinburgh. Ms Hopwood-White seen commiserating in toilet corridor with sexy Scottish boys' school teacher.

2 p.m.
Class arrives at Eiffel Tower queue.

3.30 p.m.
Class leaves Eiffel Tower queue in disgust and goes souvenir shopping at famous French department store Galeries Lafayette.

4.30 p.m.
Class asked to leave Galeries Lafayette after incident involving Thin Kylie and Mark Lambert and the lingerie changing rooms.

6 p.m.
Class eats authentic French chips and pizza from Travotel revolving buffet.

7 p.m.
Ms Hopwood-White seen leaving Travotel in company of sexy Scottish teacher.

7.05 p.m.
Sad Ed leaves Travotel via bin area on Jim Morrison pilgrimage.

7.15 p.m.
Rest of class watch screening of *Maid in Manhattan* (dubbed in French, no subtitles) in

Conference Room A (aka canteen) under supervision of Mr Vaughan.

8.00 p.m.
Screening of *Maid in Manhattan* abandoned due to riot following heated debate on size of Jennifer Lopez's bottom and class sent to rooms for night by hotel manager after Mr Vaughan found asleep on back row.

9.30 p.m.
Thin Kylie complains of stomach ache and possible French Big Mac/Travotel revolving buffet poisoning.

9.35 p.m.
Thin Kylie sick in bidet.

9.40 p.m.
Room service called to clean up vomit.

11 p.m.
Room service arrive to clean up vomit.

11.15 p.m.
Ms Hopwood-White seen entering hotel with sexy Scottish teacher via bin area.

11.30 p.m.

Sexy Scottish teacher seen leaving Travotel via bin area.

11.40 p.m.

Thin Kylie demands presence of Fat Kylie and sends Rachel Riley to find her.

11.41 p.m.

Emily Reeve (in My Little Pony nightdress) tells Rachel Riley that Fat Kylie has not been seen since dispersal of *Maid in Manhattan* screening.

11.45 p.m.

Fat Kylie traced via distinctive grunting sounds to Mark Lambert's room at far end of Travotel corridor.

11.50 p.m.

Rachel Riley informs Thin Kylie that Fat Kylie is in bed and cannot be disturbed. (Not a total lie.)

11.55 p.m.

Ms Hopwood-White bangs on doors to tell everyone to *'fermez les bouches'*.

. . . .

Sunday 26

8 a.m.

I am racked with indecision. Should I tell Thin Kylie about the illicit sex and get beaten up by Fat Kylie and

possibly stabbed by Mark Lambert or keep quiet and end up getting morning-after pills for Fat Kylie as well? It is like *Sophie's Choice*. Or Hobson's. Who was Hobson?

Plus Sad Ed is still missing. Ms Hopwood-White has gone to find him. I told Mr Vaughan he had gone on a pilgrimage to see Jim Morrison's grave but he said everyone knows Jim Morrison isn't really buried there— and that he probably isn't even dead but is fat and living in Las Vegas with Elvis. I said that was a bit far-fetched but he said, 'No one saw the body—how do you explain that?' (Mr Vaughan is conspiracy theory mad—he thinks Diana was killed by Prince Philip for wearing cleavage-revealing dresses.) We are under strict instructions not to leave the Travotel. Ms Hopwood-White is terrified she might lose more students and end up in the *Daily Mail*.

11 a.m.
Sad Ed is back. He had been arrested for defacing Jim Morrison's grave with chewing gum and a Mars bar wrapper. He claims it was a poem but the policeman couldn't read English and then a pigeon pecked it to get at the chocolate and it blew away so the evidence was gone.

Why, oh why, didn't I go with him? I could have spent the night in a foreign jail with nothing to eat and the howls of tortured inmates ringing in my ears instead of the sound of Fat Kylie and Mark Lambert having sex. Ed said that actually they gave him a falafel and four pain au

161

chocolates and he got to read a French porn mag. That is what is wrong with the French. They are too lax with their criminals. Inspector Morse would never have let his suspects read porn. We are all going home on an early train. Ms Hopwood-White says it is worth the supplement.

I feel sorry for Thin Kylie. Not only is she possibly pregnant due to my evil Smint/morning-after pill changeover but now the father of the illegitimate child is secretly having relations with her clinically obese alleged best friend. Trisha would have a field day. She could devote a whole show to it. She could call it 'Leave the underage father of my baby alone, fat friend!'

10 p.m.
Back home. Mum asked if my trip had been educational. I said it had. Luckily Ms Hopwood-White has promised not to tell anyone about Sad Ed getting arrested. This is insurance against Sad Ed telling Mr Wilmott that she broke school trip regulations by sneaking out of hotel to meet up with sexy Scottish teacher and leaving inept Mr Vaughan in charge.

Monday 27
Went round Scarlet's at lunchtime. She was off school due to pneumonia and a mild dose of trench foot following unseasonal downpours at Glastonbury. She was in bed with henna tattooes and hair braids listening to

goth music. She looked like a sickly ethnic vampire. She said Glastonbury was life-changing and that she is in love with a juggler called Axe. I asked her if they had done it and she said no, but he had let her hold his fire clubs. He lives in a bivouac in a forest near Brighton. This is typical. And totally unfair.

Tuesday 28

Thank God. Thin Kylie is not pregnant. She asked if she could 'lend' a Tampax during science. I said 'borrow' and she said, 'Well, I ain't giving it back, you perv, am I.' Then I said I didn't have any (obviously) so she had to get a giant sanitary towel off Mrs Leech. I cannot go through this worry every month. I am going to have to get the pills back.

Wednesday 29

The school is overrun with Andy Murray madness. I do not understand it—he is tall and geeky. Just because he has an iPod does not make him a sex symbol. Although he is marginally better than Tim Henman whose head is oversized. Even James is demanding tennis lessons (Mum has said no on the grounds that he has shown no promise at Swingball.) I predict this craze will be over by July and the tennis courts of Saffron Walden will be overgrown and used for football practice once again.

Told Kylie I needed the morning-after pills. She said they were round Fat Kylie's so we would have to go to Whiteshot Estate tomorrow (Fat Kylie is off school with alleged mumps). I agreed. It is the only way to end this Smint contraception mess. Have told Mum I am going to a rounders team try-out. She looked suspicious. She knows I have the upper body strength of a kitten.

Thursday 30

Went round Fat Kylie's to get Smints. The house was full of children. They were all drinking Um Bongo and watching MTV on their giant plasma screen, except Whitney, who was busy sharing a Peperami with Tupac. Mrs O'Grady was not present. Whitney, who is named after Kylie's dead dad's favourite singer, is suspiciously brown. I noted that, in addition to the plasma TV, the O'Gradys also owned three PlayStations, an extensive DVD library of Steven Seagal films, a Barbie scooter and a Nissan 4x4 with a 'Honk if you're horny' sticker on the rear window (I have seen Mrs O'Grady and I do not think she gets many honks). Granny Clegg is right, the benefits system is too generous.

Fat Kylie got the pills while Thin Kylie and I watched *Bump and Grind* with the feral children. One of them, possibly Brady, tried to hug me, leaving Dairylea Dunkables smeared on my uniform. Thin Kylie told me to be careful as he is renowned for weeing on people. Then

Fat Kylie came back and I ate the remaining seventeen Smints immediately. Thin Kylie said, 'Jesus, Riley, who did you shag, the entire maths club?' (She has no understanding of medicine, or my taste in boys.) I said, 'Something like that.' So now my reputation exceeds even Leanne Jones who actually did shag three of the senior maths club last year. She got an A* in her maths GCSE. It was the only exam she passed.

When I got home Mum saw the Dairylea Dunkables stain and accused me of illicit eating of junk food. She made me take the skirt off in the kitchen, in front of James and Mumtaz (who were eating health-giving yoghurt) so she could prevent permanent staining. I figured the truth was worse so I just apologized and said I was going to read in my room. I note she did not ask me how my alleged rounders trial went, which shows how low her expectations are of my sporting prowess.

Friday 1

Thin Kylie has found out about Fat Kylie and Mark
Lambert. Fat Kylie made the fatal mistake of coming to
school with the evidence of Mark Lambert's sexual
attentions on her outsize Primark jacket (an 'I ♥ 50 Cent'
badge). They arranged to fight it out on the sheep field at
lunchtime. So the whole school trooped up there, but by
the time the Kylies had taken off all their giant hoops and
rings (illegal fighting implements under unwritten John
Major High rules) Mrs Brain had reported suspiciously
low chip and doughnut sales and Mr Wilmott arrived to
break it up. Mark Lambert is pleading partial innocence.
He says he couldn't help it, he had needs and Thin Kylie
was being sick in a bidet from le Big Mac poisoning. Ms
Hopwood-White is on Thin Kylie's side. She said men are
all liars and cheats and should be castrated. I think she
has broken up with the sexy Scottish teacher. The long
distance must have torn them apart. Scarlet says that is
why Axe has not rung her. I pointed out that it was only
104 miles to Brighton via the M25 (James checked on
Dad's AA route planner) but she said it is a thousand
when you are in love, plus there are roadworks on
the A24.

Saturday 2

Scarlet is going to Live 8. Suzy is overexcited as she and
Bob went to the one twenty years ago. She still wears the

T-shirt despite it having revealing cigarette burns on the nipple area. Sad Ed and I are going to watch it on telly instead (Mum and Dad are going to the garden centre, Grandpa and Treena are babysitting). Sad Ed says it is a moment of musical history. Personally I think his expectations may be a bit too high. Mariah Carey is playing.

5 p.m.
Live 8 viewing has ended. Mum got back and found Grandpa drinking cider and blackcurrant, the dog eating her mung bean cultivator, and James and Treena dancing provocatively to Mariah Carey. She said it was a scene from her worst nightmare. She has weird dreams.

Sunday 3
Thin Kylie came over today to 'hang out'. I don't think she has any friends any more. Fat Kylie claimed Tracey Hughes and Lynn Herbert for her gang following the falling-out, which left Thin Kylie with Lynn Start, but she has defected to her sister's gang in Year Ten. She is their mascot. Mum did not look pleased when she opened the door. She does not approve of the Britchers. She says they are lowering the tone of the neighbourhood with their incessant arguing and the St George flag that Terry has put up in one of the bedroom windows.

Kylie said my room needed a makeover. She said all the pictures of ugly and dead women (Sylvia Plath and

Ophelia) gave her the creeps and was a 'bit lesbo'. She says I should stand up for my rights to have telly in my room as well and suggested I threaten to bunk off or not do homework. She says it has got her a new stereo and a trip to Alton Towers in the last month. Which is amazing as she is always bunking off and not doing homework anyway, so Mrs Britcher is being blackmailed under totally false pretences.

Then she got bored with the lack of TV so we went down to Barry Island to watch Darryl Stamp and his mates rev up their crap cars. (He has finished his community sentence for robbing Mr Patel's. He had to look after some goats at Harlow Town Farm. No wonder re-offending is so high. Pet Corner is hardly going to turn someone off a life of crime.) Darryl offered me and Kylie a joyride to Bishop's Stortford in his Fiesta but I said I had to get back for Sunday lunch. Kylie went anyway. She is mad. The car has no wing mirrors and a purple neon light underneath it so it looks like a really crap spaceship. There would be nothing joyful about riding in it. When I got back, Mum said she hoped I wasn't going to make a habit of 'playing' with Kylie. I pointed out that she should be pleased because at least Kylie's mum wasn't a vegetarian sex therapist. But she said she'd rather that than someone who thinks Kraft Cheese Slices are a cocktail canapé.

And I forgot to go round Scarlet's, as prearranged during exceptionally dull citizenship lesson. Scarlet rang

up to demand to know why. I told her the dog had eaten my watch. I have to stop telling lies. It is getting confusing.

- -

Monday 4

Kylie ate her Turkey Twizzlers with me at lunchtime. I had no choice in the matter. She sat down before Sad Ed could get to the chair (his weight is a speed impediment). He went to join Scarlet on the hummus table instead, even though he had chicken surprise (the surprise is the lack of chicken). Luckily Mrs Brain did not notice or there could have been another free-meals-table-style stand-off. (Discussion of which pencilled in for PTA on Thursday night, according to Mum. She is for segregation.) I am being torn between my friends. It is like *West Side Story*.

- -

Tuesday 5

Not a good day. Rumours are rife about me and the maths club. Thin Kylie says Fat Kylie started them as revenge. Ali Hassan is refusing to speak to me in case it incriminates him further. He is worried his parents will be thrown out of the Church of England. I don't think he has anything to worry about. Reverend Begley will take anyone. I have even seen him trying to convert Barry the Blade. Scarlet is livid that I did not tell her. I said it was all a mistake involving some Smints and the Kylies but

172

she says there is no smoke without fire. Sad Ed just looked sad.

Wednesday 6

Andy Murray madness has officially ended. London has won the Olympics for 2012. James now wants to train as a speed cyclist. I pointed out he will still be only fifteen when it is the Olympics but he said he would campaign to get the age lowered for that as well as Parliament.

Suzy rang to offer me sexual advice. I told her I was the victim of a vicious hate campaign started by an obese adulteress. Plus, just because I was nearly fourteen did not mean I was doing 'it' and that, unlike several of my peers, I intended to abide by the age of consent. She seemed disappointed.

Thursday 7

London has been blown up by suicide bombers. Mum says it goes to show she was right to stay in Saffron Walden, which has been, historically, major-incident free, unless you count the St George's Day fracas. Grandpa Clegg rang to shout about swivel-eyed malcontents (he means Muslims). He says he is thinking of turning the outside loo into an air-raid shelter. I think he wound Mum into a foreigner-fearing frenzy because she told James that Mumtaz couldn't come over for tea tomorrow.

Plus, the PTA meeting got cancelled due to the potential terror threat so the free school meals debacle is destined to remain unresolved until September. Personally I think Mr Wilmott is over-reacting. I do not think Al Qaeda will be targeting John Major High anytime soon.

• •

Friday 8

Tonight's 'end of year' school disco has been postponed as a mark of respect for the London bombings. It has been rescheduled for next Friday when Mr Wilmott thinks the 'hoo-ha' will have calmed down a bit.

• •

Saturday 9

Thin Kylie has given me a makeover. She has dyed my hair using her mum's Sun In spray and straightened it. She says I look like Brittany Murphy instead of the 'ugly one out of *Scooby Doo*' now. Maybe that is what was wrong. Maybe tragic heroines just need a decent hairdo and some lipgloss. I do feel better. Although that may change when Mum and James get back from Waitrose.

5 p.m.

Mum has added hair dye to her banned list. I tried to explain the Brittany Murphy thing but she said the only person I looked like was Vanessa Feltz and then she made

174

me go and use her Head and Shoulders to try and lessen the dye. It did not work. Now I look like Barbara Windsor. Although I am at least dandruff free. Even James is on her side. He says hair dye is the first sign of juvenile delinquency and that I will be heading for an ASBO if I am not careful. Scarlet and Sad Ed will understand. They wear eyeliner.

Sunday 10

Went round Scarlet's for the second annual *O.C.* final episode ceremony. Jack answered the door. He said, 'Why, Miss Riley. You really are beautiful,' and then burst out laughing. Scarlet was horrified. She said blonde hair is anathema to goths. Sad Ed was not happy either. He says I am mixing in bad company and will be listening to R and B next. Everyone is turning into my mum. They do not understand. They will be jealous when Thin Kylie turns out to be a working-class literary marvel. Though I must say I am anxious for her to start showing signs of this. At the moment her reading is limited to gossip magazines.

Monday 11

My new hair is the centre of much hilarity at school. So far I have been likened to: Vera Duckworth, Lily Savage, and Fat Kylie's poodle Tupac. I bet Peaches Geldof doesn't have to put up with this kind of harassment. She is the

style icon for our generation and is probably allowed to smoke and drink wine at dinner. Whereas I still own a Brownies T-shirt and am not allowed to drink Ribena except under strict supervision in outside spaces.

. . . .

Tuesday 12

Battle of the Boyne
Holiday (N. Ire.)

It is Mum's birthday tomorrow. I have got her a new mung bean cultivator. I am going to sign it from me and the dog in the hope it will get us both back into her good books.

. . . .

Wednesday 13

Mum's birthday

Mum got a mung bean cultivator (me and the dog), a Cif gift pack (James), an M&S voucher (Dad), a bottle of Britney Spears perfume (Grandpa and Treena), and £5 and a UKIP car sticker (Granny and Grandpa Clegg). Auntie Joyless did not send anything. She is still of the opinion our family is beyond redemption.

. . . .

Thursday 14

Mum has a rash all over her neck and face. She looks like Nigel Moore in Year Eleven who has impetigo (not potato

176

blight, as claimed by Mark Lambert). It is the Britney Spears perfume. Grandpa admitted Treena got it in the White Horse off someone called Ducatti Mick. Mum has listed him in her ASBO catalogue.

Friday 15

St Swithin's Day

It is the end of year school disco tonight. I am going to wear my vintage (Monsoon) skirt and Brownie T-shirt (worn inside-out, as seen on Peaches Geldof in *Bliss* magazine last month). With my newly blonde hair I will look just like Sienna Miller. Justin Statham is definitely going, according to Scarlet. Although she didn't seem as enthusiastic about telling me this as she normally would. Maybe she is still pining after Axe. I must be careful not to flaunt my prospective love life in front of her.

11 p.m.

Disco did not go according to plan. I did not look at all like Sienna Miller. Kylie came over after tea and persuaded me to cut a metre off the bottom of the Monsoon skirt and borrow her mum's halter top so the closest resemblance was Paris Hilton with a perm. She said, 'I ain't going out with someone with no second-hand shit on, someone might have, like, died in it. Gross.'

When we got to school, Scarlet said I couldn't stand with her in Goth Corner (aka next to the out-of-order fire

extinguishers) or she and Sad Ed might get ejected. (Sad Ed was allowed to stand there because he had a black T-shirt on). So I had to stand with Thin Kylie and help her give Fat Kylie and Mark Lambert the evils. Luckily that did not last long as they got sent home for inappropriate behaviour behind the crash mats. Then Kylie danced (snogged, with his hands up her boob tube) with Jason Kinsey who is in Criminals and Retards for trying to set fire to Rat Corner. Having a reputation as a nymphomaniac certainly boosts your popularity for slow dances. I got offers from four members of the science club and Gary Fletcher off the Waitrose pet food aisle who is in Year Eleven and has done it with Leanne Jones. I declined all and stood with Sad Ed at the 'bar' (Ms Hopwood-White's Coke stall). Scarlet was dancing with head goth Trevor Pledger who has a floor-length leather coat—the holy grail of gothwear. Sad Ed said he preferred my old look. I said it wasn't my idea and he said, 'To thine own self be true.' Which is out of *Clueless*. He is still trying to be poetic in everyday situations. Then they played The Killers and I danced with Ed for a bit, which was weirdly nice. But then Scarlet came over and said she and Ed had to go back to Goth Corner as Daisy Devlin was going to show everyone her fake tattoo of Marilyn Manson on her left buttock. I got bored and went home. Thin Kylie was in the staff car park with one hand down Jason Kinsey's trousers. She said she would get a lift on his minibike.

When I got in Mum went mental at me for walking on my own. I pointed out that, given the fact that it was still

broad daylight, and we lived in Saffron Walden, I was not likely to get mugged or raped. But ever since Granny Clegg told her the government is rehousing paedophiles in suburbia she is paranoid and made me promise to phone Dad for a lift next time. I told her I couldn't as I didn't have a mobile and Mr Wilmott has banned pupil use of the staffroom phone after Stacey O'Grady called a sexline. (He claimed it was a legitimate emergency.) Then I went upstairs before she could think of a clever answer.

At least it did not rain. Which is good news weather-wise for the next forty days.

Saturday 16

Treena came over. She was wearing jogging bottoms again. She is too fat to fit into her jeans. If she lets herself go any further Grandpa will ditch her. I have caught him eyeing Cherie over the road. So has Mum. She has threatened to move his bedroom to the dining room where he will only overlook Marjory's ornamental water feature.

Scarlet and Sad Ed went to the fair on the common without inviting me. James told me he saw them on the ghost train with some other goths. (Dad took him and Mumtaz and the dog. The dog ate three lots of candyfloss and a toffee apple and was sick on a giant saucer after it leapt onto the Mad Hatter's Tea Party under-tens merry-go-round in pursuit of James. Dad has vowed never to go again.)

Sunday 17

Kylie came over with *Cosmopolitan* so we went to my bedroom and did the sex survey. I got mostly *d*'s ('Nun') and she got mostly *a*'s ('Madonna'). She knows a terrifying amount about penises.

Then Sad Ed knocked on the window. He had climbed up Dad's ladder, left out after trying to readjust the aerial so Grandpa could watch *Home and Away* on Channel 5. Kylie opened the window and said, 'What do you think this is, *Dawson's* f**king *Creek*, you fat weirdo?' He said he had tried the door but the doorbell battery had gone and he couldn't rouse Grandpa from his post-Sunday lunch torpor in front of the Grand Prix (Mum and Dad had taken James to B&Q to buy a shelf for his expanding doll collection).

Kylie demanded to know what he was doing so he handed me a CD and said it was a pre-birthday present. Kylie told him he had better go as the ladder 'wasn't licensed for bloaters'.

Then Sad Ed said, 'To thine own self be true' again so Kylie called him a poof and slammed the window shut, narrowly missing his fingers. I wish he would stop spouting *Clueless* all the time. It doesn't help his image.

Then Kylie looked at the CD and said, 'Oh my God, it was Fat Ed what got you nearly pregnant!' I said it was 'who, not what', and that anyway it wasn't him, and told her to give me the CD back, but she waved it around chanting, 'You shagged Fat Ed, admit it, admit it!' repeatedly.

So then, and I only did this to shut her up, I told her he was gay and snogging Jonah Reed (who once played Mary in a primary school nativity and is therefore destined to be classified as gay for ever). Kylie was so shocked she dropped the CD down the back of the bed. I begged her not to tell anyone as Sad Ed hadn't 'come out' yet and his parents were Aled Jones fans and might take it badly. She promised her lips were sealed, but she said that after Lynn Start told her she had a third nipple and the whole school was calling her 'triple tits' by first break the next day. I may have made a fatal mistake. Sad Ed is going to kill me.

Monday 18

Mark Lambert has run away with the fair that was on the common at the weekend. It is all over the school. He is going to spin waltzers, according to Fat Kylie. She is devastated. He tried to get her to go with him but she said she didn't want to 'live in a caravan with some gyppos'. This is rich. She goes to a caravan park in Clacton every summer with her horde of feral siblings. Thin Kylie is comforting her. They are reunited in their grief.

More worryingly, Jude Law has cheated on Sienna with a commoner—his nanny. If even the glorious and vintage Sienna is not immune to lying and cheating then what hope is there for us mere mortals? Not that I am going out with anyone for them to be able to cheat on me.

Tuesday 19

The Sad Ed gay rumours have started. Fat Kylie stuck a picture of Graham Norton on his locker and Oona Rickets has invited him to join her Gay and Lesbian and Proud Association. Ed told her he was neither. Thank God Mark Lambert is not here to add his voice to the bigoted throng. Sad Ed says he doesn't care because all poetic geniuses are persecuted during their short but tragic lives. I am not sure how long this devil-may-care attitude will last in the face of the right-wing leanings of John Major High school governors, not to mention his parents. Then he asked if I had listened to the CD yet. I had to admit that I hadn't. It is still behind the bed due to the panic following the gay revelations.

9 p.m.

Found CD under bed. Unfortunately so had the dog and it is now chewed beyond recognition. It was probably only full of songs about death anyway. I have given it to James to use for his light-refracting CD mobile (as featured on *Blue Peter*).

Wednesday 20

Sad Ed has been forced to issue a vigorous denial of any homosexual leanings after Jonah Reed's mum wrote a letter to Ms Hopwood-White demanding that he use the girls' changing rooms for PE. He says he is not taking his

clothes off in front of sixty-seven girls as they will be too critical of his physique. He is right. It is a good thing it is the last day of school on Friday. So far the source of the rumours has not been identified but I fear Thin Kylie may blab to Fat Kylie then it will all be over.

Thursday 21

Thin Kylie blabbed. Scarlet stormed up to me in first break and demanded to know if I was claiming one of my best friends was gay to boost my popularity in the chav hierarchy. I said on the contrary, the chavs are no friends of gays and lesbians and anyway, Sad Ed might be gay, we just might not know it yet. She said he was far from gay and was in love with some stupid cow who was too obsessed with herself and her image to notice. (She must mean Sophie Jacobs. That would explain why he hates Justin Statham so much.) Then she said I had totally changed and she didn't think she could be my friend any more and stormed off with her Glastonbury goth skirt tinkling its bells angrily.

I will give her a while to calm down then I will go and explain everything. She will understand that I was lured into it by Thin Kylie.

It would be good if Sad Ed was gay though. We could be like *Will and Grace*. Maybe the Sophie Jacobs thing is a cover up. He does watch *The O.C.* and is good at clothes advice. Oh my God, it has been staring me in the face all along. Sad Ed is the key to Jacqueline Wilson-ing my life.

I am going to spend more time with him. That is if he is still speaking to me. Maybe he will thank me instead. I will prove instrumental in him coming out to his parents. They will embrace his alternative lifestyle and join Oona Rickets's club with him and get Aled Jones to be patron.

Friday 22

Sad Ed is not thanking me so far. He and Scarlet are not speaking to me. Though I did catch Sad Ed looking at me in maths so maybe he is cracking. But then Scarlet saw him and hit him with her set square.

I was glad to get out of school. The corridors were plagued by gangs of Year Elevens with cans of silly string and huddles of sixth form girls weeping because they are never going to see each other again (not until resits, anyway). Am going to have to win back Scarlet and Sad Ed soon or I am doomed to spend my summer holiday sitting on a wall with the Kylies drinking alcopops.

Plus James has commandeered the stereo and keeps playing a vintage love song compilation CD. It is unbearable. Since when did he like David Bowie? Plus it keeps getting stuck. The dog must have bitten it.

Saturday 23

Went round Scarlet's to make up but Jack answered the door and said she wasn't speaking to me. I begged him

to let me in but he said Scarlet had threatened to put incriminating Celine Dion tracks on his iPod if he did. I said I would try Sad Ed instead. Jack said I shouldn't bother as he was upstairs with Scarlet as Scarlet couldn't trust him if he was on his own. I said it was like *Mean Girls* with me as Lindsay Lohan and Jack agreed.

3 p.m.
Ooh—maybe Jack thinks I look like Lindsay Lohan.

4 p.m.
Read *Cosmopolitan*, left by Thin Kylie. Am going to wax my bikini line. Apparently using Dad's Bic on my legs and armpits is not enough in these summer months.

Sunday 24
Bought wax from Waitrose. Thank God they open on a Sunday or I may well have been forced to have an untamed pubic area for another shameful day. Am going to do waxing after lunch.

3 p.m.
Am in agony. Cannot sit down properly due to bleeding of hair follicles in close proximity to minky. I followed the instructions properly but their warnings 'mild discomfort' are clearly inadequate. I may well write to complain. Told

Mum I had to lie down due to stomach ache. I do not want hair removal added to her banned list or I will look like Oona Rickets within a week. Will wear shorts in future or a sarong.

Monday 25

Went round Sad Ed's at 9 a.m. in a bid to thwart Scarlet (she does not get up until *T4* has finished). But his mum said he had stayed the night at a friend's (i.e. Scarlet's). Her vengeance knows no bounds. She is trying to steal my possibly gay best friend for herself so she can be Debra Messing and I will be the midget one with the high voice. It is not fair. Something must be done.

Took the dog for a walk past Scarlet's in the hope of catching her as she came out of the front door and having a reunion on the block-paved driveway. But after the seventh walk past Jack came out and told me I was wasting my time as they were punting in Cambridge with Bob and Suzy. He invited me in for tea but I said the dog might get overexcited by their two cats (Tony and Gordon) so I had better go home.

When I got back the Kylies were on the front wall listening to gangster rap so I joined them until Mum got back from Boots and gave me a look so menacing it actually made Thin Kylie shiver.

Tuesday 26

Have resigned myself to spending the summer holidays

with the Kylies. It will give Scarlet and Ed time to realize that their lives are meaningless without me in them. It could be good anyway. Cherie is getting a swimming pool installed in their back garden tomorrow. She says it is a symbol of their new position in life. Mum says it is a symbol of having more money than sense. They cost a fortune to run and you only use them for a few weeks a year. This is the same argument she used against me getting a pony and Dad getting a convertible MG.

Wednesday 27

The swimming pool is in. It is like a giant kidney-shaped washing-up bowl (why does everyone want to swim in something shaped like an organ that makes wee?) and is wide enough to do three breaststrokes across it. Kylie didn't actually get in the water. She says the chlorine could damage her hair. She and Cherie lay on the patio and read *Hello* instead. It is a good job I did wax my bikini line. The costume Cherie lent me is perilously high cut. (She said my navy and yellow Speedo would make Caprice look like Marjory and was best off in the bin.)

7 p.m.

Kylie was right about the chlorine. My hair now has a weird green tinge to it.

Thursday 28

Swam some more. Fat Kylie was there with Whitney. Cherie floated her round the pool on a pair of inflatable breasts. (Whitney, not Fat Kylie. She would have sunk them.) I expect it is the closest Whitney has got to that part of the anatomy. I have only ever seen her drink Yazoo and Coke. Read *Hot Stars*, *Grazia*, and *Heat*. Tried to initiate a discussion on Sienna Miller's new haircut but the Kylies were too busy assessing Jade Goody's boob job. I miss Scarlet and Sad Ed.

Friday 29

Swam. Ate Kraft cheese slices. Read *Heat*. It is amazing how doing nothing can stretch to a whole day.

Saturday 30

Oh my God. I am a real-life criminal. It is all Thin Kylie's fault. She made me do it. We ran out of Diet Coke (me) and Benson and Hedges (her and Cherie) at the pool so we went to Mr Patel's to get some but she didn't have enough money (I expect it is all in an offshore account. Rich people never have small change, it is a well known fact) so when Mr Patel bent down to get a bag for the Coke she grabbed a packet of cigarettes and put them in my pocket (she was wearing a tube dress and, to be fair, it would have been too obvious, whereas I had a capacious gypsy skirt on). But

Mr Patel must have eyes in the back of his head and demanded to search us. Kylie said no perv was going to touch her up so Mr Patel said he was going to call the police at which point I panicked and gave the cigarettes up.

Kylie feigned innocence by saying, 'Oh my God, my friend's a f**king burglar.' I pointed out that this was petty theft as opposed to burglary but I don't think that helped my case. I offered to make it up to Mr Patel by doing a Sunday paper round for free but he said he only has seven and he does them in his people carrier as most people get theirs from the petrol station at Tesco. He made me tell him my home phone number and called it there and then. James answered. He said, 'Send her home, she will be punished.'

When I got home, Mum lost the plot completely. She has sent me to my room to reflect on my delinquency while she and Dad think of a suitable punishment. James is right. My life is on a downward spiral. It will be drugs and tattoos next.

* *

Sunday 31

Mum and Dad have decided to send me to Granny Clegg's for the rest of the summer to keep me away from the Kylies. They are going to stay in Saffron Walden. Dad is taking the day off work on Tuesday to drive me.

I do not want to go to Granny Clegg's. There is no internet, no Channel 5 reception, and no Channel 4 (the

TV can receive it but Granny Clegg thinks it is a force of corruption). Plus I will have to see Auntie Joyless and her freakish offspring.

It is my birthday tomorrow. I do not hold out much hope for any of requested presents (i.e. mobile phone).

Monday 1

Bank Holiday (Scotland)

My birthday

Presents received:

- Mum and Dad—a mobile phone! It is Pay As You Go and does not have a camera plus it is on the large side but it is a mobile phone none the less. Mum said it is so she and Dad can trace me at all times. I might have known the only way to break her was to turn it into an essential anti-ASBO item. Clearly crime does pay.

Also received:

- James—Carol Vorderman Sudoku Puzzle Book (several puzzles completed)
- Grandpa and Treena—a copy of *Bliss* magazine and a box of mint Matchmakers (both last-minute Mr Patel purchases, according to James)
- The dog—a copy of *How I Live Now* by Meg Rosoff. It is about a girl who is sent to live with her backward relatives in the middle of nowhere and then falls in love with her cousin. I hope the dog (aka Mum) is not encouraging me to seek solace in the arms of Boaz.
- Granny and Grandpa Clegg—Cornish phrases tea towel (am going to learn them later to help me acclimatize to the back of beyond)
- Sad Ed—nothing.
- Scarlet—nothing.

193

Thin Kylie came over to say happy birthday but James sent her away. She left me a novelty rude card and a bottle of Bacardi Breezer (both now confiscated).

Texted Scarlet with my new phone but got no reply. Thought maybe she was out of the country at an Ashram or something so texted Jack to test theory. He texted back saying she was in her bedroom doing Sad Ed's make-up and avoiding a suntan (the goth's worst nightmare). So she is still not speaking to me. Texted Jack to say I was being sent to Cornwall to reform. He said, 'BWARE RESTLESS NATIVES W SHARPENED PASTIES CU SOON X J.' Not sure whether the X is a kiss or a mistext. He does have long fingernails (essential guitar-playing accessory).

Exile begins tomorrow. Maybe it will not be so bad. Maybe village life will be wholesome and amusing like *Last of the Summer Wine*. Or possibly Rick Stein will have opened a bistro in St Slaughter and it will be flooded with cosmopolitan types.

. . . .

Tuesday 2
First day of exile
8.45 p.m.
Am in Cornwall in Granny Clegg's spare bedroom (mauve bedspread, picture of blue-faced lady, overpowering smell of Fray Bentos). Have gone to bed already due to lack of *a*) decent television; *b*) stimulating

194

conversation; and *c*) mobile phone reception. Am going to climb up hill in village tomorrow to attempt contact with the outside world. No sign of Rick Stein bistro. Or of jovial *Last of the Summer Wine* types. Although there was a man actually chewing straw outside the Spar.

Journey was six hours of Radio 2 hell. I did not know my dad knows all the words to so many crap songs. Only the dog seemed sad to see me leave. Grandpa refused to let it come in case Granny Clegg seized it and held it hostage.

Wednesday 3
Exile—day two
10 a.m.
Went on cultural walk round sights of St Slaughter i.e. Spar and the Community Playground (disused). I do not see the point of Cornwall if it isn't by the sea. Plus there is no mobile phone reception in entire village. Pig-faced man with barely understandable accent said I would have to get closer to Redruth to pick anything up. I do not want to get closer to Redruth. It is like a giant Whiteshot Estate but with pasties. Besides, Granny and Grandpa Clegg do not have a car. They rely on Auntie Joyless's dented Metro.

1 p.m.
Ate lunch. Fishpaste sandwich and Viennetta.

3 p.m.
Raining.

5 p.m.
Still raining. Ate tea. Steak and kidney pie and tinned peaches. Asked Granny Clegg what she does all day to pass the time. She says she enters magazine competitions. So far this year she has won a Sanderson duvet cover, a socket set, and a year's supply of Fray Bentos (this explains a lot). She is hoping to win a holiday in Florida with her witty completion of the line 'I love Germoloids haemorrhoid cream because . . . ' She wrote 'it is top for my bottom.' It is surprisingly clever for her.

9 p.m.
In bed. Will lose dark circles by Sunday at this rate.

Thursday 4
9 a.m.
Still raining.

1 p.m.
Still raining.

3 p.m.
When will this deluge end? My hair is mass of hideous damp-induced fluff and am likely to go down with

pleurisy or consumption. Although that would be excellent for making Mum regret her hasty decision to send me to stay with the Cleggs. Plus loads of tragic heroines die from consumption like Nicole Kidman in *Moulin Rouge*.

Friday 5

9 a.m.

Still raining. This cannot go on. My hair is the size of a spacehopper. Am going to have to get it cut. Plus the roots are showing. Granny Clegg says I look like a young Myra Hindley. I do not think it is a compliment.

3 p.m.

Granny Clegg has made an appointment for me at Brenda's Hairdressing. It is with Brenda herself. I am hoping she is an innovative style director like Nicky Clarke.

Saturday 6

Brenda is not an innovative style director. She is a forty year old from Penzance with nicotine-stained fingers. She suggested a radical elfin cut to remove the blonde and frizz. I was foolishly swayed by the possibility of looking like vintage Audrey Hepburn and so let her hack at my hair with blunt scissors and a razor for two hours. I do not

look like Audrey Hepburn. I look like an eight-year-old boy, i.e. James.

Auntie Joyless is coming for Sunday lunch tomorrow. At least she will approve of my hairdo. I look like a shaven penitent.

. . . .

Sunday 7

My life is not as bad as I thought. Compared to Auntie Joyless my mum is like Julie Cooper-Nichol (except without the porn star past or yacht). Uncle John and my cousins Boaz and Mary are living a life of puritanical misery. They do not even own a television. Oh my God. You'd think they'd at least watch *Songs of Praise*. Boaz smiled at me insanely throughout the meal. He has a weird look in his eye. It is lucky that guns are banned or I fear his repression may lead to a Columbine-style massacre at Redruth High. Auntie Joyless asked if I was repenting my straying from the path of righteousness. Luckily my mouth was full of claggy Smash so I couldn't answer. Then Grandpa Clegg started in on the outrage of changing the name Jif to Cif and how Tony Blair and Brussels were to blame so I escaped further interrogation.

. . . .

Monday 8

Rained. Ate mini Kievs. Read *Of Mice and Men*. We are doing it for GCSE next year. It is not about mice, it is

about a giant retard called Lennie. The Kylies are going to have a field day.

· ·

Tuesday 9
Stopped raining. Went to Spar with Granny Clegg. Bought Steakhouse Grills and frozen carrots. Came home. Ate them.

· ·

Wednesday 10
Got up. Nothing happened. Went to bed. Now I know why Mum left Cornwall the first chance she had. Every day is like Sunday. Without *The O.C.* or Waitrose.

· ·

Thursday 11
Mum rang to check on me. I said my life was one long miserable prison sentence. She said, 'Good.' I asked what was happening in Saffron Walden. She said the dog had got stuck in the washing machine, Grandpa had twisted his ankle falling off James's mini trampoline (now banned—she always knew it was a deathtrap), and her mung beans had failed to cultivate. It sounded so exciting I started to cry and begged her to take me back. I reminded her that Redruth is the suicide capital of the UK and that I was severely depressed but she told me not to be so dramatic and that she would see me in two weeks

and not to eat the arctic roll in the freezer as it was two years past its sell-by. I will not need to commit suicide anyway. I will die of boredom at this rate.

Friday 12
1 p.m.
Something interesting has happened! People have arrived at the holiday cottage opposite (aka Hester Trelowarren's battery chicken shed). There is a row of green wellies lined up outside the front door and a Range Rover parked outside. More importantly, one of their children looks distinctly like the non-ugly one in Busted. A Waitrose van has delivered their shopping. Grandpa Clegg is all riled up. He says they are taking homes away from natives. I said the only natives they had ousted from their home were chickens but Grandpa said that wasn't the point. Granny Clegg is more concerned as to why they have spurned the supermarket Mecca that is Spar. She is going over to investigate.

3 p.m.
Granny Clegg has returned (an hour and half later). She says they are called Rory and Fiona Britt-Jones and come from Fulham, he is a doctor and she is an interior designer (not a real job, according to Granny Clegg) and they have two children, Will (15—Busted one) and Poppy-Boo (11).

She said they paid £600 for the week. I bet they were sick when she told them 5,000 battery hens were living in their inglenook five months ago.

Saturday 13

Have met Will! The Britt-Jones's came over to thank Granny Clegg for the cake she had left for them (Mr Kipling's French Fancies—she is trying to lure them to Spar). Will is gorgeous. I think I am in love. It is like *Pretty in Pink* (another of Suzy's favourite films) with me as the impoverished but beautiful and vintage Molly Ringwald and him as rich but open-minded Andrew McCarthy. Or like Darcy and Lizzie Bennett. Oh hurrah. Only I am going to have to plan my wardrobe with more care. I fear on first impressions he may have thought I was a celtic inbred. My hair does look marginally asylum-like, plus I had on the enormous, formerly flea-ridden jumper and Granny Clegg's slipper socks.

Sunday 14

Lurked outside in front garden trying to look interesting and beautiful but *Of Mice and Men* got all soggy in the drizzle and then Granny Clegg opened the window and asked if I wanted her to boil wash my underwear as she was doing Grandpa Clegg's. Asked Granny if she had seen the Britt-Joneses and she said they had gone to Eden at

8.30 and wouldn't be back until 7. Why does no one tell me these things? I may have caught pneumonia now. I was only wearing my inside-out T-shirt and the reduced length Monsoon skirt.

. . . .

Monday 15

Britt-Joneses gone to bloody Tate Gallery in St Ives today. I do not blame them, there is nothing to do in St Slaughter unless you count the fruit machine in the launderette. Plus they probably want to get away from Granny Clegg's incessant questioning. She makes Jeremy Paxman look half-hearted.

. . . .

Tuesday 16

2 p.m.

I have found my opportunity to bond with Will. Smoking. Granny Clegg says Maureen Penrice from Spar said he bought a packet of Marlboro Lights and a Yorkie this morning. I am going to join him in his illicit habit. Admittedly, I don't know how to smoke but it can't be hard—the Kylies had learned by the age of 10.

8 p.m.

Have just had bonding cigarette moment with Will on the broken swings in the St Slaughter Community Playground (disused). I followed him there after tea (fish

fingers, tinned sweetcorn, Black Forest gateau). I asked if I could 'cadge a fag' (I learnt this from Thin Kylie—she has her uses) and he said, 'Yeah—don't tell the old girl though.' That is his mum. He is so cool. We had a deep and meaningful discussion ('Why are Walker's cheese and onion crisp packets blue when everyone else's are green?' and 'Oompa Loompa out of *Charlie and the Chocolate Factory*—dwarf or midget?') while I wafted the cigarette about. Then he asked if I was going to actually smoke it as he didn't want to waste a good fag so I sucked on it casually like Kylie does but it must have been an extra strong cigarette or something because then I couldn't breathe and started choking and felt totally sick. Will laughed but I think it was with me not at me. At least I hope so, because romance is definitely in the air. We are meeting again tomorrow night.

Wednesday 17

I have snogged Will! (First real kiss, unless you count no tongues with Brian Drain on the Year Seven coach trip to Peterborough Roller Rink.) I felt so sick with excitement/fear I was worried I might actually throw up on him like Fat Kylie (actually sick in Dean Auger's mouth at the Wimbish Village Disco, but it was cider not passion that was the cause). We met at the swings again. I did not smoke this time—I said my asthma might flare up. (This is not a total lie—I might have latent asthma.)

Will asked why a girl like me (!) was staying in 'Hicksville, Arizona' and why my hair was so short. I said I had done some 'wild things' and it was all punishment, which he thought was 'way cool, like Joan of Arc'. I did not tell him about the Smints or Brenda. It would ruin the effect. He is my soul mate. He knows all the words to the *O.C.* theme tune. I am going to go to the Witchcraft Museum tomorrow with his mum and dad and Poppy-Boo. It is like a date! I don't think I will be able to sleep.

* * *

Thursday 18

Went to the Wicca House with the Britt-Joneses. Fiona and Rory did not seem entirely thrilled at our love for each other but that is what happened to Lizzie Bennett with evil Caroline Bingley and Lady Catherine De Thingy so is only to be expected in across-the-divide love affairs. Poppy-Boo is a brat. She made sick noises when we tried to kiss behind the rune cabinet.

Will is going back to Fulham tomorrow. I said we should meet at 'our place' tonight to say goodbye properly. He asked what 'our place' was. I said the disused playground. He said, 'Right—of course. I was joking.'

10 p.m.

It has happened! I have let Will touch my M&S bra (32AA). He said we are in love so it is OK. I think he

wanted to touch more but Maureen Penrice came past with her German shepherd Arnie so we had to stop. I cannot believe he is leaving tomorrow. He has given me his Zippo lighter to remember him by. I will treasure it always.

Friday 19

Will has gone home in his Range Rover. We are going to call each other every day. We will not let distance ruin our relationship like Scarlet and Axe. Or maybe it will be like *Grease* and he will show up at John Major High next term but will have to pretend he doesn't know me because we are too different!

Saturday 20

I am loveless. Tried lying in bed all day moping but Granny Clegg told me to get out because she needed to Shake'n'Vac. I don't know why she bothers. Nothing will get out the ingrained smell of meat pie. I wish Scarlet was still talking to me so I could tell her about Will. Or that I had mobile phone reception to talk to anyone. I may as well be on Mars. I cannot even text Will to tell him I still love him and Granny Clegg won't let me use the BT phone because it is too expensive. This is hypocritical— she wastes pounds ringing up Mum to whitter on about nothing.

7 p.m.
Hope is in sight. We are going to Auntie Joyless's house for lunch tomorrow. They live near a giant satellite dish so there is bound to be mobile reception.

Sunday 21
Hurrah—there is mobile reception in Goonglaze Road. But it was a double-edged sword. Auntie Joyless confiscated my phone after it beeped during our puritanical lunch (boiled ham and potatoes, apples for pudding). Then, when I finally got my phone back, the text was not from Will at all but from Sad Ed to say Happy Birthday (he sent it two weeks ago). Scarlet is losing her Grace-like grip. Or, more probably, she has gone away.

Boaz offered to 'come and play' tomorrow. Auntie Joyless did not look pleased but Boaz said he would bring his Noah's ark and Creationism quiz book so she has reluctantly agreed. I wish she hadn't. I do not want to be seen with a boy who wears sandals and socks.

Monday 22
Boaz came over. The Creationism thing was a cover-up. He wanted to quiz me about my stand against repression. He says he is thinking of upping his resistance to Auntie Joyless and that I am his role model. He asked if he can come to live in Saffron Walden. I have warned him that

there is no Ribena and that Grandpa Riley is doing some very unbiblical things but he said he didn't care and would I ask my mum.

5 p.m.
Oh my God. I have got my period! Maybe Boaz has weird religious powers like Reverend Billy and his verruca-healing hands. I am going to Spar immediately. I cannot tell Granny Clegg.

6 p.m.
Am wearing giant Spar own-brand sanitary towels. It is like having a nappy on. I rustle when I walk.

7 p.m.
Granny Clegg has rung Mum to tell her I have 'the curse'. I thought it might be the rustling that gave it away but apparently Maureen Penrice told Hester who told her that I had bought 'sanitary provisions'. Is nothing sacred?

I told Mum about Boaz and she said it was just a 'phase' and not to worry. I am worried. He wears 'Jesus Loves Me' T-shirts. I will be the social equivalent of Emily Reeve. Good God, if anyone needed mobile phone reception it is now. I am going to walk to Redruth if I have to tomorrow so that I can phone Sad Ed. Only he will understand my plight. Plus Will must have called by now.

Tuesday 23

Did not have to walk to Redruth. It turns out you can get two bars on the top of the disused climbing frame. I called Sad Ed and he confessed that Scarlet has been brainwashing him but that he cannot afford to lose her friendship in case I am exiled for good, plus she is a good source of illegally downloaded music and sex advice (both via Suzy). He said we could meet in secret when I get home. Then I told him about Will and my torrid holiday romance and he went quiet, so I asked him how his life was and he said it was like living inside the lyrics of 'Teenage Dirtbag'. I do not know how, he doesn't know any girls called Noelle, or like Iron Maiden. Then the phone went dead. It must be the poor quality reception. I may write to Orange to complain about the transmitter situation in rural areas.

No call from Will yet. Maybe his parents have forbidden him to call me and are forcing him to go out with someone called Tiffany whose dad owns a Porsche and who does not have a wonky hairdo.

8 p.m.

I do not see what the period fuss is all about. It is all highly uncomfortable and undignified. I am not leaping for joy or wearing tight white clothing like in the adverts. I am wearing giant pants and Granny Clegg is making me eat liver once a day to replace lost iron. It is torture.

Wednesday 24

Went to the climbing frame again and called Will. He sounded weird. I asked why he hadn't called and he said he was in trouble because his mum had found out about him smoking (Maureen Penrice) and in the heat of the moment he had said it was my influence. I asked him if he still loved me but then the beeps went and my credit ran out. Went to the Spar to top it up but it shuts at one on a Wednesday due to the cattle market 'in the big town'.

Thursday 25

Called Will again. He said I should stop wasting my minutes on him but I said love was never a waste. Then I heard someone giggling in the background. I demanded to know who it was and he said it was Poppy-Boo but then there were kissing noises and he said he had to go as an emergency had come up.

Friday 26

I am single again. I called Will and told him that I knew about him and Tiffany. He said, 'Who's Tiffany?' and I said she was metaphorical and might be called Tara for all I knew but that wasn't the point. He said, 'What is the point?' and I said that I didn't think he believed in me any more and that I couldn't believe in someone who didn't believe in me, and he said, 'What the f**k are you on

about?' Admittedly the line was stolen directly from *Pretty in Pink* when Andrew McCarthy is too embarrassed to admit he doesn't want to take Molly Ringwald to the prom but it totally fitted our situation. So I said 'It's over,' and he said, 'It never began,' and we hung up. It was utterly Julie Burchill. I am devastated. I will never love again.

. . . .

Saturday 27

Granny Clegg is ecstatic. She has won the holiday in Florida. They are going in October. The makers of Germoloids must have been short of entries. I tried to be happy for them but I am still mourning Will so I smiled and then went back to sighing by the window and reading *The Bell Jar*. Granny Clegg said she is glad Dad is picking me up on Monday. She says it is worse than when Auntie Joyless found out that Jesus had died for her sins and would not come out of her room for a week.

Boaz is coming over tomorrow to say goodbye. I have begged Granny and Grandpa not to go out but Granny says she is not missing the St Slaughter giant vegetable competition for the world.

. . . .

Sunday 28

Boaz has just gone. He has agreed to try to convert the forces of repression (i.e. Auntie Joyless) from within.

Thank God. My fragile reputation is safe. I told him to be careful—being a rebel youth wasn't as easy as it looked—but he went all biblical and said it was like Revelation and Judgement Day. Then he asked if he could have my Sienna Miller scarf as a symbol of our joint struggle against authority. I let him. It is quite flattering to have a minion. He tied it round his head and asked me to wish him luck. I did. He will need it.

Monday 29

Late Summer Bank Holiday (UK)
2 p.m.
Dad is here. He is eating Viennetta in the garden with Granny and Grandpa and the dog. Grandpa allowed it to come on the grounds that Dad is not to let it out of his sight for a second—not even to go to the toilet. Dad says something has happened at home but that he can't tell me in front of Granny and Grandpa Clegg. Maybe Mum has had a kind of conversion and has gone all permissive. Or maybe she has a terminal illness. I could donate my bone marrow and nearly die on the operating table. They could turn it into a film.

10 p.m.
Am back in civilization—i.e. Saffron Walden. I still do not know what has happened. Mum said I was too weak from travelling to cope and that she would tell me in the

morning. James was in bed so I couldn't quiz him. He is easily bribed.

. . . .

Tuesday 30

Oh my God. No one is dying. It is worse. Treena isn't bulimic. She is five months pregnant and Grandpa is the father. They are going to keep it. I am going to have an uncle or aunt who is fourteen years younger than me. I am white trash. No wonder Will spurned me.

Also, a hurricane has flooded America. James said it is retribution for George Bush's invasion of Iraq. I said I didn't think God was on the side of Saddam Hussein but James said it was nothing to do with God—it was Allah. Mum went a bit pale. I think she is worried Mumtaz is converting him to Islam.

Granny Clegg rang in a panic. Their resort in Florida has been partially submerged. Mum said it was a good thing and wouldn't they be better off in Newquay anyway, but Granny Clegg said a bit of rain and wind never put her off. She is determined to be the first person from St Slaughter to go to America.

. . . .

Wednesday 31

Called Sad Ed to tell him about Grandpa and Treena. He agrees it is shocking. Asked him to come over later but he is going to Scarlet's to help with their Hurricane Katrina

Appeal. I said I would help as well but he said it was not advisable as Scarlet was still not talking to me. I said that I was no longer consorting with the Kylies (this is true— I haven't seen them yet—they are probably in America getting flooded) and he said he would put in a good word for me. I will win her back once school starts. She will be bored in maths without me.

Thursday 1

Mum has found Will's Zippo. I explained it wasn't mine but she has confiscated it anyway and done a forensic search of my bedroom for smoking evidence (findings—nil). Mum said I will be sent to live with Granny Clegg permanently if my poor behaviour goes on.

. . . .

Friday 2

Granny Clegg rang. Auntie Joyless has had a minor breakdown. She got back from a prayer group meeting at the Farmers' Union hall and found Boaz 'reading the devil's literature' (i.e. *FHM* magazine) and 'wearing women's clothing' (i.e. my Sienna Miller scarf). Uncle John has called in Father Abraham (I am not joking) from their extremist church to perform an exorcism. It is all my fault. I hope he does not grass me up to Auntie Joyless.

. . . .

Saturday 3

Treena came over. She is gigantic. I hope it is not twins. She let James put his hands on her tummy and feel the kicking. Mum looked horrified. She asked if they had told Treena's husband Des about the impending arrival yet. Treena said he was in solitary confinement for a week for headbutting the prison cook but that she was going on Thursday to break the news. She said she was going to have a civilized grown-up discussion and ask for a divorce and the house. I do not think Des will give her either of these things. By all accounts he is neither civilized nor grown-up. They had better sort it out soon though. He is due to be released into the community with his electronic tag in a month.

Sunday 4

Thin Kylie is not coming back to school tomorrow (she came over to show off her Corfu-acquired tan). She says Cherie is worried that I might be a bad influence on her. That is a joke. Kylie is the worst influence in John Major High. She is going to St Gregory's Girls instead. I asked how she got in (they have a rigorous entrance exam and a catchment area of three roads) and she said Terry has paid for a new roof for the needlework wing. Even the nuns are corrupt these days. I blame the New Labour era of sleaze. Kylie is gutted about the uniform though. It is brown with a straw hat. Not even she can make that look sluttish.

Monday 5

8 a.m.

I take it back. Have just seen Thin Kylie getting into the 4x4 in her school uniform. The brown skirt is halfway up her thighs and her white shirt is undone revealing a black Wonderbra. Even the hat manages to look like something

in one of Mark Lambert's magazines. I am glad she is going. I predict I will be able to win Scarlet back by first break.

4 p.m.
Scarlet is still sulking. Although according to Sad Ed she did say that my hair looked avant-garde. She is weakening.

On the plus side, Mrs Brain's fast food menu has been ousted and the school canteen has gone totally Jamie Oliver (Scarlet is triumphant—her hummus sandwich rally has finally been called off). There was a near riot at lunchtime though when Fat Kylie was offered a choice of pitta pockets or foccacia. She said, 'Don't you f**king swear at me, where's my f**king pizza?' Mrs Brain called Mr Wilmott and demanded a return to 'traditional cooking' (i.e. microwaving nuggets) but he said he was under orders from the LEA and that someone from the Government was coming to visit the school next week as it is a model healthy eating establishment so there was no way chips were going back on the menu before then. The crisp and Coke machine was sold out in a record fifteen minutes.

I hope it is not so-called 'Blair Babe' Education Secretary Ruth Kelly who is coming to visit. She has the voice of a man and the hair of a lunatic. She should get some pointers from Suzy who is living proof you can be politically minded and dress like a high-class prostitute.

Tuesday 6

The Jamie Oliver menu is still not the roaring success Mr Wilmott was hoping for. Lessons started fifteen minutes late this afternoon due to the queues of Year Tens at Mr Patel's waiting for microwave Ginsters.

Wednesday 7

I have found a way to get back in with Scarlet. She and Jack have joined the drama club (they are going to lobby for the *Rocky Horror Show* as their next production). I am going to sign up immediately. It means I get off games. Plus being an actress would be totally glamorous and ethereal. I may very well become the next Kate Winslet. I asked Sad Ed if he would join as well (I need back-up) and he has agreed as long as he doesn't have to wear skimpy underwear on stage (he is still several pounds over his target weight).

Thursday 8

Treena has been to see Des. It did not go according to plan. There was a fight during which they both had to be restrained. Des is now back in solitary and his parole has been put back until December.

Grandpa is going to move in to Treena's semi on the Whiteshot Estate. Treena says she is not ashamed of her generation gap love any more. James said she should be

but Treena did not hear him—she was too busy eating Wotsits for two.

. . . .

Friday 9

Saw Jack on C corridor at break. He asked how Cornwall was. I said I was fully reformed. He said that was a shame. I asked if Scarlet had mentioned me at all and he said only in the same sentence as the words cow and loser. I can see she is not going to be broken easily.

. . . .

Saturday 10

Grandpa has moved out. I think Mum was actually sad to see him go. He was a source of constant spillage for her so she will have nothing to do in the day now. Although it may have been disappointment that the dog is staying. Treena has refused to take it—she says it is a health hazard to the baby. This is rich coming from someone who owns a budgie called Christina (as in Aguilera) who is allowed to poo freely on the sofa.

. . . .

Sunday 11

10 a.m.
Scarlet has rung. She is coming over this afternoon to discuss our relationship. Suzy and Sad Ed have worn her down. Hurrah. We will be reunited and I can tell her

about the tragedy of Will. Plus I will have someone to borrow clothes off again.

5 p.m.

The reunion did not go according to plan. Thin Kylie showed up with a bottle of Thunderbird and *Hot Celebrities* and Scarlet went all scary and said I had to make a choice between the 'chavs and the chav-nots'. So Kylie said, 'I ain't no f**kin' chav, Dracula, and anyway, she'll choose me, cos I got a swimming pool, innit,' and sat down on the bed. This is not true. I would choose Scarlet over her any day, but I was worried about repercussions from Kylie so I kept quiet. But Scarlet looked at me with her cat-like eyes (she has inherited that gift from Suzy) and said, 'Your silence speaks volumes,' and swept out of the room in her new goth coat (vegetarian leather). Then Thin Kylie said she had to go anyway as she had Latin homework.

I rang Sad Ed and he agreed this is a major setback. He does not see much hope of a reunion before Christmas.

. . . .

Monday 12

Mr Patel has installed a Pot Noodle stop in his newsagents (i.e. a machine that boils water and a fork dispenser). I am full of admiration for his entrepreneurship—he will be able to fully exploit the gap in the market for E-number-laden junk food now that Mrs Brain has gone organic.

. . . .

Tuesday 13

Grandpa came over for tea. He says he wanted to see the dog but I think he misses Mum's cooking as well. Treena just eats Lean Cuisine and crisps. He said the Whiteshot Estate is not that bad if you ignore the constant roar of minibikes and the smell of convenience food. Mum asked if they had come up with any names yet. He said Treena wants to call it Harvey. Mum said what about if it's a girl and Grandpa said, 'That too.' This is not good. Treena's surname is Nichols.

Wednesday 14

Went to my first drama club meeting. It is a disparate group of eager theatre freaks (Jack, Scarlet, me, Sad Ed) and not so eager Retards and Criminals who are forced to do it as part of their rehab (Davey 'flasher' MacDonald and Jason Kinsey). Justin Statham and Sophie Jacobs are in it as well (they are neither nerds nor retards but a third way of beautiful people). Mr Vaughan is in charge. It is part of his teacher training. He says we can vote on the new production, as part of his democratic teaching method. I have voted for *Hamlet*. Sad Ed asked if we could do a musical version of the life of Jim Morrison, featuring songs by The Doors, but Scarlet told him to shut up and made him vote for *Rocky Horror*.

It is not Ruth Kelly who is visiting the school. It is Prime Minister Tony Blair. Sad Ed says Scarlet says Suzy is in overdrive and is planning to infiltrate the school so that she can meet him. I do not think she will succeed. Mr Wilmott and Suzy have a history of not seeing eye to eye.

Thursday 15

There has been mass Pot Noodle injury due to Mr Patel's introduction of a chilli variety. Mrs Leech was in overdrive administering ice packs and soothing cans of Sprite. Mr Wilmott looked worried. Tony Blair is coming tomorrow and the canteen is conspicuously quiet these days.

Friday 16

10 a.m.

The school is crawling with security guards ahead of Tony Blair's visit. There was a mild panic in the sixth form common room when sniffer dogs showed up but it turns out that these ones can only smell bombs not drugs. Mr Wilmott has planned ahead quite well—the Retards and Criminals are on a day visit to a fishfinger factory and Mrs Brain is on annual leave. (Ms Hopwood-White has reluctantly agreed to pose as a go-getting dinner lady instead.)

4 p.m.

Tony Blair's visit was not the resounding success hoped for. Plans were going well. Mr Wilmott had managed to

lure people away from Mr Patel's with a carrot and stick approach (a temporary 'no leaving the school at lunchtime' rule and a promise to reinstate doughnuts by Monday) so that by 12.15 everyone was eating broccoli and sipping spring water but then Suzy, who had managed to evade school security (i.e. Mrs Leech) by coming through the gap in the sheep-field fence, threw herself at Tony Blair outside the mobile science labs in an act of comradeship (according to Suzy), and potential terrorism (according to the Secret Service). Tony Blair got bundled back into his blacked-out Rover before he could sample the three-bean pilaff and Suzy got arrested.

I do not know what Suzy sees in him anyway. His teeth are sinister.

Saturday 17

Grandpa and Treena are getting married. They came round after *CD:UK* to share the happy news. Mum is in shock. I think she was hoping Grandpa would come to his senses and grow old gracefully. How he is going to do that with a toddler called Harvey I do not know. Although at least it ends the Nichols threat—Treena is going to change her name to Riley. Dad pointed out that she was still married to a convicted criminal, but Treena said she had already filed for divorce on grounds of mental cruelty. James said, 'Mental illness more like.' So Mum sent him to his room to tidy up his hobbit shrine. I am not sure if

I am happy or not. On the one hand, I am all for controversial love across class, race, and age boundaries but, on the other hand, this is the sort of story that gets featured in *Chat* magazine for £50.

Sunday 18

Saw Thin Kylie on the wall. She says St Gregory's is excellent. She has a new best friend called Aaliyah who is fifteen and has a black dad and has done it with three different boys including Mr Whippy, the ice cream man. (aka seventeen-year-old Dave Tennick who got thrown out of John Major High last year for joyriding in Mr Wilmott's Vauxhall Cavalier. At least he is putting his driving skills to good use now.) Why can't I go to a Catholic girls' school instead of a mixed comprehensive. It is so much edgier.

Monday 19

James has won the Saffron Walden under-tens literary competition with his story 'Murder Round The Bend'. It is about a man who walks around a corner and gets stabbed to death. The judges said it shows real promise and a flair for minimalist surrealism. I have serious doubts about the judges' credentials. I do not think Mr Goddard the butcher should be involved in discussions on literary merit. He cleaves entire pigs in two for a living.

Tuesday 20

It is drama club tomorrow. I hope *Hamlet* wins. I would make an excellent Ophelia. I already know what drowning in a meringue dress feels like.

Wednesday 21

We are not doing *Hamlet*. According to Mr Vaughan it only got one vote. We are doing *Bugsy Malone*, which won by a massive ten votes (the Criminals and Retards discovered it involved guns). Sophie Jacobs is jubilant. She wants to be Tallulah. Auditions are next week. I am going to try for Blousey Brown, innocent but talented new girl in town. She gets to kiss Bugsy (which is bound to be Justin Statham as he is the best looking by far, plus his dad can get programmes printed cheaply). Sad Ed is in a panic. There is a character called Fat Sam and he is worried about typecasting. Scarlet is sulking. She says *Bugsy Malone* is, at best, pro-American propaganda and, at worst, a paedophile's dream come true. I do not know what she thinks *Rocky Horror* would be. It involves gay sex and suspender belts.

Thursday 22

I have learnt all the words to Blousey Brown's song ('Ordinary Fool'—how appropriate). I am going to get the part for sure. I sound almost like Katie Melua.

Friday 23

Saw Justin in B corridor at lunchtime with Jack. With our new-found bond as drama club members I decided to talk to him and said he would make an excellent Bugsy. But then Sophie Jacobs sashayed up singing 'My Name is Tallulah' and whisked him for practice. Jack rolled his eyes and said they deserved each other. How can he speak ill of Justin? Or maybe he was being nice about Sophie. Whichever, he is wrong. Justin deserves me. I am so over Will. He was a rebound boyfriend. Justin is my true destiny.

Saturday 24

Watched *Bugsy Malone* on DVD with James to get tips for my audition. James said Scarlet is right—the film glorifies sex and violence, and is not suitable for a school production. I pointed out that 'Murder Round the Bend' glorified violence but he claims it has an anti-knives subplot.

Sunday 25

Grandpa and Treena came over. Des is contesting her mental cruelty divorce and has filed for divorce himself on grounds of adultery. Treena says she will not give him the satisfaction. I said what did it matter if the end result was the same but Treena said it was a matter of pride. But

she is adulterous. The proof is due in less than three
months.

- -

Monday 26

Rehearsed with Sad Ed after school (Scarlet had to go to
Mrs Wong's for a filling and so couldn't intervene to stop
us). He said I was excellent, but that my husky voice
sounded a bit more menacing than sexy at times. Sad Ed
is going to sing Tallulah's song. He says that is the sort of
subversive thing Jim Morrison would have done. He is so
gay. I was right all along! Hurrah.

- -

Tuesday 27

Scarlet is off school. Jack told Ms Hopwood-White she
lost a lot of blood after her filling. I should think she is
thrilled. She will look anaemic now, which is the
preferred goth skin tone.

Auditions are tomorrow. I actually feel sick. I may
have been hasty in likening my singing voice to Katie
Melua. The dog howls when I practise.

- -

Wednesday 28

Auditions did not go brilliantly. Mr Vaughan had decided
to do them *X-Factor* style with Ms Hopwood-White as
Sharon Osbourne. Three Year Eights left in tears. I got off

mildly. He said my voice was interestingly unpolished. I think that might be good. Ms Hopwood-White said it was a 'Yes' from her. Sad Ed is through as well. Mr Vaughan said his rendition of 'My Name is Tallulah' was hilarious. Although I am not sure that is the effect Ed was aiming for.

. . . .

Thursday 29

Saw Mr Vaughan outside the mobile science lab having a cigarette. I asked him if he had made his decision on Blousey Brown yet. He said there was only one girl for the part. Yes, but which one?

Sad Ed has invited me to his birthday party on Saturday. He is going to make vodka martinis and play lounge music. I asked him if Scarlet was going. He said no.

. . . .

Friday 30

Went into town to find Sad Ed a birthday present. Got him ten Flyte bars and *Will and Grace* Season One on DVD (on offer in WHSmith for £6.99, purchased when Mrs Noakes safely on lunchbreak).

October

Saturday 1

Sad Ed lied. Scarlet was at his birthday party. She was not pleased to see me—apparently he had lied to her about my presence as well. Plus there were no vodka martinis or lounge music. Mrs Thomas served jelly and devilled eggs and made us play musical chairs to 'Walking in the Air' until Scarlet claimed I had cheated by using an orthopaedic footstool as a chair and refused to join in until I was sent off. It was all over by 7 so I went home and ate the contents of my party bag (except the miniature playing cards, obviously) and watched *Casualty*. I would make an excellent paramedic. I am decisive and compassionate, plus I love tragedy and look good in green.

Sunday 2

Granny Clegg called. Father Abraham's exorcism has worked. Boaz is back singing 'The Battle Hymn of the Republic' and wearing boys' clothes (Clark's shoes and tank tops). What is wrong with the men in our family? They all give in at the first sign of torture or bribery.

Monday 3

Sad Ed thanked me for the presents. Flyte bars are key to his weight loss programme. He has eaten three today already. I asked him if he had watched any *Will and Grace*

233

yet but he said that all the discs had a bite-sized chunk out of them and were unplayable. (Aaagh—dog must have got to it after I watched several episodes—just to check quality, of course.)

. . . .

Tuesday 4

Jewish New Year
First day of Ramadan

Mum is not pleased. James is on a fast in religious sympathy with Islam. He can only eat during hours of darkness, which has messed up her strict meal and bed timetable. He will not last the week. Plus I doubt Reverend Begley will have any sympathy with his embracing of world religions.

. . . .

Wednesday 5

I am not Blousey. Sophie Microwave Muffins Jacobs got the part. She is neither innocent, nor talented. I bet her dad is providing catering. The casting is all over the place. Oona Rickets is Tallulah. Jack is Bugsy. Justin is Dandy Dan. Scarlet is a man. I am a chorus dancer. So is Fat Kylie (I pity Mrs Mathias's needlework class making her costume). Worst of all I have to slow dance with black cleaner-cum-tap-legend Fizzy (Davey MacDonald— neither black nor able to dance, to my knowledge). The only appropriate casting is Sad Ed as Fat Sam. So his

subversive and gay tendencies did not pay off. Rehearsals get under way next week. Mr Vaughan is instigating an experimental and democratic teaching method—people can choose not to come to rehearsals. He is hoping it will instil a sense of responsibility and teamwork amongst the cast. I won't hold my breath.

. . . .

Thursday 6

James's Ramadan fast has ended. He went dizzy during netball (non-sexist sports coaching) and had to be force-fed chocolate milk to revive him. He is going to pray to Mecca five times a day instead. I asked where hobbits featured in Islam's teachings. He said this was typical of such a small-minded Westerner and that Islam was not the exclusive, extremist religion it was cracked up to be.

. . . .

Friday 7

James's praying to Mecca has ended. He says it interferes with CBBC too much. Plus the dog got overexcited and chewed his prayer mat (an M&S beach towel).

. . . .

Saturday 8

Went to see Grandpa Riley and Treena. They are living in semi-squalor. There were biscuit wrappers and budgie

235

poo all over the floor. Grandpa says it is because neither he nor Treena can bend down any more due to lumbago and heavy pregnancy respectively. I felt sorry for Grandpa, he is not used to council estate conditions, so I hoovered up and washed the dishes for them. I drew the line at cleaning out the loo though. I know how much time Treena spent with her head down it.

Sunday 9

Granny Clegg called to say goodbye. She and Grandpa Clegg are off to Florida tomorrow. She told Mum her will was in the bread bin. They have never been on a plane before and are convinced it will be hijacked or flown into a tall building by Osama Bin Laden. Mum said it wasn't too late to cancel the trip (she is worried about Dad having to fly out to rescue them from a situation) but Granny Clegg said no beardy-weirdy is going to stop her from seeing one of the seven wonders of the world. Mum said she wasn't aware of a wonder in Florida and Granny Clegg said they were thinking of a day trip to the Grand Canyon. Mum went all pale. The Grand Canyon is 2,570 miles from Florida (James googled it). The possibilities for disaster are endless.

Auntie Joyless is driving them to Gatwick. At least there is no chance of getting lost on that stage of the journey.

Monday 10

The flight was not from Gatwick. It was from Heathrow.
Luckily they had left eight hours check in and sightseeing
time (the airport is a wonder of the world in itself to
Granny Clegg) so Auntie Joyless managed to get the
Metro round the M25 to Terminal 3 with four hours to
spare. The plane has taken off and there are no reports
of incidents involving midget pensioners. Mum checked
on Ceefax and rang the airline.

Tuesday 11

The provisional SAT results are out. John Major High is at
the bottom of the league, beating only the Sharon Davies
Special School in Braintree. Mr Wilmott gave a talk in
Assembly. He said we had let the school down.

Wednesday 12

Mr Vaughan is being forced to rethink his democratic
teaching method. Dandy Dan's and Fat Sam's gangs (i.e.
Davey MacDonald and the rest of the Criminals and
Retards) did not show up for group rehearsal—they were
behind the mobile science lab, smoking. Mr Wilmott
found them and returned them to the drama room with a
withering look. Then we tried the opening dance routine
(as choreographed by Sophie Jacobs) but it got stopped
after a fight between the gangs broke out behind the

wardrobe department (aka a wardrobe). Jason Kinsey said they were just getting into character so Mr Vaughan suggested their gang leaders (aka Sad Ed and Justin) start using their leadership skills but Jason said he wasn't taking orders from a 'fat bender'. Mr Vaughan has decided to schedule separate rehearsals until the gangs can channel their ASBO tendencies into their performance.

I have individual rehearsal with Davey MacDonald tomorrow. I hope his special needs do not evidence themselves.

Thursday 13

Oh my God. Davey MacDonald can dance. I was right all along. He does have special skills alongside his perverted habits. Mr Vaughan is beside himself. He thinks he has discovered Billy Elliot. He is going to phone the Royal Ballet. Davey MacDonald did not look keen but Mr Vaughan said that he would get to wear tights, which are extremely revealing. Maybe I was too hasty in dismissing Davey as a thick pervert. Ballet dancers are all deep and meaningful and have eccentric eating disorders and things. *Très* romantic.

Friday 14

A postcard arrived from Granny Clegg. It was from Heathrow Airport. It said:

Having a lovely time. Have tried foreign food already at a restaurant called McDonalds—have you heard of it? Apparently it is very popular in America. Love to Valerie.

PS. Call Hester and tell her she can have the arctic roll in the freezer. I think it may be past its best.

Saturday 15

Grandpa has asked if I will be his bridesmaid at his forthcoming wedding. I said that technically, the wedding was not really forthcoming as Treena's divorce wasn't settled yet but he said that was a mere detail. I hope he is not thinking of becoming a bigamist. It would be all over GMTV with pictures of me in my compost-stained bridesmaid's dress. Maybe I can get a new and cool dress. I will ask Mum. I could be an excellent vintage bridesmaid.

5 p.m.

Mum says she is not wasting money on trips to London to buy vintage Chanel. She says she will try Vanish

239

Oxy-Action on the compost dress or I can make do with my school uniform skirt and one of her blouses. Shudder.

. . . .

Sunday 16

Went round Sad Ed's. Scarlet was there. It was a strained hour and a half. She and Ed are going to London at half term to buy goth clothes and man make-up. I casually suggested we could visit Old Compton Street (famous gay road in London and ideal territory to gauge Sad Ed's Will factor). Scarlet snorted and said Bob and Suzy were driving them and there wouldn't be room for me. That is not true. Volvos are notoriously spacious and, anyway, I could sit in the boot.

. . . .

Monday 17

8 p.m.

Grandpa Clegg is missing in a theme park. Granny Clegg reversed charges from her motel room. He was last seen two hours ago walking towards the *Back to the Future* ride in a state of 'shock and awe'. She wants Dad to fly out to help her hunt for him. Dad has refused. He says he has an important meeting on Thursday to discuss his work's photocopier servicing contract. Mum told Granny to call the police but Granny said she wasn't trusting her husband's life to someone called Chip or Brad.

240

1 a.m.
Granny Clegg has just called (reversed charges again)—Grandpa Clegg has been found alive. He had come over funny in a tunnel and had to be taken to the emergency medical and lost children room. Dad is relieved. The future of his photocopier contract is safe.

Tuesday 18
Granny Clegg has called again. This time to ask what grits are. Mum has banned reverse charge phone calls except in matters of life or death.

Wednesday 19
Thank God I am doing excellent drama instead of hockey with the lesbians. According to Mrs Leech, there were four electrocutions, a missing front tooth, and a possible pneumonia today. I am amazed school sport has not been banned. Statistically, it is more dangerous than Formula One.

Thursday 20
Mum has gone bird flu mad. She has taken down the half coconuts and blue-tit box and done a cursory sweep of the neighbourhood for diseased pigeons etc. (findings—one suspicious sparrow in Marjory's

Leylandii). Duck feeding is out, as is tonight's planned Coq Au Vin.

. . . .

Friday 21

Mum's paranoia knows no bounds. She has broken her self-imposed long distance phone call rules to get Granny Clegg to bring back some Tamiflu in case we get infected by a rogue pigeon. They were out at a line dancing competition though so she had to leave a message with someone called Randy.

. . . .

Saturday 22

Thin Kylie came over today with her new friend Aaliyah. Her dad is an Ambassador and her mum is an ex-supermodel. This explains the errant behaviour. Thin Kylie had told her about my morning-after pill services and she asked if she could get some as Mr Whippy wasn't keen on condoms. I said that the morning-after pill was not a method of contraception and Thin Kylie said, 'But it, like, stops you getting up the spout, so, like, of course it is.' So I suggested she went on the pill instead and that Dr Braithwaite was usually happy to oblige.

4 p.m.

Oh God. What if Aaliyah tells Dr Braithwaite it was me

who suggested she went on the pill. Mum is bound to start a campaign to get the age of consent raised.

· ·

Sunday 23

Granny and Grandpa Clegg have been arrested for drug smuggling at Heathrow. The Tamiflu turned out to be Temazepam—a prescription sedative apparently favoured by hardcore drug addicts and celebrities. Granny Clegg says she is sure that is the message she got from the bellboy Randy, who kindly got her the drugs. Dad is driving down there now to sort it out.

Mum is more concerned about her lack of bird flu antidote. She is refusing to visit Grandpa Riley until Christina has been given the all clear.

11 p.m.

Dad is back. Granny and Grandpa Clegg are free. Dad pointed out their inherent stupidity and thus inability to mastermind an international drugs ring and the police reluctantly agreed. They have been let off with a fine for importing restricted goods instead.

· ·

Monday 24

It is half term. Once again I am friendless (Sad Ed is getting ready for his trip to London with Scarlet tomorrow. They are planning their 'looks' with military precision.) and being forced to take solace in literature.

I am reading *Down and Out in Paris and London*. I wish I was.

- -

Tuesday 25

It is not fair. Sad Ed and Scarlet are in London while I am languishing in the middle-class backwater that is North Essex. I could be brushing shoulders with Sienna and Kate while we scour Portobello for unique vintage finds, instead of being forced to go to DeBarrs for new school shoes (Clark's, if previous visits are anything to go by).

3 p.m.

Have new school shoes. They are black Kickers and were hard won after an hour-long battle with Mum, who was veering towards some totally orthopaedic looking Start Rite. Mum agreed on the grounds they had nicely ridged soles, no heels, and good ankle support. Kickers are very retro, which is like vintage only cleaner. Who needs London?

- -

Wednesday 26

Saffron Walden is not a shopping Mecca. I was temporarily blinded by DeBarr's experimental footwear stand. Sad Ed got a vintage Crombie (i.e. a dead man's coat) and a skateboard (impulse buy—he will never use

it). Plus, he and Scarlet had lunch in the Topshop café next to the fat one out of Blue and Ulrika Johnson (not together—or they could have called *Hello* and made some money). I asked Ed if he had gone to Old Compton Street but he said no, they were too busy buying vegetarian shoes in Covent Garden. Am going to have to find another way to get Sad Ed to come out. Maybe I will rent a Judy Garland DVD and invite Ed over. She is a gay icon. If he agrees to come and see it then I will know for sure.

Thursday 27

Got out *The Wizard of Oz* from BJ Video (aka Blow Job Video). Invited Sad Ed over but he was watching a *Buffy* marathon on Sky. So it is not a total rejection of gay lifestyle, which is promising.

Watched the DVD with James and the dog. Gay men have weird tastes in films. The dog got excited at the little people and ate the box. So now I will have a fine at Blow Job Video.

Friday 28

Oh my God. Thin Kylie is coming back to school on Monday. Mum bumped into Cherie in the bleach section at Waitrose (Cherie had taken a wrong turn in Doritos). Apparently posh Catholic girls are worse than Whiteshot chavs for drug and alcohol abuse and Cherie has taken her

out before she is led astray. I should think Terry is gutted he signed that cheque now. I bet the nuns don't do refunds.

. . . .

Saturday 29

Saw Kylie on the front wall. Cherie is a liar. Kylie has been expelled for a list of misdemeanours including refusing to wear regulation pants, sexually provoking the caretaker, and threatening Sister Ignatia with a gel pen. Although Cherie was right about the alcohol. Kylie says Vodka Slammers are de rigeur lunchtime drinking.

. . . .

Sunday 30

British Summer Time ends

James has written to Nestlé. His afternoon KitKat was solid chocolate. You would think that would be a bonus but he is very particular about his chocolate/wafer ratio.

. . . .

Monday 31

Fat Kylie and Thin Kylie are back and are harder than ever. They buried a Year Eight in the high jump pit (aka school cat toilet) at first break just so word got out that they were in charge again. Mr Wilmott did not look thrilled to see Thin Kylie back. Nor did Ms Hopwood-White. She has been enjoying a period of relative authority.

James is out trick or treating. He is dressed (surprise, surprise) as a hobbit. The dog is dressed as a werewolf (no disguise needed). Mum has gone with them. I said I was too old for such childish nonsense.

8.30 p.m.
Why, oh why, did I not go trick or treating? James got eighteen mini Mars bars, a Swizzels selection pack, a Terry's Chocolate Orange and £21.40 in cash. He has counted it five times.

CUSTARD

Tuesday 1

All Saints Day

Mum has got a new campaign. She is leading the protest against the 24-hour licensing laws due to come in in three weeks. I said she was leaving it a bit late as the law was already passed but she said she hoped to influence money-crazy pub owners into submission.

Wednesday 2

Blind but brilliant David Blunkett has resigned. Again. It is the dog I feel sorry for. It is used to a charmed life. Now it will have to go back to Sheffield and eat Pal and listen to *The Archers* like lesser dogs do.

Rehearsals started again today. Mr Vaughan unveiled the prototype splurge gun, as designed by Mr Potter's Year Ten CDT class. It has been sent back to the drawing board after it backfired and showered Mr Vaughan with Bird's custard.

Thursday 3

Eid Al-Fittr

Grandpa and Treena came over for tea. (James was at Mumtaz's celebrating the end of Ramadan.) There is still no sign of divorce progress. Des says he will make her life a misery if she does not bow to his demands (he wants the house, the black ash coffee table, the Argos sofa, the

Jean-Claude Van Damme DVD collection and the removal of Christina).

Friday 4

Mark Lambert is back. Chavs' corner is complete once more. He said spinning Waltzers wasn't all it was cracked up to be. What was he expecting? The Kylies are a bit fractious though. They have not decided who is going to shag him yet.

Saturday 5

Guy Fawkes Night

Went to the annual Round Table firework display at Caton's Lane, home of Saffron Walden FC (Vicks Inhaler league). Mum did not go—Dad is an official firework lighter and she is scared of seeing him burnt alive by a rogue Catherine wheel. She and the dog watched *Casualty* on loud to block out the noise. Scarlet was there with Bob, Suzy, and Jack. Jack waved and mouthed something but I couldn't hear due to the shrieking of eight year olds in my ears. Scarlet ignored me. She is dragging this out longer than I anticipated.

12 midnight

Cannot sleep. The dog is whimpering under my bed due to the continuing sound of fireworks and outdoor

karaoke coming from the Britchers'. Mum has put in her ear plugs. She bought them the day the Britchers arrived 'just in case'.

- -

Sunday 6

The Britchers are still in the garden. It is a scene of lottery winning carnage. From my bedroom (with James's binoculars) I can clearly see a naked man in their pool and several discarded Asti Spumante bottles. They are probably getting into practice for 24-hour drinking. Mum has catalogued them. (It is their twenty-third entry in her ASBO book of shame—a new record.)

- -

Monday 7

Grandpa and Treena have decided to postpone the wedding until after the baby is born. I asked if this was an indication that they were not going to flout bigamy rules, but Treena says it is because Berkertex can't squeeze her into anything at the moment. She is huge. She claims she is just eating for two. But I don't think babies need entire tins of Celebrations and six-packs of prawn cocktail crisps every day.

- -

Tuesday 8

Rural studies is not as easy as I was led to believe. Mr Cheesmond (scary giant beard with traces of food;

lingering smell of goat) did a surprise quiz on sheep diseases. I had no idea they were so riddled with illness. I hope Mum does not find out, she will ban me from outdoor lessons and remove lamb from her ever-diminishing menu as well. Although I would never have to do games again, which would be a bonus.

. . . .

Wednesday 9

Rehearsals went well i.e. Davey MacDonald did not get his thing out once, which is just as well as I have to dance within five inches of his exposure area. I think Mr Vaughan is regretting casting Sophie as Blousey though. He has timetabled a load of extra individual rehearsals for her. Obviously she is not measuring up to expectation.

. . . .

Thursday 10

Mum's anti-binge-drinking letter is in the *Walden Chronicle*. It says:

> As a mother of two, I am astounded that the council is sending out the message that all-day drinking is something to be encouraged. There are already no less than two homeless alcoholics

(aka Barry the Blade and Mrs Simpson)

> marauding our ancient Tudor streets, I do not think we want to see any more. In any case, the pavements are simply not wide enough for café tables—have we forgotten the catalogue of accidents when Gayhomes

(crap hardware shop)

> allowed a perilously wide display of mops to overcrowd Hill Street.

I wish she would sign her letters anonymously. Thin Kylie and Cherie (who both have severe Bacardi Breezer habits) are bound to have something to say.

• •

Friday 11

As predicted, I am, once more, at the receiving end of post-*Walden Chronicle* wrath. Mark Lambert asked if I was one of those 'Hamish' people with the bonnets and clogs and Tracey Hughes said the police were backing 24-hour drinking as their hours were so unpredictable it was the only way they could fit in a pint before work.

It is Scarlet's birthday tomorrow. She will be fifteen. I am going to get her an appropriate card and present to prove my undying friendship. Sad Ed says she is not having a party. She is going to have a silent gothic mass instead.

· ·

Saturday 12

Went into town to get Scarlet's card and present (copy of *Frankenstein* and some fake blood). Am going round there after tea to give them to her.

9 p.m.

Sad Ed lied. Scarlet was having a party. I distinctly saw merriment (upper school goths and Suzy nodding their heads to waily music) through the window. Even Justin was there. Scarlet doesn't even like Justin. I left my present on the doorstep but Jack opened the door to let Gordon and Tony out for a wee at the same time and saw me. He said, 'Shit, are you crying, Riley?' I said, on the contrary, they were tears of joy at not having to listen to such crap music with a bunch of pseudo-vampires. Jack said, 'She doesn't mean it. She loves you really. We all do.' Then he offered to walk me home but I lied and said Dad was waiting for me round the corner. Which meant I had to hover near a Passat until Jack went in.

I walked back via Sad Ed's. As predicted, he was not in but was at Scarlet's joining in the goth celebrations. It is not his fault. He is torn between his friends. And Scarlet is winning because she has an iPod and a vegetarian goth coat.

· ·

Sunday 13

Remembrance Sunday

Went to Remembrance Parade with James and Grandpa to 'honour his friends and colleagues who lost their lives in the wars'. I had said I wasn't going (being anti-war is essential in Year Ten) but then Grandpa got all animated about if it wasn't for people like him I would be eating bratwurst and Werther's Originals now (which is rubbish as he eats the latter anyway as a matter of choice and I am not even sure they are German). He is still deluded about his role in the Blitz but I agreed to go none the less. I am honouring innocent men who died heroically trying to protect my freedom and that of weaker nations—not the muppets like Finbarr O'Grady who joined up because they like guns and drinking games.

Monday 14

I have my six-monthly appointment with Mrs Wong tomorrow. Mum has scheduled it for four o'clock in anticipation of the blood loss and general carnage. So I don't even get a day at home sipping emergency Lucozade and missing double maths to compensate.

Tuesday 15

Cannot speak. Can barely write through the pain. Have had another filling. I do not understand it: I use Colgate, floss, and plaque-revealing tablet things. Maybe Mrs Wong just likes inflicting pain.

Sad Ed came over after tea (Covent Garden soup through a straw) to see if I was still alive. He says that dentists get paid more for carrying out painful and complicated procedures. This is outrageous. Does Tony Blair know of this dental corruption? I am going to take it up with Suzy, as soon as Scarlet and I are on speaking terms.

Wednesday 16

Sophie and Justin were not talking to each other in rehearsals today. As Sad Ed said, 'Something is rotten in the state of Denmark.' (He got this off *True Romance*. He is now hoping to be Christian Slater and specialize in borderline insane acting roles before dying young. I pointed out that Christian Slater was still alive but Sad Ed says, with increasing life expectancy, thirty-six is positively premature.)

Thursday 17

Mr Vaughan has asked Sad Ed to tone down Fat Sam's eye rolling and mental grinning because *Bugsy Malone* is light-hearted comedy, not *Goodfellas*. Sad Ed told him that Christian Slater wasn't in *Goodfellas* and Mr Vaughan said, 'Sorry, I didn't get that. I thought you were being Joe Pesci.' Sad Ed is sulking. He says his weight and slightly

diminutive stature (he is only 8 cm taller than me) are hampering his career.

Friday 18
Something is definitely rotten in Denmark. I saw Sophie in tears behind the mobile science lab. Mr Vaughan was comforting her. He is very understanding for a teacher. It is because he is only twenty-three and can remember what it is like to be young and in love.

Saturday 19
Granny Clegg rang to ask if we were going to Cornwall for Christmas. Mum said we couldn't as Dad is on emergency standby for work (what emergency could this be—a glitch in the Bic biro supply?) Anyway, this is not true. It is because she is paranoid about Hester Trelowarren's battery hens giving us bird flu. Her lie backfired though. Granny Clegg said that they would come to Saffron Walden instead then. Mum did not look happy when she hung up. She has not recovered from the dog visiting rights episode.

Sunday 20
James has got an audition for his school nativity tomorrow. He is going to do a scene from *Lord of the Rings*

playing both Frodo and Gollum. I offered to give him some tips but he said he didn't need advice from a bit-part player.

. . . .

Monday 21

Oh my God. My life could be about to change. According to Sad Ed, who heard from Scarlet who heard from Jack, Sophie has chucked Justin Statham. She told him on his lunch break at Goddard's on Saturday. This was a rash move, considering the proximity of the mincing machine. Apparently there is a third party involved. This is excellent news. He will be distraught and get stage fright and I will coax him out of his terror and win his heart at the same time. Hurrah.

. . . .

Tuesday 22

Saw Justin at the Coke machine at first break. He looked pale and needy. So I pretended to have got the wrong thing out of the machine (i.e. a Double Decker) and said he could have it. But he said he is allergic to raisins and gave it to Jack. Jack said he would swap it for his Twirl but it was all getting too complicated so I gave up and went to watch Fat Kylie menace some new Year Sevens.

. . . .

Wednesday 23

Rehearsals were fraught with tension. Sophie burst into tears three times and had to be taken to the upper school toilets by Fiona and Pippa for emergency mascara application. Mr Vaughan looked worried. He should have expected it though—all theatrical types are emotional and needy.

Thursday 24

Mum is in a state of panic. 24-hour licensing comes in today. She is convinced the town is going to turn into Amsterdam and that drunken youths will rampage past Woolworth's at 8 a.m., high on a breakfast of Special Brew and cocaine. If only. The only drink-related crime incident to date is when one of the O'Grady's drank ten bottles of cider as a dare and stole a police dog. The police got in trouble as well for having such ineffectual Alsatians. Anyway, it is an excellent law, which will turn dull market towns into continental café societies.

Friday 25

Once again Mum (and me, to some extent) are being forced to eat our ill-chosen words. It turns out that none of Saffron Walden's landlords applied for 24-hour drinking. Mum is claiming partial victory—she says it is her forthright campaigning that dissuaded them from the lunacy of it all. I fear it is more likely their general laziness and unenterprising spirit.

Saturday 26

I take it back. There has been some drinking law related hoo-ha—Barry the Blade was arrested at one in the morning for causing a scene outside Abrakebabra. He had purchased late-night lager from Stavros the Greek and was singing 'Push the Button' with his trousers round his ankles. Clearly Stavros is the only forward-thinking businessman in Saffron Walden. It is a shame that his main customer is a renowned psychotic tramp.

Sunday 27

First in Advent

Walked past Scarlet's twenty-seven times today. I miss her. There is nothing to do on a Sunday. Plus Sad Ed is at an enforced Aled Jones convention in St Albans. Had to come home though when the dog saw Tony and Gordon on the roof of the Volvo and set off the alarm trying to get them.

Monday 28

James has got the lead role in the St Regina's nativity play. According to Reverend Begley, he shows natural

talent. This is typical. I am being outshone, theatrically, by an eight year old.

⋅ ⋅

Tuesday 29

Oh my God! The third party in the Sophie Jacobs/Justin Statham break-up was Mr Vaughan. Apparently his 'comforting' behind the mobile science lab went a bit further than an arm around the shoulder (a hand inside the Wonderbra, according to Pippa Newbold). Luckily she is already sixteen or he would be joining former Geography teacher Mr Ingham on the sex offenders' register (Leanne Jones triumphs yet again). As it is, he has been banned from directing the school play. Mr Wilmott is putting someone less impressionable in charge (i.e. Mrs Butfield (aka Buttface)—notoriously strict Head of English). Sophie Jacobs is out as well. She is back on the hockey pitch with the lesbians from tomorrow.

⋅ ⋅

Wednesday 30

Mrs Butfield is going to recast Blousey. There is an emergency audition on Friday. Hurrah—I am bound to get the role. There is no way Fat Kylie can fit into the costume.

Grandpa and Treena came over for tea. Grandpa looked nervous. It is because Des is being released tomorrow. Treena says they are going to stand their ground and demand to keep the house.

december

Thursday 1

Treena and Grandpa have moved in with us. They are going to go on the council waiting list for a flat. They will have a long wait. There are several O'Gradys to rehouse first. Mum is not speaking to Dad. She says her house is being turned into a hostel for deviants and wild animals (Treena brought Christina with her). At least it will keep Auntie Joyless away. Mum has booked Christina in at the vet's tomorrow for a thorough bird flu check-up. Until then it is in quarantine in the garage. The dog is overjoyed at their arrival. It chased its tail inanely round the dining room in celebration for over an hour. I fear it is not loyalty but Treena's crisp habit that is making it so happy, though. She is now on eight packets a day.

Friday 2

My audition for Blousey went well. I think Mrs Butfield was impressed at my word perfect delivery and my innocent wide-eyed stare (although Sad Ed says it makes me look like Miss Beadle). Oh, I want the part so much. I will have to kiss Jack and Sad Ed (Mr Vaughan wrote in a bit where she sleeps with Fat Sam to get the job to make it more realistic) but it is small price to pay for the ultimate prize—snogging Justin at the after-show party.

Christina has been given the all-clear (at a cost of £57.65). Mr Mercer told Mum that the risk of a domestic budgie catching bird flu was more than fourteen million to one. But Mum said that was what they say about the lottery and look at the Britchers.

Saturday 3

Christina has gone missing. It is because Grandpa left the cage open so that she could fly about during *Dick and Dom*. Treena is beside herself. She says it is a sign from God. Mum is more concerned that there will be poo on the soft furnishings. She has covered the three-piece suite with cling film and spare towels.

Plus the dog is ill. It has been retching for hours now to no avail. It has taken over Christina's quarantine spot in the garage until it shows signs of improvement.

Sunday 4

Second in Advent

The mystery of Christina's disappearance is over. The dog has produced a pile of green-feather-studded sick in the garage. It also brought up a sock and part of a Pringles box. Luckily I removed the evidence before Treena or Mum could find out. It is better that Treena thinks Christina has flown to her freedom on the Peter Purvis Recreation Ground rather than that she was chewed to death by an insane mongrel.

Monday 5

Today is a milestone in the emancipation of gay and lesbian people across the country. Civil partnerships (aka big, fat gay weddings) are now legal. I think it is lovely. Sad Ed can get married now and I can be his maid of honour. Grandpa Clegg rang up to moan. He says Tony Blair is letting 'deviants like Elton John and that bloke off *Strictly Dance Fever*' run the country. Dad said he didn't know why anyone would bother with getting married if they didn't have to. Mum demanded to know what he meant by that and then we all got sent to our rooms to do our homework (Grandpa and Treena included).

Tuesday 6

Mrs Butfield is going to announce the recasting tomorrow. I am sick with anticipation. Sad Ed says he has put in a good word as well. He is just terrified it will be Fat Kylie. She will crush him, even with his bingo wings.

Wednesday 7

I am Blousey Brown! I knew it all along. Both James and I are theatrical—we are like Jake and Maggie Gyllenhaal or the Fienneses. Thin Kylie is going to take over my role. She and Davey MacDonald are made for each other. They are both perverts.

I got a cheer and a drama club hug. I note that Scarlet

269

did not join in though. She is annoyed I have a bigger part than her plus I don't have to wear fake facial hair. We have emergency rehearsals tomorrow to re-establish trust (i.e. lots of hugging and falling over). I hope I get paired with Justin.

Thursday 8

I did not get paired with Justin. Instead I had to catch Sad Ed when he fell backwards into my arms. I missed. He is very heavy. He claims it is his bones but it is more likely the layer of fat on top of them. Thank God Mrs Butfield has cut our snogging scene. Ed said she was compromising Mr Vaughan's artistic vision but Mrs Butfield said she didn't think the vision of a drug-smoking paedophile was valid.

Friday 9

Rehearsals were ruined again when Davey and Thin Kylie got done for partial nudity inside the wardrobe department (aka the wardrobe). Mrs Butfield suggested we put in some extra practice in our own time and off school premises where she couldn't be held responsible for our behaviour. Jack said that we should all meet at his tomorrow. Hurrah—I will get to be in the black bedroom with Dandy Dan (which sounds like Cluedo). Admittedly Sad Ed, Scarlet, and Jack will be there but it

is so dark Justin and I are bound to bump up against each other. I will make sure of it.

. . . .

Saturday 10

Went round Jack's house for rehearsals. Scarlet was out with Suzy and Bob at a sex toy trade fair in Chelmsford. She is obviously avoiding me—no one in their right mind would choose to view a load of dayglo vibrators. Or to go to Chelmsford, for that matter. I asked where Justin was and Jack said he was at Sophie's in a last-ditch attempt to lure her away from Mr Vaughan. He has no chance. Mr Vaughan has a car and can get into Cinderella Rockefeller's.

Then Sad Ed texted me to say he had stayed up late for an *Angel* marathon on Sky and was feeling faint and would be over later when he had eaten several bowls of Crunchy Nut Cornflakes. I bet Christian Slater doesn't ring up Oliver Stone or whoever and say he can't make it to the set because he is watching homoerotic vampire shows and needs to eat cereal to recover.

So it was just me and Jack. Jack pointed out that we had yet to 'crack' the kissing scene and that maybe we should practise a bit so that it is not totally weird when we do it for real next week. He said it wouldn't mean anything, it would just be part of acting, like wearing pubic wigs. I said he was right. It is just tongues and the brain is not involved at all.

271

So he kissed me. But something weird happened. Because no matter how hard I told my brain not to be involved it just got involved. But, luckily, Suzy walked in with a sex toy that looked like a rabbit and asked if I (gross) or my mum (grosser) wanted to test drive it. So I said I would ask her immediately and ran out before Jack could say anything.

What is going on? Do I like Jack? Does Jack like me? Oh God, it is opening night on Thursday. What if people can tell? What if Justin can tell? He will never love me if he knows I actually kind of like kissing Jack. I will have to do visual projection and pretend Jack is Auntie Joyless. It is the only answer.

Plus now I have Suzy's rabbit-shaped vibrator. I am not going to give it to Mum. She will have Suzy arrested. I am going to give it to the dog. It is the first time I have actually wanted it to destroy something.

9 p.m.
The dog did not like the taste of the sex toy and spat it out during *Casualty*. James is using it to massage his feet. Thank God Mum and Dad are at Clive and Marjory's.

• •

Sunday 11
Third in Advent
Treena's baby is due tomorrow. She is now so vast that she cannot climb the stairs and is sleeping on the sofa

with the dog. She is beginning to smell. James suggested to Mum that we could manhandle her into the shower later but Mum did not look thrilled at the thought of viewing Treena's expanded regions. She is going to get Grandpa to sponge her down after *Popworld*.

Monday 12

No baby. I do not blame it staying inside. Our house is not the serene cocoon of whale music and Mozart as recommended by Dr Miriam Stoppard. The dog is in a barking frenzy (it is Natasha Kaplinsky's fault—she sends the dog into a blind panic for some reason) and Treena and Grandpa are arguing about childcare. Grandpa is refusing to learn how to put on a Pampers. He says it is women's work. He is going to be in charge of entertainment. I hope the baby likes Lulu and Gillian McKeith. James asked Treena if she is going to breastfeed (I am not sure if this is out of fear or hope—her breasts are unfeasibly gigantic). She said she night give it a go at home but that no way is she 'flopping her la-las out in Woolies'. I do not blame her. Society still rails against breastfeeding mothers. One of Suzy's Labour friends, Astrid, says she got thrown out of Gray Palmer for breastfeeding her son Felix in the sports support department. Apparently Astrid told Mr Gray that breast was best and he said, 'Not in Saffron Walden, it isn't.'

Tuesday 13

Had my costume fitting. Surely Sophie Jacobs cannot be this thin. Mrs Mathias and her GCSE needlework class are putting in extra darts and an invisible expansion panel. It had better be invisible. It is opening night on Thursday and I do not want to look like Emily Reeve in her homemade pinafores.

When I got home Mum said she had a suspicious phone call from Suzy about a rabbit and did I know anything. I said I had borrowed a copy of *Watership Down* and forgotten to give it back. I then did a Mum-style forensic sweep of the house to locate the vibrator. It is in James's doll collection and is now called Big Bunny. It is overlord of all the toys on account of its ability to vibrate and glow in the dark. I said he could keep it as long as he says he found it in Treena's room and puts one of Will Young's jackets on it.

Wednesday 14

Dress rehearsal was not an unmitigated success. Fat Sam used his splurge gun on Dandy Dan at point blank range and he had to go to Mrs Leech for impact injury. Why does Sad Ed hate Justin so much? Unless it is not hate— it is love. Oh, that is it! He loves Justin! Oh my God—we have the same taste in men—it so totally *Will and Grace*! No wonder he has always told me to stay away from him. Who will win? I predict it will be me. Justin is definitely

not gay. He has done it twice (pre Sophie Jacobs), if school rumour is to be trusted.

. . . .

Thursday 15
8 a.m.
It is opening night. I have not slept. This is what Gwyneth Paltrow must feel like every day. Mum, Dad, and James are coming. They are bringing Grandpa and Treena, providing that she is not in labour and that they can roll her off the sofa and into the Passat. They are going to leave BBC1 on for the dog to keep it company.

10 p.m.
It was a triumph. Nearly everyone knew their lines and I did not sing out of tune. The Jack snog was still weird. But I visualized Auntie Joyless, which helped a bit. Although I think Jack wondered why I shuddered at the end of it.

When we got home the dog had had some sort of panic attack and eaten one of the arms off the sofa. Dad checked the TV schedule. Natasha Kaplinsky was doing the news. Mum has added her to the banned list. She has never liked her anyway—it is the choppy hairdo. She thinks all newsreaders should look like Moira Stewart.

. . . .

Friday 16

Tonight's performance was marred only by Dandy Dan firing his splurge gun at Mr Vaughan and Sophie Jacobs who were sat on the third row openly holding hands. It is gross. Mr Wilmott should be stricter. So should Mr Microwave Muffins. I may well write to Tony Blair on Justin's behalf to complain. Also, Mark Lambert climbed on to the stage to join in the final fight scene and knocked out Sad Ed. On the plus side, Ms Hopwood-White says it is the best school production she has seen since the Retards and Criminals did a scarily convincing *One Flew Over the Cuckoo's Nest* two years ago.

Saturday 17

Tonight is our final show. I would be sad but the after-show party could be the beginning of a new era for me. I hope Sad Ed isn't too disappointed.

11 p.m.

A tragedy has occurred. Scarlet has betrayed me in the worst way possible. I cannot bear to write it down. I may well die of sorrow and anger in the night. If I do, and someone finds this, it is all Scarlet's fault.

Oh—and someone tell Mr Wilmott never to use his ruler again. Thin Kylie used it to measure Davey MacDonald's thing in his office after the show.

Sunday 18

Fourth in Advent

I did not die. And I feel revived enough after my Shreddies to write about my ordeal.

Scarlet has snogged Justin. It is unbelievable. It was during 'I Believe In a Thing Called Love' as well, which she knows is my and Justin's song. I was talking to Jack and he said, 'Listen, Riley, I need to tell you something.' But before I could find out what it was I looked over at Goth Corner and there was Scarlet in her vegetarian leather with her tongue in Justin's mouth. Which is what Jack must have been about to tell me. So I burst into tears and then Sad Ed got back from the crisp machine and saw what was going on and threw himself at Justin (a sure sign of gay love) and floored him and Scarlet, then Jack tried to break them up but Sad Ed was too heavy.

Then Scarlet started screaming about how I was deluded and I said, 'At least I'm not a traitor,' and she said, 'At least I don't think oral sex is a biology exam.' (This was unfair— it was in Year Six and I don't have Suzy as a constant source of sex instruction.) So I said, 'At least I don't have a moustache,' (she was still in costume), so she said, 'At least I don't think my second-best friend is gay when he's actually in love with . . . ' but at that point Sad Ed covered her mouth, so Justin hit him and then Mrs Buttface came over and pulled everyone apart (she has superhuman upper body strength) and gave us all detention.

I will never forgive her. (Scarlet I mean, not Mrs

Buttface.) She has crossed an uncrossable line. Sad Ed
agrees. He walked me home and held my hand all the
way. He understands how I feel. He has been betrayed as
well. By Justin and Scarlet. Scarlet clearly does not
recognize his innate gayness like me. She has no sixth
sense about these things.

8 p.m.
Jack has just rung to check I am OK. He said Scarlet is
racked with remorse (not because of me—because she
has broken her goth vows and snogged someone who
wears Gap). He has invited me to Bob and Suzy's New
Year's Eve party (tsunamis and hurricanes allowing).
Maybe I will kiss Jack at midnight. That would annoy
Justin for sure. Plus it is quite nice, when I am not
thinking about Auntie Joyless.

9 p.m.
I have reconsidered and decided I may forgive Scarlet
after all. Have done a mental list of possible new best
friends and it is limited to Tracey Hughes, Oona Rickets,
and Emily Reeve. Obviously there is Sad Ed, my GBF (gay
best friend), but I need a girl as well. He gets squeamish
about tampons and leg hair.

Monday 19
8 a.m.
It is detention tonight. Maybe it will be like *The*

Breakfast Club with me as Molly Ringwald and Scarlet as the one with dandruff. We will bond as I remove her cloggy goth make-up and turn her into a pale-faced beauty.

6 p.m.
Detention was not like *The Breakfast Club*. There were no wise caretakers to chat to (Lou barely grunts), no one wrote enlightening essays about being a prom queen, a jock, and a basket case and no one smoked drugs when Mrs Buttface was on the loo. I had to sit in between Davey MacDonald and Thin Kylie (in detention over the ruler incident) and write about the life cycle of newts. Scarlet did not speak to anyone, not even Justin. Jack said she is in shock.

Walked home with Sad Ed. I asked him if he was going to Bob and Suzy's party. He said he would if I would. So we have made a pact.

Tuesday 20
Davey MacDonald is leaving next term. He got talent spotted on Saturday by someone from the Royal Ballet. They are going to regret it if he insists on showing all those highly strung ballerinas his special needs. Thin Kylie is devastated. She is being comforted by Mrs Leech with a packet of Minstrels.

Wednesday 21

First day of winter and last day of school.

Thin Kylie has recovered from her devastation, chucked Davey MacDonald and is back with Mark Lambert. Apparently it was Mrs Leech who told her to do it. They were all over each other during Ms Hopwood-White's all-faith-embracing Festive Assembly.

Scarlet actually said goodbye after school. It is exactly five months to the day since our fight. I hope it is nearly over. Otherwise I will have to borrow one of James's dolls and befriend Emily Reeve next term.

Thursday 22

9 a.m.

My life is reduced to watching *The Brave Little Toaster* with fat Treena and the dog. (Still no sign of the baby. If it is not out by Boxing Day, they are going to induce.) In contrast James has a jam-packed seasonal calendar. He is out looking at the Bishop's Stortford Christmas lights with Mumtaz and is going to a Library reading of *A Christmas Carol* tomorrow, starring Marlon and the least famous McGann.

10 a.m.

I have made a decision. I am going to Scarlet's to forgive her. It is the season of joy and goodwill after all. And even goths celebrate Christmas.

5 p.m.

Hurrah! Scarlet and I are best friends again. I said I forgave her for snogging Justin and she forgave me for letting a chav into my life. I asked her what it was like kissing him and she said she has blocked the incident from her memory, plus she had had an illegal bottle of Diamond White so it was all a bit blurry anyway. She has sworn not to go near him again as a sign of sisterhood and true goth faith. Plus, according to Jack, Sophie found out about the Scarlet snog from Pippa and is thinking of taking him back.

I did not tell her about Jack and the weird kissing thing. She might see it as anti-sisterhood. I asked her who Sad Ed was really in love with and she said it didn't matter as it was clearly never going to happen. She says he is definitely not gay though. She lent him one of Suzy's homosexual instruction videos and he reported no signs of arousal. This is very disappointing news.

Friday 23

Granny and Grandpa Clegg are not coming for Christmas. Mum was so relieved she opened up a box of Elizabeth Shaw mints. Auntie Joyless's Metro has finally broken down irreparably and Dad said he couldn't fetch them as he is on emergency hospital duty for when Treena goes into labour. Granny Clegg said it was a good thing that the Metro was dead as she didn't want to witness the 'child bride' and her illegitimate offspring. She is expecting it to be like Damian in *The Omen*.

Went into town and bought Scarlet emergency Christmas present—black nail varnish and a Marilyn Manson annual. I hope she has got me something. I do not want to be out of pocket present-wise.

Saturday 24
Christmas Eve

Still no sign of the baby. Grandpa is on twenty Benson and Hedges a day to calm his nerves. They have tried hot curry but to no avail. The midwife has told them that sex can bring on contractions but Grandpa says there is no way he is trying it on with Treena when she is that size and that angry.

Went to James's nativity at the church. He was not Joseph, as had been previously suggested. He was Jesus (who, admittedly, is the lead role). He got the part due to his freakish ability to lie still. Plus he was the only one to fit in the manger.

Christmas presents asked for:

- *Jaws* (seminal Spielberg movie and essential viewing for literary types according to Sad Ed)
- *Desperate Housewives* Complete Season One Boxed Set on DVD (*The O.C.* is so over, according to Scarlet. Only Year Eights and Suzy will be watching it next year.)
- An iPod. How can I possibly be part of the iPod generation with an outsize CD Walkman that has had

282

'The Best of Gareth Gates' stuck inside it (James borrowed it to block out the sound of Grandpa and Treena last summer).

I predict I will get none of the above. As usual.

Sunday 25

Christmas Day

I was right. Christmas presents received:

- Grandpa and Treena—*Finding Nemo*. It was the only fish-related film Ducatti Mick had.
- Mum and Dad—David Attenborough boxed set. *Desperate Housewives* has, unsurprisingly, made it on to Mum's banned list (too many reasons to list).
- James—a signed photo of Davina McCall (possibly forged, as obtained in the playground off someone called 'Mad Harry' for £1.80 and a broken tamagotchi).
- Granny and Grandpa Clegg—a £2 record token and a metre-long Toblerone (sell-by date last October, Trago Mills price ticket £1.99).
- Sad Ed—a diary. It has the Ophelia picture on the cover. Only not chewed or covered in caramel.
- Scarlet (thank God)—a black T-shirt. She is trying to lure me into the ways of the goth. She has no hope. My mum will never let me go out looking like a corpse.

Ate non-traditional bird-free Christmas lunch (i.e. roast ham)—turkey, goose, and duck are banned until Waitrose is declared flu free, and beef has not been seen in the house since Mad Cow disease. Then watched *Top of the Pops* with Grandpa and Treena. A song about a JCB digger is Number One. This is yet another reminder of how middle-class and thus rubbish my life is. Why can't Dad drive a digger? No one would write a song about driving around in their dad's air-conditioned Passat.

4 p.m.
Oh my God—Treena has gone into labour. She was trying to make it to the upstairs toilet (downstairs loo blocked following hot curry episode) and the effort brought it on. Dad has taken her and Grandpa to Addenbrookes. He is annoyed because it has interfered with the revealing of the new Doctor Who. Mum is annoyed because Treena's waters broke all over the cream carpet. She has stayed behind to Cillit Bang the landing.

10 p.m.
Feel sick. It is Sad Ed's fault. He came over to commiserate about presents (he got a Scalextric and a Junior Ready Steady Cook Ice Cream Maker) so I opened up the Toblerone to cheer him up and before I knew it we had eaten it all. I should not be doing things like this at my age, I am fourteen for God's sake.

11 p.m.
Have just had weird thought: maybe Valentine card was from Sad Ed, not Justin.

11.15 p.m.
No, definitely not. Sad Ed is just trying to cheer me up with pictures of tragic death. Obviously.

Monday 26
Boxing Day
Bank Holiday (UK)
I have a new uncle. He was born at five minutes to midnight after three epidurals, two tanks of gas and air, and something that looked like a sink plunger, according to Grandpa. They have called him Jesus. Really. Mum said she thought it was illegal but James said that, *au contraire*, it is a common name on the continent and that it is only the British who think it is odd. So Mum sent him to his room to write thank you letters. Auntie Joyless is going to go mad. She is always banging on about the second coming of Jesus and now here one is in Saffron Walden, dressed in a Bart Simpson babygro, with a geriatric father and a crisp-addicted mother. I expect it is not what she had hoped for.

5 p.m.
Jesus Harvey Nichols-Riley is home. He is asleep in a Moses basket on the sideboard. Grandpa is a changed man and is hovering with a Pampers awaiting any signs of activity in that area. He says it is down to witnessing the wonder of birth and seeing Jesus coming out of

285

Treena's undercarriage into the world. It is gross. Treena said he wouldn't be so joyous if he had thirty-seven stitches in his minky. She is not breastfeeding. I think Mum is relieved. She is in charge of sterilizing—it is a dream job for her.

6 p.m.
Cherie and Terry have been over to wet the baby's head. Cherie and Treena discussed the horrors of birth while Terry drank several of the miniature whiskies I gave to Dad. I asked how Kylie was. Cherie said she was down Barry Island testing out Mark Lambert's new minibike. She is a chav cliché.

Tuesday 27
Bank Holiday (UK)
The joy of new life is wearing thin already. Jesus woke up seven times in the night. Grandpa has taken two of Treena's painkillers. All the getting up and down for feeds and nappies is playing havoc with his lumbago. Only Treena is looking rested. She slept through it all and is on the sofa watching James Bond and eating leftover ham.

Rang Scarlet. She got *Desperate Housewives* Complete Season One boxed set so I will be able to immerse myself in postmodern suburban tragedy at her house, thank God.

Wednesday 28

Jesus was up six times last night. If this goes on I will have to move into the Aled Jones shrine at Sad Ed's. Mum has rung the council to demand Grandpa and Treena are placed at the top of the list for a new flat, but the housing department (i.e. someone called Mr Lemon) is on annual leave until January. She asked what would happen if Uttlesford District were suddenly swamped with refugees in dire housing need in the next week. The receptionist told her it was inadvisable to use words like swamped, but that she had the authority to put them up at the Travelodge at Junction 8 on the M11.

Thursday 29

The dog has taken a dislike to Jesus. It growls at the Moses basket menacingly and has eaten two babygros and a box of formula. James said it is jealousy and we should pamper the dog with presents. He has already given it a double packet of Penguins and a box of All Bran.

7 p.m.

The dog has had an 'incident' in the hallway. It could not get out of the house fast enough to reach the garden. Mum has added All Bran and other high-fibre products as dog food to her banned list.

Friday 30

Scarlet came over so we could plan our outfits for tomorrow night. She is wearing a black corset (one of Suzy's eighties cast-offs) and combat trousers to show both sides of her goth femininity. I am wearing my black T-shirt and the perilous miniskirt and Converse boots because it is the only outfit that does not have Cow and Gate sick (Jesus and dog) on it.

Saturday 31

New Year's Eve

6 p.m.

New Year resolutions checklist:

1. Drink coffee. Not achieved—unless you count Mum's decaffeinated Nescafé and a coffee flavoured Walnut Whip.
2. Get boyfriend. Briefly achieved. Though admittedly not Justin Statham, as anticipated.
3. Buy flattering clothes. Achieved—not counting the flea-infested jumper episode.
4. Train dog. Not achieved. Today it ate Jesus's cradle cap shampoo and foamed all over the carpet. Mum called the emergency vet thinking it had rabies but then it threw up the bottle cap thus averting a national crisis.
5. Get period. Achieved. Am no longer freak of nature being outdone by overdeveloped eleven year olds.

Although it is not all it is cracked up to be quite frankly. It is just messy and expensive. I may well write to Gordon Brown demanding that he provide sanitary products on the NHS. Or maybe I will get Suzy to do it. She has more sway in those circles.

6. Befriend more tragic and interesting people. Not sure if Thin Kylie counts. Although the shoplifting episode was certainly tragic. And Sad Ed being possibly gay for several months was a step in the right direction.

7. Visit Paris. Achieved. Although not the literary and romantic experience promised by *Sex and the City* etc. and clouded by memories of hideous coupling of Mark Lambert and Fat Kylie.

The doorbell has just gone. It will be Sad Ed to go to the party. I cannot wait. I may decide to kiss Jack after all. It is certainly a literary sort of thing to do i.e. snog your best friend's brother. The romantic poets were all at it. I will ask Sad Ed's advice. He is bound to agree. He likes Jack.

6.15 p.m.
Oh my God. It was not Sad Ed. It was Will! He is on the sofa with Grandpa admiring Jesus. He made Fiona drive him all the way here from Fulham. Granny Clegg gave him directions so it is a wonder he arrived at all. He says he made a mistake and he cannot live without me. Mum panicked and invited Fiona in for some Duchy Originals but she had to get back to London—she and Rory are

going to an organic beer and Twiglets party at David Cameron's eco-house in Notting Hill. Oh God, what am I going to do? I cannot take him to Bob and Suzy's. She would go mental if she knew I had snogged a Tory. Plus he does not look like I remember him at all i.e. the nice one out of Busted. He has been struck down with acne. It is vile. Even the dog shied away from him.

The doorbell has just gone again. I hope it is Fiona to take Will away. Or Sad Ed to take me away.

6.35 p.m.
Aaagh. It was Thin Kylie. She is traumatized because one of the traveller girls from the fair is pregnant and claims it is Mark's. (Her exact words were, 'That retard has got some f**kin' gyppo up the duff and Fat Kylie's in Ireland, innit.') She is on the sofa with Will and the dog watching Grandpa feed Jesus and drinking the last of the miniature whiskies. Kylie said she might 'get one of them' this year. Mum said, 'What, a dog?' and she said 'No, a baby, duh.'

Why does nothing good happen to me? All I wanted to do was get a boyfriend and be more vintage and I have ended up with an illegitimate uncle called Jesus, an alcoholic shag-happy chav as a friend, and an ex-boyfriend who has turned into the before bit of a Clearasil commercial.

The doorbell has gone again. Please God let it be Sad Ed.

6.45 p.m.

It is Boaz. I cannot take it any more. I am going out the window, *Dawson's Creek* style. Hopefully they will all be gone by next year (i.e. when I get back from Scarlet's) and life will be back to normal.

6.50 p.m.

I hope Sad Ed left the ladder up.

the life of Riley

My Utterly Hopeless Search
for THE ONE

For the Duke gang –
Hels, Boo, Frosties, Jude, Julia,
Stu and Sprog

Sunday 1

New Year's Day

Am in agony. And not due to highly anticipated cider and blackcurrant-induced hangover from best friend Scarlet's New Year's Eve party, but to fact that Dad had moved second best friend Sad Ed's *Dawson's Creek* ladder and I fell off the drainpipe in my attempt to escape my facially disfigured (i.e. acne-ridden) ex-boyfriend Will, God-bothering cousin Boaz, and uber-chav neighbour Thin Kylie. So, instead of spending the evening looking vintage and dancing to seminal music, had to sit in casualty for three hours with Dad, James, and local madman Barry the Blade, who, it turned out, was fine but had nothing better to do. Then the weary doctor (who looked about sixteen but was in fact twenty-six and a half—James checked) said I had only suffered minor bruising and it was lucky my fall had been broken by the mini-trampoline (disused due to injury risk—how ironic).

So am now on sofa with Baby Jesus (aka my uncle) and the dog watching one of Dad's *Lovejoy* videos and sipping Lucozade (me, not Baby Jesus. Or the dog—it is eating leftover green triangle Quality Street instead). Mum has taken James and Boaz to Mole Hall Wildlife Park (total exotic wildlife count now reduced to three otters due to unexplained marmoset death, plus the flamingos are out of bounds in ongoing bird flu crisis); Grandpa and Treena, parents of Baby Jesus, are at the January sales (i.e. Woolworth's); Will never came home

from Thin Kylie's; and Dad is fixing the drainpipe under strict orders from Mum who fears that squirrels will get in and devour the electricals.

4 p.m.
Scarlet and Sad Ed have just left. It is all too depressing. I have clearly missed a potentially life-changing experience. Apparently Scarlet's mum, Suzy, drank too much Merlot and did dirty dancing to Christina Aguilera (proto-feminist singer, according to Suzy). My mum would never do that. She only dances to Rod Stewart and it is excruciating to witness. Also, malodorous Year Eleven lesbian Oona Rickets got off with a MAN in the downstairs toilet, then had a panic attack over her sexuality and had to have emergency counselling from Suzy. She has redeclared herself 'bicurious'. What is that meant to mean? It sounds like bivalve. Apparently Scarlet didn't get off with anyone. She is still too traumatized by her illicit liaison with non-goth and possible love of my life Justin Statham. I asked Scarlet if Justin had snogged anyone and she said no he was too busy doing requests on his electric guitar. Sad Ed said why didn't I ask if he had got off with anyone, so I asked him and he said no, so I said point proven.

5 p.m.
Have just got text from Scarlet's brother Jack: Hp u bounce back soon Riley! Ha! X!
  Hilarious.

298

7 p.m.

Will came to say goodbye—his mum Fiona is driving up from Fulham in the morning to collect him. She is too hung-over to come today due to the Tory frivolities at David Cameron's organic beer and Twiglets party in Notting Hill. (Mum says it is more likely down to drugs and weird sex. She thinks all politicians spend their spare time getting drunk and breaking the law, except ginger Lib Dem leader Charles Kennedy, whom she is convinced is going to save Britain from moral turpitude and juvenile delinquency.) Will was with Thin Kylie who had four love-bites (I counted them) on her neck and her hand up Will's shirt. Will did not have love-bites. Not even Thin Kylie would dare go near that amount of sebaceous secretion. I said I was glad that love could conquer their social and mental divide. Thin Kylie said, 'I ain't no mentalist. You're the mental one to chuck him. He's like Prince William, innit.' Then they went off to do karaoke with Terry and Cherie. It will not last. He is used to organic caviar while Thin Kylie thinks crisps are a food group.

This is not a good start to the year. I will be fifteen in eight months. I should be at my peak of general brilliantness, i.e. like Peaches Geldof, not sipping glucose drinks in Mum's terry towelling dressing gown and watching Ian McShane with a mullet with my one-week-old uncle.

New Year Resolutions:
1. Attempt to discontinue friendship with Thin Kylie.

We have nothing in common and her Bacardi habit is worsening.

2. Repatriate Suzy's glow-in-the-dark rabbit vibrator asap. James has lent it to Treena to vibrate Jesus to sleep.

3. Concentrate on school—GCSEs now a mere year and a half away and do not want to end up serving dough-nuts in Dorrington's like Maria Pearce (aka Pie Shop Pearce) for the rest of my life.

4. Experiment with alcohol or drugs or sex. According to Sad Ed, it is the law to have been sick on Strongbow and have seen several willies (or minkies in his case) by the end of Year Ten. So far have only seen James's (bath-sharing economy drive by Mum), and Grandpa Riley's (horrific bathroom lock failure incident), which do not count, according to Sad Ed.

5. Find THE ONE. Will utterly not snog random Tories with congenital acne but will save myself for long-haired creative type with interest in tragedy and general literariness and with musical potential i.e. Justin. For a minute last year during on-stage *Bugsy Malone* snog thought it might be Jack but he is *a*) Scarlet's brother and *b*) Scarlet's brother.

- -

Monday 2
Bank Holiday
Auntie Joyless is coming from Redruth to collect Boaz at lunchtime. Grandpa and Treena have been sent to DFS

for the day with the baby (warm, plenty of seating, crisp machine). Mum thinks Auntie Joyless may have a nervous breakdown and have to summon emergency Episcopal services if she finds out Grandpa has an illegitimate son called Jesus with someone from Bolton.

4 p.m.
Boaz's return to Cornwall did not go as smoothly as Mum had planned. Dad is driving Auntie Joyless back to Redruth in the Passat now that her new Mini Metro is wedged into Clive and Marjory's Granada saloon in a generally mangled state and Len Viceroy (aka Fat Len) from Viceroy garage can't separate them until next week as he is having surgery on a varicose vein.

Timetable of events:
12.15 p.m.
Auntie Joyless arrives in new Mini Metro, as purchased from Denzel's Crazy Car Warehouse in Camborne, complete with 'I brake for Jesus' sticker on the window and lucky crown of thorns hanging from rear-view mirror.

12.30 p.m.
Boaz apologizes for running away and agrees to attend Reverend Ray's 'Bible Bash' camp for delinquent teenagers in February half-term. James asks if he can attend for research purposes. Request denied by Mum on 'because I say so' grounds.

1.00 p.m.
Dog eats Delia's vegetarian shepherd's pie (puritanical, but with a Christmas theme, i.e. shepherds) during Auntie Joyless's enforced saying of grace (eyes shut all round).

1.10 p.m.
James and Boaz sent to Mr Patel's to buy emergency lunch.

1.30 p.m.
James and Boaz return with four chicken korma ready meals, a tin of cling peaches and a semi-melted Viennetta (Mr Patel's freezer on blink). Dad says he is secretly glad dog ate vegetarian pie, Delia or no Delia.

1.45 p.m.
Fight breaks out in DFS between Mrs O'Grady and Ying Brewster over last remaining white leatherette corner set. Police and ambulances called and DFS closes until further notice.

2.30 p.m.
Grandpa and Treena arrive on doorstep four hours early. Mum sends James (crucial mistake in retrospect) to hide Baby Jesus in his bedroom.

2.45 p.m.
James appears in dining room and declares an emergency.

2.50 p.m.
Auntie Joyless says, 'Nothing is beyond the power of our good Lord,' and demands to know nature of said emergency.

2.51 p.m.
James says Baby Jesus has been sick on his Will Young doll, and it is now not singing 'Evergreen'.

2.52 p.m.
Auntie Joyless storms upstairs to find 'second coming' lying on *Lord of the Rings* duvet between sick-covered Will Young and giant glow-in-the-dark rabbit vibrator (on).

2.53 p.m.
Auntie Joyless declares the house is inhabited by Satanists and demands Boaz strap himself in the Metro.

2.54 p.m.
Auntie Joyless reverses Metro at full speed into Clive and Marjory's driveway whilst trying to cross herself at same time.

3.30 p.m.
Auntie Joyless and Boaz depart in Passat with Dad and the dog.

3.31 p.m.
Mum demands to know provenance of giant glow-in-the-dark rabbit vibrator. Rachel vows it is more than her life's

worth to divulge the sex secrets of vague acquaintances. Mum says, 'Was it Suzy?' James says, 'Yes.'

3.45 p.m.
Rabbit vibrator sealed in Jiffy bag with stern letter from Mum requesting that Suzy keep her menacing sex toys to herself.

3.50 p.m.
James and Rachel sent to rooms to reflect on inappropriate use of menacing sex toys in front of evangelistic humourless relations.

Thank God school starts in two days. How am I supposed to be tragic and literary with my ridiculous family? I bet Emily Brontë never had to put up with this sort of hoo-ha.

Update:
3.00 a.m.
Dad and dog arrive back from Cornwall. Dog wakes up entire house in incident involving leftover chicken korma.

. . . .

Tuesday 3

Mum is in a panic. She says Jeremy Paxman has informed her that there is a plague of sex register pervert teachers in schools. I said I didn't know she had a hotline to Paxo. She said don't try to be funny, it was on the news, and are there

any at John Major High, apart from sex-pest Geography teacher Mr Ingham, who is on permanent sabbatical? Said, 'No.' Did not inform her about Justin's ex-girlfriend Sophie Jacobs's ongoing gropings with student French teacher Mr Vaughan. Or lesbian PE teachers Miss Vicar (stick-thin; no breasts; facial hair) and Miss Beadle (overweight; bulgy eyes like Joey in *Friends* or rabbits with myxomatosis).

Went round Scarlet's to discuss sex pervert crisis. Suzy said it was all blown out of proportion and that most of them were not paedophiles but merely fulfilling the Oedipal desires of sexually charged sixteen year olds. She is thinking of writing to Tony (Blair—Suzy thinks they are on first-name terms following their brief encounter at the school dinners visit last year, during which she was arrested for possible terrorist activity). I wish my mother were an enlightened sex therapist instead of a former tax clerk with a Cillit Bang obsession.

Also, school starts tomorrow. And, with it, my quest to find THE ONE (as long as THE ONE is not a teacher or other pervert). I predict it will be Justin and we will be snogging by half term.

. . . .

Wednesday 4

First day of school.

Thin Kylie has already chucked a sickie, due to post-traumatic stress disorder (according to poorly spelt note

from her mum Cherie, given to me to hand in, through a cloud of Marlboro fumes and Impulse). Registration was awash with rumours that she had snogged Prince William. (Fat Kylie told trainee Year Eight chavette 'Primark' Donna (little sister of Leanne Jones, free giver of sexual favours), who is easily confused, and who told the entire lower school by first break.) Even Ms Hopwood-White was overexcited. I said that he was not Prince William, he was an acne-ridden Tory from Fulham. But Fat Kylie said, 'You're just jealous. Because no one's been near your chuff.' Luckily, attention was diverted by news that we are getting a new girl in class tomorrow. And not one of Mrs Duddy's Retards or Criminals this time either. She comes from London and is called Tuesday Weeks and is the product of a totally broken home! According to Mrs Leech, her dad, who is American, ran off with his psychiatrist. Oh my God. She is my ideal me! I bet she looks like drug-crazed beauty Marissa off *The O.C.* and has a band on Myspace and spends all weekends getting spotted as a model at the giant Topshop. Or, even better, maybe she is black! Fat Kylie is claiming her for chav corner. She is planning to take her to sightsee the drive-through McDonalds in Harlow so that she doesn't feel homesick. The Kylies are going to be disappointed. Tuesday is bound to be on the Zone diet and will only eat Sushi and raw vegetables. Which could be a problem in Saffron Walden, which is sorely lacking in Japanese cuisine.

1 p.m.

Thin Kylie is back in school, following a miraculous recovery, according to Cherie, or success at procuring morning-after pill from Dr Braithwaite (huge hands; lazy eye; bottle of whisky in desk drawer), according to Thin Kylie. Although Primark Donna told her she should keep the baby as it would be heir to the throne and she could sell her story to *Chat* for £500. Fat Kylie said she would get more from *Pick Me Up*, and she should know, her mum has sold several stories to them, including: 'I married a murderer' (not true) and 'I'm in love with a ghost' (possibly true, although probably under influence of Smirnoff Ice).

. . . .

Thursday 5

Tuesday is not black. Nor does she look like Marissa Cooper. She is like a stretched out version of Kelly Osbourne, complete with excessive EMO eyeliner and daring attitude. Sad Ed tried to talk to her in French but Ms Hopwood-White caught him and made him conjugate 'manger' on the new electronic whiteboard. Which he got wrong and broke in the process, due to his oversized fingers. So we are back with chalk and felt pens until the new financial year, according to headmaster Mr Wilmott.

At lunch, Tuesday sat at the end of the Alternative Music Club table (i.e. anyone with a guitar or an Arctic Monkeys CD—main members Jack, Justin, and Stan Barret

from Year Eight who once saw Paul Weller in John Lewis) eating peanut butter and jam sandwiches (compulsory American food) with her iPod on. I tried to warn her this was totally against school rules, but I don't think she could hear me. She is clearly uber-cool and wildly dangerous. I absolutely have to get to know her before the end of the week. Especially if she has access to Justin at lunch.

On the plus side, the Kylies have been unsuccessful in luring Tuesday into their fake-Burberry-clad clutches as well. They are clearly concerned that she may be harder than they are because they locked official school midget Dean 'the dwarf' Denley in a locker in last break just to reinforce their position.

Asked Mum if I could have peanut butter and jam on 'rye' for lunch tomorrow. She said I could jolly well have school dinners or take in a cheese and tomato bap. She is in a mood because it turns out she was wrong about Charles Kennedy. According to the six o'clock news, he is a total alcoholic. Granny Clegg rang in triumph—her motto is never trust anyone ginger or with a beard. Plus she voted UKIP.

. . . .

Friday 6
Epiphany

Ooh. Epiphany would be a good name. Epiphany Riley. I may well ask Mum if I can change my name by deed poll,

like Edward Pratt from four doors down, who is now called Edward Jedi.

Tuesday was sent to see Mr Wilmott in registration due to three breaches of school uniform rules (nose piercing, visible Wonderbra, visible thong) and lack of remorse about said breaches (she held up three fingers to Ms Hopwood-White and told her to 'read between the lines'. Which is brilliant, even if she did steal it off Jack Black, and Ms Hopwood-White didn't get it.) Scarlet is going to organize an anti-uniform rule rally in sympathy. We are all going to wear visible Wonderbras and pants (even the boys) to school next Monday. She is going to get Jack and Justin to spread the word among Year Eleven. So Justin and I will be reunited in political endeavour, following Jack's (failed) election last year. Hurrah.

4 p.m.
Asked Mum if I could get a Wonderbra (size 32A) in Cambridge tomorrow (Saffron Walden does not stock Wonderbras). Mum said what was wrong with my M&S training bra? I said it was for a political feminist cause and everyone had one, even Marjory next door (I saw it on the washing line once, it must only come out for special occasions). Mum said she didn't care if the Queen had one, I was not going round looking like 'Britney Aguilera' and, besides, she didn't have time to go to Cambridge as she had to regrout the bath. Then James pointed out that the Queen does not need a Wonderbra as she has enormous

breasts anyway, so he was sent to his room for thinking about naked royalty.

Will have to find new source for Wonderbra. I do not want to let Tuesday or Justin down. Possible targets are: Oxfam, Treena, and Thin Kylie.

. . . .

Saturday 7

Offered to take Baby Jesus for a walk into town in his pram, but was overruled by Mum on grounds that one of her Conversational French friends might think I was a 'gymslip mum'. I said that no one knows what a gymslip is, plus I am notoriously sexually inexperienced. But Mum just made her lips go super-thin so I took the dog instead. He is feeling left out now Grandpa is giving all his attention to Jesus. He is still in charge of bottle feeding, nappy changing, and reading all the manuals. Treena is in charge of wardrobe.

No Wonderbras in Oxfam. Mrs Simpson (aka hygienically-compromised lady tramp) must have bought them all. So went to lurk outside Goddard's to watch Justin do something revolting with a bit of a pig. At least that was the plan but the dog very much wanted to be inside and over-powered me, knocking a display of mince all over Justin in his blood frenzy (I blame Mum for banning beef and chicken-based dog food on the grounds that it might contain bird flu or mad cow disease, and the dog is mad enough as it is).

Had to pay for the mince spillage at a cost of £11.97 (most of my Christmas money). Mum is right. The dog is a liability. Justin looked excellent in his butcher's coat, though. Like a blood-spattered Kurt Cobain. I just need to prove that I am his Courtney Love. Without the looks, or clothes, or position as lead singer in a girl band.

Asked Treena if I could borrow a Wonderbra. She said yes, but the proferred item was suspiciously grey and stained and should clearly, under no circumstances, be visible to the human eye, rally or no rally. Options now reduced to Thin Kylie.

Sunday 8

Went round to Thin Kylie's (against New Year resolution to distance myself from chav neighbours, but ruled acceptable due to nature of Wonderbra emergency) but she was round Fat Kylie's helping her pierce baby Whitney's ears (again), according to Cherie. Asked Cherie if she or Kylie had a Wonderbra, size 32A. Cherie said don't be daft, her 'la-las' were 34FF (she has had two breast enlargements and is fast-approaching Jordanesque proportions) and Kylie's were all in the wash now that Mark Lambert is back on the scene. (It turns out he did not get some 'gyppo' from the fair pregnant, after all. It was Candy Floss Ken.)

Am going to have to wear visible white cotton M&S

bra instead, which is totally non-political and probably within school rules.

. . . .

Monday 9

8 a.m.

The day of the anti-uniform rally dawns, and with it will dawn my friendship with iPod-wearing, rule-breaking, half-American Tuesday Weeks. And possibly my love affair with THE ONE i.e. Justin. Am wearing M&S bra and will pull pants into visible range once I am out of Mum's jurisdiction (i.e. within school grounds). It is a shame the pants are white with a cat motif though, and not black, or a thong, like Tuesday's (thongs are on Mum's banned list on grounds of hygiene).

9.30 a.m.

Anti-uniform rally over due to disappointing turnout of masses and general unsluttish nature of underwear. But, luckily, Scarlet and Jack had gone all out in Suzy's Agent Provocateur tasselled and crotchless numbers, so they were sent straight to Mr Wilmott, along with Tuesday, who was inexplicably wearing a sequinned bowler hat. I said what about me, but Ms Hopwood-White said there was nothing wrong with nice cotton underwear, it let everything breathe. This is typical. But Scarlet has promised to befriend Tuesday for both of us during detention, and mention my general tragicness and literary leanings. I told her to

remember all the stuff about liking Sylvia Plath, and she said she would try, but she also had to get in some stories about her and Axe, the juggler from Brighton that she snogged at Glastonbury last year, so there might not be time. (School counsellor Doddy Doddington is doing detention today and he lets everyone off after fifteen minutes so he can get home in time for *Deal or No Deal*.)

6 p.m.
Called Scarlet for update on Project Tuesday, but Suzy answered and said she was in her bedroom listening to Eighties punk music with a 'fascinating American' and why wasn't I there? And, while I was at it, did I think my mother was orgasmically repressed (following repatriation of glow-in-the-dark rabbit vibrator) and would she benefit from some group therapy? Hung up. This is absolutely typical. Scarlet is obviously going to be eating grits or clam chowder with Tuesday and the rest of the Osbournes within a week, while I am stuck at home eating fishfingers with an eight year old in a mermaid outfit (no idea). Texted Sad Ed but he was busy watching *Star Trek* and told me not to disturb him for at least four hours.

. . . .

Tuesday 10
Tuesday gets more exciting by the minute. Her mum is a drink-addled former Eighties model called Edie and her

dad is now living in Malibu with his BOYFRIEND, which is why Tuesday has moved. Apparently Edie went to school here! So there is hope for us all yet. In twenty years' time, Scarlet and I could be alcoholic former models with gay ex-husbands and tattooed teenage daughters. Brilliant! I asked Scarlet if she had managed to mention my literary leanings and hidden dark side but she said Tuesday kept banging on about some seminal writer called Hunter S. Thompson and she couldn't get a word in.

Am immediately going to read something by Hunter S. Thompson to impress Tuesday. Will go and see hairy school librarian Mr Knox during 'reading time' (aka texting and flicking through *Heat* in the lower hall, due to woeful lack of functioning classrooms).

. . . .

Wednesday 11

Everyone has gone perverts-in-schools mad. Fat Kylie forgot her gym skirt so Miss Vicar made her play hockey in her giant PE knickers. Fat Kylie called her a sex case for wanting to look at her bikini line. So Miss Vicar said she would be amazed if anyone wanted to look at Fat Kylie's bikini line (which is true—it is potentially horrendous, if the rest of her is anything to go by and, anyway, it is school rules). But Fat Kylie is going to report her anyway for 'paedoism'. Scarlet said that wasn't a word. But Fat Kylie threatened to do something painful with her hockey stick so Scarlet shut up.

Tuesday didn't do games. She has a note from her psychiatrist (seriously!) excusing her on the grounds that she is exceptionally sensitive and the competitive nature of school sports might induce instant anorexia. Miss Beadle has asked her for a full medical report by next week proving her condition, otherwise she will be dribbling a hockey ball on the sheep field with the rest of us.

7 p.m.
Amendment to New Year Resolutions:
6. Get psychiatrist. Everyone has one these days. They will uncover my deep and troubled life and blame it all on my mother for banning Ribena and *EastEnders*.

. . . .

Thursday 12
Went to see Mr Knox to get book by Hunter S. Thompson, but he said the only copy of *Fear and Loathing* had been lent out to Sad Ed last year and had had to be scrapped due to an entire mini Mars bar being stuck on page 57. He offered me a *Sweet Valley High* or the new John Grisham instead. I may well write to Tony Blair to complain. What hope is there for the literary future of the country when school libraries are so poorly stocked?

Also, Mum is learning to drive. Apparently it is one of her New Year resolutions, along with unblocking the downstairs loo and growing her own beetroot. She is

going to be taught by Michael Majors (41; highlights; reputation as middle-aged lothario type) in one of his fleet of Ford Fiestas. Dad did not look happy. But he cannot complain as it was his idea on the grounds that he is sick of being the only one having to ferry her 'inbred relatives' up and down the A303. Her first lesson is tomorrow (i.e. Friday the 13th). I said that this did not bode well, date-wise. But James said that statistically there are fewer accidents due to everyone being super-cautious or staying in to watch horror films.

. . . .

Friday 13

Mum is jubilant. She says Mike (!) says he has never seen anyone stick so rigidly to the ten-to-two position in all his fourteen years as a fully-qualified motoring skills adviser (i.e. driving instructor). Apparently he also heaped praise on her staying at least ten miles under the speed limit and her almost maniacal mirror-signal-manoeuvre checking. Dad said he bet 'Mike' had never got behind the wheel of a man's car in his life (Dad's greatest regret is not becoming a Formula One driver, due to Grandpa Riley's lack of finances and there being no car tracks in North Essex), but Mum said, on the contrary, he once sat in a Subaru Impreza with Jeremy Clarkson at the Birmingham Motor Show. So Dad humphed off to check the oil on the Passat.

. . . .

Saturday 14

Went into town with James to get Hunter S. Thompson book from WHSmith but Mrs Noakes (no chin; bad perm; calls trousers 'slacks'; habit of ringing parents to inform them you are buying potentially corrupting literature) was on the till so had to dither for an hour in the magazine section until she was on her tea break. Bought *Fear and Loathing in Las Vegas*. James bought a *Lord of the Rings* calendar, discounted due to March being missing.

8 p.m.

Am reading *Fear and Loathing*. It is a modern masterpiece and is absolutely full of swearing and sex and drugs I have never heard of. Am going to have to hide it from Mum. It will be banned for sure.

Sunday 15

Went round Scarlet's. Bob answered the door in his underpants and said everyone was in the den, before running back upstairs to shrieks from Suzy and another, unidentified female voice. But when I got to the 'den' (i.e. the sitting room in any normal, British house) Tuesday was sprawled provocatively on a Habitat bean-bag and was watching some film with subtitles and ugly people in it with Scarlet, Jack, and Justin. I asked if they were thinking of turning over to E4 but Scarlet said if I wanted to watch children's telly I could go to Sad Ed's and watch *CBeebies*.

Tuesday laughed and stretched her scarily long legs out even more so that her toes (purple nail varnish) touched Justin's leg (blue Levi's). He moved it. So point one to me. Ha! Said I had to get back to babysit Baby Jesus. Scarlet said 'Whatever.' Tuesday said, 'Oh, my God, is she a happy clapper?'

9 p.m.
I cannot believe I have been 'whatevered' by Scarlet. What is going on? Also, why does Tuesday not like me? I am totally literary and would be an excellent listener to all her hilarious stories about getting drunk with Amy Winehouse. Texted Sad Ed and he agrees it is an outrage. We are going to boycott all things Tuesday and be a rival camp of tragedy and tortured youth. Then she will absolutely want to know us. It is reverse psychology. James is trying it on the dog. He is encouraging it to eat random objects in the hope it will stick to dog food. Although early signs are not promising—it ate a pot of Vaseline this morning.

· ·

Monday 16
Tried to get Scarlet to sit with me at lunch but Tuesday headed her off at chips and beans and they went to sit with Jack and Justin on the Alternative Music Club table, so had to make do with Sad Ed and the Maths Club geeks instead.

Tuesday is still trying to lure Justin into her clutches. I saw her offer him an iPod earphone and an Alphabite. She cannot have him.

. . . .

Tuesday 17

Oh my God. Justin thinks he has found THE ONE! He told Jack who told Scarlet who told me. Maybe Justin told Jack to tell Scarlet to tell me. Because it is me! I am totally his type—I like guitars and wear vintage clothing.

7 p.m.

Or possibly Tuesday. Oh, God, please don't let it be Tuesday.

. . . .

Wednesday 18

Jesus was up eight times last night. Dad has taken to sleeping with Radio 2 being piped down his headphones. He says he would rather listen to The Corrs all night than Jesus screaming. Mum is not happy as she says she now has to put up with Jesus, tinny headphone guitar, and Dad murmuring 'Andrea' in his sleep. She is going to ring Mr Lemon at the council again to press the urgency of Grandpa and Treena's housing needs.

Tuesday did not do gym again. She had brought Miss Vicar a letter from her psychiatrist (Dr Rubenstein). Miss Vicar said psychiatry was about as real as aromatherapy

or ghosts and what was the point of 'finding yourself' if you were so fat by the time you did that you couldn't see your own toes. Then Miss Beadle added that a good dose of netball never did anyone any harm. Tuesday said, 'Whatever,' and went off in the direction of the bike sheds (aka sex corner).

Miss Beadle is wrong anyway. Netball is life-threatening and horrible, especially now that Fat Kylie has been made Wing Defence on account of her gargantuan weight advantage.

4 p.m.
Mr Lemon has agreed, under severe pressure from Mum, to move Grandpa and Treena up the housing list (Mum is good at persuasion (i.e. open threats). George Bush should employ her as an interrogator at Guantanamo Bay.) Only Mr Whippy (aka Dave Tennick, who sleeps in the ice cream van) and several O'Gradys are above them now. Mr Lemon has estimated their moving date as April next year. Mum has vowed to take her fight to the local paper, the reactionary and ineffective Walden Chronicle.

. . . .

Thursday 19
I fear Mum may have competition in the form of perverts in schools. The front page of today's *Walden Chronicle* (only two weeks behind the *Guardian*) is headlined 'Who's teaching your kids?—How to spot the school sex pest'

emblazoned above a picture of a possible sex pest (i.e. moustache and staring eyes).

. . . .

Friday 20

Mum had another driving lesson after school today, but was thirty-seven minutes late coming home (James timed her and told Dad at dinner). Mum said Mike was spot testing her on the Highway Code and they lost track of time (she got an unprecedented 100 per cent), but Dad did not look thrilled at this and has decided he is going to take over and give her some lessons in the Passat instead.

. . . .

Saturday 21

2 p.m.

Dad is no longer Mum's driving instructor. Mum says she sacked him for excess sucking of air through his teeth every time she tried to change gear. Dad says he sacked her as he needs the car to commute and the transmission will fall out with her hamfisted attempts at reversing around Waitrose car park. Mum said she would be glad to be back in the hands of someone who actually knew what they were talking about (i.e. Mike) and Dad said if that man's hands ever came near her he would personally crash test the Passat against his fleet of Fiestas. Then Mum said violence never solved anything. And James said what

about in *Ninja Turtles*, and at that point everyone stormed out. This is worrying. Mum and Dad never argue. Except over things like whether own brand cornflakes taste the same as Kellogg's. Ooh maybe I am going to be the child of a broken home after all. They will battle over who gets custody of me and James (and the dog) in court. I will definitely live with Dad. He is far more lax when it comes to potential spillages and watching ITV.

8 p.m.
Although Dad can only cook boil-in-the-bag Bird's Eye things and doesn't know where the Hoover is.

9 p.m.
What if neither of them want me? I could end up in care like Tracey Beaker. Which, according to CBBC, is kind of like boarding school for poor children and life is full of midnight feasts and hilarious incidents with vacuum cleaners and you get to call everyone by their first names without having *T4* banned for a fortnight.

9.30 p.m.
Although Thin Kylie went into care when her mum's breast implant burst and she says she had to live with a 'fat God-botherer' called Merryl who had no telly. Maybe I will concentrate on staying on Mum's and Dad's good sides for the moment so they both want me.

Sunday 22

Made Mum and Dad tea in bed. Mum sat bolt upright and said, 'What have you done. Are you pregnant?' I said I was merely fulfilling my duties as a loving daughter and that no, I was not with child. So she said, 'Did you squeeze the teabag properly otherwise it drips on the lino on the way to the bin?' I don't know why I bother. Even making tea is fraught with potential stain-making activity.

Texted Scarlet to see if she wanted to come over but got no reply. She is probably becoming American with Tuesday, i.e. drinking root beer and listening to grunge. Texted Jack but he said SORRY CRUCIAL DRUM JAM, LTRS. Tried Sad Ed but he said he was in a shopping precinct in Ipswich waiting for Aled Jones to cut the ribbon to the new Iceland. So broke resolution and went round to Thin Kylie's but Mark Lambert answered the door in a pair of Get It Here boxer shorts so I left rapidly as I do not want to get anything from Mark Lambert. And James was busy making wholegrain low fat muffins with Mumtaz, so ended up watching *Lovejoy* again. Laughed enthusiastically to show Dad how we share a love of Nineties comedy drama i.e. why he will want to keep me, but Dad just said, 'What is wrong with you, Rachel? Now I will never know whether Tinker's codpiece is genuine.' Which is not true—he has seen this episode at least seventeen times. It is fake.

9 p.m.
Am ploughing on with Hunter S. Thompson. It is excellent. Apparently it is called 'New' Journalism and involves drinking too much and gambling and driving dangerously whilst writing. It is certainly not like anything I have read in the *Walden Chronicle*. Though the O'Gradys would make excellent subject matter.

. . . .

Monday 23
Sad Ed has switched to the dark side i.e. the Alternative Music Club lunch table, now officially renamed 'Tuesday's table'. He said Tuesday is a 'breath of fresh air in this God-forsaken backwater' (he is still trying to be poetic in everyday situations) and that he can't understand why I am boycotting her, she is literary and tragic and has nine different pairs of Converse including limited edition Gwen Stefani ones. I said there was more to being tragic than having yellow plimsolls and a psychiatrist and he said, 'Well, you hardly qualify to comment.' This is rich coming from someone whose parents have a shrine to Aled Jones in the spare room and still buy his Christmas presents from Toys 'R' Us.

Although he does have a point. Why, oh why, isn't Edie my real mother? Then I would be guaranteed some tragedy.

8 p.m.
Maybe Edie is my mother and Tuesday and I are actually

identical twins like in *Parent Trap*, only without looking anything like each other, obviously.

8.30 p.m.
Although I definitely have Granny Clegg's knees. And, anyway, I don't think uber-cool alcoholic Edie would have slept with my dad. He is called Colin and has been known to wear thermal vests.

. . . .

Tuesday 24
Sad Ed is on a diet. He opted for Mrs Brain's 'country salad' at lunch today (tinned coleslaw and a pickled onion). He is so transparent. It is all clearly a bid to impress Tuesday. Anyway, it will not last. He only managed two days of the cabbage soup diet in Year Eight before he was back on chocolate digestives.

I am the only one who appears immune to Tuesday's 'charms'. I will remain steadfast on the Maths Club table. Even though I had to sit next to Paul Banner at lunch today and he brings soup in a flask and makes funny noises after each mouthful.

. . . .

Wednesday 25
Lunch with the maths geeks is not as easy as I thought. They have composed a loud and totally crap rap about logarithms. I had to hide behind my sandwich. Luckily

it was a large granary bloomer so I may have got away with it.

But I will not give up in my one-woman anti-Tuesday protest. I will not be moved.

. . . .

Thursday 26

Have given up lunch protest. Paul Banner asked me if I wanted to go to PC World with him on Saturday to look at hard drives. It was all too much. Am now an official Tuesday's table member (had to trip Stan Barret up at the jelly queue in order to secure a seat). Tuesday was telling everyone about the time Pete Doherty gave her a lift on his moped. But unfortunately Ms Hopwood-White heard her and told her she was breaking school rules on incitement to drink, take drugs, or ride motor vehicles underage. So Tuesday called her a 'fugly cow' (this is London speak for not very attractive person) and got sent to Mr Wilmott. She is so rebellious.

Sad Ed has lost a kilo in two days. He says it is down to a rigorous exercise regime and his new salad lunch (cold pasta today—full marks to Mrs Brain for recycling yesterday's 'spaghetti surprise') but it may also be due to the fact that the vending machine has been out of Mars bars since Monday. A petition has been handed in and Mr Wilmott has promised to restock at Mr Patel's if next week's delivery does not include best-selling snack items.

. . . .

Friday 27

Holocaust Memorial Day

Not celebrated, due to ongoing ban on 'made-up' religious days, following excess requests from Fat Kylie on grounds of her Catholicism (she asked for days off for Saint Clare—patron saint of television and conjunctivitis; Saint Cornelius—patron saint of earache and cows; and Saint Ambrose—patron saint of schoolchildren and wax-melters. She should have gone for Hilary—patron saint of retards and criminals). Mr Wilmott says he is only 'doing' Christmas, Pancake Day, and Easter this year. Tuesday (who is half-Jewish, on her gay dad's side) claims Mr Wilmott is in denial of the holocaust and posted his name on the 'most wanted' section of an anti-fascist website during IT. I suggested she might have been a bit hasty; after all, Mr Wilmott has always been extremely welcoming to Ali Hassan (admittedly C of E but of definite brown hue) but then she accused me of being an anti-semite so I shut up for fear of alienating Scarlet and Sad Ed again, who were all for the fascist outing. I am with the French. Schools should ban all mention of religion, it is a hotbed of potential *faux pas*.

Saturday 28

Have received invite to Thin Kylie's birthday party next Saturday (her birthday is actually on Friday but Cherie says Mr Hosepipe, the fireman strippergram (aka Mark

327

Lambert's dad, Darren) was booked for a ninetieth at the Conservative Club so he could only do Saturday. Am going to have to get her a present now. What do you give the chav who has everything?

. . . .

Sunday 29

11 a.m.
The dog has eaten Baby Jesus's talking Tigger. Every time it walks past it boings or says 'Let's bounce faster!' It is getting quite annoying. Even for the dog. It is confused as to where the voice is coming from and is barking at its own stomach. Mum says we will have to wait until it comes out one end or the batteries die. Grandpa said, 'What if the dog dies first?' Mum said, 'God willing,' but Grandpa couldn't hear as the dog did a particularly loud 'boing' at that point.

3 p.m.
James is taking bets on which end the Tigger will appear. I have £1 on mouth.

7 p.m.
I have won £3.20 and a Ninja Turtle figurine (Donatello—who apparently 'does machines'). The dog has sicked up Tigger along with one of Dad's socks that went missing before Christmas. They are both in the wash. Mum said, 'Waste not, want not.'

. . . .

Monday 30

9.15 a.m.

School has been evacuated due to a terrorist bomb threat! According to Tracey Hughes, whose mum answers the phones at the police station, Mrs Leech, the school secretary (bad hair; too much face powder; biscuit habit) opened a letter addressed to Mr Wilmott claiming there was an explosive device somewhere on C Corridor. She has been taken to hospital for trauma (she was eating a HobNob at the time and breathed an oat in the wrong way). We are huddled on the sheep field until further notice, much to Miss Beadle's annoyance as Fat Kylie's stilettos are sinking into the hockey pitch under her weight.

10 a.m.

The police force (by which I mean two men and an Alsatian) have arrived and are dithering outside. Apparently the bomb disposal unit is on an awayday at Chessington World of Adventure so they have decided to call the fire brigade instead.

10.30 a.m.

Fire brigade arrives. Female teachers (with notable exceptions of PE staff) flock to catch glimpse of Mr Hosepipe (aka Mr Lambert).

11 a.m.

Anglia TV crew arrives and asks for intelligent students to

interview on crisis. Mark Lambert is heard telling reporters that it is most likely the 'lezzer PE teachers' or Mrs Cruz the lab assistant, who 'looks a bit terrorist' (she is Spanish).

Rachel Riley (i.e. me) rings the *Walden Chronicle* to warn them of this front-page story on their doorstep but their reporting team (i.e. one reporter) is otherwise occupied covering the St Regina's newt pond so Rachel Riley offers to catalogue events for them in new bid to become literary journalist Hunter S. Thompson type.

12 noon
Entire school queues at Mr Patel's Pot Noodle stop, due to Mrs Brain's canteen being cordoned off, bill to be funded by Education Authority. Tuesday takes photo of mass Pot Noodle eating to send to Jamie Oliver's Feed Me Better website.

12.15 p.m.
Mr Whippy parks up at school gates to cash in on crowd's lust for junk food and Fat Kylie's lust for Mr Whippy.

1 p.m.
Miss Beadle organizes mass game of dodgeball in bid to keep warm.

1.15 p.m.
Dodgeball cancelled due to use of Dean 'the dwarf' Denley as ball. Ambulance called.

1.45 p.m.
Firemen locate suspicious device in cupboard of Mrs Duddy's Retards and Criminals room. School declared shut until further notice and everyone sent home (except the Kylies and Mark Lambert who left an hour ago in Mr Whippy's van).

3.15 p.m.
Suspicious device turns out to be Retards and Criminals attempts at Meccano and school declared safe for lessons tomorrow.

4.00 p.m.
Ambulance arrives for Dean Denley.

. . . .

Tuesday 31
9 a.m.
School open.

10 a.m.
School shut following arrival of letter claiming to have infected school sheep with anthrax and blaming Mr Wilmott for his rabid hatred of Vanessa Feltz and various other celebrity Jewish people.

10.30 a.m.
Police arrive with Mr Mercer the vet.

10.45 a.m.
School sheep declared anthrax-free and school reopened.
Mr Wilmott questioned in makeshift interrogation room
(i.e. the language lab) under race hate laws.

11.00 a.m.
Tuesday Weeks called out of double Science (burning
peanuts) to explain appearance of Mr Wilmott's name on
anti-fascist website.

11.15 a.m.
Mr Wilmott officially declared non-racist by police and
reinstated as Head of School.

11.18 a.m.
Tuesday Weeks given a week's detention for abuse of IT
facilities (investigation also revealed she had downloaded
seventy-nine songs off iTunes using Mr Wilmott's credit
card).

11.19 a.m.
Tuesday Weeks tells Mr Wilmott to 'Keep your hair on,
Rog.'

11.20 a.m.
Tuesday's detention increased to two weeks. (She will be

excluded by mocks if she keeps this up. She is totally out of control.)

11.21 a.m.
How does Tuesday know Mr Wilmott's first name?

FREEVIEW
BOX

february

Wednesday 1

9 a.m.
School open.

11 a.m.
School shut again. One of the Criminals and Retards 'accidentally' blocked the lower school toilets with a chicken. Students forced to leave via staff room window due to flow of raw sewage down C Corridor.

3 p.m.
The *Walden Chronicle* has rejected my Hunter S. Thompson-style report on the bomb scare. They claim none of the sentences were in the right order and some of the words weren't in the spellchecker. I said it was called New Journalism and was very popular in London and America and the woman on the phone said Leann Rimes is popular in America but it doesn't make her good. I had no answer to that so I hung up.

My journalistic career will just have to wait until I can find a more forward-thinking publication than the *Walden Chronicle*, which is too focused on sheep sales and whether or not Saffron Walden needs new traffic lights at the notoriously congested Waitrose junction (answer—yes).

Thursday 2

School definitely open, though smelling slightly of drains. Mark Lambert said it was like being in Africa, but without the 'people with the big stomachs'. Then he saw Sad Ed and was about to say something else but Ms Hopwood-White quickly intervened and sent him to (officially non-racist) Mr Wilmott.

. . . .

Friday 3

Thin Kylie has got a dog for her birthday. It is called 'Fiddy' (as in Cent) and is a pedigree miniature Pinscher (aka a small but potentially threatening yappy thing). She brought it into class in her fake Moschino bag where it remained undetected until first break when it made a mad dash for Fat Kylie's Peperami Hot and was confiscated by Ms Hopwood-White. Cherie was forced to switch off Jeremy Kyle and come and collect it from the school caretaker Lou, formerly of Criminals and Retards. It is lucky she got there when she did—Lou once ate the school rabbit.

I asked Kylie if I could bring Scarlet, Sad Ed, and Tuesday (so we could mingle ironically with the chavs) to her party but she said there was a strict 'no lezzers or fat poofs' door policy. So now I am going to have to mingle with Fat Kylie and Primark Donna on my own. Which is not really ironic, just sad. Plus I still haven't got her a birthday present.

. . . .

Saturday 4

Am giving Kylie a bottle of Bacardi Breezer and a pirate

Vin Diesel video. Treena got them both cheap off Ducatti
Mick in the White Horse last night. (I admire the way she
is refusing to let Baby Jesus prevent her from continuing
her social life.) But am now in a dilemma over what to
wear. Do I remain true to myself and go vintage, thus
risking being compared to Marjory by Cherie again, or do
I do chav chic (i.e. mini skirt and bra top) and risk being
compared to Cherie by Mum.

6 p.m.
Am going to wear jeans and gold halterneck (formerly
Cherie's). I will look like Kate Moss at a Hoxton art
gathering. Will sip 'virgin' cocktails (i.e. non-alcoholic) and
do karaoke in ironic manner before retiring early to read
more enlightening Hunter S. Thompson.

1 a.m.
Feel sick.

1.15 a.m.
Have done purple sick three times.

1.17 a.m.
Oh, more sick coming.

. . . .

Sunday 5
8 a.m.
Feel awful. Woke up on bathroom floor with purple

339

sick in hair, dog licking sick, and James taking photos of ensemble with his camera. Cannot remember how got here. Am going to bed.

9 a.m.
Can hear Mum cleaning bathroom in fury. Even the spray of Cillit Bang hurts my ears. Will try to eat Shreddies to revive self.

9.15 a.m.
More sick. Some Shreddies actually came back up square. Mum Cillit Banging again. Will go to bed and sleep it all off.

2 p.m.
Oh my God. Have remembered something. Oh God, oh God, oh God. Need to talk to Thin Kylie urgently.

3 p.m.
Oh God, oh God, oh God. Thin Kylie has confirmed the worst. Have snogged an O'Grady. Not Fat Kylie (would have to kill myself) but her brother Kyle, who is only twelve and is already high up in the Criminal and Retard rankings. Cannot possibly go to school. Will have to fake serious illness like meningitis or Lyme disease.

5 p.m.
Have been grounded by Mum for a week (for underage drinking, coming in late, and excess vomit on pedestal mat).

7 p.m.
Oh God. Have had message from Kyle—TXT ME FOTO OF TITS X. Declined.

. . . .

Monday 6

Mum says James's purple felt tip does not look at all like septicaemia (apparently Grandpa has already tried this to avoid a prostate check) and I am jolly well going to school. Oh God. My reputation as a tragic and literary eccentric lies in ruins. This was not supposed to happen. Was supposed to wait for THE ONE. Justin can never know. It is like Courtney Love snogging someone in McFly. Kurt would never have forgiven her.

9 a.m.
As I feared. Kyle was waiting at the school gates. He offered to take me up the bike sheds in first break (not sure if this is a euphemism) but told him I was far too busy what with being in Year Ten and having a boyfriend already. He said, 'You ain't got no boyfriend, I checked and anyway, Fat Kylie is always up the bike sheds.' I said Fat Kylie's sexual preferences were of no concern to me and that I had double French and to please leave me alone. At least Scarlet will sympathize. She actually licked Carex anti-bacterial soap after snogging Justin due to his non-gothness. I, on the other hand, would never wash if I got to snog Justin.

3 p.m.

Overestimated Scarlet's capacity to sympathize. She just said she hoped I had taken precautions as the O'Gradys have been isolated as the source of the infamous Saffron Walden chlamydia scare. I said I had not been near any potential chlamydia-infected areas but she said after six Pernod and Strongbows, I could have given him a blow job and not know about it. (I definitely didn't—I checked with Thin Kylie; besides I don't know how to do it—do you actually blow?).

Tuesday says she doesn't know what all the fuss is about. She once snogged a twenty-five year old after too much Stella (beer not McCartney). Sad Ed seemed distant. I said at least it was one down, one to go on the sex and alcohol experimentation front, but he said binge drinking with a rat boy is hardly Kafkaesque. Jack didn't say anything. He and Justin have a gig next week (Certain Death are supporting Kilgore Trout) so he was probably just nervous about his drum solo. Thank God Justin had a dentist appointment so he is none the wiser. It is the first time I have been grateful to sadistic Mrs Wong.

. . . .

Tuesday 7

Kyle is not giving up. In first break he sent Primark Donna to find me (hiding with Scarlet in upper school toilets) to give me a Yu-Gi-Oh pen and a packet of Monster

Munch (pickled onion flavour). I told her to take them back—I did not want any tokens of affection from a twelve year old with a criminal record. At lunch he hovered outside the upper school canteen with his Dairylea Dunkables before being removed by Mr Wilmott for breaking the rules that prevent Criminals and Retards eating in public except under strict supervision (following Lou's school rabbit incident).

Am going to claim a food allergy so that I have to spend every break in the sealed language lab with Emily Reeve who lives in fear of being within three metres of a peanut butter sandwich.

Justin still off school with Mrs Wong-inflicted injury.

. . . .

Wednesday 8

Mum has refused to back my alleged food allergy—despite me relaying the horror of last year's incident with the Snickers bar and Mr Patel's sticky lino. So am at mercy of Kyle and his pre-pubescent longings.

10 a.m.

Kyle has texted me a photo of his bottom. If he thinks it will win me over he is sorely mistaken. It is spookily like Fat Kylie's (glimpsed during last year's illicit liaison with Mark Lambert in the Paris Travotel while Thin Kylie was being sick in le bidet).

2 p.m.

Kyle has just sung 'You Raise Me Up' to me outside the mobile science labs. Is there no end to his obsession?

. . . .

Thursday 9

Apparently there is. It turns out that Primark Donna has fancied him for ages and she will do anything for a packet of NikNaks. I am a stalkee no more.

Justin finally back, though lisping slightly. Mrs Wong gave him six injections and they, and the pain, have only just worn off.

. . . .

Friday 10

The dog has disappeared. Last confirmed sighting (James) was during *Blue Peter* when it was chewing the back door. Mum does not seem to be sufficiently distraught. I said he could have been stolen by pet torturers or mangled outside the notoriously dangerous George Street turning. She said at least she will not have to cordon off the Sunday roast again.

9 p.m.

Fiddy is making a racket over the road. Mum has catalogued it in her ASBO book. She says at least the dog didn't bark excessively, which is about the only thing she can find in its favour. Grandpa said, 'That dog was

344

a saint, Janet. What did it ever do to you?' She said 'Where shall I start?' So Grandpa went off to search Marjory's herbaceous borders with a Tweenies torch.

· ·

Saturday 11

9 a.m.
The dog is still missing. Grandpa has called the police. Tracy Hughes's mum answered. She said the only dog in the pound is Fat Kylie's poodle Tupac, who was involved in a fracas at the White Horse last night. She suggested he try Abrakebabra, who are apparently under investigation for suspicious meat provenance, although it is a secret so she will be in trouble yet again.

4 p.m.
The dog has been found! He was not lost or turned into a kebab at all but has been hiding in Thin Kylie's garage in an attempt to be closer to Fiddy. He is in love. James suggested we let them mate, as an experiment (he is hooked on David Attenborough). Cherie looked horrified—she said it would be like 'letting Barry the Blade have a go at Zara Phillips'. That is a bit harsh. The dog is hairy but he does not live in an Austin Allegro. Plus Fiddy is hardly royalty—she came from the Whiteshot Estate.

7 p.m.
The dog is missing again.

8 p.m.

The dog is back. Terry brought it over. He says Cherie is going to 'ASBO' us if we don't keep it locked up. Mum is beside herself with potential ASBO tit for tat. She says she will ASBO the Britchers for having a provocative dog (Fiddy wears a pink jewelled coat).

. . . .

Sunday 12

11 a.m.

The dog is going bonkers. It is not allowed out of the dining room for fear it will make a dash for the Britchers' and get us ASBOed. Mum will have to give in soon though. It has already chewed two chair legs.

4 p.m.

The dog is out. Mum could take no more after it started digging up the carpet. Grandpa had to agree to conditions to secure its release though. It has to be kept on a lead at all times and is being booked in for 'the snip'. Grandpa complained and said no man should be forced to give up their masculinity and what if it went all funny (i.e. gay). But Mum said Dad hadn't shown any signs of losing his masculinity and maybe Grandpa should have given it some thought before foisting his overeager loins on us all (she is annoyed because Jesus woke up seventeen times in the night).

Although Dad does like Jeremy Clarkson a bit obsessively. Maybe this is down to the 'snip' after all.

. . . .

Monday 13

Half term

A dead duck has been found in France. I would have thought this was an everyday occurrence what with all the foie gras they eat and their generally lax attitude to animal welfare but apparently it is a suspicious duck (i.e. riddled with life-threatening bird flu). Mum is considering a ban on all French food produce.

It is Valentine's Day tomorrow. Feel sick with anticipation. Potentially I could get a card from Justin. Am still keeping up campaign to prove I am his ONE. And we are definitely getting closer. Last week he actually smiled and said, 'Thankth, Riley,' (Mrs Wong-induced lisp still slightly present) when I told him he was totally better at guitar than Danny Wheatley in Year Thirteen, who once had an audition for Motörhead.

Called Scarlet to discuss Justin situation but she was at the vet's with Gordon and Tony who have been fighting again (cats not politicians). Jack answered. He asked me if I had sent any cards. I said, 'Of course not; as well you know, Valentine's Day is a made-up non-event perpetuated by evil card manufacturers.' (The Stones are totally anti-Valentine's Day.) Jack said, 'Oh, right,' and hung up. I think he was stunned into silence by my excellent political monologue.

Tuesday 14
Valentine's Day
9 a.m.
No cards. This is typical. Am going to text Scarlet to confirm my support for her ongoing anti-Valentine's Day stance.

10 a.m.
Scarlet has ended her anti-Valentine rally. She got a card from Brighton i.e. from unhygienic tent-dwelling juggler Axe. She is in love again and is trying to persuade Suzy to drive her to his bivouac tomorrow. Jack and Tuesday are going to go with her. I have asked if I can go too. Brighton is the UK centre of teen tragedy and general edginess. According to Julie Burchill there is lesbian snogging and drugs on every street corner.

Wednesday 15
8 a.m.
Suzy has agreed to take us to Brighton. She is totally forward thinking when it comes to teenage sexual urges. (Unlike Mum. Thank God she has not read *Sugar Rush*.)

I wonder what Axe will be like. Scarlet claims he looks like Brad Pitt but I suspect he is more like a younger Barry the Blade.

9 p.m.
Not the day of gritty multicultural urbanity I had hoped

348

for. For a start we had to go in the Mini Cooper (Bob has taken the under-seat-heated Volvo to an annual gynae-cologists conference—it is entitled 'Light at the end of the tunnel'). Then Sad Ed decided to come (to escape a day of lurking outside Radio 2 studios in London to get Aled to sign his mum's polo-neck) and insisted on playing a CD of some man called Leonard Cohen, who is as utterly cheerless as Sad Ed. Then Suzy went round the M25 the wrong way (she was trying to talk to Bob about penis dysfunction on her non-hands-free mobile and said it was easier to turn left than right) and we didn't get to Brighton until two o'clock. We then spent four hours looking for Axe's bivouac (there are a surprisingly large number of hairy men living in tents in Brighton) only to find that he had gone to his mum's barn conversion in Malvern for the week. Scarlet sat in silence all the way home. Suzy says it is because she has been betrayed. (He told her he was from an estate in the Midlands. She had pictured a crime-ridden council estate in Birmingham.)

Plus Tuesday was being weirdly nice to Sad Ed. She kept giggling mentally at his crap jokes and then she asked him to go to Jack and Justin's gig on Saturday with her. She did not invite me or Scarlet (although we will be there anyway so her snub is pointless). Maybe his diet is paying off after all. Although having spent four hours wedged in his armpit I estimate he still has twelve kilos to go to hit his target. Not aided by the fact that we have eaten seven bags of Doritos, two jumbo bars of Bournville, eight

Ginster's Cheese and Onion pasties (not pasties according to Mum and the long-running subject of her 'real pasty' campaign) and a three pack of Jaffa cakes (also the subject of one of Mum's 'misnamed food' campaigns—apparently it is down to whether they get soggy or dry if left out). All purchased from the Mecca that is the Junction 8 services. As opposed to eating fish and chips on Brighton beach with gay people, which is what we should have been doing. It is all utterly depressing.

When we got back to Saffron Walden, Tuesday refused to let Suzy drop her off at home. She made her drop her outside Mr Patel's claiming she needed to buy a Turkish Delight before her blood sugar levels dipped too low and she got violent. This is a lie as she ate most of the Jaffa cakes. It is because she doesn't want us to see where she lives. It is totally like that bit in *Pretty in Pink* when Andie won't let Blane know where she lives because he is a rich prep boy and she is a poor but beautiful eccentric from the wrong side of town (although she does own a car, which goes to show that being poor in America is actually better than being me in Essex). It is so unfair. She is probably living knee-deep in rats and gin bottles in elegant squalor, while I am living in citrus fresh Summerdale Road.

. . . .

Thursday 16

Scarlet and I are both in utter shock. It turns out that her Valentine card was not from Axe at all. It was from Justin.

Justin was at his Aunt Renee's bungalow in Hove for the weekend and posted it from there. According to Jack, Aunt Renee lives with a woman called Leslie. She is a stand-up comic and has a shaven head. Even Justin has interesting and Julie Burchillesque relatives. I want him even more now. Why oh why does he like Scarlet and not me? Actually I know why. It is because she has permissive parents and knows the exact location of the G spot. He is wasting his time though. She has taken a vow never to snog anyone who has highlights again.

. . . .

Friday 17

Kissing in school plays is potentially going to be banned. According to Suzy's *Guardian* it is because of bonkers right-wingers who are paranoid about perverts in schools. (Although according to Grandpa's *Daily Mail* it is because of bonkers left-wingers.) They were discussing it over their authentic peasant lunch of Waitrose olives and hummus when I arrived to comfort Scarlet out of her post-Axe trauma with Treena's copy of *Heat* (it has pictures of Marilyn Manson without make-up). Suzy said Bob had once fondled her breasts during a production of *Joseph and his Technicolour Dreamcoat* when they were at school. So Bob said that was nothing to do with the plot that was because the lights went out. But then Jack said, 'It's not like it means anything anyway. It's just tongues. No one really enjoys it.' At which point I choked on an olive

351

stone and had to go and cough it up in the loo. Why did he say that? Maybe he is trying to hide his true feelings. After all, our *Bugsy Malone* clinch was fairly heated. Oh God, maybe he fancies me. Maybe he is THE ONE and I have been mistaken all along!

7 p.m.
Or what if he is telling the truth and he didn't enjoy it? He is an excellent actor after all—as testified to by *Walden Chronicle* drama critic (and editor) Deirdre Roberts. That is it. Of course he doesn't fancy me. I am practically a medical midget and my hair is mental. Plus I have hopelessly un-tragic relatives and a dog who eats furniture. Am going to give up on men. So far my record is: Brian Drain on a Year Seven trip to Peterborough Roller Rink (I was momentarily distracted by Thin Kylie trying to beat up the bus driver); acne-ridden fascist Will; Kyle O'Grady under severe influence of purple alcohol; and Jack, who was only doing it in the name of art. I will be like Kirsten Dunst in that weird film and die a virgin and everyone will say what a waste of beauty and literary genius it all is.

Saturday 18
11 a.m.
It is Jack and Justin's gig at the Air Training Corps hut tonight (youth group for the criminally weapons-obsessed). Scarlet and I are going to show our support for him. And

obviously monitor Tuesday and Sad Ed. We have vowed not to snog anyone (not hard in my case—I am unlovable). We are going to concentrate on being brilliant literary types and writing genius first novels before we leave school.

11 p.m.
Oh my God. Sad Ed snogged Tuesday. Or rather, she snogged him—he seemed to be in shock and stood there with a Coke in one hand and a Flyte bar in the other while she mauled him with her purple fingernails during Certain Death's ironic cover version of 'Ugly' by the Sugababes. No one has ever snogged Sad Ed before. Unless you count his cousin Julia, which we have agreed we don't. Maybe Sad Ed is actually the sort of person everyone in London goes for. Which would mean I have been living practically next door to Saffron Walden's answer to Johnny Depp for years.

Plus Scarlet snogged head goth Trevor Pledger (he has black hair and a pet rat, so he passes all her strict criteria). So now I am alone in my adolescent torture. It is so totally *Dawson's Creek* with me as brilliant but innocent beauty Joey and Tuesday as the one on drugs who sleeps with everyone. God knows who is Dawson though. No one has a forehead that big in real life.

Although Sad Ed and Tuesday will never get together. It will definitely be a one-night stand. I will go round there tomorrow and we will laugh about it and watch a

Buffy DVD and everything will be normal again with Ed being fat and hopeless and me being tragic but potentially more likely to snog someone.

- -

Sunday 19

It is not a one-night stand. She is coming round to his after lunch to snog again and watch French films. I said didn't she mind about his upper arm issues and the fact that his mum is obsessed with a Welsh Evangelist and he said, according to Tuesday, he is a tortured soul trapped in a suburban nightmare, and inside him Pete Doherty is straining to get out, which is totally Tim Burton, and anyway Aled Jones is Methodist.

- -

Monday 20

Back to school

It is official. The dead French duck has bird flu. Mum has thrown out the Bonne Maman jam and the Waitrose Normandy butter. She has also banned any future trips to Paris.

Sad Ed and Tuesday were all over each other in first break. Well, she was all over him. He is as unenergetic in his snogging as he is in PE. She let him share her iPod headphones so they could listen to New Wave French Electropop together. But Ms Hopwood-White saw them and confiscated it. Sad Ed is clearly blinded by lust

because he actually told Ms Hopwood-White to 'chill'. He got sent to Mr Wilmott immediately and has detention after school with scarily strict Head of English Mrs Butfield (aka Buttface). He says it is worth it as he acted in the name of love. Although it means he will miss *Richard and Judy* and *Neighbours* so I bet he doesn't try it again.

. . . .

Tuesday 21

The dog has had the snip. Mum dropped it off at Mr Mercer's before school. It was all excited until it saw Rosemary, the severe veterinary assistant. I think she brought back bad memories of when it got a torch wedged in its windpipe.

When it got home it lay whimpering with its head on Grandpa's lap. Grandpa tried to console it with a packet of chocolate digestives but it was sick all over Grandpa's trousers half an hour later so Grandpa's theory that the dog would suffer an immediate personality change has proved unfounded.

. . . .

Wednesday 22

Tuesday says Sad Ed is a repressed love-god. She has given Scarlet and me detailed descriptions of their sexual activity (no genitals yet but she did let him stroke the waistband of her ironic Calvin Klein boxer shorts). She

has compared him to a young Bob Geldof (whom she claims to have snogged in a toilet at Peaches Geldof's birthday party last year). She is mistaken. He looks more like a young Chris Moyles. I asked her if she loved him. She said she is just using him sexually.

All evidence points to Sad Ed actually being my ideal man, i.e. THE ONE. How can this be? Although I suppose he does look quite good in his Morrisey T-shirt.

Ugh. Have just done involuntary shudder at thought of thinking about Sad Ed that way. No he cannot be THE ONE. He is like Buttons in the pantomime and Justin is Prince Charming.

· ·

Thursday 23

Mum had another driving lesson today. She says, according to Mike, she could benefit from extra tuition on her clutch technique. Dad is refusing to discuss it. He is convinced Mike is going to seduce her with his rugged good looks and three-point-turn ability and that she will fling herself across the Fiesta at him in abandonment. I said this was unlikely as Mum has more self-control than Gillian McKeith, plus the seatbelt arrangement wouldn't allow it, but Dad is still unconvinced. He says he has seen that look in men before. I said in who and he gave Grandpa a withering look.

· ·

Friday 24

Have decided to start my genius first novel tomorrow. Will purchase leather-bound notebook and supply of pens from WHSmith plus candles for added inspiration and general atmosphere of torture.

. . . .

Saturday 25

2 p.m.

Have bought pens (ten blue Bics—£1.99) and notebook (Slightly uninspirational cover featuring McFly as it was on discount and WHSmith doesn't stock leather due to lack of demand. I said surely the McGann or Marlon off *Emmerdale* (Saffron Walden's entire celebrity population) must ask for them to pen their diaries and other actorly things, but Mrs Noakes said the last time Marlon came in he bought a copy of *Woman's Own* and a Ronan Keating CD.) Have also lit several candles and drawn curtains. Am going to write about a homeless teenage prostitute in King's Cross (notorious inner-London drug den) who is also a hidden literary marvel and goes on to be the darling of the London arts world before dying tragically of syphilis on the eve of publication of her memoirs.

2.15 p.m.

Have opened curtains slightly. Cannot see pages of McFly notebook in gloom. How on earth did Jane Austen cope?

3 p.m.
Progress not brilliant due to arrival of Mum to investigate smell of wax. She has ordered me to put out candles due to potential fire hazard of M&S curtains and duvet set. So atmosphere somewhat less tortured than I had hoped.

4 p.m.
Will just have some biscuits. According to James the brain needs a teaspoon of sugar an hour to function. (He regularly just eats a teaspoon of demerara to ensure he is in tip-top condition brain-wise. Mum has not seen this or she would ban it for sure.)

5 p.m.
Ooh. *Strictly Dance Fever* is on. All writers need a break from deep and meaningful thoughts and reality TV is ideal. Will write after I find out who gets to the dance-off.

8 p.m.
Will just watch *Casualty*. It will be useful for medical information.

10 p.m.
Too tired to write. Will start in morning.

. . . .

Sunday 26
9 a.m.
Am in utterly literary mood. Have eaten brain-stimulating

toast and marmalade and drunk obligatory cup of coffee (Nescafé decaffeinated). Think I will focus on descriptions of urban degradation and squalor.

10 a.m.
Have realized know nothing about King's Cross. Will change location to Cambridge railway station instead. I have been there several times and the toilets are vile so it is fairly gritty.

11 a.m.
Also know nothing about drugs. Maybe will give her Benson and Hedges habit instead.

12 noon
Think have writer's block.

1 p.m.
Will just eat lunch.

2 p.m.
And maybe watch *Maisy* DVD with Baby Jesus.

3 p.m.
Will definitely go back to novel once have found out where Maisy is taking her train today.

4 p.m.
Got text from Scarlet demanding my presence to discuss

Trevor Pledger situation. (He has failed to demand sex. Not that Scarlet wants to do it with him. She just wants to show how feminist and forthright she is in respecting her minky etc.) Will write when I get back. True poets always work at night anyway. It is a well known fact.

10 p.m.
Very tired due to endless discussion of whether Trevor Pledger is actually gay. Conclusion—not, but with possible religious issues. (Scarlet found a WWJD bracelet in the pocket of his vegetarian leather goth coat. Apparently it stands for What Would Jesus Do? She is going to confront him next week.)

Will lie on bed thinking literary thoughts. And will close eyes to block out uninspiring view of Mr Men height chart (still three cms off the top).

Monday 27
7 a.m.
Oh God. Fell asleep. Woke up with dog retching in ear. It had eaten a candle and the wax was sticking to its tongue. Will have to do novel after school.

5.35 p.m.
After *Neighbours*

6 p.m.
And tea

8 p.m.

Oops. Forgot have French homework. Have to write 200 words on one of our parents in French. Am doing Mum as have no idea what Dad does. Will use excellent internet translator tool discovered by James. Novel will have to wait. I am not worried. I do not leave school for at least two and a half years (A levels being compulsory in this house) so have plenty of time to reveal precocious talents.

Tuesday 28

Shrove Tuesday

Dad's birthday. Luckily Mum had got him a present from all of us (a day with Saffron Walden golf professional (and closet homosexual) Russell Rayner) because I had totally forgotten what with all the novel writing. BUT more importantly Dad got himself a present—it is a Freeview box! We have joined the digital age—and only three years late, which is comparatively short when you think we only got a DVD player two years ago. Dad says he is sick of missing crucial golf shots because of the lack of red button in the house. Mum did not look happy. Satellite and cable are on her banned list due to excess sports and porn. She is making Dad set parental guidance controls to block E4 (to prevent Grandpa and Treena watching back to back *Hollyoaks*), BBC3 (to prevent me watching tortured teenage drama involving drugs and lesbians) and Bid-Up (to prevent James buying cooking equipment

and gold-plate jewellery). We are allowed to watch the other channels when we get home from school.

8 p.m.
Freeview is not all it is cracked up to be. The choice was: news, *Lovejoy*, or a programme about monkeys. We watched *Lovejoy*. Dad is beside himself with the prospect of Ian McShane on every night. I do not know why. He has most episodes on video anyway. Luckily the dog made up for lack of entertainment by eating twelve pancakes and an entire Jif Lemon.

For Mum

march

Wednesday 1

St David's Day/Ash Wednesday

Got French homework back. An E-. Am not using internet translator tool again. It translated 'obsessed with Cillit Bang' as 'obsessed with silly sex'. And it spelt stain remover wrong.

Thursday 2

Sad Ed came round after school. I asked him if Tuesday is THE ONE. He said one what. He does not read *Cosmopolitan*. I said, 'You know, like Cathy and Heathcliff, or Bridget and Mark Darcy. Or Richard and Judy.' He said that Tuesday did not believe in Mr Right. She says it is all about Mr Right Now. Clearly Tuesday does read *Cosmopolitan*. Then he asked if I knew who my ONE was. I said I thought there had been two potentially but one thinks Scarlet is the ONE and the other one has made it clear he definitely does not want to be the ONE. Sad Ed said my ONE is probably right under my nose I just don't know it yet. Maybe he is right. Maybe it is someone I sit next to at school. Oh God. I sit next to Mark Lambert in Citizenship. It cannot be him.

Friday 3

And have been moved next to Fat Kylie in Maths. There is no way she is my ONE. I am definitely not a lezzer.

Saturday 4

Trevor is not a closet God-botherer. Scarlet confronted him with the WWJD thing last night but it turns out the J stands for Jez, who is some goth singer who once sacrificed a chicken on stage. And then he stuck his hand up her bra so she got to shout at him for taking advantage and is now over the moon. Asked her if she wanted to come over tonight to lounge around wearing black and generally agree about how crap Saturday nights in Saffron Walden are, but she is going to Trevor's so she can spurn his sexual advances some more. Texted Sad Ed but he was waiting for Tuesday to come over so he could do the opposite. He still hasn't been to her house though. What is she trying to hide? If I had an ex-drunk mother I would be getting everyone over to watch her struggle with the cooking sherry.

. . . .

Sunday 5

This is why I need to find the ONE. Because otherwise my weekends will be spent watching Gloria Hunniford talking about God and going for family walks around garden centres. Because all my so-called friends are too busy snogging.

. . . .

Monday 6

Ms Hopwood-White reminded us it is work experience

week next week. We are supposed to have arranged to go into a local business to see what the real world is like. Except I totally forgot about it. Scarlet is going to sit in on her mum's sex counselling sessions. Sad Ed and Tuesday are both going to work in Roadshow Records. They are beside themselves as they get to choose what music they want all day (i.e. foreign and depressing). Ms Hopwood-White asked what I was going to do. I said some last minute details still had to be finalized. Did not tell her all the first minute ones were sketchy as well.

Tuesday 7

Have had stroke of genius. Will offer literary skills to *Walden Chronicle* and revive prematurely abandoned journalistic career.

Wednesday 8

Have secured work experience on condition that I use real words and do not try to 'sex up' any stories. I start Monday morning. I cannot wait. This is how Julie Burchill began her star-spangled career. Admittedly it was on the *NME* and she lived in gritty London not Saffron Walden but this is a definite step in the right direction none the less.

Thursday 9

Today is the second anniversary of the death of Fat Kylie's dad Les. He choked to death on a Findus Crispy Pancake (chicken and sweetcorn variety). The O'Gradys are all off school to mark the occasion. They are probably weeping at his oversized grave. It is utterly tragic.

Friday 10

Fat Kylie has detention for a week. It turns out the O'Gradys did not spend yesterday weeping at Les's headstone but went to TK Maxx in Harlow instead. Kylie made the fatal mistake of bringing her haul of discount chavwear to school. She told Ms Hopwood-White it is what her dad would have wanted. Which is probably true.

Saturday 11

Yet another Saturday night with no friends. Scarlet is round at Trevor's trying to buy bats off the internet and Sad Ed and Tuesday are experimenting sexually and watching films with subtitles. Not even Mum and Dad want to stay in with me. They are going for casserole at Clive and Marjory's. And Treena is going down the White Horse. So will end up watching censored Freeview with Baby Jesus, James, and Grandpa.

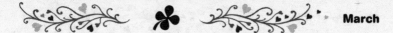

11 p.m.

I wrote too soon! James had, by a process of elimination, deduced Mum's Freeview pin number and removed all parental controls (it is '0907'—the use-by date on her women's vitamins). Grandpa made a half-hearted attempt to stop him but then he remembered that *The OC* was on so he just said James had to reprogramme the set-top box afterwards.

. . . .

Sunday 12

Dad is thinking of sending the set-top box back as it is now refusing to let him watch *Pie in the Sky*. Mum said it is showing good sense.

4 p.m.

Sad Ed has just been over for emergency counselling. He and Tuesday are having sexual problems i.e. she wants to do 'It' but he is not so sure because of *a*) upper arm fat *b*) penis size, and *c*) fears of statutory rape charges being brought by litigious gay American father and ending up on front of *Walden Chronicle*. I said I was not the right person to speak to but he said he can't talk to his mum because she refuses to even say the word penis (or vagina—she still calls them weewees and front bottoms) and Scarlet is too intimidating with her encyclopaedic knowledge of all things penis-related. So I told him *a*) he should keep a long-sleeve top on and claim he has that disease whereby

extremities get cold and go numb (Grandpa Clegg gets it), *b*) gross, and *c*) his mum is more likely to file charges against Tuesday. Then, for some reason, I got all funny about the thought of him and Tuesday doing 'It', and remembered that *Clueless* thing he kept spouting at me last year and said, 'It's like Alicia Silverstone says—to thine own self be true.' But he just said, 'That was Polonius, you moron. God, you are so unliterary,' and went off to do 'It'.

9 p.m.
Sad Ed has not done 'It'. He says he had a panic attack and visions of his mother looming above him shrieking, 'If Aled can wait, so can you!' Plus he says he didn't feel very aroused due to appearance of his dad to offer them Jammy Dodgers. He is going to stick to foreplay until he is at least sixteen (i.e. in seven months). Plus he says he hasn't even worked out how to undo her bra strap so it would be like trying to sit Maths AS without doing Key Stage 2. Am relieved. Not that I want Sad Ed for myself. That is too weird. Ooh, got that shudder thing again. But he is too good for her. Anyway, Sad Ed says if he is Tuesday's Mr Right Now she will wait for him. Did not mention the using him sexually thing.

Work experience week starts tomorrow. Hurrah. Have converted my genius first novel McFly notebook into my new journalistic career notebook. When I am famous and interviewing Nelson Mandela on *Breakfast News* I can sell it on eBay for thousands of pounds. I cannot wait to get

started. I am going to focus on investigative journalism (i.e. uncovering fraud and crime at the heart of Saffron Walden high society (i.e. the golf club)).

. . . .

Monday 13

Not the glittering start to my career that I had imagined. I had to sit with the receptionist, Mrs Connolly, who answers the phones (i.e. reads *Woman's Realm* all day). Deirdre, the editor, said it would give me an overview of the bustle of a hectic newsroom. There were three phone calls. One from Kitchens Direct offering to install shaker-style units and a microwave, one from Deirdre's husband asking her if she had seen his 9-iron and one from Mum to check if I had my lunch money. Anyone with an urgent news story would have a job getting through anyway, as Mrs Connolly spent most of the day on the phone to her sister who apparently has problems 'down there'. On the plus side, they are going to let me open the post tomorrow.

8 p.m.

Spoke to Scarlet who has been listening to sexual revelations with Suzy all day. Apparently Ying Brewster has got inverted nipples.

. . . .

Tuesday 14

Nine letters: one bill, one invite to the Young Farmers

Annual Barn Dance (i.e. a load of straw-chewing inbreds in Millets shirts listening to Shania Twain), and seven letters to the 'Why, Oh Why' letters page (there is a lot of moaning to be done in Saffron Walden). For example:

Why, oh why has the library filed Thaxted-raised science fiction writer Diana Wynne Jones under J for Jones. I spent literally ten minutes floundering in the Ws before realizing their mistake.

And:

Why, oh why is Saffron Walden in Essex? We would benefit enormously tourist-wise if we could move it five miles over the border into Cambridgeshire, which enjoys a better class of visitor all round.

Mum had sent two of them, complaining about: *a*) Waitrose moving the yoghurts without prior warning; and *b*) graffiti on the Bernard Evans Youth Centre (not so much the graffiti per se as the fact that it is grammatically incorrect, i.e. 'Leanne Jones have huge tits').

I put them in the bin. I do not want anyone thinking I am doing her any nepotistic favours.

Asked Deirdre if I could do anything resembling actual reporting tomorrow. She said I could do the office cake run to Dorrington's and stock the photocopier. This is so unfair. I bet no one makes John Pilger go and buy Viennese fingers off Pie Shop Pearce. Am going to take a

stand and demand to put my excellent journalism skills to better use.

8 p.m.
Scarlet has been banned from sitting in in Suzy's counselling. It is because she broke the official sex counselling secrets act with the inverted nipples thing. She is going to watch Bob the abortionist at work from tomorrow instead. She says it will be less distressing anyway.

. . . .

Wednesday 15
10 a.m.
My stand has paid off (or possibly fact that got five doughnuts and a jam slice free from Dorrington's due to presence of Thin and Fat Kylies on pie shop work experience). Deirdre has agreed to let me go out this afternoon with ace reporter (i.e. only reporter) Glen Davies. We are going to cover the ongoing affordable housing crisis (Suzy is for it, rest of Saffron Walden is against it), including an interview with Hugo Thorndyke, evil MP for Saffron Walden and environs, at his Tudor manor in Seward's End! It will be totally Jeremy Paxman with me and Glen asking awkward questions and Hugo looking shifty in his lap of luxury.

5 p.m.
Our in-depth interview turned out to be tea and macaroons

(home-made by red-faced Mrs Thorndyke) and Glen saying, 'Anything for the record, Hugo?' and then Hugo just banging on about John Prescott into a dictaphone. I tried to ask a question about needy refugee families but my mouth was sticky with macaroon and I just ended up coughing macaroon dust onto the Axminster. I am very disappointed at the *Walden Chronicle*'s interview technique. I hope the *Guardian* does not operate on this basis.

8 p.m.
Sad Ed called. He and Tuesday have been sacked from Roadshow Records for refusing to let Cherie buy a Daniel O'Donnell CD on grounds of taste. Sad Ed says he is glad. Tuesday was showing an unhealthy interest in Dave, the part-time sales assistant and one time pop star (he played third synthesizer on an Erasure single once). Ed is considering amending his no-sex rule in a bid to keep Tuesday. I told him to be strong and fight for his dignity. But he said there was nothing dignified about being ditched for a twenty-nine-year-old Saturday boy with a mullet.

Thursday 16
Publication day.

The *Walden Chronicle* front page is headlined 'Not in My Back Yard' and has a picture of a beaming Hugo Thorndyke with Mrs Thorndyke hovering in the background with

her macaroon plate. It is all about how enormous blocks of affordable flats will block out views of the church, cause mass riots, and send crime in sleepy Saffron Walden soaring. It has a quote from Hugo saying, 'It's not that I don't want these people to have homes, I'm just saying there is an alternative to blots on our landscape, and it's called Haverhill.' Haverhill is not an alternative to anything. Except possibly Loughton.

Mum asked why neither of her 'Why Oh Why' letters made the paper. I said there were a lot of tough hard-nosed news decisions to be taken. So she said why is there a letter from Emily Reeve's mum demanding that Nestlé develop a non-sticky fruit Polo (a sweet that has never made it into our house as they are not real Polos because all Polos should, by law, be mint flavoured). I said it is because Mrs Reeve knows Mrs Connolly's sister with the downstairs problems. Mum is outraged. She is going to complain about the complaints page to higher beings (i.e. Deirdre's boss, East Anglian media tycoon Jethro Pledger, owner of the *Stowmarket Reporter*, the *Ipswich News* and *Fens Fortnightly*). She will get nowhere. He is married to Mrs Connolly's sister with the downstairs problems.

Friday 17

St Patrick's Day

Went to *Walden Chronicle* for final day of somewhat disappointing journalistic work experience but office was

shut. Saw Glen outside the Co-Op and asked him if there had been a bomb scare or other breaking all-hands-on-deck type story but he said they have a 'casual' Friday rule i.e. no one shows up at all due to general lack of news and Deirdre having a three-hour drive to her holiday home in Cromer. I said what if terrorists took over the town hall and he said chance would be a fine thing. So came home and watched *This Morning* with Grandpa, the dog, and Baby Jesus. Mum was out with Mr Wandering Hands. Which was a good thing as one of the items was about a team of synchronized labradors who could leap over metre-high fences and Grandpa got excited and tried to get the dog to jump over the coffee table but it missed and knocked over Grandpa's carton of illicit Ribena. I got out the Cillit Bang. I am well versed in stain removal.

. . . .

Saturday 18

Mum and Dad are going to dinner with Dad's boss Mr Wainwright tonight. This is excellent news, Freeview-wise. James is already lining up *Wife Swap Extra*. We should nominate Mum for that programme. Maybe we would get a spill-happy TV-loving crisp fiend for a week!

5 p.m.
In addition to Treena that is.

. . . .

Sunday 19

Mum has changed her Freeview pin. She found Grandpa and Baby Jesus watching *Pimp my Ride* at 2 in the morning.

Saw Thin Kylie walking Fiddy (i.e. letting her poo on Marjory's gravel). She and Fat Kylie got sacked from Dorrington's for a catalogue of misdemeanours including doughnut theft and making comedy penis shapes in the celebration range icing. Fiddy is getting fat already. I expect it is her unwholesome diet of Microchips and Kraft Cheese Slices.

Monday 20

Work experience week has been declared a success. There were only seventeen sackings this year—a new low (the Kylies, Sad Ed and Tuesday, and some Retards and Criminals who seemingly find it impossible not to let off fire alarms at every available opportunity). Plus Mark Lambert has been offered a job at Brenda's Hairdressing when he leaves school (which could be fairly soon if Ms Hopwood-White has her way). Apparently he shows remarkable promise shaving Union Jack designs into the heads of rat boys.

Also Mr Wilmott has installed a new 'Cooler' at school. It is a room for delinquents (i.e. the disused needlework mobile) where they are deprived of all privileges and just have to read calming poetry. Apparently he got the idea

377

off the BBC and is going to supervise the delinquents himself. I predict Mark Lambert and the Kylies will be in there before the term is over.

· ·

Tuesday 21

The cooler has been temporarily closed due to overcrowding. Mr Wilmott is having to revise his referrals policy—currently Mrs Leech is in charge and in her enthusiasm is just sending anyone who is lurking outside Mr Wilmott's office, including three Year Sevens with suspected nits. From now on, you can only get in if you have verbally or physically abused a member of staff or fellow student.

· ·

Wednesday 22

Twenty-three people got referred to the cooler today including:

Fat Kylie—calling Thin Kylie a 'lezzer';

Thin Kylie—calling Fat Kylie a 'lezzer';

Mark Lambert—asking Kylies to demonstrate 'lezzer sex';

Tuesday and Scarlet—actually demonstrating 'lezzer sex';

Lou the caretaker—adjusting the Coke and crisp machine so that you can get NikNaks for 1p. (Personally I think this shows a good grasp of physics, maths, and metalwork, and should be rewarded.);

Most of Criminals and Retards—too numerous to list—
it is like a badge of honour to get referred for them.

Mrs Duddy has complained to Mr Wilmott. She says the
cooler is disrupting the Retards and Criminals curriculum.
Mr Wilmott mentioned the calming Shakespeare but she
said most of them are still struggling with *Olga da Polga*.

Thursday 23

10.30 a.m.

Apparently Justin has been referred to the cooler for
likening hairy librarian Mr Knox to a yeti. Am going to
get myself referred immediately so I can bond with him
over our delinquency. Will call Tuesday a 'lezzer' within
Ms Hopwood-White's earshot. Tuesday will know I am
being ironic.

11.30 a.m.

Have black eye (Fat Kylie thought I was referring to her
and is not so understanding of irony and Ms Hopwood-
White distracted by Mark Lambert trying to undo Thin
Kylie's bra one-handed for a can of Coke and a Picnic off
Fat Jim Warner). Am not in cooler but in Mrs Leech's
office eating reviving bourbons.

1 p.m.

The cooler has been closed until further notice so now
I will never get to show Justin how we are both

379

misunderstood by conventional society. Apparently a fight broke out between the Year Eight Retards and the Year Nine ones and Mr Wilmott is now in Addenbrookes with a compass wound. He is going to leave the delinquents to Mrs Duddy from now on.

· ·

Friday 24

James's birthday. Got him some stickers for his *Lord of the Rings* album (stickers being recently unquarantined but still under strict review pending any incidents of rogue stickers being found on furniture). He is not having his official party until tomorrow. He and Mumtaz are having a joint celebration at the Lord Butler Leisure Centre. Mum is not happy but Mrs Patel has organized it. It involves twenty nine-year-olds rollerskating, swimming, eating vast quantities of chips and neopolitan ice cream, and a disco (i.e. a Tweenies CD on repeat). Mum says it will end in tears and/or vomit. She is taking a box of Kleenex and a squeegee.

· ·

Saturday 25

Went into town with Sad Ed for annual ritual of finding Mother's Day cards and presents. He says Tuesday is getting impatient with his True Love Waits attitude towards sex. She is going to a seance with Scarlet and the goths tonight and has not invited him. I said I wasn't

invited either but he pointed out that I don't own enough black clothing. Got Mum a non-whimsical card with daffodils on and a bar of Green and Blacks.

5 p.m.
James is back from his birthday party with broken fingers ('Mad Harry' rollerskated over them). Apparently it is not the only injury. There were two concussions (trampolining) and a near drowning (neapolitan ice cream). Mum says she is sticking to educational museum visits next year.

Sunday 26

Mother's Day
10 a.m.
Mum has threatened to consign the Freeview box to the bin. James got her a five-piece copper-bottomed Anthony Worral Thompson saucepan set for Mother's Day (£5.99 off Bid-Up via Grandpa's credit card). She asked how anyone could have worked out her new pin. James said it was easy—it is the last four digits of the Vanish Oxy-Action barcode. Dad is fighting back over Freeview. He says he will only give it up if she agrees to give up driving lessons with Mike the Molester. Mum says she would rather walk to Cornwall than learn with rival instructor Carl Kent (of Kent's Kar Klasses). His failure rate is second to none in North Essex; he deliberately misspells

for alliterative effect; plus he has Micras instead of Fiestas and Mum has never trusted the Japanese.

. . . .

Monday 27

I fear Sad Ed may have overanticipated Tuesday's willingness to wait for true love. I saw her smoking behind the ATC hut with Dave from Roadshow Records after school. But I cannot tell Sad Ed. It may break his heart. He is notoriously sensitive.

4 p.m.
Have told Sad Ed. He is going to confront her immediately (or at least after *Charmed*).

9 p.m.
Sad Ed has not confronted Tuesday yet due to fact that she let him borrow her copy of *The Catcher in the Rye* and touch her left nipple. I said wasn't he concerned about being two-timed with a sexually experienced former rock god. He said he couldn't afford to be choosy. I said that is not the attitude but he said I was in no position to comment. Which is true. No one wants to snog me. Maybe it is because I am rubbish at snogging. That is it—that is why Justin has rejected me. Jack must have told him about my crap snogging. Oh my God. I need to learn to snog properly. And fast. It is the end of term disco on

Friday and the air will be thick with adolescent hormones (and CK One). Plus Justin will be there.

. . . .

Tuesday 28

Have asked Scarlet for snogging advice. She said it is not really a matter of technique, it is about chemistry, but that Sean Woodley in Year Eleven will snog you for 50p and taught Leanne Jones everything she knows. Am going to his 'office' at lunch tomorrow (aka the upper school toilets).

. . . .

Wednesday 29

Went to Sean Woodley's 'office' but it was being 'manned' by his Neanderthal sidekick Vincent Miller. Apparently Sean has mumps and is off for a fortnight. And there is no way I am snogging Vincent. He only has one eyebrow. So yet another school disco will be spent eating crisps and watching the Kylies get felt up to 'Dirty'.

. . . .

Thursday 30

Oh my God. Tuesday and Sad Ed have broken up. She says she chucked him because she is sick of boyfriends getting all 'possessive' on her and if she wasn't going to take it from Elijah Wood, she certainly wasn't going to take it from Sad Ed. Sad Ed says HE chucked HER for

383

adultery. I pointed out that they were neither married nor adults but it seemed to fall on deaf ears. He is refusing to go to the disco tomorrow due to heartbreak. And the fact that *Buffy the Movie* is on.

. . . .

Friday 31
8 a.m.
It is the school disco and I still haven't found anyone to teach me how to snog. Plus I will have to stand on my own in goth corner—a vintage rose in a sea of black bat people (Scarlet is going to let me in—being the girlfriend of head goth Trevor Pledger bestows you with immediate 'door' privileges). Am going to force Sad Ed to go. Will tell him Tuesday is showing interest in rekindling their romance.

12 midnight
OH MY GOD. I have to stop doing this. Have snogged someone else totally non-tragic, although this time not an O'Grady and above the age of twelve. It is Sad Ed. Oh God. Feel sick. Am going to bed before I bring up the four bags of Quavers and two apple Tangos I had from the 'bar'.

Saturday 1

April Fool's Day

Oh God. So this is what happened. Sad Ed and I were busy being depressed (him) and vintage (me) in goth corner, watching Fat Kylie pretending to be Beyonce by gyrating her giant behind, when I said it was very likely no one would ever snog me again. So, for some reason I have not yet fathomed, Sad Ed said he would snog me. And for some reason, possibly because Tuesday says he has excellent tongue technique, and because I was desperate, I agreed. And so we snogged, which I have to admit, technically wasn't horrible (apart from the fact that Fat Kylie was still dancing at the time and I could see her buttocks banging together out of the corner of my eye). In fact, on reflection, it was quite like Madonna kissing her best friend Rupert Everett, if Rupert Everett was fifteen with weight issues. Then Tuesday saw us and stormed over and shrieked, 'I can't believe you've dumped me for that pubic-headed loser.' (So it is true, Sad Ed did chuck her!) I said it meant nothing and was just practice so I could snog Justin without him being so revolted he decided to become gay or celibate. But Tuesday said talk to the hand, but accidentally smacked Fat Kylie when she thrust her bejewelled fingers at me, and Mark Lambert saw this and thought it was a free-for-all against the goths and then a mini riot broke out and Mr Wilmott had to use a fire extinguisher to separate some of the Retards and

Criminals who had improvised weapons with giant Tizer bottles.

So all in all it was a total disaster. I have snogged Sad Ed, who is not the ONE and is practically my brother, and alienated my only lifeline to tragedy (i.e. Tuesday) and now neither of them are speaking to me. And Scarlet was not too happy either due to the closure of goth corner—it was full of foam. They had to relocate to maths geek corner (the maths geeks agreed to combine forces with the farm club people). Worst of all, Jack and Justin saw the whole thing, including the actual Sad Ed snog and the bit about me actually wanting to snog Justin. Jack just said, 'Another triumph, Riley.' But he did not smile this time. Why is he still being mean to me? It is his fault I am having to practise snogging in the first place. Thank God it is the holidays. I predict everyone will have forgotten the hoo-ha by next term. Will go round Sad Ed's later and ensure he knows it meant nothing to me. Then maybe he and Tuesday can patch it up.

4 p.m.
Sad Ed is in mourning. I told him that I was sorry and that I would never snog him again, however desperate I was. And he said, 'Well, I feel so much better,' then went back to listening to the Smiths in the dark and eating Minstrels. I will give him some more time. He will soon be back to normal and we can get back to being tragic and single together.

Plus it is Grandpa Riley's birthday but no one remembered. Not even Treena. He thought it was just an April Fool at first but by four o'clock no one had given him any socks or miniature whiskies so he locked himself in the shed with the dog. He says it is the only true friend he has ever had. He will be out by 8. It is cold outside and *Casualty* is on.

8.05 p.m.
Grandpa is out and on the sofa. Treena bought him an Il Divo CD and some Liquorice Allsorts to say sorry. Plus the dog was going bonkers through sensory deprivation. It started to chew its own leg.

· ·

Sunday 2
Passion Sunday
Oh, the irony. The only passion in my life is Grandpa and Treena's audible conjugating over the sound of Italian Robson and Jeromes.

· ·

Monday 3
No school. Called Scarlet but Suzy said she was consoling a devastated Tuesday. And Sad Ed is still off limits. According to Mrs Thomas he hasn't come out of his room since tea last night, not even for *Songs of Praise*. She says he has taken the entire biscuit cupboard in with him. I do

not know why he is being so weird. After all, Tuesday was definitely flirting with Mullet Dave, and like Jack says— it's just tongues.

Watched *News 24* on Freeview with James for five hours (Mum in Cambridge making potentially life-changing purchase of new Hoover). Ate tea (fishfingers and beans). Admired new dog-hair eliminating Hoover with five turbo attachments. Watched *Lovejoy*. Went to bed.

. . . .

Tuesday 4

Took dog for a walk. Ate tea (toad-in-the-hole). Went to bed.

. . . .

Wednesday 5

Called Sad Ed. Mrs Thomas says he is improving. He has switched from the Smiths to the Killers and has been out of his room twice. Once for more KitKats and once for a poo. She is hoping he might have a shower tomorrow. Then she started on about how clean Aled always looks so I said I could smell burning and hung up.

Called Scarlet. She was down the Mocha with Trevor and Tuesday drinking coffee and being generally alienated from society.

. . . .

Thursday 6

12.30 p.m.

Watched *Teletubbies* with Baby Jesus for three hours. James says I need to get out more. He has invited me to test out the new 'slide of death' in the park on the common with him and Mumtaz this afternoon. I actually cried at his kindness. I may well go. It is my only source of social life.

4 p.m.

Slide now on Mum's banned list. James has broken another finger after shooting off end of 'perilously steep' helter-skelter thing and landing on top of Mad Harry.

. . . .

Friday 7

A dead swan has been found somewhere grey and wet in Scotland. *News 24* are beside themselves with potential time-filling television. So far they have interviewed a policeman, a man from the newsagent's, and some woman who likes swans. Mum is glued to Freeview. She has finally found a use for it.

. . . .

Saturday 8

Went round Sad Ed's to see if he has showered. He hasn't. Told him to pull himself together but he said I wouldn't understand, having never been in love. I said,

on the contrary, I was deeply in love with potential rock guitarist/mince machine operator Justin Statham, but Sad Ed just said, 'Oh, spare me,' and shut the door. At least he is out of bed though. That is a good sign. Once he stayed under the covers for two days when Willow ruined her image as netherworld lesbian by being in *American Pie*.

. . . .

Sunday 9
Palm Sunday

Granny Clegg rang to say 'Happy Birthday' to James. James answered and pointed out she was over two weeks late. Dad said, 'Bloody Cornish still think it is 1985.' At which point Mum commandeered the phone. When she got off she looked pale and panicky. It turns out that Granny and Grandpa Clegg are planning an Easter visit i.e. in five days. Mum warned them there was no room, what with the dog and Baby Jesus, but Granny says they will be happy to 'bed down' with one of the neighbours (this is the sort of weird thing they do in Cornwall). Only Clive and Marjory don't like the Cleggs after Grandpa accused Clive of being 'a poof' two years ago, for wearing a pink Pringle jumper, plus we are in their bad books due to fact that their Granada is still on blocks at Viceroy's, awaiting demangling, and they are having to use Marjory's Fiat Uno, which has a 'tricky' biting point. And Granny Clegg doesn't like Aled Jones because his voice

isn't high any more, which rules out Sad Ed's. So that leaves Terry and Cherie!

. . . .

Monday 10

Mum is refusing to ask Terry and Cherie if the Cleggs can stay there. She is going to book them into the Chestnuts B&B on the Ashdon Road (aka a 1930s semi with a view of a conker tree four doors down). I fear the worst. It is run by Les Brewster and his wife Ying (erstwhile proprietors of the Siam Smile, formerly the Dog and Bucket) and Grandpa Clegg is notoriously racist.

. . . .

Tuesday 11

Sad Ed has showered. Mrs Thomas rang to announce the news. I am going round tomorrow to see him. Obviously he is back to being just normally depressed as opposed to suicidal.

. . . .

Wednesday 12

Went to see Sad Ed. He says he is committing his life to being a misunderstood and celibate genius poet like Morrissey. He is writing a song about it all. It is called 'Hope She Dies Before I Get Old'. (It must be about Tuesday.)

. . . .

Thursday 13
Maundy Thursday

Fat Kylie is over the road with baby Whitney who is pushing Fiddy around in her Barbie pram. Fiddy is huge. She can barely walk so it is probably a relief to have someone wheel you about. Also it is good practice for Whitney. She will be pushing a pram for real by the age of sixteen if Mrs O'Grady is anything to go by.

. . . .

Friday 14
Good Friday
10 a.m.

Dad left at five to pick up the Cleggs from St Slaughter (Auntie Joyless is refusing to assist any contact with the 'heathen' wing of the family). He has taken Mum with him so she can memorize the route. He says the only good thing that will come out of her 'relationship' with Mike is that she will have to queue behind Margaret Beckett and her caravan for three hours on the A303 come August. Grandpa has put *Hollyoaks* on. He says we should enjoy our last hours of freedom before the Clampetts arrive.

7 p.m.

Mum and Dad are back. Granny and Grandpa Clegg have been deposited at Chestnuts with their Spar bags. Mum is nervous. She says Grandpa Clegg had a definite look of menace about him when he met Ying.

10 p.m.
Granny Clegg just rang. She says conditions at Chestnuts are intolerable and has sent for Dad to collect them. Dad said they cannot be worse than in Cornwall, which is practically the third world, but Mum sent him out with one of her evil glares.

10.30 p.m.
Granny and Grandpa Clegg are here. Grandpa Clegg says he will not share a bathroom with anyone who owns a bikini-line trimmer (Ying's, I assume, not Les's). Granny Clegg is backing him all the way. She says she would rather be under the same roof as a dirty old man and an illegitimate messiah than a foreign prostitute.

So I am in with James and the dog again. Mum is going to call Cherie in the morning.

· ·

Saturday 15
Woke up with James, a Will Young doll, the giant Des Lynam, and the dog in my camp bed. James said he had a bad dream involving Konnie Huq and a *Blue Peter* badge and needed to bring his 'friends' with him. Plus Grandpa Clegg and Grandpa Riley are still refusing to be in the same room at the same time until they can agree on whether or not Terry Wogan is the greatest living broadcaster or an annoying Irish twit so there is a ridiculous hoo-ha every time one of them needs to move

around the house. The sooner Mum calls Cherie the better.

11 a.m.
Cherie has agreed to let the Cleggs sleep in their spare room. She is moving the abdominizer and the sunbed into the garage. Granny and Grandpa are going to get a shock. I have seen the spare bed and it has black satin sheets and a vibration setting. They are going over in an hour to inspect the facilities but Granny Clegg has warned Mum they will be straight back if there are any signs of deviancy. I don't know if Channel 5 is included in this list. I hope not.

1 p.m.
Granny and Grandpa Clegg have moved over the road. Her fridge check revealed a Fray Bentos pie and some Kraft cheese slices. She thinks she has found her soulmate. Plus Fiddy has taken a liking to her. It is her vast bosoms. Animals like to sit on them. We are all going over for 'nibbles' later.

5 p.m.
Granny Clegg is in heaven. She is eating processed cheese and discussing *Heartbeat* with Cherie. Grandpa Clegg is happy too. Terry is just as racist as he is and they are singing 'Light My Fire' in comedy Indian accents. It is pitiful. Thin Kylie is not happy though. She said, 'Oh. My.

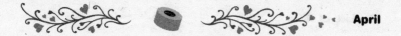

God. Your relatives are, like, retards. They wash their pants in the sink. It is minging.' For once I had to agree with her.

* *

Sunday 16
Easter Day
10 a.m.
Five eggs. Am going to hide them in my wardrobe to avoid repeat of last year's shameful binge.

11 a.m.
Oh my God. Fiddy has given birth on Granny Clegg's cardigan. She was not fat after all but pregnant. All fingers are pointing at the dog. The puppies have the same wiry hair and perpetual look of idiocy. Granny Clegg is going to have one of them.

Cherie is in shock. It is the thought of Fiddy and the dog doing 'It'. It must have been on his walk that time when he went missing for five minutes when James found 20p glued into the tarmac and tried to get it out. The dog is clearly a fast mover. Fiddy must have stood on a chair or something though—there is nearly a metre height difference. Grandpa Riley is taking the dog over to meet his offspring later. He says he will instinctively know they are his—it is how he felt when he first saw Jesus.

6 p.m.
The dog did not take too well to the puppies. Apparently

it went into a barking frenzy and Grandpa had to stop it trying to chew one of them.

8 p.m.
The dog has found all the Easter eggs. There is a pile of foil-studded sick outside my bedroom door. Only the generic Trago Mills one is left. I wonder what is wrong with it? Will just try a little bit.

1 a.m.
Have been sick. Granny Clegg has poisoned me with out-of-date confectionery. Even the dog had better sense than to eat it, and it seemingly enjoys being sick.

. . . .

Monday 17
Easter Monday
Granny and Grandpa Clegg are going home today. The Spar bags are already in the car but Granny Clegg is spending her last few minutes with 'Bruce' (as in Forsyth)—the puppy who has been singled out for her affections, and a lifetime of boredom and pasties in Cornwall. She has asked Dad to bring him down as soon as he has had his injections. Grandpa Riley said he would need typhoid and malaria to cross the border. Luckily Bruce had his tongue in Granny Clegg's waxy ear so she didn't hear him.

School starts tomorrow. Hopefully the end of term snogging fiasco will be consigned to history: Justin will

have suffered amnesia about the confession, Tuesday will forgive me as an act of sisterhood, and she and Sad Ed will ignore each other like grown-ups. Excellent.

· ·

Tuesday 18

Snogging utterly not consigned to history but luckily it is outdone by a shock revelation—Tuesday is not living in elegant squalor at all. She is living in a mock-Tudor four-bed on Pleasant Valley with Mr Wilmott. It turns out she is his niece! The news unfolds as follows:

9.10 a.m.
Sad Ed tells Tuesday he never loved her, she was his rebound girlfriend. (Who from? His cousin Julia?)

9.11 a.m.
Tuesday punches Sad Ed in stomach causing partial regurgitation of Wheat Crunchie (Worcester Sauce flavour).

9.12 a.m.
Mark Lambert offers to set up a bout with her and Fat Kylie, uncontested school fighting champion.

9.13 a.m.
Fat Kylie punches Mark Lambert to prove her fighting skills.

9.14 a.m.
Ms Hopwood-White sends for Mr Wilmott.

9.15 a.m.
Mr Wilmott says he is sick of Tuesday taking advantage of her relationship to him to get away with murder.

9.16 a.m.
Mark Lambert says, 'Oh my God, she's shagging Mr Wilmott.' Mr Wilmott says, 'Relationship to, not relationship with, you moron,' and that he is not shagging her, she is his niece and is staying at his house on a temporary basis.

9.17 a.m.
Tuesday storms out in an 'oh my God you are so embarrassing' fit.

9.18 a.m.
Order is restored and class goes back to discussion of whether Lennie in *Of Mice and Men* was autistic or seriously mental.

. . . .

Wednesday 19

Tuesday is leaving school. She says Dr Rubenstein says her mental health is at risk in the comprehensive system. But she was mental before she got here. She is going to

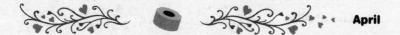

the Quaker school instead. I would think that is far more damaging. They have to wear green. Mr Wilmott is relieved. So is Fat Kylie. No one has ever threatened her position as fighting champion of John Major High before, not even Fat Jim who is eighty-nine kilos and in the Air Training Corps.

Thursday 20

Tuesday has gone. Scarlet, Sad Ed, and I have agreed we will never be blinded by pseudo-tragedy again. Although Sad Ed says he will die a virgin now. This is probably true.

Friday 21

Grandpa and Treena have set a date for the wedding. It is December 30th. Jesus is chief page boy. They are going to see if they can get a contraption so the dog can carry him down the aisle. I am a bridesmaid. I asked Treena if Des has signed her mental cruelty divorce papers but she was too busy showing Mum a picture of Jordan in a pink meringue dress. This does not bode well for my bridesmaid's outfit.

Saturday 22

Scarlet came over with a book of witchcraft symbols. Apparently she and Trevor are planning tattoos to demonstrate their commitment to each other and to

general gothness. James said she is not old enough and besides, she will look undignified in her old age but Scarlet said she is planning to die young anyway. We chose a pentangle. Trevor is getting a bleeding skull. They are going to Maudsley Mick's in Harlow tomorrow. Apparently he will do underage jobs for a bottle of Tesco whisky.

. . . .

Sunday 23

St George's Day

Not marked in this house following last year's fracas with the dog, Marlon, and Hugo Thorndyke. Mum is hovering near her ASBO catalogue. It is because the Britchers have painted a red cross on the garage door (and not of the biblical variety). Mum says it is encouraging jingoism not to mention graffiti.

5 p.m.

Went round Scarlet's to admire her tattoo. She was reluctant to show me at first so I had to sneakily pull down her skirt when she walked upstairs (thank God for elasticated goth clothing). I said I couldn't see anything so she pointed out a blue dot on her upper thigh. Apparently she fainted when the blood started seeping. Trevor did not even make it that far. He passed out when he saw Maudsley Mick's array of needles. How they expect to drink blood like Dracula I do not know.

. . . .

Monday 24

Called for Scarlet on the way to school but she has an infection in her thigh and is going to see Dr Braithwaite. So had to walk with Jack instead (Suzy's idea). Jack asked how my relationship with Sad Ed was. I said I did not have a 'relationship' with Sad Ed unless you count listening to dirge-like music and anyway, what did he care? Jack said he didn't. Then we walked in silence until we got to Mr Patel's where I pretended to need to talk to Thin Kylie about something (she was outside menacing some Year Sevens). What is going on? Jack and I used to be friends. It is because we crossed an uncrossable line and kissed. I have learnt my lesson. I will never snog a friend again. You either end up heartbroken or in a fire extinguisher fight.

I didn't mean heartbroken. Obviously. Jack did not break my heart.

Tuesday 25

Scarlet was back in school. Her tattoo is seeping though, so she has a note to get off games tomorrow. I asked if Suzy had grounded her but she said no, Suzy said self-mutilation was a rite of passage. She has an Egyptian fertility symbol tattooed on her left buttock and Bob has a ring on his unmentionables.

Also £1.50 has gone missing from Mum's purse. She suspects Grandpa. He came home with a four-pack of

brown ale. She asked him where he got the money and he said Dad had lent him £5 yesterday. Mum is not convinced but has given Dad a verbal warning anyway.

. . . .

Wednesday 26

A national scandal has occurred. Gigantic politician John Prescott has been having an illicit affair with his secretary, Tracey. James said that Tracey must have gone on top due to John Prescott's vastness so Mum sent him to his room. How does he know so much about sex? At his age I thought babies came from John Lewis. I feel sorry for Mrs Prescott. She looked very sad on telly, under her enormous hairdo and thick make-up. She must have thought she was safe with someone that revolting. How wrong she was. Granny Clegg is right—all politicians are sex cases.

. . . .

Thursday 27

Mum's purse has been raided again. And for £1.50 again. How does she know the exact amount? She has a tighter grip on finances than Gordon Brown. Mum has called an emergency family meeting at 6.30 (after tea and before David Attenborough) to identify the culprit.

6.45 p.m.
The culprit is James! He is being bullied for money with

menaces by Mad Harry (second toughest in the juniors, according to James, after Stephen 'Maggot' Mason, who eats mud). He has to pay him £1.50 a day or Mad Harry is threatening to beat up Mumtaz. James said it was a matter of love and honour. I'm not sure what Mum is more angry about—the money or the religious divide relationship. She is going into school tomorrow to talk to Reverend Begley about the bullying policy at St Regina's.

Friday 28
Mad Harry's mother has been called into school next week for a meeting with Mum. Reverend Begley is going to mediate. I do not rate Mrs Mad Harry's chances. Or Reverend Begley's. Mum is terrifying in a heated debate.

Saturday 29
Something utterly exciting is happening to Saffron Walden. Suzy is going to be on TV! She has been given her own sex show on Channel 5. It is going to be on at 2 a.m. on Fridays. She got spotted by one of the producers when she helped him with his perverted sexual problems. So now we will have three celebrities. Although the McGann has not been spotted for several weeks and there are fears he may have moved to Sawbridgeworth, which

has a Pizza Express. Mum will ban it for sure. I do not care. I will watch it at Scarlet's. They are going to video every episode so they can send it to Granny Stone in St Helier. Apparently she is very sexually progressive as well. She was the first woman in Jersey to get a delivery from Ann Summers.

Sunday 30
9 a.m.
Something is wrong with the dog. It has refused to eat its breakfast and is just pacing up and down.

9.30 a.m.
The Freeview box remote control is missing. Yet the channel keeps mysteriously changing of its own accord. Which is annoying enough except the dog is still pacing up and down and so I can't see what is going on anyway.

9.45 a.m.
Two mysteries solved. Dog belched and suddenly forbidden E4 came on. It has swallowed the remote. Dad is outraged. He is going to miss the Open unless Mr Mercer can do an emergency operation this afternoon and retrieve the controller. Grandpa is rubbing the dog's tummy to calm it. Which has stopped the pacing but the channel is now flicking furiously.

11.00 a.m.
Mr Mercer can do the operation but not until 3 p.m. as he is watching the golf. Dad is livid.

11.15 a.m.
James has had a genius suggestion. He is rubbing the dog's tummy until the golf comes on then he is going to take the dog out of range of the telly (i.e the shed) until it goes to the vet's. It will mean we have to watch Eurosport all day but Dad says it is a small price to pay to ensure he can study Tiger Woods's vice-like grip on his three iron.

2 p.m.
Dad happily watching golf. Treena is going to drive the dog to the vet's in the Passat.

2.15 p.m.
Dad not happily watching golf any more. The dog made a run for it when Treena let it out of the shed and it raced through the sitting room to get to Grandpa who was asleep with Baby Jesus and turned the telly to E4 on the eighteenth hole. And James can't get it to switch back. He fears the batteries may be flat. So now Dad is taking the dog to the vet anyway. At least we can watch *The OC* this afternoon.

4 p.m.
Dog is back. It has a shaven patch on its side again. It

seems happier though. The remote has been forensically cleansed by Mum and appears to be functioning normally. Which is a miracle given the other contents of the dog's stomach (a Bic biro, two buttons, and a sweetcorn holder, according to Mr Mercer).

SAFFRON
WALDEN

may

Monday 1

May Day Holiday

Went round Sad Ed's. He is totally over Tuesday now. Apparently he got a text from someone called Lisa in Year Nine yesterday asking if she could test out his legendary snogging powers. His reputation will overtake Sean Woodley at this rate. He will be able to oust him from the upper school toilets. I reminded him of his pledge to be celibate and misunderstood. He said I had misunderstood him, so he was already halfway there. Ha ha.

. . . .

Tuesday 2

Mrs Mad Harry has taken full blame for the bullying incident. Apparently he was also extorting money from Douglas Pole, who has diabetes, and Archie Knox, son of hairy librarian Mr Knox, who has premature shaving issues. She has suggested the two boys 'get to know each other better' to quash their differences. Mum is not entirely happy but has agreed. She says James needs more contact with normal boys (as opposed to Mumtaz).

. . . .

Wednesday 3

Have dentist appointment with sadistic Mrs Wong tomorrow. Am going to dose up on Nurofen in anticipation. James is coming too. He is not scared. Mrs Wong says he has the teeth of a Great White. Which is

411

totally unfair, given his demerara habit. Although he is vigorous bordering on the obsessive with his brushing routine.

. . . .

Thursday 4

Yet another filling. I will have no teeth left by the time I am sixteen. Mrs Wong said she blames the parents for letting children overdose on Coca-Cola and Gummi Bears. I said chance would be a fine thing. Or at least I would have had my mouth not been filled with blood and gritty filling bits.

. . . .

Friday 5

John Prescott has been sacked for his giant sex romp with his secretary. Tony Blair has given his job to sinister Ruth Kelly. That is a good move. There is no way she will be caught in a sex scandal. She makes Mum look permissive.

Plus, the road sign to Saffron Walden from the A11 has gone missing. Mum has rung up the council to complain. She says it could lose the town literally hundreds of pounds in tourist revenue. She says Mike is backing her campaign (the missing sign was spotted during her dual carriageway lesson this afternoon). They are going to the press (i.e. the *Walden Chronicle*) if the council doesn't act within the week. Dad says she will be the talk of the town if she joins forces with Mr Wandering Hands. Mum says

she doesn't care, they have taken Saffron Walden off the map and it is a matter of principle. (Actually this once really happened—Saffron Walden wasn't on a WHSmith Road Map. I have never seen Mum so militaristic. WHSmith had to do a national recall and reprint the whole thing. Apparently Plymouth and Milton Keynes were missing as well. I am not surprised. It is because they are totally pants places and no one would want to visit them anyway.)

Saturday 6

Mad Harry came over for tea. It was not the bonding experience Mrs Mad Harry had hoped for. First he encouraged James to feed jigsaw puzzle pieces (Windsor Castle) to the dog, then he climbed on the shed roof and refused to come down until he got a packet of Hula Hoops. Mum had to call Mrs Mad Harry to collect him early. James begged Mum not to send Harry away though. So her plan to oust Mumtaz has backfired. She has acquired Satan in nine-year-old form instead.

Mum is right to be concerned. At one point Mad Harry tried to look up my vintage skirt. He is a menace.

Sunday 7

Barry the Blade has been kidnapped. Treena says he got bundled into a car outside the White Horse last night. I

413

asked Treena whether she had called the police and she said they were singing 'Chirpy Chirpy Cheep Cheep' on the karaoke in the saloon bar at the time so she didn't bother. Have made her call them now. Her description of the car was disappointing however—she said it was blue with a 'thingy' on the bonnet.

∙ ∙

Monday 8

Mr Wilmott reminded us we all have mock exams in two weeks. He says we should not be misled by the word 'mock', they are totally important and real and should be treated as such. He is lying. He is just trying to avoid a repeat of last year when only ten people passed maths and no one turned up at all for mock Rural Studies. Am going to revise though. Have decided my best route to tragedy is to get into Cambridge or Oxford and study classic literature. I will be totally like Sylvia Plath and that one off *Mission Impossible 3* and will meet all sorts of future politicians and philosophers and be inspired by the ancient architecture and traditions. Unlike at Stoke on Trent University (formerly Derbyshire Adult Education Centre), whose alumni include Justin's cousin Bez. According to him, the only traditions are the annual Angel Delight eating competition. He got a 2.2 in media studies and is now working in Dixons. So he is in a related profession at least.

∙ ∙

Tuesday 9

The police rang for Treena. Barry the Blade has been found alive and well. Apparently he was a willing participant initially as Stacey O'Grady had promised him a 'bunk-up' with Mrs Simpson if he got in the boot of his Toyota. Only then he and Darryl Stamp drove Barry to Haverhill and left him on the B1054 with no trousers. The police seem quite excited though. They think they could secure Saffron Walden's first ever ASBO, thanks to Treena. Mum is seething. She has been trying to secure a brace of ASBOs for over a year to no avail and now she has been beaten to it by a Northerner in leggings.

Wednesday 10

Communal showers have been banned after PE due to the ongoing water shortages. This is excellent news so now we will not have to witness the vastness of Fat Kylie's bottom and I will not have to be subjected to 'hilarious' jokes about my 32A chest. Not that anyone actually showered anyway—we just got our feet wet and ran round the changing room in case Miss Vicar came in for inspection. On the downside it means that Oona Rickets will have to be quarantined.

Thursday 11

Barry the Blade's kidnap is the cover story of the *Walden Chronicle*. It says:

415

> ## WALDEN JOINS ASBO WARS AS POLICE PULL THE PLUG ON O'GRADY SHOW
>
> Clean-living Saffron Walden is set to hand out its first-ever ASBO to habitual nuisances Stacey O'Grady and Darryl Stamp, the criminal minds behind last year's heist at Mr Patel's. It follows their kidnapping of Barry Hooton (also known as Barry the Blade, or Mental Barry) and attempts to 'pimp' out local madwoman 'Lilo' Lil Simpson. The police say crucial evidence came from community-minded Treena Nichols, twenty-nine-year-old mother of baby Jesus, who witnessed the events from her bar stool at the White Horse.

Treena is worried the O'Gradys are going to stalk and possibly grievous bodily harm her. She is going to call the police and demand witness protection for her, Grandpa, and Baby Jesus. Grandpa said it would mean they would never be able to walk the streets of Walden again, but Treena said they would get a new house and the dog could come—they could dye its hair. Mum is hoping they do have to change their identities. She is getting sick of

the endless smell of toxic nappies and dribble on the M&S sofa. Plus now she has been out-manoeuvred on the anti-anti-social behaviour front by Treena, which has called her entire existence into question.

• •

Friday 12

Mum is putting in for an early driving test. She has scored a hundred per cent on all her Highway Code quizzes including the notoriously tricky flying motorbike sign. Dad said the sooner she was out of Mike's wandering hand range the better. But Mum said she was thinking of doing the advanced driver course immediately so Dad stormed off to polish his golf clubs. Anyone would think Mike Majors was some kind of irresistible George Clooney type. I have seen him, he looks like Eamonn Holmes with a moustache.

Also, the police have refused to put Treena and Grandpa under witness protection. They say they are under financial pressure and struggling with the Alsatian budget as it is—they are on own-brand Netto instead of high quality Pedigree Chum. Treena is disappointed. So is Mum. She was planning to re-woodchip their room (Jesus and James have picked out all the chips in the current wallpaper). Luckily Fat Kylie is not speaking to Stacey at the moment after he ran over Tupac's foot in his Toyota. So she is on our side.

• •

Saturday 13

James has gone round Mad Harry's for the day. Mumtaz called for him so I lied and said he was at the library. But she said she had already checked there and I should be ashamed of myself. I said I was and confessed the truth. Mumtaz did not sound happy. She said Mad Harry is a bad influence and is heading for a life of crime.

Told James Mumtaz had called. He said he was 'laying off the "ho"s for a while' so Mum sent him to his room to reflect on his sexist attitude. Grandpa said it was good James was building up his defences against the never-ending demands of the opposite sex so young so Mum sent him to his room as well.

Sunday 14

Terry has got a black eye. Grandpa and James saw him when they were walking the dog round the block and Terry was letting Fiddy and the puppies poo on Marjory's gravel. Grandpa asked him if he had been mugged. Terry said he was the victim of domestic violence. James said it goes to show Mad Harry is right. All women are mentalists. Terry said, 'Too right, son.' Then the dog tried for a repeat performance with Fiddy so they all came home.

Grandpa is jubilant. He says not even the snip can keep a Riley down.

Monday 15

The A11 roadsign is back. It says 'Saffron Wallden—twinned with Bad Wildungen and Chichicastenango.' Mum has already rung the council. She says she would rather have no sign than a misspelt one.

On the plus side, I did not know we were twinned with Chichicastenango. Have looked it up on Google. It is a deprived village in Guatemala. Excellent. I am going to suggest a cultural school exchange to Ms Hopwood-White. It will be far more mind-expanding than the usual French one, which just involves wandering around Carrefour and dancing to crap Euro-pop. We will be able to live in stone huts with indigenous peoples and grind coffee beans. It is utterly romantic.

Tuesday 16

Ms Hopwood-White did not seem too keen on cultural Guatemalan exchange programme. She says she went to Nicaragua after her finals and spent two weeks in hospital after drinking a shamanic asthma remedy. Plus Mr Wilmott is still wavering on rubber-stamping foreign field trips following last year's Paris disaster. Will get Mum to write a letter. She is good at the art of persuasion.

5 p.m.

Mum says I am going to Guatemala over her dead body. It is riddled with revolutionaries and I will be killed or

infected with dysentery within five minutes of landing. I should have got Scarlet to talk to Suzy instead. She is always going on protests to back Fidel Castro and other South American freedom fighter types.

. . . .

Wednesday 17

Saw Tuesday after school in her new uniform. She was in Mr Patel's, which is totally out of bounds to Quaker school students, according to unwritten John Major High rules. She is lucky Fat Kylie wasn't there to enforce them. Tuesday evil-eyed me over the Pot Noodle machine so I evil-eyed her back. So she said 'bothered' and went back to reading *NME* with Daisy Truelove Jones. They are suited to each other. Daisy is a pseudo-tragic type as well. She claimed that her dad works in films but it turned out that he owns BJ Video (aka Blow Job Video, actually Bob Jones Video).

. . . .

Thursday 18

Oh God, just remembered have mocks on Monday. Will start gruelling revision schedule after school in bid to escape middle-class clutches of Saffron Walden and get into Oxford.

7 p.m.

Why, oh why did I opt for geography? I cannot remember where the Isle of Man is let alone the rest of the world.

Called Sad Ed for advice and possible joint revision session but he was doing text sex with some Year Nines. He has reinvented himself as a sort of love guru. He says the celibacy thing just seems to make them keener.

. . . .

Friday 19

Have had emergency pep talk from Mr Wilmott about mocks. He says our lives depend on them (he is in panic mode because we are being Ofsteded next month). Am totally going to revise all weekend. Scarlet is coming over tomorrow so we can do cosines and remember whose side Stalin was on.

. . . .

Saturday 20

Strict revision schedule not going according to plan due to interruptions from:

a) The dog (trying to get at our brain-stimulating chocolate);

b) Mad Harry (offering Scarlet fifty pence for a look at her bra);

c) Baby Jesus (inexplicable hatred of Grand Prix coverage).

. . . .

Sunday 21

Went round Scarlet's. Suzy says the secret of passing

exams is not to worry too much. Plus to write stuff on your legs and surreptitiously look up your skirt if you get stuck. This is how she got As in all her O Levels.

Suzy was rehearsing for her TV series. She starts filming in three weeks in Les Dennis's old *Family Fortunes* studio. The show is called *Sex with Suzy* and she is going to delve into celebrities' sex lives and give them useful tips on the way. Her first guest is Jeffrey Archer. I said I was surprised he had a sex life. She said she is going to talk to him about prisons and masturbation.

Monday 22
9 a.m.
Feeling totally prepared. Have followed Suzy's advice and have large sections of *The Crucible* on thighs in blue Bic.

3 p.m.
Was not drama. That is tomorrow. It was maths. Am going to fail it.

Tuesday 23
Am also going to fail drama.

Wednesday 24
And French.

Thursday 25

And Rural Studies. Jack was lying about it being a cinch. There were all sorts of revolting questions about goat gestation periods and mastitis.

. . . .

Friday 26

8 a.m.

At least will pass English. Literature is my life so will breeze it easily even though have only read three pages of *The Tempest*.

3 p.m.

Who is Ariel? Must be comedy laundrywoman or something. That will be where name comes from.

5 p.m.

Oh God, have just checked. Am going to fail English as well. Have written 200 words on importance of mad magical laundrywoman in Shakespearean tragedy.

. . . .

Saturday 27

10 a.m.

Something is going on over the road. A suitcase has just flown out of Cherie and Terry's bedroom window.

10.05 a.m.

Followed by several vests and other undergarments.

10.15 a.m.
Terry is now on the front 'lawn' (scorched brown patch)
piling alarmingly small pants into the suitcase while Cherie
and Thin Kylie throw socks and shoes out of the window.
Am not sure what is going on. Mum is hovering by the
phone—the situation is fraught with ASBO potential.

10.20 a.m.
Marjory has arrived to peer through our double glazing
(the view is better as we have no obscuring hydrangeas in
the way (outlawed for being unnaturally blue)). She says
Clive saw him coming out of the Saffron Hotel with Lorna
Green, who works on the Waitrose checkouts, so he has
possibly been having an affair! That would explain the
black eye as well.

10.45 a.m.
Terry has loaded his Cherokee with the suitcase, the
abdominizer, and two of the puppies and has driven off. I
hope one of them wasn't Bruce. Granny Clegg is expecting
delivery any day soon. Although frankly they all look the
same—hairy and mental. Cherie is now playing Take That
at full volume. Am going over the road to offer sympathy
to Thin Kylie at this tragic time.

11.15 a.m.
May have worsened situation. I said I was sorry to
hear about Terry and Lorna from Waitrose. Cherie said,

'Who? I thought he was just doing that girl from the bookies. The lying bastard!' Then she turned up the volume on Gary Barlow. Thin Kylie is gutted. She says Terry was supposed to be taking her, Cherie, and Fat Kylie to Faliraki for half term and now she'll have to go to Butlins with the O'Gradys. I asked her if it was this bad when her real dad left. She said, 'Are you, like, mental? My real dad only took me to Clacton. God, you are so f**king retarded.' So I left her to her grief. Will go back tomorrow when she is ready to share her feelings.

- -

Sunday 28

Went to console Thin Kylie but she was out at an illegal minibike race with Mark Lambert and Mr Hosepipe. Cherie looked terrible. She was in her pink dressing gown eating cherry liqueur chocolates and watching *Popworld* with Fiddy and the puppies. I asked her if she needed anything and she said, 'A packet of Benson and Hedges and a vibrator.' I said I would have to pass on the cigarettes as Mr Patel knows I am underage but that she should call Suzy about the vibrator. She is always willing to help in that department.

James says the lottery is to blame. Statistically lottery winners are thirty-seven per cent more likely to be adulterous than non-winners. He Googled it.

- -

Monday 29
Bank Holiday
Half term.

Called Scarlet to see if she wanted to go and lurk outside Goddard's later (Justin is working all half term—he has been promoted to the till temporarily because Mr Goddard is at his sister's in Weston-Super-Mare) but there was no answer. Then remembered they have all gone to Jersey to see Granny Stone. Why do we never go away on holiday? (Actually, see February 20th for catalogue of reasons.) Asked Mum if we could go to Cornwall (even St Slaughter would be more interesting than Saffron Walden). But Mum says there is no way we can all fit into Bellevue unless I want to share a single bed with James (not) or a room with Granny and Grandpa Clegg (double not) plus Auntie Joyless has vowed never to let a Riley darken her doorstep again. I said this was exactly why my Guatemalan exchange was a good idea otherwise how would I ever get to learn about other cultures. So Mum said she would take me to Cambridge to look at the Aztec pipe players busking outside Gap. This is typical. It is because Mum did not leave a ten-mile radius of Redruth until she was eighteen.

Went round Sad Ed's to commiserate. We have decided to make the most of our lot and culturally explore Saffron Walden for the next five days. We are going to start with the cemetery tomorrow. Sad Ed says someone famous and poetic is bound to be buried there.

Tuesday 30

There is no one famous buried in the cemetery unless you count Niall O'Grady, notorious uncle of Fat Kylie etc. O'Grady, who accidentally blew himself up with a can of hairspray in 1989. We are going to go to the museum instead tomorrow to immerse ourselves in Saffron Walden's grim medieval past.

Wednesday 31

Have given up on cultural Saffron Walden experience. Since when are stuffed ducks historical? Plus Mr Cremin, who dusts the exhibits, got annoyed with Sad Ed's text sex beeping and asked us to leave as we were disturbing the other three visitors.

Thursday 1

Cherie came over to ask if Dad could pop round later and help her undo some jars. She said she would ask Clive but he looks like he has weak wrists and Dad's look much more manly. Mum did not seem too thrilled but said she would send him over after his casserole. Cherie looked a lot better. Her make-up was in the right place and she didn't smell of Bacardi. Plus she was wearing a Wonderbra so she is definitely back on form.

7 p.m.

Dad has gone to unscrew Cherie's jam or whatever it is.

8 p.m.

Dad is not back. Mum says nothing takes that long to undo, not even Granny Clegg's rhubarb and potato chutney (1985 vintage).

8.30 p.m.

Dad still not back. Mum is going to send James over if he is not home by 9. Grandpa asked why she wasn't sending him but she said James is more authoritative.

8.55 p.m.

Dad is back but has drunk four daiquiris and a Harvey Wallbanger and has been sent to bed. It was not jam. It was maraschino cherries and peaches in brandy.

Friday 2

8.30 a.m.

Dad is too hungover to go to work. Mum has phoned in sick claiming he has food poisoning—not a total lie, it could have been a rogue maraschino cherry that put him over the edge. I asked why she never did that for me and she said Dad would wish he was in work by the time she had finished with him. She is not happy about him lingering at Cherie's with his manly wrists.

10 a.m.

Dad has gone to work. Mum's Spanish Inquisition style questioning was too much for him. He insists that nothing untoward occurred and that Cherie just had a lot of cocktail-related jars that needed undoing but Mum is unconvinced. Then Dad said Mum was in no position to talk, seeing as she was about to spend forty-five minutes within a foot of Mike Major's molesting fingers so Mum said, 'That man is a saint whereas Cherie Britcher makes Madonna look like a nun,' so Dad got the Passat keys and his briefcase and left. He is still wearing his M&S moccasin slippers. I do not know how he is going to explain that to Mr Wainwright. All this arguing is very disturbing. I am definitely going to be in care by the end of term at this rate. Maybe Suzy and Bob will take me in. Then I could become totally interesting and sexually advanced. And vegetarian.

. . . .

Saturday 3

Mum and Dad have made up. Mum says it is tension due to general overcrowding and the constant demands on her array of cleaning products. Dad has promised to tackle the situation head on. He is taking Grandpa to see an estate agent about renting a flat for them this afternoon.

3 p.m.

The rental situation is not promising. Grandpa turned down all three flats on the books of Mullock, Mullock, and Cheffin. One because it was painted yellow, the second because it had the 'wrong sort of electricity', and the last because it is above Abrakebabra and Treena doesn't like looking at the elephant leg in the window (though she will happily eat it). Dad said beggars can't be choosers but Grandpa said he wasn't begging. He is quite happy in Summerdale Road. Mum is going to pester Mr Lemon again. Dad offered but she said he had already proven his ineffectiveness.

. . . .

Sunday 4

Whit Sunday

Granny Clegg rang to check up on Bruce. James answered and said that he had seen him eating gravel the day before and that he is living in a broken home now that racist Terry has run off with Lisa from Tony's Turf Accountants. Granny Clegg demanded to speak to Dad and has instructed him to

433

remove Bruce from the Britchers' forthwith and bring him down to Cornwall so she can put him in the St Slaughter fete 'most lovable pet' competition. There is no chance he will win. He has bad breath. Plus, if he takes after his father he will be sick during the ceremony. Dad is going to pick him up later and then drive him down next Saturday. Mum is not happy. She says Granny Clegg will not know if we leave Bruce there an extra week but Dad said that Granny Clegg had threatened to get on the bus and collect him herself tomorrow and we all know what happened last time she tried to use public transport.

4 p.m.
Dad has gone to fetch Bruce. Mum has sent James with him to make sure he doesn't lurk at the Britchers' too long, plus she has made Dad wear gloves to cover up his manly wrists.

5 p.m.
Bruce has arrived. Mum has cordoned him off in the kitchen using Jesus's playpen (Jesus is in a makeshift arrangement of clothes airers, but as he seems to take after Treena in the not moving and watching telly stakes, it is fairly safe). The dog is going mental and throwing itself at the kitchen door. Grandpa keeps telling him that Bruce is his own flesh and blood but the dog does not seem moved by this at all. It has already broken one hinge and is fast loosening the second.

6 p.m.

The dog has knocked itself out on the kitchen door and is being revived with brandy. To make matters worse, Bruce squeezed through the playpen bars and got into the cereal cupboard. The kitchen is a sea of Shreddies. He has now been moved to safer quarters i.e. Marjory's cat carrier. Mum has suggested Dad takes the day off work tomorrow to drive Bruce to his new home. Dad says there is no way he can cancel Jeremy from Head Office to chauffeur a puppy to the Cleggs'.

* *

Monday 5

8 a.m.

Dad is driving to the Cleggs'. Overnight, Bruce ate the cat carrier door, a box of apricot muesli, and two tea towels. Plus the dog, who was locked in the shed for safety reasons, bit the lid off a tin of creosote and is now highly flammable.

11 p.m.

Dad is back. He says that is positively the last time he is traipsing down to the back of beyond to do favours for a Clegg. Apparently Bruce ate the tuning knob off the radio. So Dad had to listen to Kiss FM for a total of twelve hours. He says he may well need counselling.

* *

Tuesday 6

We are going on a school trip to the ballet in three weeks! It is to see former Retard and Criminal Davey MacDonald in his debut performance in *Swan Lake*. He is in the corps de ballet so he is probably a tree or something. Mark Lambert has forbidden Thin Kylie to go. He is worried she will fall for his penis-revealing special needs again and dump him. Thin Kylie said, 'Don't be a twat, he's, like, a poof now, innit, like that Billy Elliott.' So Ms Hopwood-White sent them both to Mr Wilmott before it got out of hand. She says she is resorting to preventative punishment in order to keep the peace. Maybe Davey MacDonald is gay now though. That would be excellent. Then I would know a genuine homosexual. As opposed to Oona Rickets who is swinging all ways.

. . . .

Wednesday 7

Suzy has gone to London to start filming for Channel 5 today. Scarlet says she did not sleep at all last night and has taken two valium to calm her nerves. Luckily they sent a car to pick her up or she would never have got there. Bob had to carry her and strap her in as it was. I asked if it was a stretch limousine with a uniformed chauffeur but apparently it was a dented Granada driven by a fat man called Steve. We are going to Scarlet's on Friday to watch it being broadcast. It is at 2 a.m. so we are sleeping over. I said I hoped Jack had invited Justin.

Scarlet said she hoped he hadn't as Trevor was going to be there and she didn't want them to brawl over her in her goth pyjamas. I said this was unlikely as Trevor would definitely lose given his gothic pallor and weedy forearms. Then Scarlet got all shirty. I don't know why—I am just pointing out the facts.

Thursday 8

Cherie came over after school to ask if Dad could change the fuse on her hair straighteners. Mum said he was out all evening at the Round Table voting on who will be Carnival Chairman, now that Graham Ferris is moving to Sudbury, and that she should try Mr Atkinson at number 18. This is a lie. He is due back at 9. Mum is clearly not taking any risks with Dad and his manly charms. Since when did Dad become a sex god? It is very disturbing.

It is Suzy's sex programme sleepover tomorrow. Have told Mum we are going to bed straight after the *News at Ten*. This is not a total lie. But have not mentioned that Jack is under strict instructions to wake us up at 1.30 a.m. Oh please let Justin be there. I am going to wear my Top-shop-style boxer short pyjama things especially (note the word style, rather than actual. In fact a pair of Dad's old boxer shorts and a vest top—Mum has refused to let me go to Cambridge to buy 'draughty nightwear' just because I have seen it on TV).

Friday 9

10.30 p.m.

Have just watched this year's *Big Brother* for the first time. Now I know why Mum banned it. It is like being a fly on the wall in the Retards and Criminals room. Maybe that is how they pick contestants. Justin is not here. Apparently he is grounded on Fridays until GCSEs are over. What an unenlightened mother he has. Something else we have in common.

Plans to actually go to sleep have been abandoned. We are all going to watch DVDs in the den. Scarlet and Trevor are hovering in the seventies loveswing thing like a pair of giant bats, Sad Ed is on a pouffe with a box of Green and Black organic pralines, which leaves me and Jack on the sofabed. Am determined not to feel any untoward urges to touch his hair or anything weird like that so have wedged a pillow between us. Jack has wedged several cushions. Not that he has any untoward urges obviously. He has made that clear. It is to ward me off.

. . . .

Saturday 10

8 a.m.

Oh God. Have just woken up with head on Jack's shoulder and drool making a wet patch on his Snow Patrol T-shirt. Thank God he is still asleep. Must have climbed over pillow and cushion barrier in sleepwalking-style incident. Plus have totally missed *Sex with Suzy*. Why did no one wake me up?

Would ask Sad Ed but he is asleep under pile of chocolate wrappers with remote control welded into his hand. Scarlet and Trevor are still hovering menacingly. It is not normal.

9 a.m.
Apparently no one managed to stay awake. Except Sad Ed, who switched over to a *Babylon Five* marathon on Bravo and forgot to switch back. So we have just watched it on video. Suzy was brilliant. She got Jeffrey Archer to discuss deep thrusts. Bob says she is like Paula Yates, before the heroin but after Michael Hutchence. We are all going into town for 'brunch' (aka toast and mini pots of marmalade at Eaden Lilleys—I don't think Saffron Walden does eggs overeasy yet) to celebrate.

1 p.m.
Suzy is an overnight star. Barry the Blade, Mr Whippy, and (weirdly) Mrs Noakes have all commented on her performance. Even the least famous McGann (not in Sawbridgeworth after all, but apparently filming an episode of *Holby City*) gave her a funny look. He is worried his superstar status is going to be usurped. Got home to find Mad Harry and James trying on my underwear. James is going to be heading the way of Kyle O'Grady if this carries on. Am going to have to rekindle his interest in Mumtaz. She would never walk round with an M&S training bra over her ears.

Sunday 11

Granny Clegg rang. Bruce did not win the most lovable pet competition. One of Hester's chickens that looks like it is doing the macarena triumphed. Granny Clegg is outraged. She cannot understand how the judges could have overlooked Bruce's charms for a dancing hen. Although possibly the fact that he ate the microphone and a kilo of Maureen Penrice's heavy duty flapjack had something to do with it.

Monday 12

Scarlet and Jack are enjoying new-found fame at school now that they are the offspring of a TV sex guru. Jack has been invited to the Upper Sixth Cheese and Wine anti-war night—unheard of in John Major history. And Mr Wilmott asked Scarlet if her mother might like to take over from Miss Vicar for this year's sex education lesson—he is trying to be progressive now that the Burger King Sports Academy in Bishop's Stortford has had a guest lecture from braless TV legend Charlie Dimmock. I predict he will regret this decision though. It is fraught with potential perverts-in-schools issues. At least he did not ask my mother. Her version would involve plenty of moist wipes and a bucket.

Tuesday 13

Mum is jubilant. Mr Whippy has been rehoused. He is moving out of his ice-cream van and into a three-bed

440

semi behind Homebase. Now there are only two O'Gradys to go. Mum is thinking of suggesting they all move in with Mr Whippy considering the spacious accommodation he has been given, but James pointed out that that would be like a mini criminal lair and would only encourage anti-social behaviour as they swapped tips on burgling.

Wednesday 14

Granny Clegg rang to update us on Bruce's progress. Apparently Grandpa Clegg is training him to fetch his socks for him. I do not envy Bruce. I have seen Grandpa Clegg's feet and I would not want anything that touched them near my mouth.

Thursday 15

Granny Clegg rang again. Today Bruce has only weed on the telly four times. Mum says Granny Clegg does not need to ring every day—a weekly update will be fine.

Friday 16

Granny Clegg rang again. But it was not about Bruce. It is because St Slaughter has a new dentist and he is black! He is called Mr Nuamah and has moved from Cardiff. Grandpa Clegg is going bonkers. He says he would not

have written to his MP to complain about the lack of dental provision if this was what was going to happen. I pointed out that this was racist but Grandpa Clegg says he is not being racist, he is being practical. He would rather his teeth fall out than have them put under a voodoo spell. I said the Welsh were not renowned for their practising of dark magic but Grandpa Clegg says he once knew a woman from Abergavenny who could turn herself into a goat. There is no answer to that.

Suzy is doing snooker legend Steve Davis tonight. Thank God Mum has not noticed this addition to the TV schedules yet. It is because she snips the Channel 5 column out of the *Radio Times* so that no one is tempted to watch *Trisha* or *Columbo*.

. . . .

Saturday 17

Went into town with James to buy Father's Day cards and presents (chocolate golf balls—me, a *Dr Who* poster— James). Bumped into Thin Kylie in the *Hello* magazine section of WHSmith. I said it must be awful not knowing where to send a Father's Day card. She said she knows exactly where he is—in the Chestnuts B&B with Les and Ying because Lisa from Tony's has thrown him out. He has been secretly ringing Kylie to get her to persuade Cherie to take him back, but apparently Cherie says she has moved on and is pursuing more sophisticated men who do not have tattoos of Pamela Anderson on their

bum. I hope she does not mean Dad. She will never wrest him from Mum's vice-like grip anyway.

. . . .

Sunday 18
Father's Day

Dad is delighted with his presents. He has already eaten the chocolate golf balls (Mum was out taking Jesus for a walk, or they would have been rationed). He says he will take the poster to work though. Mum will never let him put it up in the house—not because of the subject matter but due to her ban on Blu-Tack and drawing pins. However, he has been outdone in the present stakes by Grandpa who got three (Dad, Jesus, and the dog. Uncle Jim did not send anything. He is still too busy finding himself up a mountain in Tibet with his wife Sunflower (not her real name—she changed it from Felicity)).

. . . .

Monday 19

It is Jack's first GCSE today. Bob and Suzy are very philosophical and have told him that if he fails he can always go to Braintree College and do a foundation course in Rock Music (avec Justin), but apparently Jack is determined to stay on for sixth form because you can't do politics at Braintree (ousted from the timetable in favour of NVQ hairdressing, and bricklaying for beginners). He is hoping to become the first ever person

to simultaneously win the Mercury Prize and become Foreign Secretary.

. . . .

Tuesday 20

Oh God, it is parents' evening tomorrow. Mr Wilmott gave a talk in assembly about how it is nothing to worry about and is all about constructive criticism and making sure everyone reaches their potential, however thick. (He didn't say thick, he said challenged. He means thick.) He is wrong. It is totally something to worry about. What if Mum finds out about the E in French and the internet translator? I am doomed. At least mock results have been delayed until next term. Mr Wilmott says there has been an administrative error but I bet Mrs Leech has mislaid them under a packet of Gypsy Creams again.

. . . .

Wednesday 21

6 p.m.

Mum and Dad (his first ever) have gone to parents' evening. Oh, please let something miraculous happen so that Mum forgets to see Ms Hopwood-White.

8 p.m.

My prayers were answered! Mum and Dad are back from parents' evening already, but are not speaking to each other. Dad has a black eye and Mum is lying down in the

dark and no one will tell me what has happened. Will have to phone Scarlet. Suzy will know everything and has no inhibitions about blabbing.

9 p.m.
According to Suzy, Terry showed up to assert his parental responsibility for Thin Kylie (this is a joke—he is utterly irresponsible, he once let her ride around on the roof of the Cherokee with no restraints) so Cherie decided to assert her maternal responsibility and smacked him with her faux Chanel handbag. So Dad tried to calm them both down but Cherie said, 'See, that's what a real man does, Terry, he fights with his brains,' so Terry said, 'Well—can his brains outwit this?' and then thumped Dad (answer— no), so then Cherie got out her Clairol and hairsprayed Terry and Dad at which point Mr Wilmott arrived with Miss Vicar who wrestled both men to the floor at once. Miss Leech had to be called to administer hot tea and Optrex to several bystanders who got caught in the giant cloud of Clairol. No wonder Mum is not speaking to Dad. It is totally Jerry Springer.

10 p.m.
Mum has just demanded to know why Suzy was signing autographs at parents' evening. I said it is because of her attempts to overthrow evil Conservative MP Hugo Thorndyke. Mum said she doubted it. One of them was for Miss Vicar and she votes Socialist Worker. I do not

want her to find out about *Sex with Suzy*. She may ban me from seeing Scarlet who is my only source of advice, black clothing, and croissants.

. . . .

Thursday 22

Too late. Suzy is on the front page of the *Walden Chronicle*. It is under the headline 'Sex-crazed and Stoned—is Suzy giving Saffron Walden a bad name?'

The article says:

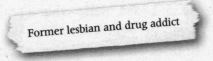

Former lesbian and drug addict

(this is following Suzy's on-screen confession to a snog with her flatmate Carol in 1989 under the influence of three bottles of Mateus Rosé and her election confession to inhaling marijuana)

is causing a stir in sedate Saffron Walden with her X-rated TV show in which celebrities literally bare all

(Suzy managed to get some bloke off *EastEnders* to reveal his unusual penis in last week's show).

The paper has been inundated with literally nine complaints about the sordid series. Hugo Thorndyke MP says it is nothing less than he expected from his political adversary. 'This is typical of the Labour Party and just goes to show how right the electorate were to reject Mrs Stone and her manifesto for a sexual free-for-all.'

(Not strictly true—her manifesto was mostly about tax credits and free fruit in schools).

Mrs Sylvia Thorndyke, chief of the Uttlesford Women's Institute and 4th (Baptist Church) Troop Brown Owl agrees. 'It is her children I feel sorry for. What hope for them turning out normal?' (Turn to page 14 for Sylvia's delicious recipe for macaroons).

Scarlet says Suzy is not bothered. The *Guardian* has called her Channel 5's answer to Nigella with her 'heaving bosom and come hither eyes'. Suzy is doing Nigella later in the series so it will be an overdose of heaving bosoms and come hithering. Grandpa Riley will not be able to contain himself.

Friday 23

Mum is still annoyed about the Suzy thing. She is getting Dad to video tonight's episode (Lorraine Kelly) so that she can inspect it and decide whether to fire off complaint letters. James said the programme was actually quite informative so Mum asked how he had seen it and Grandpa Riley went very quiet. They are now shampooing the dog as punishment.

5.30 p.m.

Shampooing the dog has been banned. There is foam in every kitchen cranny. From now on he has to go to Dog About Town in Stansted.

Saturday 24

Dad accidentally videoed Open University. Mum is going to complain about that instead. They misspelt Venn, as in diagram.

Sunday 25

There is a black-dentist-related emergency in St Slaughter. Granny Clegg has a gippy wisdom tooth and says Hester's traditional remedy (gin) is not working. Mum has told her she has to make an appointment with Mr Nuamah tomorrow morning. Granny Clegg says she will blame

Mum if she comes back dead. Mum said she was willing to take that risk. Dad said we can only pray.

Monday 26

Granny Clegg has an appointment with Mr Nuamah at 10 tomorrow. Grandpa Clegg is going with her to protect her from hexes.

Tuesday 27

Granny Clegg has rung. Apparently Mr Nuamah has hands 'like the good Lord himself' and has 'miraculously' cured the gippy wisdom tooth (i.e given her a filling). Also he gave Bruce a sugar-free lollipop. She is a complete convert. Grandpa Clegg is livid.

It is the school ballet trip tomorrow. It is totally exciting as it is in London and we are allowed to go early and sightsee (i.e. go to the giant Topshop). I am going to buy a prom dress and fluorescent eyeshadow as seen on Lily Allen who I am absolutely like. Except that she lives in Camden and has probably done it with at least five people and has a renowned psychotic actor for a dad. Why, oh why, can't Keith Allen be my dad. The whole parents' evening/Cherie fight would have had a very different outcome then. I bet Tuesday knows Lily. They probably snogged each other in an ironic manner at Peaches Geldof's party. God, it is so unfair.

Wednesday 28

No prom dress or fluorescent eyeshadow. Ballet trip as follows:

3 p.m.
Bus driver 'Fat' Len Viceroy arrives at school in ancient coach, complete with utter lack of in-flight entertainment and overwhelming smell of sick.

3.05 p.m.
Year Ten boards coach.

3.10 p.m.
Year Ten unboards coach after sick discovered on back seat.

3.15 p.m.
Year Ten reboards coach.

3.20 p.m.
Year Ten unboards coach because there are twenty people too many.

3.25 p.m.
Ms Hopwood-White weeds out the Retards and Criminals trying to catch a lift to Harlow and Year Ten reboards coach.

3.30 p.m.
Coach finally departs for London.

4.00 p.m.
Coach stops at services with suspicious rattle coming from luggage area. Mechanic called. Year Ten allowed to access motorway services.

5 p.m.
Mechanic arrives. Suspicious rattle identified as Dean 'the dwarf' Denley who has been stowed away against his will by Fat Kylie. Mrs Denley called to collect him.

5.15 p.m.
Mrs Denley arrives (surprisingly tall) and coach given the all-clear to proceed to London.

5.16 p.m.
Thin Kylie and Mark Lambert reported missing, last seen heading towards the Travelodge. Fat Kylie reported missing, last seen in arcade eating a Double Whopper and playing 'Resident Evil'.

5.40 p.m.
Thin Kylie and Mark Lambert located in Travelodge bedroom. Ms Hopwood-White agrees to pay for 'soiled sheets'. Fat Kylie located in Dunkin Donuts queue.

5.45 p.m.
Coach proceeds to London.

6.45 p.m.
Ms Hopwood-White points out to Len Viceroy that, as far as she remembers, St Albans is not a suburb of London.

7 p.m.
Curtain goes up on *Swan Lake*.

8.45 p.m.
Coach arrives at Sadler's Wells. Year Ten enters auditorium to general shushing and tutting noises.

9 p.m.
Davey MacDonald appears on stage in a tutu and swan helmet-type thing. Year Ten braces itself for Mark Lambert's reaction.

9.01 p.m.
Mark Lambert lives up to reputation and shouts, 'Oi, MacDonald, you retarded bender, guess who's knobbing Thin Kylie now?'

9.02 p.m.
Davey MacDonald departs stage and storms up auditorium still in swan helmet and tutu.

9.04 p.m.
Mark Lambert declared victor having knocked Davey MacDonald out with a pair of opera glasses.

9.15 p.m.
Year Ten told to leave auditorium and reboard coach.

9.20 p.m.
Coach departs London for Saffron Walden.

12 midnight
Coach arrives in Saffron Walden following detours to Potters Bar and Royston.

12.05 a.m.
Len Viceroy treated for shock by Mrs Leech with her preferred method of custard creams.

. . . .

Thursday 29

Mr Wilmott has given Year Ten a stern talking to. All future mind-expanding trips are under review, including Year Seven's annual Peterborough ice disco. Also Mark Lambert has been moved out of 10 Hopwood-White. He is going to Retards and Criminals next term to do macramé and times tables. It is a wonder he was not in there in the first place. Thin Kylie is devastated. She says she can't last the hour and ten minutes between official breaks without groping him several times.

. . . .

Friday 30

The A11 road sign has been replaced again. It now reads

Historic Saffron Walden Twinned with Bad Wildungen, Chichicastenango and Hull. Mum is outraged. Not at the grammar, which even she has to admit is faultless, but that we have been twinned without her knowledge, and to somewhere renowned only for fish and John Prescott. She is ringing the council to complain.

THE HIGHWAY CODE

BROWN AND BEAUTI FUL

july

LIGHTSABRE

Saturday 1

England are out of the World Cup. James is jubilant. He bet Grandpa £3.10 and a Curly Wurly that this would happen. Grandpa has offered him double or quits on Andy Murray winning Wimbledon. He has no sporting sense. As Dad pointed out, there is more chance of Mum lifting the ban on Vimto. So Grandpa put £5 on that as well.

. . . .

Sunday 2

Grandpa is another £5 down.

. . . .

Monday 3

James came home from school with a Light Sabre. Mum asked him where he got it and he said he swapped it with Mad Harry for his Will Young doll. Mum is not amused. She says it will get out of hand. I do not know what the fuss is about. James got the better deal. Will Young can't sing any more, is naked, and only has one eye.

. . . .

Tuesday 4

James has swapped his Lego hospital for a doll that wets itself and cries. It is called Baby Wants a WeeWee and is utterly disturbing. I do not know why he needs a doll anyway—Baby Jesus performs all those functions and more.

. . . .

Wednesday 5

Andy Murray is out of Wimbledon. As predicted. The fickle tabloids have turned on him already. When I am a journalist I will stand by my convictions and not be swayed by mob rule. James has offered Grandpa odds on Saffron Walden FC making it through to the third round of the FA Cup next year (no chance—their striker is Fat Len Viceroy) but Grandpa says he can't afford it. He has a long-standing bet on Baby Jesus's first word being 'Daddy'. Another guaranteed loser. It will be 'Fetch the J-cloth, Colin'—the most commonly heard phrase in this household.

* *

Thursday 6

James has swapped Dad's *Swing Like Tiger* golf DVD for a pair of Barbie shoes (size 8). Mum is right. It is getting out of hand. Am going to ask for a lock on my bedroom door to protect my underwear and collection of tragic literature (i.e. *The Bell Jar* and *Fear and Loathing*).

* *

5 p.m.
Mum has said she is not putting a lock on any door in the house as it encourages drug use and underage sex. I said she was making a huge leap of imagination but she said, 'Look at Uncle Jim; Grandpa gave him a lock and now

look where he is, up a mountain with someone who thinks fairies actually exist.' She has a point.

. . . .

7 p.m.
Dad has asked where his *Swing Like Tiger* DVD is. He has a crucial game with Mr Wainwright on Saturday. Luckily for James the dog belched at that point, and Dad is now under the assumption that the dog has eaten it. I feel sorry for the dog. It has been sent to the shed under false pretences.

. . . .

Friday 7

James has swapped his Barbie shoes for three tins of tomatoes (Sainsbury's peeled plum). I said he was underselling himself and what on earth did he want tomatoes for. He says it is striking the deal that is the reward itself. He needs help.

Also, Suzy is doing Conservative Party Leader David Cameron on her sex show tonight. Apparently his aides think it will improve his ratings as the housewives' choice. Or the perverts'. Suzy is fast becoming the most famous person in Saffron Walden. She is on *Richard and Judy*, and Phil and Fern next week. Marlon and the least famous McGann will be forced to move to Broxbourne if they want to retain their status.

. . . .

Saturday 8

The dog is missing. James took it for a walk round the block and claims it made a dash for a passing Renault Clio. This is not beyond the realms of imagination. The dog has an inexplicable hatred of French cars.

11 a.m.

The dog did not run away. James swapped it for a packet of Rolos. Mum found him binge eating caramel and made him confess all. Mum says it is a swap too far and has banned all future swapping. He has been despatched with Dad to Mad Harry's to retrieve the dog, via Mr Patel's (for Rolos).

1.15 p.m.

Dad, James, and the dog are back. Mrs Mad Harry could not get the dog out of the house fast enough. Dad said he bets Mum is regretting being so discipline-mad. She is desperate to get rid of the dog and a swap is an ideal solution. Then everyone went swapping mad. Grandpa Riley said he wished he could swap his cup of tea for a pint of stout. Mum said she would happily swap Grandpa Riley for a cup of tea. And Dad said there were times when he wished he could swap Mum for Kirsty Wark. Then Mum's lips went thin and she said she was going to practise her gear changes. Dad went a bit pale. I think he is worried she might swap him for Mike 'Wandering Hands' Majors.

· ·

460

Sunday 9

Grandpa Clegg rang to report the outrage that Mr Nuamah has joined the Redruth Freemasons. Grandpa says he is trying to infiltrate normal society and then brainwash them with his weird ways. Dad answered and said there was nothing normal about a bunch of half-witted Cornishmen sitting in darkened pub rooms doing tricksy handshakes and they should welcome someone who is *a*) educated to more than the 11-plus and *b*) does not think 'arr, it be' is an answer to anything. So Grandpa Clegg hung up. He does not like Dad because he does not come from 'the old country'.

Monday 10

Mark Lambert has been sent for an induction week with the Retards and Criminals. (They can't take him permanently yet due to overcrowding—it is all the O'Gradys). He says he prefers it down there. There is plasticine and Disney videos. I pointed out that this was not academically stretching and he should be thinking about his GCSEs which are only a year away, so he said he didn't need GCSEs to shave heads, and why didn't Aladdin have nipples when Tarzan does? I said I had no idea. But it is weird. Why doesn't he have nipples? I will ask James. He is bound to know.

461

6 p.m.
Suzy has just used the word clitoris live on *Richard and Judy*. Even the dog seemed shocked.

9 p.m.
James is still stumped on the nipple question. Google has failed to come up with the goods. He is writing to Disney.

. . . .

Tuesday 11
Suzy is in the *Daily Mail* following her *Richard and Judy* appearance but according to Scarlet all publicity is good publicity because Channel 5 have rung and are moving her show to prime time in the autumn, twice a week. She is thrilled. Although apparently Bob is not best pleased—he says Suzy's household management skills have gone out of the window now that she is a star (they were sketchy in the first place—I have witnessed her use a pair of pants to rinse round the bath—Mum would have spasms).

. . . .

Wednesday 12
It is Mum's birthday tomorrow. Went into town with Scarlet, Trevor, and Sad Ed at lunchtime to get her a present. Got her *How Clean is Your House?* by TV's Kim and Aggie (answer—forensically clean). Then we went to Roadshow Records so that Scarlet and Trevor could

browse tuneless goth music but Tuesday was in there talking to Dave. When she saw Sad Ed she grabbed Dave and snogged him energetically. So Sad Ed threw me against a giant cut out of Justin Timberlake and tried to snog me but luckily Justin fell over and dislodged the discount bucket and I managed to escape Sad Ed's clutches. What was he thinking of? And since when does he act on impulse? It takes him an hour to choose between black combats or other black combats. Actually I know what he was thinking and that was to win Tuesday back by apparent lack of interest. But I do not see why he has to involve me. Scarlet and Trevor did not see anything. They had headphones on and their eyes shut and were swaying gothlike to something called 'Death Monkey'. When they saw the scene of devastation before them they just said, 'Cool.' Year Ten is fraught with sexual tension and potential broken limbs. Unless you are a goth, clearly.

Thursday 13

Mum's birthday.

Mum says the Kim and Aggie book is the best present she has ever received. She has already found two new methods of getting red wine stains out of pale shagpile. Dad is annoyed. His M&S voucher and box of Black Magic have paled into insignificance. Even James's Badedas bath foam is looking shoddy and ill-thought-out by comparison. (And rightly so, he swapped it with Mad

Harry for a jigsaw of Anne Boleyn, several pieces known to be inside dog).

Sad Ed has apologized for the attempted snog. He says he was overcome with rage at confirmation of Tuesday's adulterous nature. I said that was no excuse for foisting himself on me. He said, 'Sorry I revolt you so much. Would you prefer it if I dyed my hair blond and minced some sheep for you.' I said yes. Although he has no chance of emulating Justin. You either have panther-like magnetism or you don't. Sad Ed does not.

· ·

Friday 14

It is sports day—annual ritual of humiliation for all concerned. Particularly Mr Wilmott last year when the Retards and Criminals stole the javelins and used them to try to spear the school sheep. Plus it is 100 degrees outside. It is utterly unfair to make us run around and perform sporting feats in heat like this. I bet even Paula Radcliffe is taking it easy with a bottle of diet Coke and *Hello!* Mentioned this to Miss Vicar and Miss Beadle but they said she can afford to lounge around with her bilaterals, whereas we look like the before bit on *Fat Camp*.

3 p.m.

As predicted, sports day was a total disaster. There were forty-seven casualties—forty heat exhaustion (including Scarlet and Trevor who insisted on doing the three-legged

race in full gothwear), six shot-put-related concussions, and a Cox's Pippin lodged in the windpipe (apple bobbing for Mrs Duddy's lot). On the plus side I won the hurdles—all but one of the other competitors were busy being revived by Mrs Leech and her coolbox of Fanta at the time so I only had to beat Sarah Eccles, who has one leg shorter than the other.

Saturday 15

St Swithin's Day

Have prayed for rain to end this heatwave. Even the dog is refusing to go for a walk and is lying lethargically behind the shed with a strawberry Mivvi (panic purchased in bulk from Mr Patel by Treena). Am regretting resolution not to remain friends with Thin Kylie, i.e. the only person in Saffron Walden to own a swimming pool, apart from Lord Butler and his Leisure Centre.

Mum has got her driving test date. It is on the 24th. She has been on the phone to Mike for half an hour. Dad is hovering near the door trying to listen in. I do not know what he thinks he will hear. They are only discussing emergency stops.

11.59 p.m.

No rain. So we are stuck with third-world-like conditions for forty days. Joy.

Sunday 16

11 a.m.

Can see Thin Kylie and Cherie lounging by the pool, eating Doritos. Asked Mum if we could get out James's paddling pool but she says it is out of use after she used it to get the creosote off the dog before he spontaneously combusted.

11.30 a.m.

Now Fat Kylie has arrived over the road and has commandeered the Doritos while Thin Kylie floats around on the giant inflatable breasts. Maybe Suzy will have a swimming pool installed now she is famous. It is a totally celebrity thing to do.

11.45 a.m.

Scarlet says Suzy has rejected the swimming pool idea on the grounds it would mess up her anti-nuclear weapon peace garden (i.e. some windchimes and a Buddha statue).

12 noon

Cannot take this torture any more. Am going over to Thin Kylie's in my Speedo on pretext of borrowing her maths homework (far-fetched, I know, but needs must) and hopefully Cherie will take pity on me and force me to take a refreshing swim.

5 p.m.

Cherie did take pity on me but not as anticipated. She

said, 'Jesus, look at the state of you, you look like Whitey Wilson.' (i.e. town albino.) 'Fetch the St Tropez, Kylie, it's an emergency.' And then before I could protest she had sprayed me with fake tan and was drying me off with her Nicky Clarke diffuser. And you can't come into contact with water for twenty-four hours so I couldn't swim, or even waft my foot under the garden sprinklers for fear of streaking. I just had to stand on the crazy paving with my arms out while the Kylies read out bits from *Chat*. On the plus side, I will be sporting a natural sunkissed shade of caramel tomorrow, according to the label on the bottle.

. . . .

Monday 17

Oh God. Am not caramel. Am hideous unnatural shade of Dairy Milk, verging on the Bournville. Have scrubbed myself with a pumice but it has just added a reddish tinge. Dad is in hysterics. He asked me which shade of Cuprinol I had gone for—Dark Oak or Black Ash. Mum is less amused. Have begged her to keep me off school on grounds I may go down with some kind of allergic reaction to all the tanning chemicals but she has refused. James is backing her. He says it will teach me a lesson on the perils of vanity.

4 p.m.

Scarlet is refusing to let me stand with her and Trevor at break in the all-new goth corner (formerly maths geek corner). She says fake tan is the goth's worst nightmare.

She says I can come back when I have faded to a more acceptable colour. I asked her for a rough guide and she said Waitrose toffee sauce. At this rate it will be next term before I am readmitted. To make matters worse, token Year Nine skinhead Paul Lefevre thought I was being racist and invited me to join the BNP.

. . . .

Tuesday 18

Am still an alarming shade of mahogany. It is totally depressing. Bumped into Jack on the way to school. He said, 'Christ, Riley, what have you done this time? You do know you look like a wardrobe with a perm.' I said I was perfectly aware of the colour of my skin, that it was inflicted on me by a deranged madwoman and had he looked at his own hair lately because it was dangerously similar in style to Jennifer Aniston's. Then, for some reason, I started crying. Jack said, 'Shit. I didn't mean it. You look great, honest. Sort of like Nicole Richie. If she had curly hair. And was shorter. And less skinny.' Which is the nicest thing Jack has said to me in a long time (even if it was only an emergency measure to staunch the flow of tears), which only made me cry even more. So Jack phoned up Scarlet on his mobile and made her come and get me. She says I can hover at the edges of goth corner at break, as long as I keep my cardigan on and pull my hair over my face a bit more.

. . . .

Wednesday 19

Am now Walnut Whip on the Cuprinol scale.

. . . .

Thursday 20

It is official. Saffron Walden has got its first ever ASBO courtesy of Stacey O'Grady and Darryl Stamp. Mum is jubilant, though still annoyed that it was secured with the aid of Treena, rather than herself. Treena said she wishes Mum had done it not her then Mum could be the one living in mortal fear. I said her fears were ill-founded as having an ASBO is highly regarded in chav circles and they were probably celebrating with a bottle of Lambrusco and some illegal bangers. Mum said if they were she would report it. I said she would have plenty of chance to fulfil her anti-anti-social calling as Stacey O'Grady is bound to break his strict conditions (he has a 7 p.m. curfew and is not allowed within a mile of Abrakebabra). I predict by next week at the latest.

Tan-wise am still Walnutish but verging on the Antique Pine.

. . . .

Friday 21

It is the last day of school. Which is always the same. Someone will set off the fire alarm, the staffroom will be festooned with silly string, and hordes of Year Elevens will hug each other dramatically and say, 'It is the end of

an era' etc., etc. Which it is not. They will all be back in
September for A levels and resits. Apart from the Retards
and Criminals cohort, obviously, who are going straight
to stack shelves at B&Q/community service. And Justin,
who is going to Braintree to follow his dream. They are
all having a lunchtime farewell 'rave' in the upper school
canteen (i.e. Duncan Evans and his CD player). I will go
and linger—it is my last chance to snog Justin before he
falls for some arty sixth form college type with piercings
and ironic dungarees. If only I were more pale and tragic
looking and less like Liz McLarnon.

3 p.m.
Oh my God. Justin is back with Sophie Microwave
Muffins Jacobs. She let him feel her 34Bs behind the fire
curtain in a fit of last-day-of-term adrenalin and nostalgia.
I only know this because I was at the time behind said fire
curtain with Sad Ed waiting for my chance to infiltrate
proceedings. Sad Ed said it was the natural order of things
and I should set my sights higher. There is no one higher
than Justin. He is a supreme being. Also Kev Starr is now
engaged to Lucy Davies and the staffroom is out of bounds
due to excess funny foam. Mrs Leech is campaigning to
ban Year Elevens from school after GCSEs. She says it
causes nothing but heartbreak and maintenance issues.
She was consoling Mr Vaughan at the time with a
Cadbury's Highlight (Turkish Delight variety).

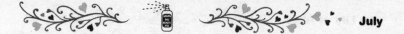

Saturday 22

This is typical. It is the first day of holidays, I have faded to an acceptable light ash on the Cuprinol chart, but it is now pouring with rain. I have a good mind to write to WHSmith and suggest they remove any mention of St Swithin from their diaries as it is confusing, weather-wise. Am going to go round to Scarlet's—the goths welcome rain—it is further encouragement to stay inside in the gloom.

3 p.m.

Bob is right. Suzy has totally forsaken her household duties now that she is a celebrity sexpert. There were piles of dirty Jamie Oliver crockery stacked all over the indigenous Iroko wood worktops and even more sex manuals littering the carpet than usual. Plus the smell coming from the den, which I had attributed to drugs or strange incense, turned out to be one of Tony's or Gordon's poos (the cats, not the esteemed Prime Minister or Chancellor—that would be *Chat* material for sure).

Jack and Justin were eating Hula Hoops in the kitchen when I arrived (another sign of Suzy's neglect, pre-celebrity it would have been Kettle Chips or M&S mini bruschetta). Jack said was I all right because I looked a bit pale. I said his puerile jokes were beneath me. But it was actually quite amusing. In truth, Jack is a lot funnier than Justin. When I said to Justin that I was delighted that the path of true love had been restored and that he was back

471

with Sophie (a lie, I was being poetic—or possibly ironic—I get confused) Justin said, 'Yeah, whatever.' Maybe he is regretting following his end of term urges! Or more likely he has no interest in speaking to me at all.

Watched *Raven* in the dark. Then Scarlet and Trevor said they wanted to snog so came home. I think I preferred Scarlet when she was single.

. . . .

Sunday 23

Still raining. May revive my genius first novel if this inclement weather carries on. Although my McFly notebook is now dedicated to my journalistic career so would have to buy a new one. Which would mean going out in the rain. It is a wonder we get anything done in this country at all. It is so wet and inhospitable. Although these are ideal conditions for tortured literary works. Look at the Brontës stuck in the Peaks with endless drizzle. It is a total Catch 22.

It is Mum's driving test tomorrow. She is getting an early night (7.45—a new record, and beating Baby Jesus who is staying up for *Trial and Retribution*) to prepare. There is no possible way she can fail. Dad tested her on her Highway Code and she got every question right. Then she tested Dad and he only got four out of ten. Mum says she is signing him up for refresher lessons with Mike. Dad says he would rather chew tinfoil than spend any time with Mr Wandering Hands, but his resistance is futile.

Once Mum has made her mind up about something there is no swaying her. Like when she decided Dad had to stop wearing shorts.

. . . .

Monday 24

Mum has failed her driving test. She says it is down to mini-roundabout madness in Bishop's Stortford. Apparently they have sneakily installed a badly-signposted gyratory system near the Hockley Road, confusing Mum, who ended up circling DFS for ten minutes before the examiner took over and drove them to freedom. She is writing to the council to complain. Dad is not pleased. It means she is back behind the wheel of Mike's Fiesta and back within his Casanova-like clutches for another month. But on the plus side, his refresher lessons are off the agenda while he pays for her to actually pass in the first place.

. . . .

Tuesday 25

As predicted, Stacey O'Grady has broken the conditions of his ASBO, and several laws besides. According to Tracey Hughes (who told Mark Lambert who told Thin Kylie who told Cherie who told Mum outside Gayhomes) he tried to rob Barclays with a pump-action water pistol and is facing a six-month prison sentence. He has blamed boredom for his criminal tendencies. I know how he

473

feels. Saffron Walden in the holidays is torturous. Mum is over the moon though—it is one O'Grady down, one to go in the housing stakes. She has totally forgotten about failing her driving test.

· ·

Wednesday 26

Asked Mum if we were going away anywhere this holiday. She said she and Dad were taking James to Granny Clegg's for a fortnight at the end of August. I said what about me, and she said there was no room, that I had spent all last summer there (yes, but in enforced exile) and that anyway she needed me to supervise her cleaning schedule, given Grandpa and Treena's spillage tendencies. It is utterly unfair. Not that I want to share a Fray Bentos-smelling bed with James or spend two weeks listening to Grandpa Clegg's borderline racist rantings but even so, it shows that I am the outcast of the family. It is totally like *Cinderella* (the Hilary Duff version).

· ·

Thursday 27

Rain has stopped. So have put off novel in favour of wandering aimlessly around town with Sad Ed and Scarlet.

5 p.m.

Scarlet thinks I should have a birthday party. Fifteen is

almost coming of age after all. I suggested an ironic tea and fairy cake party (totally vintage and very vogue, according to *Vogue*) but Scarlet said the irony will be lost on most of the guests and they will just think I am a prat, plus there is no way she is wearing a floaty lacy dress and a hat. Sad Ed agreed—on the hat grounds. Am going to ask Mum later. Will say I am treating it as a test of responsibility and promise to clean up all post-party stains.

6 p.m.

Mum has agreed to a party, but has imposed a fifteen-person headcount limit (following *Supernanny*'s one guest for every year rule—normally only applicable to under-eights), banned all food products, and is only allowing pale drinks i.e. water or lemonade. Did not argue as it is a wonder she has agreed to anything at all. Am going to do guest list later. With a strict no Retards or Criminals door policy.

8 p.m.

Guest list is harder than I thought.

- Me, Scarlet, and Sad Ed, obviously.
- Trevor, because Scarlet will not come unless he comes.
- A bat friend for Trevor because he will not come unless he has another goth to commune with when Scarlet is in the loo.

- Jack
- Justin (Am not inviting Sophie, obviously. Once he has seen me and my vintage and edgy party he will realize that I am his destiny, despite me still being an A cup.) Then realized have no other actual friends. So guest list is seven, including me.
- Maybe will invite Thin Kylie. After all, she did invite me to her party.
- And I suppose I had better invite Mark Lambert to keep her occupied.
- And Fat Kylie.
- Could invite Oona Rickets—every party needs a gay person there to start the dancing—it is a well-known fact.

So just need four more people. Will ask Scarlet tomorrow.

Friday 28

2 p.m.

Scarlet says I absolutely have to invite Sophie Microwave Muffins or Justin won't come. Which makes twelve. And that Sophie won't come without Pippa. So that is thirteen. But I still need two more. Why am I so utterly friendless? Maybe it is because I am a tragic loner. Like Lord Byron or Winona Ryder.

4 p.m.

Or mad Miss Crawley who has a moustache and seven cats. Oh God.

5 p.m.
Have decided to invite Ali Hassan and his maths geek
friends. At least they will keep the numbers up. And are
unlikely to cause any stain- or sex-related issues.

* *

Saturday 29
10 a.m.
Have posted invites (James got all the addresses off some
stalker's website). So now will wait for my RSVPs.

10.15 a.m.
Forgot to put RSVP on invite. Was too busy trying to do
clever things facewarping Lindsay Lohan on James's
computer. So am reduced to hoping for the best. Only
three days to go. It is quite fraught having a party. There
are so many things to worry about. Particularly when the
venue is owned by someone with borderline OCD
cleaning issues.

Sunday 30
Have begged Mum and Dad to go out during the party.
Dad has suggested the golf club but Mum is insisting on
being within a twenty-five metre radius so they are going
to Clive and Marjory's. Mum says that way she can
measure decibel levels and be home in eleven seconds
(tested) in a spillage emergency. It is better than nothing.
James is going to Mad Harry's for a sleepover. They are

going to build a robot alligator. So I will just have the dog, Grandpa, and Treena and Baby Jesus to worry about. Please God do not let Grandpa try to dance. Also am going to hide Treena's leggings. Do not want anyone witnessing her in those. And will ask her not to say 'bag of shite' or 'piffy on a rock bun' (no idea) or any other weird Northern things.

* *

Monday 31

Only a day to go. Went round Scarlet's to get in the mood. They are getting a new cleaner now that Suzy is too busy investigating celebrity sex issues. I said that wasn't very left-wing and I hope she wasn't an illegal and repressed Filipina. Scarlet said *au contraire* it is very New Labour to keep the proletariat in work and she is not a Filipina but is called Edna and is sixty-seven. So I said that was all right then.

Tuesday 1

8 a.m. (9.5 hours to go to party)

Presents received:

- flip-flops (not £15 black Havaianas from Topshop as requested but £2.99 red ones from Woolworth's so obviously will not be wearing them).
- 'Now That's What I Call Music' something like 179 featuring utter chart pap so obviously will not be listening to it.
- Lifetime membership of Mole Hall Wildlife Park (which still has out of bounds flamingos and no man-eating animals, so obviously will not be visiting it).
- A jelly bean dispenser, beans already consumed by James, so cannot use it even if wanted to.

But will get more relevant and thoughtful presents at party later, for which now only have nine hours to prepare—i.e. choose outfit, music, experiment with mood lighting, purchase lemonade etc. Must get started immediately. Will call Sad Ed for reinforcements.

8.15 a.m.

Sad Ed not thrilled at being woken. He says he will be over after *T4* and has forbidden me to do CDs until then as he says my taste in music is questionable and I cannot be trusted not to throw in some Bee Gees. (Who are utterly retro and therefore cool. He just doesn't like them because they have big hair.)

481

8.30 a.m.
Have chosen outfit. Am going to wear leggings and stripy
T-shirt in manner of continental-style Kate Moss. Also
have blacked out most of flip-flops with marker pen. Will
look utterly excellent and mature i.e. fifteen. Only nine
hours to go.

11.30 a.m.
Have done playlist with Sad Ed. He has vetoed the Bee
Gees (hair) and Corinne Bailey Rae (hair and annoying
serenity) and instead has made me a special Ed Party Mix
CD to play. He says it is guaranteed to get people in the
mood. Yes but for what? Suicide?

12.00 noon
Have run out of things to organize. Will have a power nap
to prepare me for the excesses of the evening.

5 p.m.
Oh God, have slept for five hours. Have only two and a half
hours to have bath, remove excess body hair, control absurd
Leo Sayer-style hairdo and usher family out of house.

7.15 p.m.
Done. Mum and Dad have been banished to Clive and
Marjory's. James is experimenting with batteries and
kitchen implements at Mad Harry's. The dog is in the shed
with the radio (Radio 4—it likes *The Archers*). Baby Jesus

is asleep. Grandpa and Treena are upstairs conjugating. Sad Ed's special party mix is on the hi-fi (currently playing something about stabbing yourself with a fork—thank God it will be over before anyone arrives) and there are fifteen paper cups laid out on the table amid an array of Perrier, Evian, and Waitrose Lemonade (cloudy, but non-staining—Mum did a patch test). Now just need guests.

7.30 p.m.
Oooh, doorbell. This must be everyone.

7.31 p.m.
Was Cherie asking if Dad could unblock her pipes. Hope it is not euphemism. Sent her round to Clive and Marjory's.

7.45 p.m.
Where is everybody? They are now fifteen minutes late. Which is fashionable. But annoying.

7.50 p.m.
Oooh, doorbell again.

7.51 p.m.
Was Sad Ed.

8.05 p.m.
And Scarlet and Trevor. So far not really a party. We are just watching *Casualty* and drinking fizzy water.

8.15 p.m.
Doorbell. Can see Mark Lambert, Thin Kylie, Ali Hassan, and at least twenty other people in the drive. Well, just a few more won't hurt. It will all be civilized. After all, there is no Bacardi in the house. What could possibly go wrong?

* *

Wednesday 2

Am grounded for ever. On the following grounds:

- Headcount exceeded fifteen. (Actually thirty-eight. The Kylies rounded up everyone at Barry Island including Darryl Stamp and some other O'Gradys.)
- There is Bacardi Breezer vomit in the dining room (belonging to Ali Hassan and several maths geeks). Thin Kylie smuggled twenty bottles in inside Fat Kylie's smock top and told them it was Britvic.
- There are stiletto holes in the hallway parquet due to Fat Kylie's weight/heel ratio.
- The dog has had a 'go faster' stripe shaved down its back (Fat Kylie using Treena's Ladyshave—lucky she did not use Mum's epilator or the dog would not have been so compliant).
- Baby Jesus is fractious after the Kylies insisted on waking him and sticking him up their T-shirts so they could see what it felt like to be pregnant.
- All Mum's Duchy Original biscuits have gone missing (Mark Lambert claimed he had 'got the munchies' after smoking a menthol cigarette).

It is lucky Mum got back when she did (summoned by the insane revving of one of the O'Grady's Datsuns) or there would have been a serious stain-related incident with Treena's Ice Magic chocolate mint sauce. It took me and Jack until midnight to clear up the debris, no one else passed Mum's sobriety test (or dared take it—Thin Kylie disappeared taking her chav minions with her at the first sight of the Cillit Bang). Not even Sad Ed who had only drunk Shloer. It is because he is notoriously clumsy—Mum has not let him near anything breakable since he fell onto her glass-topped coffee table at the age of nine. Grandpa and Treena are in trouble as well for failing to oversee events properly. They had locked themselves in their room with the telly and four bottles of Kylie's Bacardi.

Plus did not get to snog anyone unless you count fending off Kyle with James's light sabre. Justin was too busy with his tongue in Sophie Jacobs's ear (gross) to notice me. And have indelible black flip-flop marks on feet.

Thursday 3

Oh God, am bored. Am not even allowed round Scarlet's to mope about there. It is so unfair. It is not my fault I got gatecrashed by malign forces. Mum says I should use the time wisely to reflect on my irresponsibility. She has banished me to my bedroom with *Vanity Fair* (the book, not the glamorous magazine, chance would be a fine

485

thing), which we are doing for GCSE English next term. She says no doubt I will relate to it in some misguided tragic way. What can she mean?

. . . .

Friday 4
8 a.m.
Will read all day.

10 p.m.
Still reading.

. . . .

Saturday 5
10 a.m.
Still reading.

11 p.m.
Have finished. Mum is right—I am TOTALLY Becky Sharp i.e. I am downtrodden and socially inferior but my superior brain skills (i.e. general literariness), wit and guile will help me rise above my lowly birth. Scarlet is clearly Amelia. Which would make Jack her brother Joseph, whom I am destined to marry then kill, but inherit his fortune, following ill-advised liaisons with all manner of random men. Interesting. I wonder who Justin is. Possibly the devastingly handsome Captain George, who dies horribly.

. . . .

Sunday 6

Mum is in an exceptionally good mood. It is thanks to the *Sunday Times*, which has informed her that the government has brought in a new law whereby rogue minibikes can be seized and crushed immediately. She says it is another vital blow against Saffron Walden's scourge of anti-social youths (aka Mark Lambert and the O'Gradys). Took advantage of her momentary joy to ask her if I could go round to Sad Ed's as I was possibly getting Vitamin D deficiency due to being locked up all day. She got me a chewable Sanatogen and sent me back upstairs.

Monday 7

Oh God, the interminable holidays stretch out before me like an interminable stretchy thing. I don't even have anything to read. I have to get ungrounded. I am fifteen and should be out getting mugged at Camden Market, not alphabetizing my *Famous Fives*. Am going to plead with Mum again.

11 a.m.

Told Mum if she didn't let me out to go to the library or WHSmith I would die from lack of literary stimulation. She gave me three Maeve Binchys. May well phone Childline. Even Nelson Mandela got the *Economist*.

Tuesday 8

Scarlet rang. She and Trevor have caught colds from lying on gravestones at St Regina's at midnight trying to commune with the netherworld. Plus Trevor has been bitten by Elspeth the church cat and has had to have a tetanus jab. God, it sounds so exciting. What I would give to lie on a gravestone or get attacked by Elspeth.

5 p.m.

Mark Lambert's minibike has been seized and crushed. *Quelle surprise*. Although, according to James, who witnessed the proceedings in Waitrose car park, it was Mr Hosepipe who was riding at the time.

Wednesday 9

Rang Scarlet to see if she has any more graveyard injuries or animal wounds (she doesn't—they have decided to give St Regina's church a wide berth since they found out that Fat Kylie and Mr Whippy have been shagging on George Henry Cummings (1898–1957)).

Thursday 10

11 a.m.

Oh my God, have to get ungrounded as a matter of emergency. Scarlet rang. Suzy's producer at Channel 5 owns a huge house near Padstow but he is in Majorca filming *Celebrity Monkey Tennis* (no idea) with Carol Vorderman and is letting the Stones have it for two weeks starting Saturday and I am invited. Everyone is going—including Trevor and Sad Ed and Justin (and Sophie Microwave Muffins, annoyingly). Scarlet says to tell my mum it will be educational and supervised by responsible adults (aka Bob and Suzy).

5 p.m.
Mum says under no circumstances is she letting me loose in North Cornwall (renowned for underage beach sex) with the Stones as my guardians. She says I can come to the Cleggs' and sleep on a lilo on the landing (Mum and Dad are in the spare room, James is on the sofa). I said no thanks I would rather stay with Grandpa and Treena and Baby Jesus but she says she is putting Marjory in charge of her cleaning utensils and I am going to St Slaughter like it or not as I have proved myself untrustworthy and incapable of basic mess prevention. It is hopeless. I am doomed.

9 p.m.
Have had an epiphany during *Animal Hospital*. Becky Sharp would not be lying on her M&S duvet whingeing that she was hard done by, she would be doing something sneaky and excellent to get her own way. So am going to be model child and totally transform Mum's image of me as spill-prone vandal in twenty-four hours.

Friday 11

10 a.m.

Mum and James have gone out to shop for things we will not be able to buy in St Slaughter (i.e. everything except tinned vegetables, giant sanitary towels, and pasties) so have checked all food cupboards for out of date produce (findings: some weird-looking chocolate, owner unknown, no date but have thrown out anyway due to its greasy consistency and Mum's fear of processed sugars), brushed the dog (much to its annoyance, it was trying to get inside the airing cupboard at the time), arranged the cleaning products by height and colour, and watered the mung beans, so that when she gets back she will say, 'Oh, but Rachel, I am utterly wrong, you are indeed a responsible young adult and of course you may go to Cornwall with Scarlet etc.' Or something like that.

11.30 a.m.

Mum is back. She did not say, 'Oh, but Rachel, I am utterly wrong, you are indeed a responsible young adult and of course you may go to Cornwall with Scarlet etc.' In fact her words were, 'Where is the Chocolax? James is all bunged up and I do not want to be stopping at Taunton Deane for a poo emergency like last year. Honestly, Rachel, I go out for five minutes [actually two hours] and when I get back the cupboards are all willy nilly, the mung beans are drowning and the Cillit Bang has been moved without permission. This is exactly why you are coming to Granny

490

Clegg's. Now fetch the Dustbuster before we all choke on dog hair.' Then, as if on cue, the dog had an accident on the kitchen floor. It must have retrieved the Chocolax from the bin when I was watering the mung beans.

It is hopeless. Even Becky Sharp would have a hard time against Mum. Am going to spend two weeks of perpetual misery with backward relatives eating Viennetta. Plus Dad is making us get up at four in the morning to miss the traffic.

. . . .

Saturday 12
7 a.m.

Am miserable already. Have spent three hours in close confinement with James and the dog. (Amazingly, we are bringing it with us. Mum says she will sleep more soundly knowing it cannot in any way eat, dismantle, or vomit on any part of the house while we are gone. It is lucky we left at 4 otherwise Grandpa might have protested. As it is he is going to get a shock when he wakes up.) Plus Mum has ignored pleas (including Dad's) to stop at the drive-through McDonald's on the M5 so we are now eating Marmite sandwiches and Fruesli bars at a so-called beauty spot on Dartmoor (i.e. some gorse, a mangy sheep and several other overloaded estate cars). This is not a good start to the holiday.

10 a.m.

We are in St Slaughter after six hours and seven wee stops (three for James, four for the dog), and a near collision on

the A30 at Polyphant (the dog tried to climb into the driver's seat to get a better view of a Jack Russell in the BMW in front). Granny Clegg is delighted at 'Valerie's' arrival. She is making a bed for it next to the telly. (It gets better accommodation than we do. I am outside the bathroom door under several pictures of Great-Granny Clegg, who looks like former foreign secretary and 'demon headmaster' Jack Straw. I will have nightmares.) Bruce and the dog are less pleased. The dog is trying to assert its authority by sitting on the coffee table but Bruce has topped it by perching in the serving hatch, guarding the kitchen from all who dare enter.

11.30 a.m.
Grandpa Riley has rung to report that the dog is mysteriously missing. He says he has done a sweep of the house in case it accidentally locked itself in a cupboard but has now resorted to calling the police. Mum said did he not see the note? Grandpa said which one? (There are notes and instructions on every available surface including one on the freezer saying 'This is the freezer'.) Mum said the one on the dog food, which he would have seen if he had bothered to try to feed the dog. Grandpa says he got distracted by *Pingu* and forgot until half an hour ago. Then he read the note and said it is dognapping and he could sue. Mum said, 'Try me.' So Grandpa hung up. He will not try. Even he knows better than that.

1 p.m.

Lunch. Mum offered to heat up a Waitrose quiche but Grandpa Clegg said quiche is for 'poofs and foreigners' and anyway Granny Clegg had done something special. It was not special. It was Brain's faggots. Do people actually eat this stuff out of choice? The dog seemed to like it though. It had two helpings and a Mr Kipling French Fancy (how this passed the 'poofs and foreigners' test, I do not know. Or the faggots for that matter.) I may well go vegetarian. Then at least I would only have to suffer claggy Smash.

3 p.m.

A family has arrived at Seaview Cottage (aka Hester's battery chicken shed, actually eleven miles from the sea and with a view of a silage bin). Sadly they are not from Fulham, nor do they have any Busted-resembling teenage children. They drive a Renault Espace (purchased from Clive Studley Premium Motors, Solihull) and have identical triplets who were fighting with flashing, winged Barbies in the back seat. James is going over tomorrow to see if they want to swap one.

5 p.m.

Tea. Spam and boiled potatoes (tinned). Ate potatoes. Will be non-Government-approved Lily Cole-esque size 0 by end of summer, and not through choice.

Sunday 13

10 a.m.

James has gone to Seaview Cottage to try to procure a Barbie. I do not know what he is swapping though as his *Lord of the Rings* doll collection and sticker album are still here.

11 a.m.

James has returned without a Barbie but with a Puppy in My Pocket and the information that the triplets are ten and called Parker, Presley, and Peyton (i.e. pseudo-American and on Mum's absolute proscribed list); that Parker is allergic to fishpaste; and that Presley once got electrocuted when she weed on a Flymo. He is like Granny Clegg in his ability to wheedle information out of complete strangers. James says he is in love. I said with which one. And he said he wasn't fussy, they all looked the same, so what did it matter.

12 noon

Granny Clegg has asked where her electric can opener is. I have my suspicions.

1 p.m.

Am going vegetarian. Lunch was Chilli Con Carne (tinned) with Alphabetti Spaghetti. Will tell Mum before dinner.

4 p.m.

Told Mum that I was becoming a vegetarian. She said,

'Don't be ridiculous, you will become anaemic and fail your GCSEs.' I said it was a matter of principle (i.e. I refuse to eat Granny Clegg's food as it is vile) and she should respect my wishes. She said, 'On your head be it,' but I can tell she is planning to force-feed me goulash when we get back to civilization. If I was in Padstow Suzy would be congratulating me on my forthright stance against animal cruelty. Grandpa Clegg said, 'She'll be shaving her head and piercing her backside next.' I said, *au contraire*, vegetarianism was no longer the province of the lesbian community, and that, as everyone knows, meat is murder. James said, actually it isn't murder, as defined by the *Oxford English Dictionary* online version, and anyway, it is all quite humane with an electric shock probe thingy and it only hurts if the probe slips and only gets half the brain, and then the cows stagger about mentally for a bit. Which made me feel ill and has only fortified my beliefs.

5 p.m.
Tea. Reminded Granny I was now a vegetarian and she said, 'This is tongue.' I said tongue was in fact meat. She said, 'Norman, did you know that? Tongue is meat.' He said, 'No it's not, it's tongue.' I ate carrots (tinned) and strawberries (tinned) with condensed milk (tinned and utterly banned in our house so actually a rare treat). Dad looked like he might join me in my vegetarian stance. He struggled with every mouthful.

Monday 14

Went to Museum of Mines. Looked at bits of tin and ancient pasty remnants. Came home. When we got back Parker was on the doorstep with Granny's electric can opener. She says her mum says it is not an electric wand and it has congealed stuff on it and could she have her Puppy in My Pocket back. Mum has sent James to his room to reflect on his swapping problems. James says no punishment can keep him down, he cares only about the triplets and will do anything to secure their love.

Ate mushy peas for tea. Vegetarianism isn't as nutritionally fulfilling as I thought.

. . . .

Tuesday 15

Went to Spar with Granny Clegg to do her weekly shop (four Fray Bentos, a Viennetta, sixteen Andrex, a packet of Heinz potato waffles and the *St Slaughter Reporter*). Maureen tried to get Granny to buy some olives and a tin of capers (specially imported 'from up country' for the hordes of tourists St Slaughter is confidently expecting now that Hester has got the ball rolling) but Granny said she would sooner eat rabbit droppings. Maureen agreed. Then they started on what lovely hair Mr Nuamah the dentist had so I went outside. James and the triplets were on a bench. He was letting them kiss him in turn. Even my brother is more successful, snog-wise, than me and he is only nine.

Got home and informed Dad that James was groping

the triplets on the High Street. Dad said, 'Lucky him, triplets, eh.' But Mum said, 'Go and fetch him, Colin, before he picks up anything.' She doesn't mean disease, she means a Birmingham accent.

Wednesday 16

9 a.m.

Finally we are going to do something interesting i.e. go to the beach, i.e. I will be able to swim and dive off rocks and will be utterly like Gwyneth Paltrow in *The Talented Mr Ripley*. We are leaving the dog and Bruce at home. Mum has warned Granny Clegg that this is asking for trouble but Granny Clegg says they are warming to each other. I do not think so, I saw the dog wee on Bruce's bowl last night.

5 p.m.

Was not like *Talented Mr Ripley* at all. For a start Gwyneth did not have Grandpa Clegg and his 'beachwear' (i.e. a vest and suit trousers) to contend with. Plus James went AWOL and was discovered skinny dipping in a rock pool with Parker. Luckily it was me and Granny Clegg who found him. Granny shouted, 'Put your trunks on, no one here wants to see your widgie,' thus adding to my utter shame and embarrassment.

When we got back the dog and Bruce had eaten my lilo. So am now sleeping on the carpet. It is all too depressing for words.

Thursday 17

9 a.m.

Am going to the community playground (still disused but the only point in St Slaughter to receive mobile phone signals) to call Scarlet and Sad Ed. Hopefully they will be having an equally pants time and we can commiserate together about the crapness of Cornwall.

11 a.m.

Aaagh. They are not having a pants time. They are having an excellent time involving an outdoor pool, croquet, and barbecues with Natasha Kaplinsky who is staying at the house next door. The only downside is that Justin is not there. He got a better offer—he is in Florida with Mr and Mrs Microwave Muffins.

This is typical. I am stuck in Hicksville, Arizona with an oversexed nine year old and not one but two mental and vomiting dogs, plus I am getting no sleep due to the itchy carpet and Grandpa Clegg's weak bladder. I cannot take it any more. Am going to have to run away to Padstow. It will be like *Without a Trace* and Mum and Dad will be utterly sorry they ever grounded me and made me suffer Granny Clegg's 'cooking'.

4 p.m.

Have checked the bus timetable. There is one bus a day to Bodmin, at 7.30 a.m. It gets in at 11 (which seems quite a long time for twenty miles). Have rung Scarlet and told

her my plans. She says it is totally excellent and rebellious and is getting Bob to pick me up from the bus station in the Volvo.

. . . .

Friday 18
6 a.m.

Have packed my essentials (i.e. bikini, hair products, copy of *Vanity Fair*) and have written a note for Mum. It says:

By the time you read this I will be gone. Please do not be sad or angry. I am in a better place.

I intend to stay with Suzy and Bob, who can better cater to my new vegetarian stance, plus they will not make me sleep on the landing.

PS Can you pick me up on the way home? According to Scarlet it is the big white house with the statue in the front garden, a hundred yards down from the sign saying 'Trespassers will be persecuted'. Tell Mum this is not a spelling mistake.

See you there. You cannot miss it. It has huge gates and a sign saying 'Heaven'.

7.30 a.m.
Everyone was still asleep when I got up so I packed emergency rations (pink wafers) and pinned the note to the dog's collar. Am now on bus. Unfortunately so is Maureen Penrice from Spar. She is sitting next to me.

8 a.m.
Have moved seats. Cannot listen to any more stories about her trigger-happy son Damian. (He is in the army, not just a random mentalist.)

9 a.m.
Now I know why the bus takes so long. We are stopping at every village, hamlet, and pig shed on the way to pick up indigenous people and their pets. I imagine this is what it is like in Chichicastenango, but with goats instead of bull terriers.

10 a.m.
Am surprised that Mum has not rung my mobile in panic. It is clear that they absolutely do not care about me.

11.10 a.m.
Ah, civilization (well, Bodmin) at last. I can see Scarlet, who is in goth beach wear, i.e. a black lace vest and floor length skirt, and Jack, who is in normal beach wear i.e. a Muse T-shirt and shorts. Sad Ed must still be asleep. Feel a bit sick. It must be the joy at being reunited with interesting and literary people.

5 p.m.
Have just spent glorious day by the pool rereading *Vanity Fair* and eating an exotic fruit platter. This is utterly what life should be like. Suzy says I should ring Mum and Dad but I said I had left a fully explanatory note and that they had my mobile number if they needed to call. Which they haven't so obviously they are not concerned at all at my disappearance.

6 p.m.
Oh my God. Have just watched *West Country Today* (i.e. crap local news) and I am the top story! According to the reporter I am missing, presumed dead, and there is a countywide search going on for a body. Then they interviewed Granny Clegg (Mum and Dad clearly too distraught to speak) and she said that I had been showing worrying signs like going off my food and reading dark matter (she means *The Bell Jar*) and then she held up what she claimed was a suicide note. I do not understand. How can this have happened? Why didn't anyone ring me? Worst of all why did they use a photo of me taken last summer by Granny Clegg i.e. with an eight-year-old boy/lesbian haircut?

6.03 p.m.
Have checked mobile. The battery is dead! Aaagh. Bob is calling the police now to confirm that in fact I am alive and well and eating mangos in a luxury holiday villa. Sad

501

Ed says at least it shows my parents care about me. I said it did not show that, it showed they are utterly mental.

6.15 p.m.
Have spoken to Dad (Mum too angry to speak). I said I had made it perfectly clear where I was and what was all the hoo-ha about the suicide note. Dad said all they had found was a chewed bit of paper (cursed dog) that said:

> By the time you read this I will be gone. Please do not be sad or angry. I am in a better place ... See you there. You cannot miss it. It has huge gates and a sign saying 'Heaven'.

Which I can see might be misleading. Dad says he is coming to get me in two hours. I pleaded with him not to take me back to St Slaughter but he says he is under strict instructions from Mum and he is not going to take his chances against her. But Dad says on the plus side Mum and Auntie Joyless are on speaking terms again, now that they have runaway children in common. I have nothing in common with Boaz. He reads the Bible and wears beige.

9 p.m.
Am still at the villa! Oh joy! It is all thanks to Suzy and her persuasive ways. When Dad arrived Suzy said had he and

Mum thought what effect a return to St Slaughter might have on me? Dad said Mum had considered it but had decided that a ban on fake suicide should do the trick. Suzy says this was retrogressive something or other and that if he did drag me back to the Cleggs', it would only aggravate my misery and drive me to run away again, or worse! I think it was the 'worse' that got him, or perhaps the fact that Suzy was wearing an underwired bikini top and sarong at the time, because then he agreed that conditions at the Cleggs' were not ideal (this is an understatement) and that maybe it was best that I did stay with the Stones. Thank God Mum didn't come with him. There is no way Suzy's bare midriff would have won her over. I bet Dad wishes he could stay here too.

Excellent. I have won my freedom and can enjoy an actual bed, an inside toilet, and conversations that don't revolve around Terry Wogan for the next few days.

10 p.m.
Dad rang. Mum is not best pleased but has agreed on the condition that I use the time to reflect on my behaviour. I said absolutely. They are collecting me at 10 o'clock next Saturday night, to avoid the traffic on the A30.

. . . .

Saturday 19
The *Cornish Times* have rung. They want to interview me now that I am 'back from the dead'. I said I was not back from the dead, that I had been sunbathing the whole time

and had only left St Slaughter to get away from my embarrassing family. Then they asked if it was true that I was staying with TV sexpert Suzy Stone. I said yes. So they asked if they could interview her instead. I put her on the line. This is typical. My possible tragic and untimely death is being eclipsed by best friend's mother and her vibrator collection.

Jack asked if I wanted to go down to the beach to escape the media frenzy. I said yes. We will have a beach party and barbecue Linda McCartney sausages and drink and Sad Ed can play his guitar.

4 p.m.
Did not have a beach party. Scarlet and Trevor refused to come in case they accidentally got a tan and Sad Ed was helping Suzy answer fan mail and problem letters (now that he is a Year Ten sex guru he thinks he is fully qualified to dole out advice on penile dysfunction). So it was just me and Jack in the sand dunes. Which was actually OK. We talked about school and what we are going to do when we leave i.e. move to London, probably Camden, and when I looked at my watch four hours had gone. This is unprecedented. Normally Sad Ed drives me to desertion within an hour. Jack said he thought my fake suicide was 'legendary Riley' and a complete stroke of genius. I was about to tell him about the bit of the note that the dog had eaten but for some reason I didn't. It is nice being thought of as a legend.

Sunday 20

Suzy is in the *Cornish Times* women's pages talking about the dos and don'ts of holiday sex (do use condoms, don't expect an orgasm from some man you have just met in Whispers in Newquay). It is alarmingly progressive for Cornwall. This just shows that in fact St Slaughter is in some sort of timewarp and everywhere else is normal, relatively speaking. Except for Bodmin Moor, where their idea of fun is a museum with stuffed kittens in period costume.

Monday 21

11 a.m.
There is a French girl by the pool. She has long French hair and equally long French legs. Plus she seems to know Jack very well. They are talking in French, which I do not understand, and which is worrying as my French GCSE is in less than a year. I may well write to Tony Blair to complain about the quality of language teaching in the state education sector.

11.30 a.m.
According to Scarlet the French girl is called Marie-Claire, is 17, and is the niece of the Pitt-Watsons who are from Surrey and staying one luxury villa down from Natasha Kaplinsky. She and Jack went to a club in Newquay last week and Scarlet is predicting they will snog before Friday.

Feel annoyed. But no idea why. I do not care about Jack in that way any more.

5.30 p.m.
Do I?

. . . .

Tuesday 22

Went to beach with Sad Ed and Jack (beach still out of bounds to goths, who are spending most of holiday inside with curtains drawn). Marie-Claire turned up in a French bikini and rattled on in French with Jack. Then, worryingly, Sad Ed joined in. (I am clearly a dunce and am going to fail French and have to work with Pie Shop Pearce.) Or maybe Marie-Claire has some kind of hard-to-understand regional Parisian dialect that Sad Ed and Jack have managed to pick up through practice. That will be it. Luckily she had to go, as (according to Jack, who helpfully translated) the Pitt-Watsons were going to eat line-caught mackerel at some uber-hip beach shack in Rock. Sad Ed said he'd walk back with her, as he had forgotten his sunglasses and might damage his sensitive eyes and have to be like Stevie Wonder (but white and less talented). This is a lie. It is because it was hot and he didn't want to have to expose his upper arms to the general public.

So it was me and Jack again. I said Marie-Claire was very pretty. He said, 'I suppose so, if you like that sort of thing.' I said, 'What's not to like? She has absolutely coltish

506

limbs [learnt from *Vogue*], hair that does not attempt to defy gravity and at least 34C breasts.' He said, 'Put it like that, yeah, she is pretty.' Then we just lay there in silence and I pretended to be engrossed in his *Mojo* magazine until Suzy came to tell us it was time for hummus.

4 p.m.
That was not what he was supposed to say. He was supposed to say, 'Yes, but she has a slightly wonky tooth and says "paff" instead of "whatever".' But he didn't. Which proves he is going to snog her. Scarlet is always right about these things.

Wednesday 23
Oh my God. Tuesday is in Cornwall! Me and Scarlet were in Padstow with Suzy buying essential food items (organic muesli, marinated artichokes, and pain au chocolats) when Suzy suddenly shrieked, 'Tuesday, my dark angel, is it you?' Answer—yes. It turns out she is staying with Mr Wilmott at the Bedruthan Holiday Park (i.e. totally not literary and tragic) while Edie 'overcomes some problems' (i.e. is back in rehab). Suzy has insisted she comes over to visit tomorrow. Sad Ed is going to get a shock. Me and Scarlet have agreed not to warn him in case he panics and tries to run for freedom. Then Suzy got star spotted by a coachload of pensioners from Rhyll and had to sign autographs for an hour.

When we got back Marie-Claire was in the pool again—topless! I do not approve of all this continental breast-baring. It is very distracting, not to mention depressing when she is clearly several sizes bigger than me. Jack and Sad Ed did not seem to mind though. Nor did Bob.

. . . .

Thursday 24

Jack's GCSE results arrived this morning. He has got nine As so he is definitely staying at John Major High to become a genius politician and musical legend. (Justin got four Cs and three Ds. He is doing resits at John Major High as not even Braintree want him at the moment. Maybe I can become his tutor and help him pass his exams and he will fall hopelessly in love me and realize I am THE ONE after all. Excellent.)

Suzy is going to throw a party to celebrate. She is inviting Natasha Kaplinsky, the Pitt-Watsons, Marie-Claire, the man from the *Cornish Times,* and the druid of St Petroc, who is influential in these parts. She is also inviting Tuesday. Scarlet and I begged her not to invite Mr Wilmott but Suzy said that would be rude and she is sure he likes a good party as much as the next man. I am not so sure he will like one of Suzy's.

2 p.m.
Tuesday is here. Mr Wilmott dropped her off in his Skoda. (Tuesday made him park several hundred yards up the

508

road, but I spotted him from the balcony.) Sad Ed dropped his Magnum in shock when he saw her but they have now gone for a walk to 'discuss their relationship'. What relationship?

7 p.m.
Sad Ed and Tuesday are back together! I said didn't he care about her adultery and the fact that she is actually not tragic at all, but he said she has been thinking of chucking Dave for a while as he has stretch marks, and she once jumped into the fountain in Trafalgar Square in her underwear which is totally brilliant and edgy. There is no telling some people. They have sealed their love with a grope by the pool.

* *

Friday 25
Rang Mum and Dad to check what time they are picking me up. Dad said 10. I begged him to delay until midnight but he said the roads would be perfectly clear by then and Mum says if we leave any later the dog and James are in danger of getting overtired and fighting. Asked him what everyone was up to. He said Mum was removing some unidentified sticky stuff from the bath, the Cleggs were at the Spar buying Bird's Eye things, and James was sunbathing with the triplets. He says he is looking forward to going home.

Tuesday is here again, lying on top of Sad Ed by the pool. She says there is no way Mr Wilmott is coming to

the party. She is going to stay the night and he is picking her up from the top of the road tomorrow. At least we will be able to drink celebratory alcoholic punch without fears of repercussionary detentions next term.

Marie-Claire is here as well. She is listening to Jack play 'Chelsea Dagger' on his guitar. They are obviously waiting for the right moment to snog, i.e. the party tomorrow with its atmosphere of general sexual abandon, knowing Suzy.

10 p.m.
Why do I care whether Jack snogs Marie-Claire? Maybe I don't care.

10.15 p.m.
Oh, I think I do care. Oh God. What am I going to do?

. . . .

Saturday 26
10 a.m.
Cannot decide if I actually fancy Jack. Am hoping it is mere annoyance at Frenchness of Marie-Claire and general absence of Justin that is confusing my feelings.

11 a.m.
Just seen Jack in swimming trunks. Definitely do fancy him. Oh God, this is not good.

12 noon
Maybe it is good. Maybe he really loves me too.

1 p.m.
No is not good. Will stop thinking about him and concentrate on first celebrity party (i.e. Natasha Kaplinsky and druid man).

5 p.m.
Oh, but have just seen him do backwards dive into swimming pool. He is sensitive, artistic, and excellent at sport. Unlike Justin, who can only do breaststroke and bombing.

7 p.m.
No definitely must not tell him. He thinks Marie-Claire (i.e. tall with straight hair and no mental relatives) is pretty and therefore will absolutely not want to be near me. Will just ignore him and enjoy company of friends. And Tuesday.

10.00 p.m.
Am in the wet room hiding from *a*) Jack and *b*) dog-related chaos (Mum and Dad have arrived and I forgot about the dog's aversion to Natasha Kaplinsky and there has been an incident that has left Natasha's glamorous good looks slightly chewed. She will not be able to do the news without a wig for a few weeks.) Everything was fine until Scarlet, Trevor, Tuesday, and Sad Ed (who had clearly been talking to the druid) decided to go and stand on a 'ley line' next to the surf shop and Jack and I got somehow left alone on the balcony, in a sunset. Which should both be

511

banned as they are totally romantic and make you want to do things that under normal circumstances (i.e. level ground and drizzle) you are easily able to not do. Jack said Marie-Claire had asked him out. I said that he should totally go out with her. That she had French legs and French hair etc. and was seventeen. Then he said, 'But she never faked her own death, or dyed herself to look like a wardrobe or thought Karl Marx was one of the Marx brothers.' I said, 'No, she isn't that stupid.' Then Jack touched me on the shoulder and it was like that bit in films where all the background noise disappears and it was just me and him in extreme close up and he asked me if I was really saying he should go out with Marie-Claire. And I really wanted to say, 'No, go out with me!' but for some reason, what came out was 'Yes.' And then I was back on the balcony with the sound of the dog barking manically and Natasha Kaplinsky's screams ringing in one ear.

Maybe it is all for the best. After all he is Scarlet's brother.

10.05 p.m.
It is not for the best. I think he is THE ONE. Oh my God. I am going to tell him immediately before Dad drags me to the car with the dog.

11.30 p.m.
Have not told him. It was too late. When I went downstairs he was by the pool with Marie-Claire's arms around

512

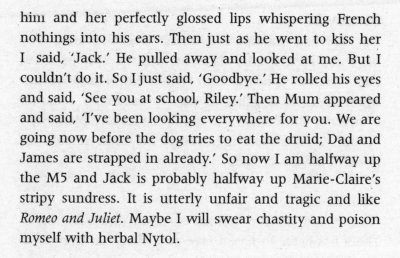
him and her perfectly glossed lips whispering French nothings into his ears. Then just as he went to kiss her I said, 'Jack.' He pulled away and looked at me. But I couldn't do it. So I just said, 'Goodbye.' He rolled his eyes and said, 'See you at school, Riley.' Then Mum appeared and said, 'I've been looking everywhere for you. We are going now before the dog tries to eat the druid; Dad and James are strapped in already.' So now I am halfway up the M5 and Jack is probably halfway up Marie-Claire's stripy sundress. It is utterly unfair and tragic and like *Romeo and Juliet*. Maybe I will swear chastity and poison myself with herbal Nytol.

12.30 a.m.
Have gone off chastity—remembered Miss Crawley again. Am going to write him a letter declaring my love. All poetic types can only communicate their true feelings on paper, it is a well-known fact. Will post it when we get home.

4 a.m.
Have posted letter. Mum asked what was so urgent that I needed to get it in the postbox tonight. I said 'destiny'. She said Miriam Stoppard was right, the teenage years are worse than the terrible twos. Then she got inside and found that Grandpa and Treena had left the oven on and several windows open, breaking all manner of security rules.

Sunday 27

Not only had Grandpa and Treena broken security, they have also broken four plates, stained the upstairs toilet, and filled the cupboards with Wagon Wheels and Wotsits. Mum says she is going to see Mr Lemon as a matter of urgency. Otherwise, she cannot be responsible for her actions. This is worrying. She is the most responsible person I have ever met.

1 p.m.

Oh my God, Saffron Walden is on the lunchtime news. There has been an illegal rave on a sheep farm in Great Chesterford. This is typical. I leave for two weeks and I miss the only interesting thing to happen ever. According to the BBC, literally a dozen drug-crazed youths fled to freedom from riot police across treacherous train tracks (not likely—there is one train an hour and James can outrun it—he proved it once). Then they showed grainy footage of what looked suspiciously like Fat Kylie's enormous miniskirted behind wobbling towards Hadstock in the moonlight. Mum says this is what happens when her ceaseless campaign against anti-social behaviour decamps to the south-west.

Jack gets back tonight. Which means he will get the letter tomorrow morning. My fate is sealed. His holiday romance will be long forgotten and he will fall into my English arms.

Monday 28

Bank Holiday

Except that it is a bank holiday. So he won't get it until tomorrow. I should have posted it by hand. Curse Barclays and their need for random Mondays off.

The rave is in Grandpa's *Daily Telegraph*. There is a quote from evil Tory MP for Saffron Walden and environs Hugo Thorndyke. He says,

'I am outraged that local youths have endangered not only their lives but those of our respected

(hardly)

and hard-working

(barely)

local police officers. But it is clear that many of those involved had crossed into our Conservative, in all senses of the word, constituency from Labour-run Harlow, where mob rule runs free. You can be sure I will be speaking to Barry Goggins at the first available opportunity.'

It is the farmer I feel sorry for. I bet his fields are ruined with Fat Kylie bouncing around on them.

3 p.m.
I have been a fool for love. The unthinkable has happened. Jack has gone to Paris with Marie-Claire until Friday! I rang Scarlet to discuss the rave but she was round at Trevor's painting his toenails black so I casually asked Suzy about Jack and she said she dropped him at Dover last night with a copy of *Madame Bovary* and a packet of condoms. She is hoping he will have his sexual awakening. Hung up as the thought of Jack awakening with Marie-Claire made me feel sick.

Thank God for bank holidays. I will intercept the post tomorrow and destroy the letter before Suzy does anything stupid like forward it to Paris or read it down the phone to him. He will never know of my utter devotion. Until I die tragically (and for real this time) and my diaries are published and he will be racked with guilt and remorse and will kill himself so he can be with me in everlasting peace (or vampire-ridden netherworld, according to Scarlet and Trevor). Except that by then I will have married Justin in a barefoot ceremony and have several children called tragic Shakespearean things like Ophelia and Romeo.

4 p.m.
Oh not Romeo. That is totally Beckham i.e. chav.

7 p.m.

Have given up vegetarianism. Mum made lasagne for tea. It was organic lamb mince though, so it is almost veggie, because the sheep were happy before they died and got pulverized. Also it is pointless being vegetarian if Jack does not love me. Especially as would have to shop in lentil-smelling health food outlet Nuts In May, run by hunchback Mr Goldstein and his ailment-ridden assistant Rosamund.

· ·

Tuesday 29

9 a.m.

Went round Scarlet's to intercept post. Their new cleaner, Edna, was there, rearranging the cutlery. She would not pass Mum's strict cleaning ability tests. For a start, she was smoking a Rothman's while she worked. The letter had not arrived. This is typical of the Royal Mail. According to James the post office is rife with criminal activity and my letter has probably been stolen by organized gangs of postmen. This is not good. Our postman is Beefy Clark who is a notorious gossip and will no doubt report the sordid details to everyone else on his post round and they will be all round the school by next week.

· ·

Wednesday 30

Still no letter. Scarlet checked with Edna but she says she

put all the post where it belonged, on top of the fridge. I said I didn't know the post belonged on the fridge, but apparently Edna is imposing a strict, if slightly random, new system.

Mum has been to see Mr Lemon. He says he will call her when there are any developments and to please stop harassing him as he is finding his job increasingly stressful with all the O'Grady issues.

. . . .

Thursday 31

No letter. James is right. It is probably stolen or thrown into a bin. On the plus side, this means that it will never reach its destination, i.e. Jack, and my secret will die with me.

Edna's new system is causing havoc. Scarlet says Bob was an hour late for work because all his pants had disappeared and he refuses to do pelvic surgery going commando. They were eventually located in the bedside cabinet.

The rave is in the *Walden Chronicle* with several grainy photos of perpetrators and an invitation to 'name that hoodie'.

september

EAT MORE CHIPS

Friday 1

2 p.m.

Jack gets back in three hours. I am going to resist the temptation to go and lurk at the Stones' in order to catch a glimpse of him. It will only fuel my sorrow.

3 p.m.

Two hours to go before Jack is back. Am still being resolute. Will stay in my bedroom and read poetry.

4 p.m.

But maybe he and Marie-Claire discovered that their lives are separated by more than the English Channel and that actually they have nothing in common, and the condoms have been abandoned, unopened, on the Champs Élysées and Jack is all fired up after reading *Madame Bovary* and is rushing home to throw himself at my English mercy.

5 p.m.

Yes, that is utterly what will have happened. Am going to Scarlet's immediately.

8 p.m.

That is not what happened. Jack is still snogging Marie-Claire. He is already talking about having gap years in Paris and going to the Sorbonne. And, worse, it is all my fault. When I arrived he said, 'Riley, you were right— Marie-Claire is amazing.' Then he went on for two hours

about how they saw a baby deer in the Bois de Bologne on their last night and how her mother is an actress who once appeared nude in a Fellini film and her dad is a left-wing anti-government radical—typical. This is typical. I left before I threw up.

Saturday 2

Called Sad Ed so I could feel better about my utterly non-progressive existence (his family make mine look like the Stones) but he was round at Tuesday's painting an art installation on her bedroom wall. Even Sad Ed is more tragic and interesting than me. Although I do not envy him when Mr Wilmott finds out they have defaced the Hint of Barley.

Sunday 3

School starts tomorrow. A new and crucial year. Have got a Year Eleven appropriate schoolbag i.e. black and inconspicuous instead of Milletts rucksack with an 'I've climbed Snowdon!' sew-on patch.

Monday 4

School starts

Davey MacDonald is back and the vending machine is gone. They are both the victims of political correctness gone mad, according to Scarlet. This is not true. Davey

MacDonald is the victim of his own idiocy—on top of the Thin Kylie fracas at Sadler's Wells, he kept revealing his penis to the rehearsal pianist. The vending machine is a victim of Jamie Oliver. It has been replaced with a fruit and nut dispenser.

Mr Wilmott gave all the Year Elevens a talk about how this is the most crucial year of our school career and that it is time we knuckled down to our GCSEs, which are only ten months away etc., etc. Then he announced we would be getting our mock results tomorrow. They were located in Mrs Leech's bottom drawer under her Nurofen and tampon supplies. A general feeling of fear hangs over 11 Hopwood-White. Except for the Kylies who are too busy going through Year Seven applications to their gang.

. . . .

Tuesday 5

Got eight Bs and a D (rural studies). This is shameful. Even Stacey O'Grady passed rural studies. Bs are not so bad though. Loads of philosophical and literary types are mediocre at school and their talents only come to light in the nurturing intellectual atmosphere of Cambridge University. Or maybe I can claim I am dyslexic like Keanu Reeves or Eddie Izzard. Or Fat Kylie. Although hers is still under review as to whether or not she is just thick.

No one is using the fruit and nut dispenser. They are going to Mr Patel's instead for kingsize Mars bars and Coke. His profits must be soaring and it is all thanks to New

Labour. He already has a new people carrier and a conservatory. With the vending machine ban I predict he will be moving to a five-bed on Seven Devils Lane, formerly home to pint-size Eighties pop sensation Nik Kershaw.

5 p.m.
Mum says I am not dyslexic, as proven by my freakish ability to spell Mississippi at the age of five, but that I will be soaking up the less than intellectual atmosphere at Harlow Further Education College unless I start to take my GCSEs seriously.

Wednesday 6
The apples are rotting in the fruit and nut dispenser. Mr Wilmott has taken the drastic measure of banning anyone from leaving the school premises during breaks, including staff (they are dependent on Mr Patel for their supply of cigarettes and microwave samosas). Fat Kylie says she is suffering malnutrition and is threatening to get her mum in. Ms Hopwood-White says you cannot get scurvy from crisp withdrawal and has sent her to Mr Wilmott.

Thursday 7
Fat Kylie's mum has set up a crisp and Coke stall and is doing a roaring trade selling Fanta and Wotsits through a gap in the sheep field fence. Mr Vaughan has asked if she

can start doing Benson and Hedges as well. Mr Wilmott is not so enlightened. He has ordered Mr Cheesmond (scary giant beard, lingering smell of goat) aka the head of Rural Studies aka Cowpat Cheesmond, who is in charge of sheep, to turn the electric fence on at all times.

Friday 8

The crisp and Coke stall is no more. Fat Kylie's mum got electrocuted seven times in five minutes. She is suing the school for singeing her velour jogging bottoms. Mr Wilmott has offered her a generous out-of-court settlement of £100 but she says she is going for a million. She will not get it. I know for a fact that they cost £12.99 off the market.

Saturday 9

Went round Scarlet's for lunch. Edna is causing havoc with all her rearranging. The CDs have been rehoused in the bathroom and no one has seen Gordon for a week. Bob wants to sack her but Suzy says Bob can't complain as it was his idea and they can't sack Edna on grounds of an illogical system, it is against union rules. Bob said there is no way Edna is unionized but Suzy said on the contrary she is a long-standing member of the carpet-fitters and weavers union.

Jack was on the phone to Marie-Claire when I arrived, doing loads of giggling and sighing. It was disgusting.

Scarlet says she rings him every day. I said it was lucky her parents were happy to fund her astronomical phone bills but Scarlet says Marie-Claire earned £20,000 last year from a L'Oreal mascara advert and was financially independent. Could my life possibly get any worse?

Sunday 10

Apparently it could. Baby Jesus has inserted a mini pizza into the DVD player, consigning it and my copy of utterly tragic *Romeo and Juliet* to history. He is potentially more destructive than the dog. Which is saying something.

Monday 11

The Retards and Criminals are being temporarily reintegrated into society following flooding and smoke damage on D Corridor. It is because Mark Lambert set fire to Davey MacDonald's crêpe paper collage of Girls Aloud and set off the sprinklers. We are getting three—Mark Lambert, Davey MacDonald, and Caris Kelp, who eats glue.

Tuesday 12

Ms Hopwood-White has been forced to lock the stationery cupboard. Two Pritt Sticks went missing during registration. All signs point to Caris.

Wednesday 13

Drama Club started today. They are doing *The Sound of Music* and have instigated a school-wide search for Maria, culminating in a live final next Friday lunchtime in the lower school canteen. I am not auditioning, despite my excellent acting ability and Julie Andrews-like air of innocence and practicality. Jack is bookie's (i.e. Ali Hassan's Maths Club gambling ring) favourite to play Captain Von Trapp and I do not think I could bear to be within his treacherous arms, not even in the name of Art.

Thursday 14

Ms Hopwood-White says she is thinking of suing the government over their ad campaigns to recruit teachers. I do not blame her. They are full of clean and clever multicultural children asking inspired questions like 'What is the difference between fluff and dust?' Or 'What is dark matter?' It is misleading. In reality most questions are 'Are fish actually reptiles, miss?' Or 'Was Shakespeare, like, a bender, miss?'

What is the difference between fluff and dust though? I bet James will know.

Friday 15

Apparently it is down to fibre content.

Saturday 16

Mum has got her new driving test date. It is on 25th October. She is writing to the council to demand details of all proposed road amendments and additions. But, in a potentially marriage-breaking move, she is not telling Dad about the test. She says he will only panic unnecessarily about Mr Wandering Hands. James said she would live to regret her deception. Mum told him not to be so melodramatic and to go and tell the dog to stop licking the hifi.

Sunday 17

Treena is going back to work tomorrow. It is so she can save up for a pink wedding dress, as seen on Jordan. It is a bad idea. Jordan is *a*) thin, albeit with enormous breasts, *b*) pretty, in a porn star sort of way, and *c*) married to a youthful pop star, whereas Treena is *a*) still carrying three stone of baby/Golden Wonder weight, *b*) looks like Gillian Taylforth, and *c*) is marrying a pensioner. Grandpa is not happy about her going to work. He says her place is in the home looking after him, but she says he doesn't pay £6.80 an hour. She is going to take Jesus with her. Mum said wouldn't that be difficult trying to take care of him at the same time as looking after all the old people but Treena says it will be like taking drugs into a prison. The inmates (aka old ladies), will be fighting to get hold of him and all she'll have to do is dole out the nappies.

Monday 18

Mr Vaughan asked if I had given any thought to auditioning for *The Sound of Music*. I said I didn't think I would have time with all my other extra curricular activities. This is a lie. I do not do any activities. I just cannot bear to be near Jack. Scarlet says he and Marie-Claire phone each other up every day. It is lucky Suzy is a rich celebrity now so she can afford to foot his phone sex bills.

. . . .

Tuesday 19

Maria madness has taken over the school. Everyone is auditioning, including Fat Kylie and Sad Ed, although he is only doing it because Tuesday says being in a musical is actually totally offbeat. He has no chance. Even Mr Vaughan, who is known for his sexing-up of school productions, would draw the line at a gay male nun. Thin Kylie says she is too busy to audition. I have seen the evidence. She now has seventy-three badges on her parka, dominated by the national potato week motto 'Eat More Chips'. They should have Fat Kylie as the face of their campaign.

. . . .

Wednesday 20

Baby Jesus is missing. Treena forgot to bring him back from work. She was watching *Neighbours* when Grandpa asked her where he was so he could give him his Heinz

jars. They have searched the Twilight Years Day Centre but he is not there. Grandpa is pacing uncontrollably. Mum has pointed out that he can't have gone far, as he is incapable of moving more than a few feet but Grandpa says you read about this sort of thing in the papers all the time and Des has probably kidnapped him and taken him to live in Libya. Treena said don't be daft Des doesn't even know where Libya is. They are doing a phone round the old people to see if anyone can remember seeing him.

8 p.m.
Baby Jesus has been located. And not in Libya. Although he was in a dictatorship i.e. the Pink Geranium Sheltered Housing Unit, where Grandpa used to live before he got thrown out by the fascist warden Mrs Peason for abusing the buzzer system and Treena. Mrs Peason rang after finding him in Elsie Stain's blanket box. Elsie said she thought he had been abandoned so she decided to give him a good home. Dad asked Mrs Peason how she knew who Jesus's parents were. She says he has Grandpa's obsession with breasts and Treena's moronic stare. It is true. Grandpa has banned Treena from taking Jesus to work. He says old women and babies are a recipe for disaster.

. . . .

Thursday 21
5 p.m.
Bumped into Jack in the car park after school. I tried to

hide but he saw me and asked what in God's name I was doing crouching down behind Mr Vaughan's Civic. I said I had lost an earring, which was the first thing that came into my head. Even though I don't even have my ears pierced (banned until I am sixteen and then only a single hole in regulation earlobe i.e. not ten in one ear like Tuesday). Then he asked me if I was auditioning for Maria. I said I wasn't, and that I was going to concentrate on my GCSEs. He said that was a shame as it would have been a laugh if I was doing the show. Then he said he had to go and meet Justin and Sophie to rehearse their audition pieces but as he walked off he turned and smiled and said, 'You don't wear earrings, Riley.'

Aaagh! So now he knows I am trying to avoid him. Which means he knows there is a reason for me avoiding him. Which means I have to not avoid him. Which means I have to audition. Also Justin is auditioning. So he might get to be Captain Von Trapp. He is more classicly good-looking than Jack after all. And is an inch taller. Although I suppose Mr Vaughan is not likely to give him or Sophie lead roles given their sexual *ménage à trois*.

11 p.m.
Have learnt 'The Hills are Alive' and 'My Favourite Things' off by heart, with the aid of James, who knows the entire score and dialogue. It is a throwback from his short-lived obsession with becoming a nun (swapped for another obsession with marrying Granny Clegg—thankfully

also only temporary). So am totally prepared for Mr Vaughan's live final, with Mr Wilmott as Andrew Lloyd Webber and Ms Hopwood-White as Graham Norton.

. . . .

Friday 22

The audition did not go brilliantly. I forgot what my favourite things were and had to make some of them up (bright coloured kettles and warm woollen kittens). On the plus side, I was definitely better than Fat Kylie, whose impression of a lonely goatherd will go down in John Major history. Anyway, at least I did audition. So now Jack knows I am not avoiding him i.e. I am totally over him.

. . . .

Saturday 23

James has received letters of devotion from all three triplets. Mum is not amused at his new-found status as a nine-year-old Casanova but Grandpa says he is following in Riley tradition. Mum said there was no such tradition and that Dad was a model of self-restraint in his youth. Grandpa said, 'That's what you think,' and then wandered off mysteriously. It is Mumtaz I feel sorry for. She has been thrown aside carelessly like a dirty sock.

. . . .

Sunday 24

Mum's web of deceit is spinning out of control. Dad asked

her if she was thinking of reapplying for another driving test. Mum said no. Strictly speaking this is not a total lie as she has applied already and applying again would be pointless and wasteful but I fear Dad will not see it like that. I don't like all this subterfuge. James is right. It will all end badly and I will end up homeless or in the evangelical care of Auntie Joyless.

Monday 25

The Sound of Music cast list goes up tomorrow. Not that I am eager with anticipation or anything. It is just an observation.

Tuesday 26

4 p.m.

Sophie Microwave Muffins is Maria. It is an outrage. She is neither practical, nor eccentric, plus she hates goats. It is obvious that Mr Vaughan is only doing it to prove he bears no grudge against her. Or else get back in her good books and/or knickers. Not that I wanted the part anyway. Especially now that Jack is definitely Captain von Trapp. On the contrary I am delighted to be eldest Von Trapp Liesl. Especially as Justin is Nazi youth Rolf, on account of his Aryan hair. So I will have to snog him (kissing in plays not banned thanks to intervention from all-round sexual libertarian David Blunkett).

5 p.m.

I mean get to snog him. It is good thing. I mean I have wanted to kiss him for ages and now I can, so it is excellent. Isn't it?

. . . .

Wednesday 27

Had first rehearsal for *Sound of Music*. Am not entirely convinced that Mr Vaughan's casting of Dean 'the dwarf' Denley as five-year-old Gretl is entirely politically correct but I suppose he is the only person short enough to do it without resorting to shuffling about on his knees—the favoured method of portraying children and old ladies in John Major theatrical tradition. And I don't think any audience will be able to suspend their disbelief long enough to believe Fat Kylie is Mother Superior. Everyone knows she is far from nun-like in her habits (ha ha). Also Sad Ed is regretting auditioning now that he is Chief Nazi. He is not so sure it is offbeat to have to feign a cod German accent and bleach his hair. Scarlet is doing set design. She says her goth beliefs forbid her from religious entertainment. This is not true. It is because she does not want to have to be a man again.

. . . .

Thursday 28

New CCTV cameras have been installed at 'crime hotspots' according to the *Walden Chronicle*. Mum is delighted. She

says it will drive troublemakers out of the town centre and back where they belong—i.e. Harlow. Sad Ed and Tuesday do not agree. They say it is the first step to a police state and that we will all be taking orders from Big Brother within a year. I think they mean in the Orwell book, not the bloke with the Newcastle accent on Channel 4. The cameras are pointed at Barry Island, the bins outside Abrakebabra, and the entire Whiteshot Estate. I bet the Kylies are outraged. That is all their potential shagging spots ruled out. Unless they have ambitions to become porn stars or on *You've Been Framed*.

Friday 29

Tracey Hughes says the police are thinking of suing the *Walden Chronicle* for publishing the locations of their highly secret CCTV cameras. I said they weren't that secret, given that they are six metres high and bright blue. She said that is what the *Walden Chronicle* said. Anyway, the mental capacity of criminals like the O'Gradys is such that they will forget by next week and still get caught.

Saturday 30

It is Sad Ed's birthday tomorrow. He will be sixteen i.e. allowed to have sex and smoke but, weirdly, not join a library without his parent's permission. Although I doubt Mrs Thomas will let him do any of the above. He is having

a party tonight and some of Tuesday's friends are going to be there. This is a major risk, given the unwritten John Major rules that you are not allowed to fraternize with anyone from the Quaker school due to their *a*) crap school uniform and *b*) weird religion where you don't say anything in church, you sit there all silent. I mean how boring is that? But he says he is trying to bridge a social divide and this will be like when they got rid of apartheid in South Africa and we will all be able to drink latte together instead of us having to go to the Mocha while the Quakers dominate the Coffee Stop. He is right. It is time to break down the barriers of repression.

. . . .

11 p.m.
The barriers of repression are still standing. It is because one of Trevor's bat friends tried to snog Daisy Truelove, who is apparently strictly property of the Quaker boys, and then a goths v. Quakers fight broke out, which was sort of like a scene from that film *The Village*, and Mrs Thomas ended the party before anyone damaged her Aled Jones figurines.

October

Sunday 1

Called Sad Ed to check if he had indulged in any coming of age activities. He said chance would be a fine thing. His mum sent Tuesday home with the Quakers and him to bed at nine with a hot chocolate and a *Beano* annual. He says he will be lucky to lose his virginity by the age of thirty at this rate.

. . . .

Monday 2

7.30 a.m.

Granny Clegg rang in a new-found religious fervour. She has seen the face of Jesus (the bearded Messiah, not my uncle) in a slice of Nimble toast. Auntie Joyless is on her way over to confirm if it is the good Lord himself. James answered. He is excited. He says she is sitting on a potential gold mine. Apparently a girl in Portugal found God in an aubergine and is now a millionaire. He has told Granny Clegg not to do anything daft like expose it to damp or spread it with Nutella.

4 p.m.

It is definitely Jesus, according to Auntie Joyless and Father Abraham (seriously), her ecclesiastical consultant. And they should know. Grandpa Clegg is stocking up on refreshments for all the pilgrims they are eagerly expecting and Granny has called the *St Slaughter Reporter*. James said she was underselling herself and she should call Jeremy Paxman

but then Mum grabbed the phone and told her under no circumstances to call the BBC. She said they will try to sabotage the story. This is not true. It is because she is worried that Paxo will wheedle all sorts of idiotic things out of her and expose her for the yokel she is.

. . . .

Tuesday 3

Bruce has eaten Jesus. Granny Clegg is devastated but Grandpa says it serves her right for putting the toast on a plinth on the windowsill so that passers by could catch a glimpse. Granny says she has toasted the rest of the loaf in case it is all divine but all she has got so far is Maureen from the Spar and a wonky Gary Lineker.

. . . .

Wednesday 4

3 p.m.

Had my first rehearsal with Nazi youth Rolf i.e. Justin. Mr Vaughan said he was concerned at the lack of chemistry between us, despite my excellent innocent smouldering. Justin said he was finding it hard convincing himself he was in love with me. Mr Vaughan said, 'You will never be Robert de Niro if you can't mentally turn Ugly Betty into Cameron Diaz. If this is stretching your talents then I suggest you go back to dodgeball.' Justin said, 'Oh, bog off, Vaughany, you perv,' so Mr Vaughan threw him out. But Mr Wilmott threw him back in and took Mr Vaughan

outside for a quiet chat (overheard by Fat Kylie who was having a fag break) and told him that he had to stop personal feelings interfering with his teaching or he would be back doing supply at Newport Boys.

3.15 p.m.
What does he mean about Ugly Betty?

. . . .

Thursday 5
Suzy is doing the Year Nine sex lecture tomorrow. I hope Mr Wilmott knows what he is letting himself in for. There are bound to be graphic details and free condoms.

. . . .

Friday 6
Suzy has been banned from any future sex education classes. Things got out of hand when she simulated the missionary position with Kyle O'Grady. Plus she suggested the age of consent should be fourteen. So the Year Nines are back with Miss Beadle and her plastic penis model.

. . . .

Saturday 7
James is one triplet down. Presley has dumped him for an eleven year old called Biffer who has a BMX. He got a letter this morning on Hello Kitty notepaper. He says he is not hurt as he still has Parker and Peyton under his

spell but I know he is just putting on a brave face. He asked Mum if he could get a BMX but she said no, on the grounds that my old Raleigh is still perfectly functioning, so he has gone round Mad Harry's to sulk.

. . . .

Sunday 8

Am officially bridesmaid to Grandpa and Treena. They have confirmed the wedding date with the White Horse. James pointed out that Treena still hadn't had her Decree Absolute in the divorce proceedings but she says it is a technicality. I do not think the police will see it like that. The good news is that Treena's job means that she now has a bridesmaid's dress budget so I will not have to wear one of Mum's horrendous cast-offs. The bad news is that she says she is not shopping in Steinberg and Tolkien (i.e. utterly famous vintage shop in London favoured by Kylie (the real goddess-like one, not the Primark Pretenders)) and I can go to Berkertex in Cambridge with her next Saturday. She is still going for voluminous pink, inadvisedly.

. . . .

Monday 9

The CCTV cameras have caught Mr Whippy doing 'It' on Barry Island. Tracey Hughes says she watched the video with her mum last night and the female recipient of Mr Whippy's attentions is definitely NOT Fat Kylie—the thighs are too small. I said she had better not tell Fat Kylie

but Tracey said it was too late as she had lent the video to Thin Kylie at break.

. . . .

Tuesday 10

Mr Whippy is in hospital with a broken nose and fractured ribs. I asked Fat Kylie if her brothers had come to her aid to protect her honour. She said, 'My honour don't need protecting, I done it myself.' So I asked her if she had found out who the girl was. She said her minions were searching Saffron Walden for a 'slag with a fat arse and white cowboy boots'. That could be any number of people.

. . . .

Wednesday 11

Davey MacDonald has a Nazi dance solo. I said I didn't recall this being in the original version but Mr Vaughan says he is not going to let good talent go to waste, even with the potential for genital exposure.

The Mr Whippy sex tape is selling well in the sixth form common room. Justin says it is like Paris Hilton but with wobbling.

. . . .

Thursday 12

Mr Whippy has been sacked by the ice cream company for bringing them into disrepute. This is a bit far-fetched

as they are already facing a legal suit following last summer's mass 99 poisoning. On the plus side, he is moving back in with his mum above Dorrington's for a bit until the hoo-ha calms down (and until Fat Kylie calms down), which means the other O'Grady can move into his three-bed semi, which means Grandpa and Treena are now at the top of the housing list! Mum is delighted. She is scouring the obituaries in the *Walden Chronicle* for any potential council house deaths.

· ·

Friday 13

Spent the entire day avoiding ladders, magpies, black cats, and other superstitious Friday 13th portents of doom. Then got home and found that the dog had unravelled one sleeve of my enormous fluffy jumper. This is typical.

· ·

Saturday 14

9 a.m.

Have got my bridesmaid's dress fitting later. Am determined to persuade Treena to go for demure off-white silk with absolutely no lace, bustles, or bows.

2 p.m.

Have got bridesmaid's dress. It is not demure off-white silk but is a vile pink net thing with puff sleeves and a fairy wand. Begged Treena not to choose it but she is going for

a pink theme. I suppose I should be glad I am not James or Jesus. Or the dog. They have pink sailor suits, complete with ribboned hats. Dad says we will look like a gay burlesque show. He is right. Even Grandpa is wearing a pink waistcoat.

Sunday 15

Madonna has caused an outrage by adopting a brown baby called David. She is just trying to outdo Angelina Jolie who has several. Mum said if she wanted a baby that badly she could have Jesus. But James said having Madonna and Jesus in the same family would be ridiculous. Treena said there was nothing wrong with it and if the next one was a girl she was going to call it Madonna, or Elvis for a boy. Mum went white and said, 'Please God do not tell me you are pregnant again,' and Treena said, 'Not yet, but if Ern keeps at it the way he is I'll be walking down the aisle at the White Horse two months up the duff.' Mum is not happy. I do not blame her. Having one baby in the house is bad enough. He has joined the dog in being a perpetual source of noise, sick, and destruction.

Monday 16

Mr Whippy's paramour has been identified. According to several Year Twelves and Mr Camden (history and metalwork) it is Leanne Jones. Fat Kylie is going round

her house after school with several other O'Gradys. It is Kyle I feel sorry for. This could compromise his star-crossed relationship with Leanne's little sister Primark Donna. Where will his loyalties lie?

. . . .

Tuesday 17

With Primark Donna, apparently. He has a black eye after trying to fight Fat Kylie at the Joneses' household last night. The police were called and, according to Tracey Hughes, one of the O'Gradys is now in custody. She cannot remember which one, as there are so many. Mum is hoping it is the one on the housing list, then Grandpa and Treena can move straight into Mr Whippy's. Fat Kylie is no help either. She is off school with alleged whiplash.

. . . .

Wednesday 18

It was not the right O'Grady. It was one I had never heard of called Dane. So Mum is back to waiting for a convenient death on Harvey Road.

Rehearsals went well, apart from the absence of Mother Superior, due to her ongoing whiplash, and a minor fight between the nuns and the Nazis (aka the Retards and Criminals). Mr Vaughan and his assistant director Oona Rickets say they are still concerned at the lack of seething sexual desire between me and Rolf. I said, well it wasn't my fault, I was positively oozing with it. Which is true.

Especially, and weirdly, in his uniform. But Mr Vaughan says we need to sort it out soon or he will have to rethink his casting.

. . . .

Thursday 19

The *Walden Chronicle* have started their annual search for Saffron Walden's 'bonniest' baby, sponsored by crap hardware shop, the unironically titled Gayhomes. The prize is £200 and a year's supply of squeegees. Grandpa is entering Jesus. He will fit in well in the yearly parade of Jades and Darryls.

. . . .

Friday 20

It is half term next week. To mark this auspicious occasion, Mark Lambert and Davey MacDonald (now working as one formidable super-Retard-like force) blew up a science lab by trying to gas a frog. They are suspended for a week. Sad Ed says it is down to poor parenting. He is right in the case of Mr Hosepipe. He strips to Britney Spears songs.

Also Mum had a driving lesson today. Dad got back from work early and asked where she was. I said she had gone for emergency Cif following a particularly nasty dog incident. When she got back Dad asked her where the Cif was. She said in the cupboard between the Bold 3 in 1 and the Cillit Bang, where it always is. So I diverted attention by dropping a glass of lemon barley. Thank God

her test is next week. I cannot keep this charade up any longer.

. . . .

Saturday 21

Baby Jesus has had his photo taken for the bonny baby competition. Grandpa borrowed James's camera and a selection of fancy dress outfits. I like the one of him as a policeman best, but Treena thinks Bob the Builder will nail it. They are desperate for the £200 to pay for their wedding reception entertainer—Pelvis Presley (aka Paul Presley from the garage on London Road).

Also, James is down to one triplet. Parker has decided to focus on her pony Sizzles as she has a crucial gymkhana season coming up. James is panicking and has demanded that Dad drives him to Solihull at half term for the sake of his love life. Dad has refused. This is because the last time he drove to Birmingham he got lost and ended up circling Spaghetti Junction for two hours with Mum shouting, 'Left, Colin, for God's sake, left.'

. . . .

Sunday 22

Bumped into Cherie who was struggling to lug her Debenhams bags out of her jeep. I asked her how life was treating her. She said, 'Like a bastard. Don't ever get involved with a plasterer. Women flock to them like moths to a flame and then they betray you and leave you

with nothing but a dodgy satellite dish and half a bottle of Tia Maria.' Strictly speaking Terry did not leave, she threw him out. And her drinks cabinet is vast. But I did not say this as Cherie did not look like she would be concerned with that sort of technicality.

Love is fraught with dangers. In fact I am lucky not to be gripped by its charms.

. . . .

Monday 23

Half term

Went round Scarlet's to celebrate the first day of the holidays by lying around watching telly. Jack has gone on an emergency trip to Paris to see Marie-Claire. According to Scarlet their long-distance relationship is fraught with petty jealousies and he has gone to check that she is not secretly fluttering her l'Oreal eyelashes at some boy called Henri-Claude. What is with the French and all their double-barrelled names?

. . . .

Tuesday 24

Mum's driving test is in twenty-four hours. She is having an intensive half-day revision session with Mr Wandering Hands. Thank God the web of deception will be torn down tomorrow. Dad has already rung twice. Once to ask her to cancel his subscription to *Golf World* as he can get it for nothing off Malcolm in IT and once to ask whether

Alan Whicker was dead (office bet). I said Mum was busy trying to get a piece of Lego out of the dog's windpipe and put James on instead. He knows things like that.

Went round Sad Ed's. He was busy making a CD of songs to tell Tuesday how he feels about her. I said I didn't think 'Girlfriend in a Coma' necessarily conveyed feelings of love and devotion. He said, 'That is why you are single, and I am a love god. Now go away, you are disturbing my creative juices.' I left before any of Sad Ed's juices could get near me.

. . . .

Wednesday 25

8 a.m.
Mum is nervous. She has actually spilled a cup of Nescafé, which is unprecedented. Dad said she should call a doctor immediately. He thinks it may be the onset of Parkinson's or Mad Cow disease. James asked what her other symptoms were and had she experienced any loss of bowel control, so Dad said he was late for a meeting to discuss new chairs and disappeared before James could go into any more detail. I knew this was all a mistake. It will end in tears. And divorce.

6 p.m.
Mum has passed. Thank God. Now the horrible deception can end. She has cooked Dad's favourite meal (vile liver), and is going to break the news to him after *Lovejoy*, when he will be in a good mood.

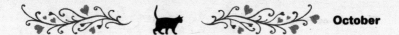

8.30 p.m.

Dad has taken the whole test thing remarkably well and has forgiven her for her evil tissue of lies. It is because Mum let him drink two glasses of Waitrose brandy, which is usually only allowed out on special occasions. He says at least now there is no risk of her and Mr Wandering Hands brushing fingertips over the Fiesta gearstick, plus she can ferry James and Mad Harry around at the weekends while he watches sport.

- -

Thursday 26

Mum is on a winning streak. There has been a potential council house death. According to the *Walden Chronicle*, ninety-three-year-old Dennis Waters is in hospital after electrocuting himself with a Dustbuster in the shower and is only clinging on by a thread. Treena says she knows him from the Twilight Years Day Centre. He is Elsie Stain's 'fancy man'. She is going to ring the hospital later to check on his condition.

3 p.m.

Treena has rung Addenbrookes. Dennis is still at death's door. I said I didn't think they were allowed to impart this sort of information unless you were a family member but Treena said she told them she was his girlfriend.

7 p.m.

Dennis has sat up and asked for a slice of Battenberg.

Mum is livid. But Treena has assured her that it was a brief moment of clarity and that he is still in intensive care and, where there's a life support machine, there's hope.

. . . .

Friday 27
9 a.m.
Dennis has died. Apparently his last words were, 'Where's the marzipan, you thief.' Mum is ringing Mr Lemon now.

9.15 a.m.
Mr Lemon said that he was slightly shocked at Mum's swift and emotionless reaction to death, but that, technically, Grandpa and Treena could be in within the next fortnight. Mum is jubilant.

Went round Sad Ed's to tell him the good news that the house will soon be a Jesus-free zone but he and Tuesday were busy taking advantage of the fact that Mrs Thomas was in Braintree verifying the signature on an Aled Jones boxed set. He answered the door in his pants looking sweaty. I asked him if he had 'come of age' yet. He said not technically, but on a points basis, he was almost there. I left before I could work out what that meant.

. . . .

Saturday 28
Mum and Dad have gone to Cambridge. They are going

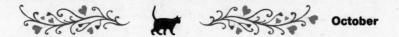

to take it in turns to drive. I am not sure this is going to be the bonding experience they are hoping for.

2 p.m.

I was right. Mum and Dad are back and are in a mood. Dad says it is because Mum drives like Marjory, i.e. refuses to overtake anything and hums incessantly. Mum says it is because Dad broke the speed limit five times and only checked his mirror to see if he had missed a bit shaving. She is booking him in for his refresher course as a Christmas present. Dad said, 'Why don't you just give me socks, Janet, and really spoil me.' Mum is not happy. They are going to look at new cars tomorrow before they start fighting over custody of the Passat.

- -

Sunday 29

Mum and Dad have gone to Motor World in Bishop's Stortford. They have taken James with them as he is encyclopaedic when it comes to engine efficiency and boot volume. He says his extensive internet searches have already whittled it down to the Renault Clio (1.4 litre engine, 35 miles per gallon and convenient cup-holder), an Audi A2 (1.4 litre engine, 38 miles per gallon but questionable MW radio reception), or a BMW 3 series (3 litre engine, no miles to the gallon but has heated seats and a ten-stack CD changer). I do not see Dad agreeing to the last one. Or Mum.

3 p.m.

Mum has got a Fiesta. She says she feels comfortable behind the wheel in a Ford. Dad says I bet you do, maybe I should get a giant cut-out of Mike to sit beside you. She said, 'Well I'd rather that than you telling me to speed up every five minutes.' Dad has gone to the golf club. Grandpa says this is what happens when you let women get behind the wheel, the way of the world gets off kilter. If he had his way, we would all still be milking cows and weaving bonnets.

. . . .

Monday 30

Back to school

Bumped into Jack at the fruit and nut dispenser. I asked him if he and Marie-Claire had overcome their sexual jealousies and he said yes, because it turned out that Henri-Claude is experimenting with being gay. I said that was excellent news. Then he said that Marie-Claire was worried about me. I thought at first he meant that she had some kind of sixth sense and could sniff terminal illness on me or something (I saw a dog do this on *Richard and Judy* once) but he said that she could feel something between us. I said, 'As if.' Jack said, 'That's what I said.' And then the machine dispensed his yoghurt-coated blueberries so he went back to the sixth form common room. No doubt to drink black coffee and discuss Sartre, which is, according to Scarlet, what sixth form is all

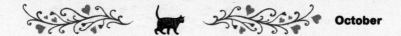

about. Unlike Year Eleven, which is about drinking Fanta and discussing *Celebrity Big Brother*.

Also Mr Lemon called. Dennis's funeral is on Wednesday and the will is being read on Thursday so he says Grandpa can move in Friday. I think he is seeing the advantages of Mum's obituary system. He said he would have waited months before anyone in the rents department even noticed that payments had stopped. So not only has Mum secured Grandpa and Treena a home, she is saving taxpayers at least £254.

Tuesday 31

Hallowe'en

Scarlet is off school. It is because it is Hallowe'en, a traditional goth holiday. I texted her and asked how she had managed to persuade Bob and Suzy. She said she didn't, Bob is busy aborting and Suzy is signing sex manuals at Bluewater. And Edna doesn't know which day of the week it is so is not likely to comment. Trevor is going round later to try to raise the dead. Have volunteered to take James trick or treating. It will be excellent. He is bringing Mad Harry, who is widely considered an expert at extortion, so I am confidently expecting a huge haul. James is going as Catwoman (in Mum's old yoga leotard and a pair of tights) and Mad Harry is Pinhead. I am going as me, in my huge fluffy jumper (one-sleeved but it is a statement) and black leggings, i.e. very this season.

8 p.m.

Trick or treating was not an entire success. Mad Harry was more keen on implementing the trick element of proceedings and egged four houses, including Marjory's. Although, frankly, what do you expect if all you offer is a Blue Riband. Thank God they didn't try Mum though. She is positively puritanical when it comes to treats and has been known to dole out satsumas. Got £2.80 (a fifth share, due to lack of costume, according to Mad Harry) and four mini Milky Ways. Which is a poor haul for having to run for my life with a catboy and a menace in a wetsuit hood with nails in it. Plus several people commented on my costume. Who do they think I was?

LEMON JUICE

november

Wednesday 1

Jack did 'Edelweiss' in rehearsals today, reducing several impressionable Year Eights to tears. I did not weep. I am hardened to Jack's (admittedly many) talents now. Plus he is doing it Kooks-style which is not as heart-rending. Mr Vaughan has asked to see Scarlet's set design. She said she had been plagued by women's problems and had not been able to finish the blueprints for fear of leaking on the drawings (this is a lie—it is because she has been mentally preparing for Hallowe'en). Mr Vaughan went a bit pale and said she could have an extra week.

Treena went to Dennis's funeral to check that he doesn't have any relatives who might try to move in. She said there were only three people there—her, the vicar, and Elsie Stain. They played 'The Only Way is Up'. Treena said she nearly cried. Not because of Dennis but because the song reminds her of losing her virginity in a Capri on the Bolton to Ramsbottom road. When I die I am going to have inspiring Mozart and Arctic Monkeys played at the funeral. Plus I will get Scarlet and Sad Ed to read appropriate bits of *The Bell Jar* and *Jane Eyre*. Or maybe Summer out of *The OC*, who by then will have played me in the film of my brilliant life story.

Treena is going to the will reading tomorrow as well. I said wasn't this unnecessary but she said it will give her an idea of whether or not she needs to get a new sofa, or if they can keep Dennis's. Gross.

Thursday 2

Dennis left everything to Elsie Stain. But as she is ninety-five and lives at Pink Geranium Housing Shelter, where non-regulation furniture is strictly outlawed, she has agreed to let Treena have everything in return for a bottle of gin. Treena says it is an excellent deal but I am not so sure. She has not seen the state of the mattress yet. They are moving in tomorrow. Mum is driving them over in the Fiesta. So it is Baby Jesus's last night in the clean and law-abiding atmosphere of Summerdale Road, before he is destined for a life of crime at 19 Harvey Road (the address is strangely familiar but cannot work out why). The dog is staying. Mum is worried that if it goes it will cause trouble and get them evicted within a week.

. . . .

Friday 3

8.30 a.m.

It is moving day. Grandpa is all upset and says he is having second thoughts but Mum has already loaded the Fiesta. We are going round for tea later to inspect the new house.

5 p.m.

Oh my God. Now I know why the address was so familiar. It is from last year's contraceptive pill/Smint mix-up! Grandpa and Treena are now semi-attached to Fat Kylie and her horde of feral siblings. Thank God the dog hasn't gone. He wouldn't stand a chance against Kylie's poodle

Tupac. I asked Grandpa if he had met his new neighbours yet. He said no but that a small child had already weed on the driveway. It is Keanu, the youngest and deadliest O'Grady boy.

Am not very impressed with the new house. It smells of old man, the carpets make a funny noise when you walk on them, and there is a 1972 topless calendar still on the kitchen wall. Mum has volunteered to forensically clean. She is determined that they are not coming back to Summerdale Road under any circumstances. The dog thinks otherwise. It is now plodding miserably around Grandpa's old room, occasionally whining. Mum says it will not last. It will be back to its usual vomiting and idiotic self after half a tin of Pal and a bourbon.

Saturday 4

Mum has packed her entire cleaning cupboard plus two dozen bin liners and the Vax. She says it will be her toughest task to date. She is relishing the thought. I have not seen her so excited since Granny Clegg let her rearrange the larder. I have volunteered to take Baby Jesus out while she fills the house with potentially deadly chemicals.

2 p.m.

Have just spent depressing two hours walking round town with Fat Kylie and Whitney, her brown half-sister. I

bumped into her at the bottom of the road. She said, 'I didn't know you had a kid. Was it, like, in *Chat* where you didn't know you was up the duff then he fell out on the loo?' I said he was my uncle, and that I had never been, nor had I any intention of being, up the duff. She said she couldn't wait for the responsibility. Then we walked to the Parade (i.e. Smeg Launderette and Mr Patel's 2, run by Mrs Patel) where she bought herself twenty Marlboro and Whitney an E-number saturated packet of Skittles. Cherie's estranged husband Terry was sitting outside Smeg looking miserable. I asked him how he was and he said, 'Crap.' I said Cherie was much the same except that also her satellite dish is broken so she has been without *Extreme Makeover* for a week. Terry said, 'Christ, she must be desperate.' I said she was.

In contrast, Mum had the time of her life cleaning. She has used a record three bottles of Dettol, two Mr Muscles, and an entire six-pack of double-sided scouring sponges. The house looks like Carol Smillie has been at it. The carpet has changed from a sludgy khaki to lime green and the walls are now yellow instead of nicotine-swirled brown.

6 p.m.

Dad has gone down the football field for this year's Round Table Firework Spectacular. He is official rocket lighter. Mum asked if his will was up to date before he left. I do not know why she is worrying, it is not the lighters who

are at risk, it is the gawping masses. Last year Mrs Leech got singed by a rogue Catherine wheel. I am not going. According to Scarlet, fireworks are unenvironmentally friendly and a drain on taxpayer's money. The dog is already cowering in the shed. He can smell the tang of gunpowder in the air.

10 p.m.
Dad is back, without predicted third degree burns. All went well, apart from a mild panic when they realized someone had put Dean 'the dwarf' Denley on top of the bonfire.

· ·

Sunday 5
11 a.m.
Terry is up a ladder at the side of the Britchers' house. Mum has catalogued him in her ASBO book for potential burgling behaviour and called the police to be on the safe side.

11.28 a.m.
Police have arrived. Terry is shouting something at them.

11.30 a.m.
Terry has fallen off the ladder and is writhing in agony on the blue gravel.

11.40 a.m.
Terry's screams have roused Cherie and Thin Kylie,

presumably from the *Hollyoaks* omnibus. Clive and Marjory are outside as well with their matching coffee mugs and disapproving expressions. It is totally like *Desperate Housewives*, but without the excessive murders and glamorous cars. Am going outside to investigate. So is James. Mum is content with watching from the landing. She has James's binoculars for close-up action.

1 p.m.
It turns out Terry wasn't burgling at all. He was trying to fix the satellite dish in a bid to win back Cherie. He has been taken to Addenbrookes. On the plus side, Cherie and Thin Kylie have gone with him. So there is hope for a reconciliation yet.

3 p.m.
Cherie is back. And so is Terry, with his leg in plaster. He actually punched the air when he got out of the car, but then fell over because he had let go of a crutch and knocked Thin Kylie into the hedge. I wonder if he is back for good.

. . . .

Monday 6
Walked to school with Thin Kylie. I said it was brilliant that Terry was back and they were a real family again. She said Cherie says he may be a twat but anyone who would risk their life to make sure she could see *Extreme Makeover* and *Plastic Surgery Gone Wrong* is a twat worth

keeping. Will not tell Mum it was my good deed that has smoothed the path of true chav love. She still thinks Terry is a threat to civilization (i.e. Summerdale Road).

. . . .

Tuesday 7

Caris Kelp is off school. According to Mrs Leech, who knows these things, she had moved on from glue and ate a tube of expandable gap filler. She is like the dog. It has no ability to differentiate between what is or isn't edible. This morning it ate four pieces of Marmite on toast and a holepuncher.

. . . .

Wednesday 8

Scarlet has unveiled her *Sound of Music* set design. It involves a lot of creaky staircases and a crypt. She says it is based on *Nosferatu* (i.e. old film involving badly made-up vampire—in other words, essential goth viewing). Mr Vaughan said she might have been better off basing it on the film *Sound of Music* and where were the nuns supposed to go but Scarlet got all militant about artistic licence so Mr Vaughan just sighed and went outside for a cigarette. He is losing patience with the drama club. It is because it is a constant reminder of his forbidden love with Sophie Microwave Muffins. Plus the Nazis keep looking up the nuns' habits.

. . . .

Thursday 9

Oh my God. Jesus has won the baby competition. He is on the front page of the *Walden Chronicle* under the headline 'Jesus knocks out Whitney in battle of the babies'. The article says:

Adorable

(in no sense of the word)

Jesus Harvey Nichols Riley has been crowned this year's Gayhomes Bonny Baby. Proud mum Treena said, 'Jesus is the light of my life. He brings joy to all he touches.'

(More like jamprints)

His fame comes at a price though – and that price is heartbreak for exotic Whitney Chanel Martini O'Grady, who was disqualified at the last minute for being seventeen months over the age limit.

This is excellent news, prize-wise, but I predict it is not going to be good for neighbourly relations with the notoriously vengeful O'Gradys.

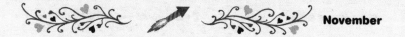

8 p.m.

Grandpa rang. He has asked for Mr Lemon's number to complain about excessive noise from next door. Apparently Mrs O'Grady is playing Status Quo at full volume.

. . . .

Friday 10

It is Scarlet's birthday party tomorrow. She is sixteen on Sunday. I asked her if she was going to use this momentous occasion to allow Trevor further than her black and purple lace bra. She said not likely. They are waiting for the winter equinox. Plus she is worried he will tell all his bat friends who will then discuss Scarlet's nether regions in alarming detail. Sad Ed is still a virgin too. Though he is planning to use this momentous occasion (i.e. the fact that we are all staying over and Suzy's free and easy attitude to teenage sex) to amend his status. Obviously, I will not be doing anything of the sort being *a*) boyfriendless; *b*) crap at snogging (allegedly); and *c*) not French or Sophie Microwave Muffins. Instead I will sip Waitrose organic cider, discuss twentieth century literature and watch Suzy try to stage dive off the sofa.

Also Grandpa has been told to keep a noise diary. He has to write down all his noise complaints for a month and then, and only then, will Mr Lemon take any action. Mum is going to supervise. She is good at cataloguing that sort of thing.

. . . .

Saturday 11

8 a.m.

Have woken up with two spots on face. This is typical. Am now grotesque gargoyle, as well as having crap hair.

Mum and Dad are having a romantic night in. They have rented *Love Actually* from BJ Video and have a selection of M&S nibbles. James is being despatched to Mad Harry's and the dog is going on an overnight visit with Grandpa. I think they are trying to rekindle their passion following the Cherie/Mr Wandering Hands arguments. Although the thought of them rekindling anything is utterly revolting.

11 a.m.

Have been to WHSmith to buy Scarlet a bat-related birthday card and browse the glossy magazines. According to *Cosmo*, I am going about the whole boyfriend thing in the wrong way, i.e. not paying enough attention to what my clothes say about me. Apparently I need to exude unobtainability, at the same time as being totally 'up for it'. Annoyingly I got caught by Mrs Noakes before I could find out what outfit exactly captures this look. Now have three spots. How are they multiplying so quickly? Am going to drink a litre of orange juice in a bid to poison them with Vitamin C.

2 p.m.

Have tried on entire wardrobe but nothing seems to quite

capture a sense of 'look but don't touch, and then I might
let you touch later when I've had a bottle of Mule'. Am
going to have to wear ironic Brownie T-shirt and leggings.
Which say, 'My mum won't let me actually go to Topshop
and I used to be a Leprechaun.' Spot count now five.

3 p.m.
Eight spots and rising. Oh God, have caught acne overnight. Am going to have to make emergency trip to Boots
for Clearasil and industrial concealer.

6 p.m.
Now have spots on chest and stomach and am itching
uncontrollably. Maybe have caught leprosy or SARS. Am
going to show Mum in case it is one of those things
where you die within twenty-four hours.

6.30 p.m.
Oh my God. It is worse. I have been struck down with
chickenpox—a disease for five year olds! Mum has checked
in her Hypochondriac's Bible (aka Dr Le Fanu's *Book of
Family Health*) and confirmed the worst. I said I thought I
had had it when I was little but Mum said no, just ring-
worm and nits. Cannot go to Scarlet's party as am now
salmon pink and crusty due to Calamine lotion daubed
liberally all over body and pair of mittens to stop scratching. A look which only says 'stay away I am contagious or
mental, or possibly both'. Mum is not happy. Not because

I am at death's door but because I have thrown a spanner in her M&S nibbles and romcom fest.

7 p.m.
James is back and is also covered in chickenpox. Mrs Mad Harry caught him and Mad Harry scratching each other under the table. Mum and Dad have abandoned their romantic evening. Dad says it is hard to be overcome with desire with two children scratching themselves and eating HobNobs in the same room. We are going to watch *Casualty* instead. Have texted Scarlet to tell her of my horrifying news. She says she will phone with a full report tomorrow, including details of any sexual activity.

8 p.m.
The dog is back. It does not have pox, but it has eaten two square feet of carpet and is looking green. The source of the infection has been isolated though. It is Jesus. Apparently he has been scratching for days but Treena thought it was fleas.

Sunday 12
Remembrance Sunday
Scarlet rang. Sexual activity as follows:

- Scarlet and Trevor—mutual viewing of goth underwear but no touching.
- Justin and Sophie—no activity due to row about size of Mr Vaughan's nipples and whether small ones

(Justin) were better than big ones (Mr Vaughan). I do not see what the problem is, they are pointless anyway so size does not come into it. Unless they are on man boobs. Which are wrong. Sophie is mad to even think about rejecting Justin's undersize nipples anyway. I have seen his sweaty chest on stage. It is a thing of beauty.

- Sad Ed and Tuesday—some activity reported, but interrupted by Tuesday being sick due to a claimed overdose on Waitrose cocktail blinis, or more probably the mini bottle of Jack Daniels she had stolen from Edie's 'cupboard of shame'.
- Jack—two phone calls to France. Both ending in shouting.

Then Jack came on the line to see how my spots were. I asked him what the shouting was about. Apparently Henri-Claude thinks he might not be gay and has asked Marie Claire to test the theory. Jack has forbidden her to do it but Marie-Claire thinks he is being repressed. So does Suzy. On reflection, Suzy is very French. They are totally at one with sexual experimentation. Apparently it is practically compulsory to be adulterous there.

. . . .

Monday 13

Went to see Dr Braithwaite to have Mum's home diagnosis confirmed. He gave us lollipops and told us not to go back

to school until the weeping had stopped. What weeping? I have not cried since I thought I had leprosy.

11 a.m.
Oh. That sort of weeping. The spots are oozing liquid. It is vile. Will never be able to go out in public again. Will have to stay on sofa watching daytime TV and drinking Lucozade. James says he is enjoying it. This is because he has called Phil and Fern's *Splash the Cash* hotline seven times so far and is confidently expecting to win top prize. Mum does not know about this or she would ban it for sure. It is £1 a call.

5.15 p.m.
James has been banned from phoning TV quizzes. He got through to *You Say We Pay* on *Richard and Judy* but Mum had picked up the other phone to disinfect it with her special wipes and heard all the incriminating evidence. James said she overreacted as he could have paid off the £29 phone bill he has clocked up, as well as bought several mobiles, with his prize money. Mum said there is no guarantee of winning. James said she is wrong, and he would have got at least £6,000 as the questions are aimed at idiots. He is right. Once they had a picture of Camilla Parker-Bowles up and Christine from Crewe said 'that horse-faced one what married the king' and Judy still got it.

Tuesday 14

Grandpa came round to show us his O'Grady noise diary.
It lists, among other things:

- Unidentifiable child shouting, 'I done it in me pants.'
- Music about 'lady lumps' being played repeatedly, disturbing *Countdown*.
- Sound of child headbutting wall. (This is Keanu, who has a death wish and possible mental issues.)
- Thunderous stamping to *Dirty Dancing* soundtrack. (This is Fat Kylie, who is trying to lose weight with the help of Eighties legend Patrick Swayze. It is a shame there isn't a bit on the DVD of Patrick shouting, 'Put down the doughnut,' in an inspiring but slightly sexy manner.)

Wednesday 15

Scarlet and Sad Ed came round after school. Apparently there is an almighty row going on between Miss Vicar and Cowpat Cheesmond over who gets priority over the sheep field—the sheep or the hockey team. At the moment they are sharing it, which is less than ideal as the sheep huddle in one of the goals, and end up getting injured. But, more interestingly, Justin and Sophie have broken up! It is because of Saturday night's nipplegate. Sophie broke down in rehearsals and Mr Vaughan had to comfort her, no doubt with his supersize nipples.

Thursday 16

My spots are definitely less red but still alarmingly visible. I hope the weeping stops soon. Cannot face another week of playing Monopoly with James. He takes it far too seriously and has made himself a rent book for all his hotels.

4 p.m.

Thank God. The dog has eaten Park Lane and several Community Chests. Monopoly has been abandoned in favour of *Mary Poppins*—James's favourite musical film. He knows all the words and can do the chimney sweep dance routine thing. Dad says he cannot bear to watch— it sends shivers down his spine.

. . . .

Friday 17

Weeping subsiding but still look like possible leper. Oh God, I hope I am not permanently disfigured. Scarlet says Mr Vaughan is already thinking of recasting Oona as Liesl if I am still spotty by next week. This is a huge mistake. She may not be spotty but her underarms are repellent. And there is no chance of chemistry between her and Justin, even with her new-found possibly heterosexual ways.

. . . .

Saturday 18

Ventured into town with James. Mum says it is part of our rehabilitation into society. It did not go well. Mrs Noakes had to ask us to leave WHSmith as our spots were putting

customers off their copies of *Horse and Hound*. Went to Goddard's to watch Justin making sausages for a bit. I said I was sorry to hear about him and Sophie. He said, 'I hope those have gone by Wednesday.' Then Mr Goddard asked us to leave as we were putting people off their mince.

. . . .

Sunday 19
Granny Clegg rang. I told her we had chickenpox. She said I should rub lemon juice into the spots to make them disappear. It is an old Cornish remedy. Am going to get the Jif Lemon out later to try it.

2 p.m.
The Jif Lemon stings. But that is probably because it is working.

2.15 p.m.
Rang Granny Clegg to ask her if it should hurt this much. She said it never hurt her and Hester but that was in the 1950s and maybe modern lemons were more powerful. Will persevere.

2.30 p.m.
Am in agony. Cannot move as entire body is screaming in pain..

2.35 p.m.
Mum has called Granny Clegg to shout at her. Apparently

the lemon juice is for freckles, not spots, and she has potentially set me back weeks. Have been sent to have shower before the citric acid eats away any more flesh.

3 p.m.
Look like burn victim. Am never going to school again and it is all Granny Clegg's fault with her backward Cornish cures. It is like the time she told James beetroot would cure his squint and he ate four jars in a day and his poo went red and everyone thought he was dying.

Monday 20
9 a.m.
Mum says I have to go to school as she cannot afford to keep me and James at home any longer. We are getting through too many packets of Duchy Originals and the phone bill is immense. Plus it interferes with her strict cleaning schedule. So am preparing for a day of utter misery. Now I know how the elephant man felt. We are both super sentient beings trapped in our hideous earthly bodies.

4 p.m.
Mark Lambert is in detention. It is for claiming I slept with Herpes McGill (aka Mr McGill, woodwork teacher who has psoriasis). Mr Wilmott called me to his office to demand to know my version of events. He is perverts-in-schools

paranoid now that Sophie is single again. I said I had not slept with any teachers, and that, in any case, Mr McGill was not contagious. He said, 'Yes, well I wouldn't take my chances if I were you.' It is pitiful. What hope do we stand if even the teachers do not grasp basic biology.

. . . .

Tuesday 21

Oh my God! The John Major High Drama Club production of *Sound of Music* is facing closure! It is because of frog-like impresario Andrew Lloyd Webber. Mrs Leech got a letter from his office today threatening to sue Mr Wilmott if he ploughed ahead with the production, as it poses a potential threat to his own West End version, starring TV favourite Connie. Scarlet is beside herself with potential rally excitement and wants to go to London to picket the Palladium. Mr Vaughan says that is not an option, due to the various bans on Viceroy buses, school trips, and political activity of any sort. I do not know why Mr Lloyd Webber is worried. I do not think potential audiences will be confused and detour to Saffron Walden instead of the glittering West End. For a start we do not have any exotic nightlife. Unless you count Barry the Blade moon-walking outside Abrakebabra.

. . . .

Wednesday 22

Mr Vaughan has come up with a genius idea. We are

going to rewrite the entire musical. It is still going to have nuns and Nazis but is going to be called *Over the Hills and Far Away* and will be a rock version! Jack and Justin are mental with excitement. It is because Captain Von Trapp and Rolf are going to be members of rival rock bands and the school orchestra is being replaced with electric guitars and a set of decks. Maria is going to be a former prostitute who is only pretending to be a nun to escape her pimp and Mrs Von Trapp is not dead at all but is fighting for custody of all the smaller Von Trapps, despite being an alcoholic and adulteress. She gets to sing Amy Winehouse's song about rehab! Mrs Matthias in costumes is not so happy though. She is having to totally rethink her lederhosen and run up hotpants and catsuits instead. It means we are having loads of extra rehearsals and Mr Vaughan has secured Mr Wilmott's permission to use the lower school canteen on Sunday!

Thursday 23

Grandpa has abandoned his noise diary. It is because Mrs O'Grady threatened to start one of her own due to the constant sounds of sex and *Teletubbies* coming from number 21. They are having a noise truce. It will not last. There is no way the O'Gradys can watch *QVC* at anything less than ear-damaging decibels.

Friday 24

James has joined the St Regina's school orchestra. He is on triangle. They are giving a recital of various popular TV theme tunes. Mum has been ordered to go.

. . . .

Saturday 25

Have learnt my new duet for *Over the Hills*. It is 'Dead Ringer for Love' with me as Cher and Justin as Meat Loaf, and is all about how he cannot live by rock 'n' roll and 'brew' alone. I think he means beer. Which does not seem appropriate for a sixteen-year-old Nazi youth.

. . . .

Sunday 26

It is weird going to school on a Sunday. Maybe this time it really will be like in *The Breakfast Club* and we will all forget our social cliques and the Retards will mingle happily with the maths geeks and the goths will be at one with the beautiful people.

4 p.m.

It was not like *The Breakfast Club*. No one mingled any-where, the goths got all up in arms because they don't like having to sing a Girls Aloud song, and then Davey MacDonald let the school sheep into the language labs via the B Corridor fire exit and they chewed the head-phones and peed in several booths.

. . . .

Monday 27

Mr Wilmott has banned use of the school premises at
weekends and says he is minded to abolish the Drama
Club as well as it seems to overexcite the Retards and
Criminals. This has not deterred Mr Vaughan. He is only
more determined to make *Over the Hills* a success, now that
we are fighting for our very existence. To be fair though,
Mr Wilmott does have a point. Maybe Mrs Duddy should
take over—she has a zen-like influence over her charges.
It is all the *Angelina Ballerina* tapes she lets them watch.

Tuesday 28

Yet again the Drama Club has been struck with misfortune.
Two of the smaller Von Trapps are moving to Newmarket.
Scarlet says it is Andrew Lloyd Webber trying to sabotage
us from afar. I do not think so. He did not offer their dad
a job at Spillers Pet Food. Mr Vaughan says he cannot
face another gruelling audition schedule and is rewriting
again with fewer Von Trapps. He says at least our dance
routine to Sham 69's 'Kids Are United' will not be so
overcrowded now.

5 p.m.
Oh my God. Maybe Scarlet is right. James googled
Andrew Lloyd Webber and he owns a company in Bury
St Edmunds, which is in close proximity to Newmarket.

Wednesday 29

There has been another *Over the Hills* catastrophe. Sophie Microwave Muffins has resigned as Maria. It is because Mr Vaughan is resisting her charms and has his eyes set on a higher prize i.e. biology teacher Miss Lexington (aka Sexy Lexy) who is not a potential sex offenders risk.

Thursday 30

Sophie is back. It is because Mr Vaughan threatened to cast Pippa as Maria and Sophie says Pippa has had her eye on him for months now and there is no way she is letting her get near his giant nipples. Why does anyone want to get near his nipples, big or otherwise?

december

Friday 1

The dog has eaten the entire contents of James's non-denominational Barbie advent calendar and it is only Day One. Sad Ed has also eaten his Buzz Lightyear one. Christmas is not what it used to be. St Regina's nativity this year features a Jedi Knight and several Incredibles.

Saturday 2

Went round Treena's to help her finalize the wedding guest list. She is inviting all the residents at the Twilight Years Day Centre and her cousin Donna, who is, according to Treena, 'double mental'. Apparently this is a good thing. I asked her if her mum and dad would be making the arduous journey from Torremolinos to see their only daughter wed, again, but she says they aren't allowed back in the country. There is going to be a pink-themed buffet, featuring strawberry Angel Delight, Iced Gems and taramasalata, and the wedding list is at Argos. I am going to get them a cruet set. It is on special offer at £2.99.

Sunday 3

Sad Ed has done 'It'! He phoned at 8 o'clock this morning to tell me the good news. It is obviously a life-changing experience because normally he is never up until *Popworld*. Plus it turns out that Tuesday was not the slut she made out to be (i.e. still a total virgin) so according

to Sad Ed it is a totally poetic experience and he is going to write a song about it later and that maybe she is THE ONE after all. So it is between me and Scarlet now. It is bound to be Scarlet first. She has Suzy and years of sex manual browsing behind her. Although Trevor asked her to touch him and she said no. I asked where and she said in the metalwork rooms at lunch on Friday.

Monday 4
Scarlet and Jack came to school wearing non-regulation yellow shirts. Apparently Edna had been storing her dusters in the washing machine and they have dyed everything. Bob is not happy. His surgeons' whites were in the wash as well. He has demanded that Suzy takes immediate action. But Suzy says if he wants to sack Edna he will have to do it himself as she is too busy delving into the many sexual secrets of Trevor McDonald this week.

Tuesday 5
Bob has not sacked Edna. It turns out her (dead) husband Stan was a miner (for three weeks before his claustrophobia got the better of him) and they are like talismans for New Labour and can do no evil so she has a job for life. She has agreed to store her dusters in a more appropriate place though. And to stop watching

Loose Women when she is supposed to be hoovering the den.

. . . .

Wednesday 6

Rehearsals went excellently today. The nuns do a brilliant version of 'Losing My Religion' where they discard their habits to reveal catsuits—Chicago style. Justin and Jack's battle of the axes (i.e. guitars) went well too. It is hard to choose between them.

4 p.m.

Not that I want to pick Jack.

4.30 p.m.

And he wouldn't want to be picked anyway.

. . . .

Thursday 7

London has been ravaged by freak weather! A tornado has swept through somewhere called Kensal Rise ripping the roofs off several BMWs. Why does nothing like that ever happen in Saffron Walden? The best we get is when it rains really hard the shopping-trolley-clogged Slade floods, putting the roundabout and seesaw out of action for literally hours.

. . . .

Friday 8

It is James's recital today. He is very excited and has asked
if he can have a violin for Christmas if it goes well. Mum
says she will think about it.

4 p.m.

Mum has thought about it and the answer is no. Apparently
James (fake police siren) and Mad Harry (coconuts) got
carried away during the theme to *The Bill* and scared a
lot of the Year Threes on chime bars and maracas. Two
of them wet themselves and James and Mad Harry have
been banned from the orchestra.

Saturday 9

Granny Clegg rang to see if there was anything special
me and James wanted for Christmas. I said an iBook (the
laptop of choice for aspiring journalists and totally what
Hunter S. Thompson would be using today if he hadn't
spent all his money on drugs). James has asked for a pony
(he is hoping to win back Parker with his equestrian
skills). This is pointless. They don't sell livestock in Trago
Mills. Or electrical equipment. We will get out-of-date
selection boxes like we do every year.

Sunday 10

Grandpa came round to visit the dog. Mum was right. It

is showing a remarkable lack of distress at Grandpa's departure. It gets more sofa room now and does not have Jesus sticking crackers on its fur. It barely looked up from *Countryfile* when Grandpa came into the room. Dad asked Grandpa where he was taking Treena on honeymoon. Grandpa said he is considering his options. Dad asked what they were and Grandpa said, 'Limited.' It is because he keeps spending his pension on internet poker.

- -

Monday 11

8 a.m.

It is show week! Everyone is overexcited at our ground-breaking and possible school-rule-breaking production. Me and Justin are having our snog rehearsal later. Have eaten two packets of tic tacs and read several back issues of *Cosmo* to ensure I am neither repulsive nor lacking technique. It is a seminal moment to get to finally snog Justin Statham—legendary guitar player and meat-mincing genius.

4 p.m.

Have snogged Justin. I am clearly making acting progress because I managed to stay completely detached i.e. did not feel all hot and bothered like I did when I had to kiss Jack. In fact, kissing Sad Ed was marginally more stimulating.

Maybe I do have Gwyneth Paltrow potential after all. Will practise stage crying next. That is the next step. Am currently having to resort to putting Vick inhaler under eyes at crucial crying moments.

Justin went red though and bit breathless. Maybe he is an acting genius too.

. . . .

Tuesday 12

Mr Vaughan has axed my and Justin's stage snog! He says it is still lacking passion plus the height difference makes it look slightly freakish. Jack agreed. He suggested we just gaze at each other instead. Justin said they were making a huge mistake and hadn't yesterday proved the seething sexual chemistry etc. But Mr Vaughan said no. That is what comes from my excellent detachment.

5 p.m.
Or maybe I don't fancy Justin after all.

7 p.m.
No, that cannot be true. He is a living god. It is impossible not to fancy him.

8 p.m.
But kissing Jack was definitely more like it is supposed to be, according to *Cosmopolitan* and Tuesday. i.e. make you breathless and feel a bit sick. Oh God. Am utterly

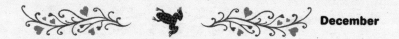

confused. In fact it is lucky whole snogging thing is cancelled. I am better off never getting involved in it again.

. . . .

Wednesday 13

Today is the dress rehearsal. Mrs Matthias and her needlework A-level group are on standby for any wardrobe emergencies. I predict several. Fat Kylie has burst out of her hotpants four times already.

4 p.m.

Mr Vaughan has given everyone a director's debriefing. He says he has woven his magic and now it is down to us whether we are stars or the Drama Club gets banned. It is a lot of pressure. Sophie Jacobs was hyperventilating by the end of the talk. Although it might have been because Mr Vaughan's shirt was slightly undone and she was trying to glimpse his fat nipples. I predict it will all be a success. As long as the Retards and Criminals don't try to reverse their cardboard Nazi patrol cars off the front of the stage again.

. . . .

Thursday 14

It is opening night. Mum and Dad are coming with James and Mad Harry. Grandpa is going to babysit the dog after last year's Natasha Kaplinsky fiasco. I said didn't Grandpa want to come and see the show but he says he had enough

of Nazis as a child and it might awaken repressed and dangerous memories. Mum pointed out that he was at Primary School during the Second World War and that, as far as she knew, there was no Nazi invasion in North Essex, but Grandpa is adamant. Also his Freeview is on the blink and there is an *OC* double bill on E4 tonight.

10 p.m.
Mr Vaughan is livid. It is because *Over the Hills* was beset with technical difficulties including Scarlet's vampiric staircase partially collapsing sending a Von Trapp spiralling into the front row. He says our stage careers are doomed. I do not know why he is so upset. The audience loved it.

Mum and Dad said they thought it was 'interesting'. I asked Mum what she thought of my duet with Justin and then she had to admit that she was in the toilets with James and Mad Harry for most of the second half because Mad Harry had got a Chupa Chup stuck in his hair. She has no sense of parental responsibility. I bet Gwyneth Paltrow's mum did not spend half of *Sliding Doors* in the toilets with an idiotic nine year old.

When we got home Grandpa and the dog had eaten an entire tin of festive shortbread and eight slices of ham. Mum said wasn't Treena feeding him and Grandpa said no, that her cooking skills were limited to heating things up in the microwave, and as they didn't own a microwave, they had been living on toast for a month. Mum

packed him some sandwiches and a flask of Bovril before he could try to infiltrate the spare room.

. . . .

Friday 15
6 p.m.
Mr Vaughan says we have one last chance to rescue our reputations and ensure quality drama has a place at John Major High. Mr Wilmott is in the audience (with Tuesday) and he is going to make the crucial decision right after the show.

9 p.m.
We are saved! *Over the Hills* was an entire success. Jack is being besieged by love-drunk Year Eights backstage right now. Plus Mr Wilmott got called out to a sheepfield emergency (sheep entangled in goal nets) and had to rely on the testimony of Tuesday as to the quality of the show. She said it was 'a landmark in British theatre'. She is right. I expect Andrew Lloyd Webber is wishing he had never started the whole hoo-ha now. His traditional nun-based production must look tame and uninspired compared to ours. We are all going to the backstage party now!

12 midnight
Something weird and enormous has happened. I was in goth corner mark two with Scarlet and Trevor, who were

trying to snort Coca Cola up straws (according to Tuesday the bubbles make you high), and Justin came over and asked if he could have a word behind the fire curtain. Then he said that he was sorry our snogging scene was cut but that now the play was over, Mr Vaughan couldn't stop him doing 'this'. And then he sort of loomed in my face, but just as his lips got within snogging distance, Mark Lambert set off the fire alarm by trying to burn Dean 'the dwarf' Denley's shoe and by the time everyone was allowed back in, Bob showed up in the vomit Volvo to take us all home. So our love is totally unconsummated. And am now utterly in dilemma. It is not the nipples—small ones are not a barrier to true love in my book—it is Jack. I know he is with evil French Marie-Claire and does not love me but I think I might still like him. And maybe it is better to be single and true to yourself than go out with someone just because they are beautiful and talented and can make sausages. Worst of all cannot ask Scarlet for advice as she is *a*) anti Justin because he wears Gap and *b*) Jack's sister and totally pro Marie-Claire, despite the annoying French hair and legs, because she wants to go to Paris at Easter. Am racked with indecision. Will sleep on it and find someone to ask in morning.

Saturday 16
9 a.m.
Love dilemma still unresolved. James says I should be

glad anyone wants to snog me as vital statistically I am a medical marvel and do not fit into any accepted concept of beauty. Am going Christmas shopping to take my mind off the matter.

3 p.m.
Have done entire Christmas shopping in WHSmith. Not because it had a comprehensive range of excellent present ideas but because Goddard's is opposite and I could clearly see Justin lurking by the chop display and I had to wait for two hours until he went on a break round the back before I could leave the shop. Have bought a laundry marker (Mum—the only cleaning related item), a light-up calculator pen (Dad—so he can do accounts in the case of a power cut), *What You Wear Can Change Your Life* (James—he is currently obsessed with Trinny), a Fimble (the dog—it likes Florrie for some reason and gets all calm when she comes on the telly), a Lemar Calendar (Grandpa and Treena—it was cheap), and a *Baby Einstein* DVD (Baby Moron Jesus—someone has to take charge of his education and it clearly isn't going to be Treena). Have not got anything for the Cleggs as Mum is giving them a *Dog Borstal* video from all of us. She is hoping they will have Bruce under control by the time we visit again. She will be sorely disappointed. Granny Clegg lets Bruce get in the bath with her. She does not believe in tough love.

595

Sunday 17

10 a.m.

Mum is resigning from the Lib Dems. It is because wonky jawed MP Lembit Opik (aka Lemsip Toothpick) has left glamorous Sian Lloyd, famous for authoritative yet reassuring weather reports, to go out with one of the Cheeky Girls, famous for asking people to touch her bum. Mum is going to join the Greens. Dad says at least they are all so busy knitting yoghurt they do not have time for sexual scandal.

. . . .

Monday 18

8 a.m.

Oh God, have got to go to school and Justin will be there. Have tried to feign illness (chickenpox relapse) but Mum checked in Dr Le Fanu and it is medically impossible. Feel sick with nerves. And not sure if it is because I do love him or because I don't.

4 p.m.

Thank God. Justin has gone to Lanzarote for Christmas with his parents and lesbian Aunt Renee (Leslie is not going as she is in panto in Rotherham). So I do not have to make any decisions until the New Year.

. . . .

Tuesday 19

It is the last day of school and the Retards and Criminals'

final taste of integrated freedom. They are going home to D Corridor next term. They have got a fully refurbished unit complete with therapeutic colour lounge and their very own fruit and nut dispenser. Fat Kylie has requested to join them but Ms Hopwood-White says she is not stupid or criminal enough. This is not true. She is notoriously idiotic and dangerous.

. . . .

Wednesday 20

2 p.m.

Am feeling utterly festive. Have decorated the tree (fake— i.e. environmentally friendly and non-messy) using ten- year-old tinsel and some biscuit decorations James made at school (apparently shaped like Baby Jesus but actually looking more like a jellyfish). Have also eaten four mince pies whilst watching *Home Alone* (James's favourite film— it is his ambition to be abandoned for forty-eight hours and have to battle the O'Gradys single-handedly with a variety of cunning inventions). It is definitely the season to be jolly etc. and am possibly thinking of snogging Justin. After all, even if he is not THE ONE, the practice will come in handy.

4 p.m.

Tree has been devastated by dog madness. It has eaten all the edible Jesus-shaped biscuit decorations and the

597

non-edible tinsel plus it tried to swallow a fairy light and got an electric shock, which has melted the plastic needles so tree has caused molten green spillage, which is far worse than dropped needles. Mum has gone to B&Q in the Fiesta for a new, real one.

Thursday 21

Grandpa rang in a panic. There has been a wedding set-back. Apparently the White Horse is turning into a Star-bucks and is being bulldozed a week today, ending his dreams of walking Treena down the aisle (i.e. between the vast array of fruit machines). He said Treena is devastated and is lying on the sofa in shock eating a jumbo bag of Skips. I told him not to panic and that it could be like when Ross and Emily got married in *Friends* in the derelict church—we could festoon the rubble and discarded dartboard with fairy lights and play Il Divo (Treena's new favourite band) and it would be totally romantic. But then Treena got up from her Skip stupor and said she wasn't getting married in a building site, gay Italian singers or not, and that the wedding was off unless alternative arrangements can be found. She has no imagination. It is because her mum and dad only had the *TV Times* in the house when she was little and she had to learn to read by checking the *Coronation Street* schedule. Also she is from Bolton.

Friday 22

The wedding is back on. In a stroke of either genius or idiocy, Grandpa has secured permission to use the Twilight Years Day Centre for the whole thing. One of the dominoes team is going to perform the ceremony in the TV room. I said I wasn't sure this was entirely legal, particularly given the fact that Treena still hadn't got her decree absolute through. Grandpa said he had rung the court in Harlow to chase it up but they were all drunk after their Christmas lunch at TGI Fridays and so he is going to try again next week.

. . . .

Saturday 23

Oh my God. Dad knows Tuesday's mum Edie! We were in Waitrose delicatessen section when a voice from the other side of the olive cart said, 'Sex Beast Riley?' and Dad said, 'Weirdy Edie,' and then their eyes met over the marinated anchovies and it was all a bit freaky so I went to calm down in the pet food aisle and watched Gary Fletcher rearranging KiteKat. When I met Dad at the checkout he looked a bit panicked and said they knew each other at school and he would prefer it if I did not mention it to Mum, in case she had one of her funny turns (i.e. scrubbing the bath with a passion verging on the maniacal). Am going to phone Suzy immediately for more information. She was a year below Dad at school and knows everything.

3 p.m.

According to Suzy they do not just know each other, they have done 'It'. Suzy says they were like the Seth and Summer of John Major High (then the Clement Attlee Comprehensive), but that their love was thwarted when Edie ran off to London to marry a gay lawyer. I said I found this hard to believe but Suzy insists that Dad was a sexual legend in Saffron Walden before he met Mum at Accountancy College.

First Cherie and now Edie. Mum is going to have to get Trinny and Susannahed fast if she does not want to lose him now he is fast regaining 'sex beast' status. Have swapped her present with James and am giving her *What You Wear Can Change Your Life* which means James will have to settle for the laundry marker. He won't mind. I will say it is an indelible spy pen.

. . . .

Sunday 24

Christmas Eve

Less than a day to Christmas and I do not see any packages under the tree resembling my requested presents, i.e.:

- iBook—laptop of choice for aspiring journalists etc., etc.
- Giant furry boots from Topshop as worn by Kate Moss during drunken rampage with Pete Doherty.
- Subscription to *Vogue* and the *Times Literary Supplement*

(so I can look excellent whilst reading about Salman Rushdie).

James keeps checking the shed for any signs of pony activity. He is going to be disappointed. There is no room in there anyway what with the quarantined mini trampoline, the lawnmower, and Dad's ill-advised mountain bike purchase—disused after he failed to make it up Hill Street let alone a mountain.

Am going to midnight mass later with Scarlet, Trevor, Sad Ed, and Tuesday. According to Scarlet it is essential Christmas activity—even for vampire worshipping goths. Everyone goes and stands at the back and sings 'Hark the Herald' whilst drinking cider. Jack isn't coming. He is going to Stansted Airport to pick Marie-Claire up.

. . . .

Monday 25
Christmas Day (and first birthday of Baby Jesus, non-religious variety)
Have been banned from St Regina's Church. Apparently Marjory saw me and Tuesday doing the conga to 'We Three Kings'. Plus Trevor was sick in the font.

Presents received:

- Laptop computer (Mum and Dad)—it is not an iBook, it is Dad's old one from work and weighs about a tonne but at least will mean my journalism will not be hampered by James's endless googling.

- Dictaphone (James). It is an essential piece of equipment for any journalist and creative type so I can record my amazing ideas at all times. Although I fear for its provenance. The tape in it has someone sounding suspiciously like Mrs Mad Harry talking about custard recipes.
- Rosemary Conley DVD (Grandpa and Treena— assume it came from Ducatti Mick and his limited pirate DVD service. Unusable until we get a new non-pizza-filled DVD.)
- Seven-pack of Playboy Bunny pants (Granny and Grandpa Clegg—now confiscated by Mum as unsuitable). They have a Trago Mills price tag but at least they do not have a sell-by date.
- A tape called *Recorder Magic* (Auntie Joyless). It features three beardy men playing assorted-sized recorders. James has got it. He says he can swap it at St Regina's, where recorders are de rigueur.
- An iTunes voucher (Scarlet and Sad Ed). Which would be excellent if I had an iPod. Which I don't. Will swap it with Sad Ed later for a giant Toblerone. He always gets one.

James did not get a pony. He got a fish tank (empty). Mum is taking him to PetWorld tomorrow to fill it. She says at least fish are clean and can be flushed down the toilet when they die, unlike rabbits or other larger pets i.e. the dog.

3 p.m.

Laptop is broken. It is because James tried to use it to google fish facts and it is obviously only used to adding up paperclip budgets because it made a strange whiny noise and then went black. Dad is going to get Malcolm to fix it.

4 p.m.

James has just pointed out it is Baby Jesus's birthday, which got forgotten in the laptop computer hoo-ha and general over-consumption of sherry (Grandpa), stout (Treena), and liqueur chocolates (everyone, including dog). Have given him Rosemary Conley DVD as emergency present. He will watch anything. He gets that from Treena.

Rang Scarlet. She got: black skull-decorated Converse, Urban Decay make-up set, tickets to the Whitby Goth Convention, and a pair of skinny-fit Levis. Apparently she is thinking of branching out from gothwear, as it is limiting, fashionwise, and going more EMO. I said Trevor wouldn't be too pleased but she says he will do anything she tells him as she is wielding the most powerful tool known to teenagers around the world—access to her underwear. It will be weird to see her not swamped in layers of voluminous black and purple. It will be like on *She's All That* when the badly dressed studious type is revealed to be drop-dead gorgeous. Trinny and Susannah will be jubilant.

Also, I asked how Marie-Claire had enjoyed her nut roast and apparently she never arrived! It is down to

striking French baggage handlers, which has caused a row because Jack is pro-striking (i.e. it is totally Labour) and Marie-Claire is anti it. So they are not soul-mates after all. Maybe this is the beginning of the end for their Anglo-French concorde. He will realize he prefers nice English granary to a baguette after all.

. . . .

Tuesday 26
Boxing Day

Have been using my Dictaphone. It is excellent—like having a constant voiceover. Life would be so much better if everyone had voiceovers. It makes everything sound dramatic and like you are about to get murdered or something.

James has filled his fish tank with African frogs. Mum is not happy but James says the frogs are more intelligent and will eat meat from your fingers. The dog does not like them and is eyeing them suspiciously. Particularly because they are getting bits of lamb chuck and he is on dried biscuits after eating an entire bowl of brandy butter yesterday.

Granny Clegg rang. Mum asked her what she was thinking of with my Playboy pants but she said, 'What's wrong with rabbits? There's nothing dirty about them, they are a very clean animal.' Then James said they eat their own babies and poo and he got sent to his room.

. . . .

Wednesday 27

Grandpa called the court again. The divorce is in the post. James says they might as well have just thrown it in the bin as it will never arrive. He is right—my confession to Jack is clearly festering under a mound of landfill—thank God. Grandpa says nothing is going to stop him marrying Treena. Not even potential bigamy.

The frogs have been moved to James's room. It is because the dog keeps sticking his face in the tank trying to eat the floating meat bits and it is upsetting the frogs.

. . . .

Thursday 28

James is single again. He got a card from Peyton. It said, 'Happy Christmas. I don't want to go out with you any more because I am in love with Harry.' For a minute there was concern that his best friend had betrayed him but it turns out she means Potter. James says he does not care and that he and Mad Harry have more important matters at hand anyway (they are trying to invent gold) but I know that secretly he is devastated because I heard him talking Elvish to the frogs earlier. Will ask Mum to lend him the Trinny book. He will be able to revamp his wardrobe and win back Mumtaz.

4 p.m.
James has been dealt a double blow. Not only has Peyton heartlessy left him for Daniel Radcliffe but his

frogs have mysteriously disappeared too. There is a soggy trail across the landing carpet. Mum says she told him to keep the lid on but James says he cannot think about amphibian security at a time like this. My suspicions are on the dog. It has never liked the frogs—they are rivals to its position as number one pet. Although I think it is worrying unnecessarily. Frogs actually make the dog look lovable.

6 p.m.
Mystery solved. And not due to usual incriminating dog vomit. Frogs tried to flush themselves down toilet in bid for freedom and have blocked u-bend causing a back-up in the bath. They are still alive but traumatized. Mum says they are going to have to go back to PetWorld. They are clearly unhappy on Summerdale Road. James says he does not care. He is at his lowest ebb and nothing can make him feel better. Not even pink milk.

. . . .

Friday 29
The wedding is tomorrow. Still no sign of divorce but they are ploughing ahead anyway. Grandpa is staying the night so that he does not see the bride before she walks down the aisle. He is bringing Jesus too because Treena has got her cousin Donna over and they are notoriously irresponsible.

. . . .

Saturday 30

Look like mental person in hideous pink fairy costume.
Thank God no one I know is going to the wedding.
Although, unless the divorce arrives in this morning's
post, no one will be going to the wedding at all.

9 a.m.

Postman (aka Beefy Clarke) has been. No divorce. Luckily
Mum is busy trying to pin on James's and Jesus's totally
gay sailor hats so she does not know the wedding is
potential Jeremy Kyle material.

10 a.m.

Crisis averted. Des has just been round. Apparently the
divorce had been posted to him by mistake and he took it
round to Treena's. He says it was lucky he did because
apparently she and Donna were comatose on the floor in
a sea of dry roasted peanuts. I think it is excellent that Des
is being so forward thinking about Treena remarrying
Grandpa. It is very modern and shows that even men
with tattoos and criminal records can be in touch with
their feelings.

10 p.m.

Des has tried to sabotage the wedding. Events unfold as
follows:

3.00 p.m.

Guests assemble at Twilight Years Day Centre awaiting
arrival of bride.

3.30 p.m.
Bride's cousin rings to say bride has had to stop bridal carriage (i.e. Donna's Nissan Bluebird) to be sick outside Woolworth's.

3.45 p.m.
Bride arrives in enormous pink and slightly vomit-stained dress, accompanied by cousin Donna (all seventy-six kilos of her) in a Tinkerbell outfit.

4 p.m.
Octogenarian dominoes player and one time Irish priest Finlay O'Grady (yes—of the O'Grady O'Gradys) asks if anyone present knows of any reason why the happy couple should not get married.

4.01 p.m.
Des Nichols (formerly of HMP Harlow) appears, as if by magic, by the tea trolley and declares undying love for Treena, threatening to kill himself if she goes ahead with ceremony.

4.15 p.m.
Ceremony goes ahead.

4.30 p.m.
Ambulance called to take Des to Addenbrookes with cake slice related injuries.

4.45 p.m.
Guests take seats at communal trestle tables for wedding feast of pink food. Dog eats entire bowl of taramasalata and is sick on the whist table.

5.00 p.m.
Phyllis Dubbs falls asleep in strawberry mousse.

6.30 p.m.
Phyllis Dubbs still asleep in mousse, holding up clearing of trestle tables for evening entertainment.

6.45 p.m.
James reports that Phyllis Dubbs not asleep but actually dead. Second ambulance called.

7.00 p.m.
Pelvis Presley rings to say he is stuck at the garage because his trusty assistant Darryl Stamp (former joyrider extraordinaire) has phoned in sick with a broken elbow (is that possible?) and he will not be able to make it until possibly tomorrow.

7.15 p.m.
Grandpa does Elvis impression. No one applauds. Treena puts Take That on the portable CD player. Old ladies get overexcited and start conga.

9.00 p.m.
Mrs Peason, fascist warden from Pink Geranium Sheltered Housing arrives in minibus and demands party is closed immediately as several of her residents have broken their curfews and are in danger of compromising their hip replacements with ill-advised conga dancing.

9.01 p.m.
Old ladies and ageing religious O'Grady loaded onto minibus and despatched to living hell with Mrs Peason.

9.10 p.m.
Minibus returns to repatriate Baby Jesus. Mum and Dad take him home, along with dog and James, both of whom are showing signs of sugar overload and mental exhaustion.

9.15 p.m.
Rest of party departs for karaoke at Axe and Compasses. Rachel Riley forced to walk home through town in absurd fairy outfit, attracting attention from Mr Whippy, several Retards and Criminals (on the plus side they did stop fighting in shock when I went past), and Barry the Blade.

10.30 p.m.
Rachel Riley goes to bed in hope sleep will obliterate memories of Barry the Blade trying to get her to turn him into Dale Winton with her fairy wand.

Sunday 31
New Year's Eve

It is New Year's Eve. A time for reflection on what has been achieved in the last year:

1. Attempt to discontinue friendship with Thin Kylie. (Achieved—although she does still walk home with me occasionally when she is not menacing Year Sevens or winning badges off Mark Lambert behind the mobile science lab.)

2. Repatriate Suzy's glow-in-the-dark rabbit vibrator (achieved—though not without consequences).

3. Concentrate on GCSEs (partially achieved, though with blossoming journalistic career will not need to know about maths or rural studies).

4. Experiment with drugs, alcohol, and sex. (Momentarily achieved—vis á vis the Kyle O'Grady fiasco. But the year is not over yet and it is Bob and Suzy's party tonight, which is bound to be full of all of the above.

5. Find THE ONE. Utterly not achieved and am still in confusion as to who exactly this might be. Though have definitely ruled out Sad Ed. And Kyle, obviously. So just leaves Jack and Justin. Except that am not sure I fancy one of them and not sure the other fancies me.

Mum and Dad are coming to the party. Dad thinks he is going to get to meet Jeremy Clarkson, who is Suzy's latest sex celebrity. James and the dog are staying at home.

Marjory is babysitting. She is bringing Giant Jenga with her. I am taking my new Dictaphone with me to record important events in journalistic fashion. And do voice-over thing. It is weirdly addictive. She said, in her sultry but intelligent voice. See.

8 p.m.
Oh God. Weirdy Edie is here with Tuesday. She has spotted Dad. Have steered Mum to the buffet before there is any sex-beast-related hoo-ha.

8.15 p.m.
Oh God. Mr Wandering Hands is here too. Apparently he is one of Suzy's clients. Probably for sex addiction. Or maybe he is one of those people who get turned on by the smell of leather. Or vinyl, in the case of Ford Fiestas.

8.30 p.m.
Mum has spotted Dad talking to Edie. She has gone over to investigate.

8.45 p.m.
Mum has stormed off and is being comforted by Mr Wandering Hands and a bottle of sherry.

9.00 p.m.
Marjory has rung to say that James has been on the

phone to Birmingham for two hours and she can't prise him off and the dog has eaten a Giant Jenga piece and is now whining hysterically. Mum is in a panic. She was supposed to be driving but is too drunk on sherry, and Dad has been on Suzy's life-threatening punch all night and is still pacing the house looking for Jeremy Clarkson, so Mr Wandering Hands has offered to take her home! Worse, she has accepted! Oh God, am going to be in children's home by next year; i.e. tomorrow. Am hiding in Scarlet's wardrobe with a bottle of Britvic and a bowl of Twiglets for emergency sustenance while I plan ways to reconcile parents. Oh, someone is coming.

9.45 p.m.
It was Edna looking for Jack. She says she has got something for him. I hope it is not one of her vol au vents. (She is in charge of canapés, another mistake on Suzy's part— she should have left it to Marks & Spencer like she usually does). I said he was on his mobile in the den, arguing with Marie-Claire.

10 p.m.
Am still in wardrobe. But think have thought of plan. Am going out. Oh no am not. Someone is coming.

10.30 p.m.
Oh God. It was Jack. He said he needed some peace as he

was waiting for another call from Paris. I asked him why he needed to use the wardobe and he said everywhere else was taken—Sad Ed and Tuesday were doing 'It' in the walk-in closet in Bob and Suzy's room, the den was full of Labour Party members playing political 'Who'd You Rather' (i.e. who'd you rather—John Prescott or Gordon Brown— answer: 'I'd rather stick needles in my thighs'), Marlon from *Emmerdale* was signing autographs in the toilet and my dad was asleep on Jack's bed. (Which is a good thing—at least he can't engage in any marriage-nullifying activity with Edie if he is comatose). But then Edna appeared in the doorway smoking a pink cocktail cigarette, and waving a horrifyingly familiar envelope, which she said was for Jack. It was my confession letter from August! (Not stolen by organized criminal postmen, or festering in landfill, but filed mistakenly by Edna on the freezer, not the fridge.) Jack said, 'Oh, look, Riley, that is just like your handwriting,' and was just about to open it when his mobile went off again so he had to go into the corridor to get better reception for shouting. Now what do I do? Am going to have to stay inside wardrobe for ever with only Twiglets to survive on. Oh God, now someone else is coming. Is there no peace?

11.30 p.m.
It was Jack again. He demanded to know if what I said in the letter was true. I said, 'Do you want it to be true?' He said, 'Maybe.' I said, 'What about Marie Claire?' And he said she lived in Paris, which is not really an answer. I

said I needed to think about it because I am at a crossroads and am very tormented and Sylvia Plath, which I know he will totally understand, as he is totally literary and tragic, really. He said I have until midnight.

So now, not only are my parents about to get divorced, but I have to decide between Jack—who is lovely but is my friend's brother and possibly actually in love with someone else, who is French, or Justin—who is lovely, and knows all the words to every Rolling Stone song including possibly racist 'Brown Sugar', but is potentially actually not the love of my life, except that I don't know that because I only kissed him on stage, which is not actual real kissing. Will have to make list. It is the only way to deal with these matters, according to James, who makes lists for everything, including a daily wardrobe rota.

OK. So Jack has good hair, laughs at my jokes, is intellectual (i.e. has read Jack Kerouac and not just Dan Brown, who is good, but not self-improving) and does not have nipple issues. BUT he is Scarlet's brother i.e. vast potential for awkwardness etc. and has done it with a French girl so may be disappointed with my general non-Frenchness.

Justin on the other hand is excellent at guitar, has muscly arms from all the meat mincing, and has a lesbian aunt, i.e. is totally progressive. BUT he is not very good at getting my cleverly ironic comments. And has done it with Sophie Microwave Muffins, who is normal height,

615

has 34B breasts (i.e. two sizes bigger than me) and does not have weird hair.

11.59 p.m.
Have made decision. Am definitely going to . . . Oh God. Can hear someone coming. Am turning off torch. Pants. Where is Dictaphone button? Oh God, who is that? Can only hear heavy breathing. OK, am going to stop talking now because whoever it is will think I am mental talking to myself. Shut up, Rachel. Oh . . . Mmm . . . Jack?

Hang on.

Justin . . . ?

Joanna Nadin was born in Northampton and moved to Saffron Walden in Essex when she was three. She did well at school (being a terrible swot) and then went to Hull University to study Drama. Three years of pretending to be a toaster and pretending to like Fellini films put her off the theatre for life. She moved to London to study for an MA in Political Communications and after a few years as an autocue girl and a radio newsreader got a job with the Labour Party as a campaigns writer and Special Adviser. She now lives in Bath with her daughter and is a freelance government speech writer and TV scriptwriter. She has written five books for younger readers, several of which have been shortlisted for awards. Joanna was shortlisted for the Queen of Teen crown for her fantastic books about the life of Rachel Riley.